What the critics are saying...

ଚ୍ଚ

"...A fast-paced thriller! The two villains are scary and disturbing...The relationship that grows between Tara and Marcus is well balanced and their sexual attraction is off the charts HOT! Ms. Agnew smoothly weaves the eroticism between Marcus and Tara into the story, making it part of the tension of the complex intrigues of this plot. This is a hot, intense thriller that paranormal romance readers will enjoy." ~ *Just Erotic Romance Reviews*

"The twists and turns of this story will keep the reader glued to the pages...Between the strong passions that develop between Tara and Marcus, and the dangerous man that is hunting Tara, the story will leave the reader breathless. I cannot wait to read more books by Ms. Agnew." ~ *ECataRomance Reviews*

"Denise Agnew continues to deliver inventive, passionate stories that never fail to delight readers..." ~ *Fallen Angel Reviews*

"This book is a real page-turner...it is an adventure that readers won't soon forget." ~ *The Romance Studio*

Denise A. Agnew

Sins
and
Secrets

Ellora's Cave
Romantica Publishing

An Ellora's Cave Romantica Publication

www.ellorascave.com

Sins and Secrets

ISBN 1419954229
ALL RIGHTS RESERVED.
Sins and Secrets Copyright © 2005 Denise A. Agnew
Edited by Martha Punches
Cover art by Syneca

Electronic book Publication August 2005
Trade paperback Publication July 2006

Warning:

The following material contains graphic sexual content meant for mature readers. This story has been rated S-ensuous by a minimum of three independent reviewers.

Ellora's Cave Publishing offers three levels of Romantica™ reading entertainment: S (S-ensuous), E (E-rotic), and X (X-treme).

S-*ensuous* love scenes are explicit and leave nothing to the imagination.

E-*rotic* love scenes are explicit, leave nothing to the imagination, and are high in volume per the overall word count. In addition, some E-rated titles might contain fantasy material that some readers find objectionable, such as bondage, submission, same sex encounters, forced seductions, and so forth. E-rated titles are the most graphic titles we carry; it is common, for instance, for an author to use words such as "fucking", "cock", "pussy", and such within their work of literature.

X-*treme* titles differ from E-rated titles only in plot premise and storyline execution. Unlike E-rated titles, stories designated with the letter X tend to contain controversial subject matter not for the faint of heart.

Sins and Secrets

Special Investigations Agency

ഇ

Dedication

ॐ

For the soldier of my heart, Terry.

Acknowledgements

Thank you to the following people for information on domestic violence:

Sabrah Agree
Janet Mills
Elizabeth Stewart
Barbara Woodward

Trademarks Acknowledgement

The author acknowledges the trademarked status and trademark owners of the following wordmarks mentioned in this work of fiction:

Subaru: Fuji Jukogyo Kabushiki Kaisha TA Fuji Heavy Industries Ltd.

Alterra: Nissan Motor Co.

Glock: Glock, Inc.

Chapter One

ঙ

Whoever fights monsters should see to it that in the process he does not become a monster. For when you look long into the abyss, the abyss also looks into you.

—Nietzsche

In seconds, Tara Crayton's dream lover made her hotter than any living man could.

White cotton sheets, plain and soft, touched her feverish, naked skin as the man tipped her back onto the bed. His big body, tall and heavy with muscle, came down next to her. Inhaling deeply, she caught a faint whiff of all man, something strong, hot and knock-her-to-her-knees sexual. A shiver raced over her skin as anticipation made her moan and move against the strong body pressed against her.

She didn't see who loved her each midnight-dark evening with a passion she never experienced in waking hours. Sensations rather than visuals dominated this dream, frustrating her efforts to know her lover once and for all. Would he be someone she knew, or a man created from long-suppressed sexual desires?

She savored erotic shivers as his big hands skimmed over her back, then down to her ass with fleeting touches, arousing every sense. She plunged her hands into the soft, wavy length of his hair.

He moaned as he kissed her, as if he'd never tasted anything so delicious in his life. His mouth coaxed rather than stormed, tasted rather than demanded, as he brushed her lips with light caresses. Tara craved more and sealed her mouth to his in a deeper, more demanding kiss. Taking the invitation, he slanted his mouth against hers. He took his time, lingering with a building eroticism until her heart pounded. Tara gasped as his tongue plunged inside. With slow, pumping strokes, his tongue danced and moved against hers. Moisture slicked her vagina and the muscles there tightened and released in preparation for the deep, hard penetration of unyielding man.

Tara wanted him inside her so much, tears came to her eyes. Desire drove her like a wild beast. She craved raw pulse-pounding sex. Sex so profound and altering she knew when he took her she'd never want another man.

She begged with her body, twining her legs around his. She enjoyed the roughness of his hair brushing the insides of her thighs, the power in rock-hard musculature moving sinuously.

He slid down, nuzzling her neck with licks and kisses. Shivering, she arched against him as she pleaded wordlessly.

Hot, sweet kisses fell on her lips and enticed her senses with their featherlight contact. She moaned while the man's hands traced tender caresses over her ribs, her back, then landed on her ass again. He touched as if he cherished and protected her. Exquisite love and hot swirls of desire dipped into her stomach and spread outward.

Cupping her ass cheeks in his hands, the man squeezed. Tara wriggled, her nipples brushing against his pecs with a bone-melting arousal.

As his lips trailed down to her breast, Tara moved her hands from his hair to grasp his broad shoulders, hanging on for dear life as her nipple hardened under the first brush of his tongue. She strained to speak, her throat tight. She wanted to plead that he take her now before this sweet dream could fade into inky night.

He licked her other nipple, and the hot sweep of his tongue, rough and soft at the same time, made her gasp. "Oh my God."

Tortured by the need for more, she moaned. He cupped her breasts in each hand, then set to work. He sucked hard on each nipple, then soothed with a long, savoring lick. He grasped the other nipple between his fingers and rolled and pinched.

Sharp, stinging pleasure bolted through her. He started a new rhythm. Dream man licked one nipple, then sucked. He stroked the other breast with his thumb. Lick. Suck. Stroke. Drawn into stiff tips, her nipples tingled.

She captured his long, thick cock between her thighs. He groaned and moved against her as she kept him trapped. She could feel him *growing harder, engorged and ready. Maybe if she shifted against him he would slip inside her.*

She wanted that so much.

Dream man switched his torture to the other breast. Long, indolent lick. Strong, persistent sucking. Lingering, soothing strokes.

Almost weeping with need, she writhed in sensual torment.

Finally, he released her breasts, trailing kisses down her stomach. He spread her legs. Oh yes. Maybe now he would –

A loud ringing vaulted her from the dream and straight up in bed. Her breath rasped in her throat, her body hungry for completion. The phone on her bed stand shrieked for attention. Sunlight pierced the lace curtains covering her bedroom windows.

Irritated, she reached for the phone. "Hello?"

"Whoa, sis." Her sister Josie's amused tone came over the line. "Get up on the wrong side of the bed?"

Sighing, Tara ran a hand through her rumpled hair. "Yes."

"Well, you're not going to like what I'm going to tell you now, so brace yourself."

She knew from her older sister's tone that it couldn't be bad news about Mom or Dad, thank goodness. "Oh?"

"Drake is out of prison."

Tara's brain froze up with sudden fear. She couldn't recall the last time she felt this frightened. *Maybe the last time his hand came at my face? The last time I winced because I knew he would yell? The last time he ridiculed me for my psychic abilities?* Six years had passed since she'd grown up fast and left a bad situation.

She slumped against her pillows. "What? When?"

"Monday. Remember Barrie Kiplinger?"

How could she forget the kind old Sergeant Major who'd lived near them during time Drake pulled his antics? Barrie had told her to leave Drake, because someday Drake would kill her if she didn't run and run far.

"I remember Barrie."

Josie sighed. "Barrie called me late last night. He asked for your number, but I got out of him what he needed. He told me Drake was out and might head your way."

Fresh anxiety rose inside Tara. She must do something. But what? She'd known this day would come. She'd moved away from Fort Leavenworth, Kansas, to Denver, Colorado, to escape bad memories and Drake's hostile family. Settling into a life so different from the one she'd known had given her a false sense of security…one she knew might someday end.

"Shit," Tara whispered into the phone. "Shit."

"You can say that again. What are you going to do? You can't stay there. Come to Montana. The ranch up here is secluded—"

"No. Are you nuts? I won't lead him to your family." The idea of Drake coming after Josie, her husband Jordan, and their twin baby girls made Tara's skin ripple with apprehension. "No way. Look, I need to think this over and plan. I'll let you know later what I'm going to do."

When she said goodbye and returned the cordless phone to the cradle, she wondered if this new nightmare would soon replace the beautiful dreams she expected every night. She closed her eyes and rolled toward the wall, snuggling under the flannel sheets so she wouldn't have to face the cold world too soon.

Planning her next move should have taken up her next thoughts. Instead, her dream man haunted her, lingering around the edges of her tired body. She knew what was wrong.

She needed a good, hard lovemaking session.

Drake once told her she must be a whore to like sex so much, and to crave it messy, fast and raw. No decent woman, he maintained, liked sex *that* much.

He'd wanted vanilla sex with the traditional man on top scenario. Not that she objected to the missionary position, but she longed to have other experiences in the bedroom. She'd suggested adventures that shocked the hell out of Drake.

Although she should have known better, she allowed his ranting about her "puerile wants" to downgrade her. His disgust had made her feel that she shouldn't desire to experiment with new and exciting lovemaking.

Drake almost ruined her desire for love and sex, but she'd fought her way through it with a therapist's help. Maybe she was ready for the challenge of a good, loving relationship with a man who cared for her.

Could these erotic fantasies be conjured by her psychic abilities? Her visions brought her trouble more than once, especially with Drake. Still, she wouldn't abandon her dreams. They reminded her that at least in her mind she could pretend such a wonderful man existed for her.

When the phone rang again, she flinched. She picked it up quickly, expecting her sister.

A familiar, rough-edged voice filled the line. "Hello, Tara."

Drake. A shiver wiggled through her body like a worm. At first, she remained silent, frozen to the spot by a well-known fear she thought she'd conquered when he'd left the courtroom and her life.

She couldn't speak.

"I know you're there," he said. "Happy to hear from me?" When she still didn't speak, he whispered, "I'm coming back to you, sweetheart. Real soon."

It was an ugly coincidence he'd called right after her sister, and it creeped her out to no end. She shivered, colder than she'd been in a long time.

Instead of answering, she slid the phone back into its cradle. She lay back on the bed, anticipation tightening her muscles as she waited for the phone to ring one more time. If she'd learned one thing in her marriage to Drake, the man stayed persistent. This wouldn't be the last she heard from him.

Five minutes went by. Ten. Fifteen.

Thirty minutes passed before her muscles relaxed.

* * * * *

"Bitch."

Drake Hollister sat in the chartreuse beanbag chair, black leatherette Bible in his lap. Dim light from the naked bulb above illuminated the rented basement room. Thank the Lord for his old friend Hickey. Without him, he'd have no place to stay.

He closed his eyes and allowed more emotions to swamp him.

Hate.

No guilt, no remorse. Pure, seething hate. *God, how good.*

The phone call earlier pissed him off. The bitch hung up on him.

No doubt about it, if Tara didn't marry him again, she would have to die. The serpent had bitten her, its teeth sharp as razors from hell. Satan sent many temptations to corrupt, and Tara had taken to them all.

No one else could cleanse her sin but him. The bitch needed to learn her lesson, and he would make her see the error of her ways. Emotion seared his psyche as he gritted his teeth and let righteousness spill over him in gigantic waves.

Childhood memories flickered through his mind. He couldn't remember feeling regret or responsibility in any great quantity. He wasn't sure he knew what those words meant. He inhaled deeply. A laugh bubbled up from his gut and exploded from his throat. He threw back his head and let it rip. Righteousness boiled inside him. Tara needed cleansing, needed to find God, and no one could show her the way other than him.

He glanced at the stark concrete walls, the impersonal surface a balm to his soul. Once Tara realized how much she needed and loved him, she would follow him into heaven.

Loathing seared his mind with sharp needles. He clutched the Bible, fingers searching the surface. He rubbed the cover and breathed deeply. His salvation came through this book. Planning would bring him results.

Craving built within him to take action now. *Now. Now. Now.*

But no. Patience. The Lord would provide the answer.

He shifted on the beanbag, opened the Bible and started to read. Syllables passed his lips rapidly. The faster he read, the harder his heartbeat quickened. His palms became sweaty, his stomach muscles tight. Anticipation and need gathered inside. Planning Tara's capture and redemption took hard work and preparation. He must search his soul for the answers. Anything less would bring God's wrath upon him and ultimate failure.

He tried to conjure fresh, bloody images. He closed his eyes at first and felt the cold plastic under his arms. Goose bumps slid along his skin, then down his body like an insidious worm, slithering and slimy. He shivered again. Damn. A swarm of thoughts filled his head, buzzing like bees. His breathing deepened, his heart rate increased. All his senses heightened. His dingy room smelled yellow. His own clothes, tainted by sweat, reminded him of brown. The furniture embraced him, brought him closer to nirvana. What the fuck was nirvana anyway? He'd never understood it. Images floated into his mind's eye that haunted him night after night in his dreams. He kept his eyes firmly closed. He'd find the spot again, the one where nightmares couldn't penetrate.

God, the nightmares got worse. They tormented him with shadowy images and darker fears born from the depths of misery. Hell had something to do with it, most certainly. And the way to remove his torment was to redeem the one thing that reminded him of what he'd had.

He would convert the sinful woman and God would make her pay. She might ignore his biblical warnings, the heavenly signs he would show her. The devil would claim her soul if she resisted and damn her to eternal hell.

Just the thought of her one brown eye and one blue eye made him shudder with a peculiar dread. Devil's marks, he knew. Only Satan could mar a woman's eyes like that.

Drake took a long, shuddering breath. "Maybe if I show her the way of the Lord, she will repent and be cleansed. Then I won't have to send her to heaven early."

Smiling with satisfaction, he sighed.

* * * * *

"He is the most gorgeous piece of manhood I have ever seen." Cecelia Davenport twirled a tendril of her long, wavy blonde hair around one finger. The tight spiral sprung back into position when Cecelia released it. "The muscles on that man are something else. And his hair. Thick, gorgeous blond."

"You've seen his penis?" Sugar McPherson asked in a hushed whisper.

If Tara didn't know her flakey coworkers well, she might have been surprised by their outrageous conversation. She yawned and strode toward them as they clustered near the coffeemaker in the break room. Sugar and Cecelia were twenty-five and twenty-nine respectively, so at thirty-five years old Tara often felt out of step with their take on men. Sure, she loved to ogle gorgeous men as much as the next hot-blooded American woman. Yet she found Cecelia and Sugar's crass approach a little immature.

She took a sip of coffee from her huge travel mug, needing the caffeine for a morning jumpstart. Cecelia and Sugar watched her approach. Their expressions said they knew she'd heard the conversation.

"Time to use your *inside* voices." Tara gave them a conspiratorial smile and then lowered her tone to a volume that wouldn't carry across the line of endless cubicles. "Don't tell me, you guys are gossiping about Jason Forte again? Chief Financial Officer Jason Forte?"

"How did you guess?" Cecelia reached for the cooler and filled her mug with water. "I mean, in this company he's the only great piece of ass around."

Weary, Tara tucked her hair behind her ears and went along for the ride. "He's a too polished for me."

Cecelia sniffed. "Polished is good, isn't it?"

"It means money and maybe even brains," Sugar said. "I may be engaged, but I'm not dead. And let me tell you, Jason is hot."

A toss of Sugar's burnished, short brunette hair punctuated her sentence. She wiggled her left hand so they could see the dazzling ring.

The glittering marquise diamond solitaire was a testament to her new status. She flaunted the ring whenever possible. Tara couldn't blame her. If two carats of colorless, flawless diamond glimmered on Tara's hand, she would display it, too.

Cecelia sighed. "Give me one chance to try that man on for size."

Tara knew what her friend meant, and while she could drool right along with the rest of them, the idea of Jason's skin against hers didn't sound the least appealing. Nope. Something about him left her ill at ease. Suspicions about him nagged at her, though she didn't have any evidence to back them up. He'd spent too much time lately cozying up to her in the employee lounge and water cooler, eyeballing her with those disconcerting, cool chameleon eyes. Icy and assured combined in Jason's face with the carved cheekbones of Adonis. With a sharp nose and a wide jaw, he missed perfection by the tiniest smidgen. Ego shone through his expressions, every word and gesture designed to plot and plan. She didn't like him.

Tara wrinkled her nose. "To each his own. I'm looking for something more."

Sugar brushed her hands down the side of her immaculate blue gabardine skirt. "So what have you got planned for the weekend?"

"You're thinking about the weekend already?" Tara asked.

Sugar sniffed. "Of course. What else is there in life but weekends?"

The women tittered, and Tara managed a halfhearted smile.

"So how about it," Cecelia said. "Do you have a hot date, Tara?"

Tara groaned. "Yeah, right."

"We would have heard about it." Cecelia's green, exotic tip-tilted eyes glittered with a teasing light. "When is the last time you had a date, Tara?"

Tara finished her coffee. She pursed her lips. "Let's see…maybe about a year ago?"

"Holy pepperoni," Cecelia said as she shook her head. "Why?"

Tara shrugged, tired of explaining to people why men didn't seem to find her interesting. "Maybe because my tits aren't big enough and my ass isn't small enough. Who knows?"

Cecelia and Sugar laughed at Tara's self-depreciation. Even Tara could smile at her joke, well aware her reasons might be the truth. Many men didn't see beyond the packaging to the goods inside. Truth be told, her butt wasn't huge and her breasts weren't tiny, and her figure was slim by most people's standards. Still, she didn't expect perfection from herself any more than she expected flawlessness from others. Working out didn't even guarantee perfection. She rode her bike, lifted weights and walked to stay healthy, not to obtain a bod to die for.

Some men found her unusual eyes alarming, and she couldn't say she blamed them. Every time she met someone, she witnessed startled looks or intense curiosity. Most people didn't know it was possible for a person to have mixed eye colors in one individual and it shocked them.

Sugar glanced at Tara's turquoise blue suit. "Maybe you should try wearing a shorter skirt."

Tara preferred the comfort and covering of long, flowing skirts. Today her short, fitted turquoise blue blazer and swingy pleated skirt made her feel good despite a headache coming on and her weariness.

As she glanced back at the rows of cubicles, an odd desolation clouded her mood. Amazing how a person could be in a room full of people and yet be alone. She'd felt that way for longer than she cared to admit, but she'd also grown used to the fact that she didn't fit in as well as she'd like. *Always awkward Tara.* That's what her family called her, and she'd gotten used to the moniker long ago.

"Now there's always Marcus," Cecelia said, then winked. "He's almost cute in a totally geeky kind of way."

Sugar huffed. "He's *gay.*"

Cecelia sighed. "Too bad."

"Morning, ladies," a harping voice said from behind them. "It's eight-ten in the morning. I've got some extra work lined up for you. I've already put it on your desks."

Bettina Carlyle didn't suffer gossips. The somewhat cynical fifty-something woman walked toward their grouping. She was a lazy person's worst enemy. As word processing general manager, she possessed an iron-hard personality and a tongue as sharp as a viper for those who didn't do their jobs. Today she wore a plain but professional navy pantsuit. She looked up at them from her petite stature. A network of wrinkles around her eyes and a tendency to frown a little too much gave her thin face a harsh look. Her short salt-and-pepper hair covered her head in a curly cap that didn't do much to flatter. At the same time, her commanding presence and quick wits ensured few people defied her.

Douglas Financial Services employed one sharp lady in this woman, and Tara respected her fairness and her honesty. She made people toe the line, and Tara couldn't fault her for that.

"Tara." Bettina displayed a genuine smile, then frowned at Sugar and Cecelia.

Sugar and Cecelia gave weak smiles and soft greetings, then trotted away to do her bidding.

Tara grinned. "I guess I'd better get my butt in gear."

"I won't stop you from getting another cup of coffee before you do." Bettina's eyebrows went up as she perused the giant purple travel mug. "What's that thing hold? About sixty-five gallons of fuel oil? My God. If I drank that much coffee, I'd be halfway to the moon by now." Tara started for the employee lounge and Bettina followed. "Something wrong?"

Tara stopped at the coffeepot, opened her travel mug and filled it halfway. She snapped the lid back on the mug. "Ah, caffeine."

"That doesn't answer my question." Frown lines formed between the older woman's eyes.

When Bettina continued to scowl, Tara said, "All right, all right. There is a problem. But nothing I can't handle."

"What is it?"

Tara's hands trembled a moment before she put down the mug. "My ex-husband is out of jail."

Bettina's normally unflappable expression held true concern. Her blue eyes narrowed. "Oh dear."

"As far as I know he's in Kansas so there's no reason to believe he'll turn up here."

"Tara, this is serious. When did he get out of Fort Leavenworth?"

Tara rubbed a hand over her eyes, realizing that she didn't feel well. Since her sister called to warn her that Drake Hollister had finished his jail term, Tara's insides seemed to churn on a regular basis.

"When did *who* get out of Fort Leavenworth?" A deep, masculine voice said from the doorway.

Bettina grinned at Marcus Hyatt as he entered the lounge. "Well, hello. Decided to come to work today?"

He flashed a wide, pleasant smile. "There was a bad accident at Twenty-Second and Austin and the traffic backed up for miles. Damned intersection is a deathtrap."

Tall and gangly, Marcus reminded Tara of boys in high school who spent time in chess or Latin club. He had tied his thick, espresso-dark hair back in a long ponytail at the nape of his neck, and the big tan glasses on his face swallowed his blue eyes. With his hair pulled back, his nose seemed thin and so did his high cheekbones. Tiny lines around his eyes and sometimes a crease between his eyebrows when he frowned gave extra character to his face. From his wardrobe selection, it appeared as if Italian designers filled his closet on a regular basis. Today his dark blue suit, gray silk blend shirt and slightly darker gray tie spelled chic. He dressed to the nines every day, even on dress-down Friday. She shared a cubicle with him, and he stayed so quiet most the time she didn't often notice when he entered or left.

Marcus reached for the coffee carafe and poured a cup of black java. "I see. You're going to dummy up because I walked in."

Bettina pressed Tara's shoulder. "It's up to Tara if she wants to share her personal life. See you later."

Bettina closed the door as she left.

"So, what did I miss at the water cooler this morning? Ladies accessing the virtues of men's asses again?" Marcus asked.

She made a soft laugh. "You goof, someone is going to hear you someday and think you're..."

Did she dare tell him what people suspected?

He put down his mug and stepped closer until less than a few inches separated them. As she inhaled, the sensual, subtle richness of musk in his aftershave tantalized her. Damn, he smelled good.

"I'm what?" Marcus looked down at her with attentive evaluation. One big hand planted on the counter next to her. "Come on, 'fess up."

"You don't want to know."

Amusement danced in his eyes. "Now I really have to know just because you said that."

All Tara's warning systems went on alert. A telltale prickle touched the back of her neck, and she knew if she didn't force it down, a vision would swallow up her sight.

Before she could move a muscle, before she could make an excuse to leave and hide, the vision encompassed her. Her body went cold and she shivered. In flashes of perception, she saw Marcus crouching behind an old building, his face determined and yet tired. He held an automatic weapon at the ready. She recognized the battle dress uniform he wore as desert khaki. Steel-eyed, he gazed at a perpetrator she couldn't see. He leveled his weapon and took aim, no hesitation or mercy in his expression. Icy blue eyes she'd once thought harmless glittered with danger. His hair was cut very short. Marcus looked ready to kick some serious butt. Nothing about him appeared the teeny, tiniest bit nerdish.

She gasped. He didn't resemble the mild-mannered man she knew, but everything like a serious, in-your-face warrior.

As the vision popped out of her inner sight, a wave of dizziness passed through her and she staggered. She grabbed for support just as she felt Marcus' arms go around her. Arms iron-hard with strength encircled her waist. She clutched at his suit jacket lapels. Dizziness refused to leave and her knees weakened.

"Whoa," Marcus said as Tara's eyelids fluttered and almost closed. "Easy, now. What's wrong?"

She clasped his biceps, but before she could say a word, he swept her up into his arms. Surprise kept her silent while he strode across the break room and headed for the couch. No indeed, nothing skimpy or wimpy about this man's arms. Solid, dependable and gentle enough to cradle a woman close.

He laid her on the couch, and she leaned her head back on a pillow. "I'm fine. Really."

Hands on his hips, he wore a puzzled frown. "Yeah, sure you are. You almost passed out on me, and I'm supposed to believe you're okay?"

"Take my word for it."

One corner of his mouth turned up. "Right."

After a vision, she sometimes felt weak, but she'd never passed out. This time the vision had been clear and staggering enough to push her close to fainting.

One thing wouldn't leave her mind. Why had she seen him playing soldier in the vision? Despite curiosity, she couldn't ask him about the vision. No one, not even Bettina, knew about her abilities. Experience taught Tara long ago that you didn't tell your coworkers, your neighbors, and not even your family about strange visions. What happened six years ago was bad enough, and jeers and looks of disbelief didn't rank up there with her favorite experiences. No, she'd keep Marcus in the dark as she did others.

Nervous, she sat up and then eased to her feet.

"Hey." He took hold of her upper arm, his gaze assessing her like a doctor. "You almost fell on your face. Give yourself time."

"I've got work to do." She didn't shake off his grip, half grateful for the support. "Bettina is going to come in here and wonder what's going on."

Although he looked at her like she'd lost her mind, he didn't move away or blink an eye. "Maybe you'd better make an appointment with a doctor. You're pale as hell."

She took a deep breath. "I'm feeling perfectly fine."

"Does all this have something to do with the guy in Fort Leavenworth? Do you know someone in the clink?"

"Yes." The word popped from her before she could stop it. "He used to be in the clink. He got out a few days ago."

Marcus' eyes hardened with concentrated scrutiny. She felt like a suspect under interrogation. "A friend?"

"As far from a friend as he can get." When he continued to stare at her, she confessed. "My ex-husband, Drake Hollister."

He frowned. "How long have you been apart?"

To her surprise, her eyes moistened with tears, and she blinked. "He's been in jail six years. We were married for five years."

"What did he do?"

"He...um...he beat—" She swallowed hard, amazed that she still couldn't say it. Perhaps she felt putting Drake's domestic abuse into words made the situation more real than it already was. She didn't feel like putting her toe in that reality anytime soon.

Marcus' frown deepened. "My God." With a slow, gentle brush of his fingers, he caressed the side of her face. "He hurt you?"

Shivers of sweet comfort slid through her body. Then new and different emotions replaced consolation when looked down on her with compassion and growing awareness.

Desire.

Sweet and hot, arousal stirred in her stomach. Astonished by her response, she dared look into his serious eyes and saw a flickering of either anger or understanding. Maybe he'd once known someone who'd been abused by their spouse.

"He hurt me. More than once," she said.

His fingers dropped away from the fleeting caress, but he still stood so near he could easily kiss her if he wanted.

Kiss her.

Where had that harebrained idea come from? Why would he want to kiss her? Tara shivered. She would have the phantom lover or no man at all.

Oh Lord. What would a shrink say about that?

Another frown creased his forehead. "You're not afraid of me, I hope?"

She shook her head. "No, no. Of course not."

He took a deep breath and allowed it to slip from him in a heavy sigh. "Good. I'd never hurt a woman." His eyes took her in, locking dead on to her gaze. "Men who abuse women are scum." He brushed his index finger over her nose in a teasing gesture. "I like touching you, though."

Wow. His voice sounds husky and sexy. Like a man who just had sex. Or wants to.

Several realizations jolted her like a blow from a sledgehammer. Quiet filled the room, the atmosphere overlaid by a scintillating sensuality delicious and forbidden.

A woman could sink into his shimmering gaze, pulled into the fathomless aquatic blue even though his glasses made his eyes look larger.

His six-feet, three-inches made her five-feet, seven-inches feel petite. And his attentiveness, his strength changed her perspective. As his suit jacket moved over his shoulders, Tara realized her impression of him being skinny might be false. Marcus' shoulders suddenly looked broad and steady.

Of course, there are those strong arms…

She asked without thinking, "You like touching me?"

He nodded, his finely sculpted mouth parting. He looked shell-shocked, as if seeing her for the first time. "Very much."

His voice rumbled with a deep masculinity, brushing over her ears like a feather. For Tara, the outside world receded, leaving them the last two people on earth.

If this man was gay, she'd eat her bra.

Teased and tempted, she almost leaned nearer to him. "Are you flirting with me, Marcus?"

He blinked slowly. She took a breath to ease the heavy anticipation pumping through her blood, hot and liquid.

"I might be."

Her head filled this time with her imagination and not a vision. His tanned, muscled body sprawled on satin sheets, arms and legs stretched wide, ready for her to feast like a ravenous woman-beast.

Marcus shook his head, as if trying to throw off the effects of a drug. He managed to drag his gaze away from hers. Stunned by the turn in her thoughts about her colleague, she walked back to the sink.

He followed her to the sink. "You going to be all right?"

She kept her gaze evasive. She didn't want to see what emotions resided in his eyes. "Of course."

"Good. Now, tell me what you started to say earlier. About what people were going to think of me if I was talking about men's asses?"

Cheered by the change in conversation, she gave him a teasing grin. "No way. You'd get mad."

"Tell me, or there will be consequences. I'll steal the ink cartridge out of your printer."

She quirked an exasperated smile. "It's your printer, too."

A bashful look came over his face. "Oh yeah."

Buoyed by his teasing, she held her hands up in a gesture of surrender. "All right, all right. But don't get mad." She paused. "Everyone thinks you're gay."

A laugh rippled from him. She tried to remember the last time she'd heard that husky, sexy laugh. Marcus didn't chortle like a fool or bellow like a buffoon. No, the guy possessed a deep, nerve-tingling nuance in his chuckle that spelled sex in huge neon letters.

"Everyone?" He didn't look surprised or angry. Marcus edged closer, and she saw the intent, insistent expression in his eyes. "Do you think I'm gay?"

"I hadn't given it much thought. It's all right, though. You don't have to prove anything to me." Heat filled her face and nervous words followed as she comprehended how provocative her statement sounded. "Then again, some women speculate that you might be a metrosexual."

His brow furrowed and he leaned one hand on the counter near the sink. "What the hell is a metrosexual?"

She rushed to explain. "It's nothing bad." She couldn't help but smile. "A man who is heterosexual but doesn't eschew fashion sense."

Instead of looking offended, his grin returned and grew wider, eyes sparkling with humor. He looked down at his shirt and then shrugged. He laughed and his voice took on a soft nuance that held sensual promise in every syllable. "Actually, I think I need to prove to you I'm not gay."

She swallowed hard. "No you don't."

As his gaze took a detour from her eyes down to her lips, she felt the burn and tingle of that visual caress all the way to her womb. "Maybe later we can…" His attention dropped down to her breasts. "…discuss this topic in detail."

Amazed and shocked that he was coming on to her she said, "It's not important, is it? I'm not homophobic."

When his gaze snapped back to hers, she detected a challenge. "Neither am I. But I'm not gay. Not by a long shot."

He watched her with a disconcerting, sharp assessment that penetrated right through his glasses and straight to her soul. For about two seconds she thought she also saw a warm and tender glimmer in his eyes. A shimmering heat enveloped her as his gaze went from her hair down to her breasts, and then cruised down her body until he fixated on her ankles.

As Cecelia would say, *Holy pepperoni. Okay, now you've gone straight over the edge, girl.*

She felt flustered, and her mouth went dry as sandpaper. "We'd better get to work."

He made a gesture toward the door. "Lead on."

Once they settled in the cubicle, she wondered why a smart man like Marcus stayed in a lower-paying job in the word processing area. While he worked like the wind and seemed the most efficient employee in the area, she knew he possessed a bachelor's degree in criminal justice.

Perhaps he had been in the military and his experiences there had scarred him? Or perhaps he'd been wounded and couldn't go back to a job that demanded physical work. She'd felt the strength in his arms when he'd carried her. Physical problems didn't seem to add up as the answer. Exasperated by the vision's ability to ruffle her composure, she shoved thoughts of her cubicle mate out of her head.

She needed to spend time locating a lawyer, but the first call she tried making to the local domestic abuse organization resulted in a busy signal. She decided she'd try back in a half hour.

Twenty minutes into a document, she stopped when the phone on her desk rang. Jumpy, she let the phone ring three times before she answered it.

"Hey, you didn't really think you could get away with hanging up on me this morning, did ya?" Drake's biting voice, strong with sarcasm, pierced her ears.

Remembering the lessons she'd learned at the domestic violence shelter in Kansas City, she didn't engage him.

A soft chuckle left his throat. "I know how to get to you. I'm coming for you, so you'd better watch your back. You're mine, honey, and I'm coming to claim you. Mine, do you hear? If any other man so much as touches you, Tara, he's going to die."

She couldn't help the gasp that came from her throat.

She thought after years away from him she would have learned to disengage her emotions and protect herself from his negativity. *Close him off, Tara, or he's going to get through that mental crack of yours and feed like a leech.* She took a shallow breath and tried to visualize a shield of white and gold between her and Drake that would bounce his negativity right back at him. She lost the visualization as he spoke.

He sighed. "Damn, honey, you never get it, do you? See, that's why you need me. Other men think you're not too pretty and not too bright."

Sticks and stones may break my bones, but names will never hurt me.

Alarm rippled unbidden over her skin, shortening her breath and making her shudder. She'd escaped the living hell he'd put her through. Now, like a weed that wouldn't die, he'd jumped back into her world as if he'd never left.

She felt waves of anger, a black miasma like revolting sulfur fumes from hell, rolling through the airwaves. His twisted hate manifested so thickly she couldn't erect a shield quickly enough to avoid the psychic impact.

"I know you're listening, so you better pay attention," he said with intense menace, his gravelly, deep voice vowing to finish what he'd started six years ago. "No more fucking around! You hear me?"

Shivers rolled through her skin, and sweat popped out on her forehead. She felt icy and hot all at once. The idea this man might know where she worked made her skin crawl with apprehension. "Drake, I don't have time for this."

He laughed, harsh and guttural. "Damn, baby, you took long enough to answer. What's the matter with you?"

Oh, damn, damn, damn. I should have hung up, I shouldn't have answered. I know better.

Her hand shook and she gripped the receiver harder. How dare he? How dare he come back into her life and ruin the peace she'd fought for years to obtain?

Tara almost slammed down the receiver. Instead, she forced herself to replace it in the cradle with the slowest of movements. Breathing hard, she stared at the phone as if it was a Komodo dragon ready to bite her. She hated feeling this vulnerable and out of control. She put her head in her hands, hiding her face and trying to keep her composure. She'd let the used-up, clammy bastard get to her. Whether he meant any of it or not, she hadn't prepared herself for the possibility he might take this tactic when he left jail.

She grabbed her purse, jumped up and left the cubicle. She thought she heard Marcus' voice asking her what was wrong, but she ignored him. Nothing mattered but seeing a lawyer about what she could do to stop Drake. She walked swiftly to Bettina's office, hoping she could catch her there and ask for time away.

Cursed with a high work ethic, Tara felt guilty if she took off work for any reason. She knew guilt like this wasn't healthy—insistence on perfection in herself. At the same time, Tara acknowledged that her brain would be mush for the rest of the day. Her head throbbed, her jaw ached and her entire body seemed drained. Maybe she *was* coming down with something.

When she reached Bettina's office, she saw the older woman standing near her secretary's desk. "Hi Tara. What can we do for you?"

Tara greeted them both and gave her best smile, even though she didn't feel it. "I'm sorry to break in like this but can I have a private word with you, Bettina?"

Bettina gestured toward her office, concern evident in her normally stern face. "Please come in and have a seat."

Once inside, Bettina closed the door and sat behind her modest-sized desk. Tara settled in a small chair off to the side under a large window. Bright July sun, muted by a vertical blind, filled the small office. Despite Bettina's frequently crusty exterior, her office was cheerful with pictures of Rock Mountain landscapes on the walls.

"Now, what can I do for you?" Bettina asked, leaning on her desk and clasping her hands together.

When Tara explained the phone calls, alarm raced across the older woman's features. "He called you here?"

"I don't know how he got the number, or how he even knew where I was working."

Bettina frowned darkly. "My heavens. You must be a wreck. Is there anything I can do?"

"Allow me this afternoon off to square some things away."

"Absolutely. And if you need tomorrow off to get things started, let me know this afternoon."

"I'm going to try to get an order of protection or a restraining order, whatever I can get in Colorado. I know every state is different. I may have to go before a judge and I don't know when I can get that done."

"Then let me recommend a lawyer I know can help you. Ethel Allegra." Bettina flipped through her address book, then wrote down some information on a yellow sticky note. "She has her own firm."

"I think I remember hearing something about her. Isn't she just down the block from here?"

"Two buildings south. She's handled quite a few high-profile cases and she's the best lawyer I know."

Tara frowned. "I don't know if I can afford a lawyer with that kind of reputation."

Bettina shook her head. "Don't you worry. Tell her I referred you and explain the situation. She'll either give you a sliding fee schedule you can afford, or she'll do it for nothing. She's been helping battered women for a long time, and she's especially hard on stalkers. Your ex-husband will think he's been hit by a freight train."

A new lightness entered Tara's heart. Maybe she could find defense against the man who'd almost ended her life and wanted to do God knows what again.

"This is great. I certainly need some good news."

Bettina shook her head, sadness clear in her eyes. "Do you think he might come to Denver?"

"I wouldn't put it past him. The thing that kept him away from me the last time was…" Her voice drifted as she flashed back to the traumatic incident that put her in the hospital, his hands hard and ruthless, his shouted insults cruel and demeaning. "He was arrested after the last time."

"I'm really sorry this is happening, dear. Is there a friend you can stay with? I don't feel comfortable knowing he might show up in town and you're all alone."

"No. But it's all right. I'll work things out."

Bettina's concern warmed Tara's heart and made her feel a little better at the same time it made her feel worse.

She hadn't tried hard enough to socialize and make friends, people she could rely on locally. She might be an oddball, but that didn't mean she couldn't have found people with similar interests. She'd taken her protectionism a little too far.

Nothing like having an epiphany this late in the game, Tara.

Tara rose from her chair. She clutched her purse in both hands like a lifeline and her fingers actually ached. She tried relaxing but then her shoulders and back tightened. "I appreciate your understanding and for the referral."

The older woman came around the desk. The sympathy in her eyes gave some comfort. "Anything I can do let me know." She pressed Tara's shoulder gently. "Don't let him get to you. That's one of the worst things you can do."

A mirthless laugh came from Tara. "If there's one thing I learned about my time with Drake, I discovered I have a well of strength. I'll get through this."

By the time she took the elevator to the parking garage and zeroed in on her red Subaru Outback, her nerves were frayed. On overload, Tara quickened her steps as her breathing came faster and her heart echoed the pace. Although her fingers tightened around her keys in a defensive mode, she felt too damn vulnerable for comfort. By the time she reached her car, she felt lightheaded.

You can't afford to do this, Tara. Don't let panic overwhelm you.

She pressed the auto unlock on her keys and her car beeped as the driver's door unlocked. The keys slipped from her fingers and landed with a clink on hard concrete.

"Shit," she muttered.

She heard a footfall and the whoosh of air behind her, then a hand landed on her shoulder.

Chapter Two

સ૦

Tara jumped, a startled squeak coming from her throat as she spun around, half expecting to see her ex-husband grinning at her with feral intent. Her nerves felt like they hung on the outside of her skin, hyperaware and ready to send her running.

Marcus' hand left her shoulder. Relief made her sag against her car.

Heavy unease intensified his gaze, and a frown creased his mouth. "What's going on?"

She inhaled deeply, then exhaled with a whoosh. "God, Marcus. What are you trying to do? Scare me to death? What are you doing here?"

"One question at a time please." He reached down, picked up her keys, then handed them to her. A gentle smile touched his lips. "Are you all right?"

Pissed, she sighed heavily. "I was until you scared me, thank you very much. Why are you following me?"

He took off his glasses and tucked them into his suit jacket. "Bettina said you weren't feeling well. But I think it's more than that. Did it have something to do with your ex-husband calling you?"

She gulped. "Yes."

"I suppose you're going to tell me to mind my own business."

She glared at him. "The thought did cross my mind." Curiosity made her ask, "Why are you hovering around me today like a guardian angel, Marcus?"

He held up one hand and ticked off points. "One, you look like you don't feel well and that worries me. Two, you're hiding something. Three, you're beautiful, so you're easy to look at."

Stunned by the accuracies of the first two points and amazed by the third, she said nothing at first.

When she found her voice, it came out rough. "I feel fine, I'm not hiding anything, and thank you for the compliment."

"Tara, I know you think this isn't any of my business, but I see real fear on your face." His voice went husky. "Talk to me."

She hesitated. Part of her wanted to tell him about Drake's threats. Then again, could she trust Marcus? Drake seemed like a nice guy, too, until the other side of him emerged, and she learned that she couldn't rely on her judgment about men.

Something strange had happened between her and Marcus today that couldn't be denied. He'd seen her experiencing one of her psychic episodes. No one had witnessed one of those since she'd left Kansas. Mortification and trepidation made her uneasy.

"What makes you think I'm hiding something?" she asked.

His mobile, finely carved mouth turned up in a smile. He crossed his arms and she itched to touch him, to feel a man's strong embrace. He shrugged. "I just know these things."

She gave an unladylike snort. "That's like telling a child 'just because'. I don't accept being treated like a child, Marcus."

He nodded, those eyes so serious and deep with questions, so concerned for her well-being she almost gave into the desire to throw herself into his arms and forget the world.

"It's…too complicated," she said.

She leaned against the car and weakness assaulted her legs. No, no. She couldn't pass out again. She'd be at the mercy of Marcus or any other man who wanted to take advantage of her.

She dropped her keys once more. Frustration filled her. God, could she be clumsier? He stooped to retrieve the tangle of keys, and then handed them to her again. His fingers brushed hers.

Warmth flowed through her hand, a pleasant tingling. "Thanks."

Compassion shimmered in that intense, all-knowing gaze. "You're welcome."

Determination also entered his expression, and Tara remembered the last time she'd seen him this stubborn. Earlier in the month one of the women in the word processing area insulted Tara to her face. Marcus cut the woman down to size. Cleanly, subtly, and without the biting sarcasm the woman had used on Tara. Tara's respect for him grew the day he'd defended her against the insults.

In the short time she'd known him, he'd been nonthreatening, laid-back and simply her casual friend. Now, as he stood close, his scent teased and his masculine heat made her feel things she didn't want to feel. Arousal. Intrigue. In less than the space of a few hours, her perspective on him began to change.

"Let me help you." His voice sounded self-assured and final. "Whatever is wrong, you don't have to handle it on your own."

She'd been thinking about the fact she didn't have any friends. Still, she'd meant female friends, not men.

"I'm on my own here, Marcus. When my ex-husband beat me, I survived. I got away from him."

He winched. "That doesn't mean you don't need help. What did he say to you on the phone?"

She almost lost her grip on her shoulder bag. She told him what Drake had said. "Now that you know, what good does that do either of us?"

His mouth thinned into a tighter line, as if he tried to jam back some emotion. After he swallowed hard, he continued. "Because something is wrong here. It started earlier when we were in the break room. You almost fell flat on your face, then you rushed out of the cubicle as if the devil was right behind you."

For a long time she waited, unsure. "I've only known you a month and a half."

"Two months," he said. "I've worked here two months."

Resistance rose up inside her. "I don't usually discuss personal issues with someone I haven't known very long."

"I understand that."

She dared look into his sea-tossed eyes, swells of emotion roiling inside her. Calm, collected and so together Marcus appeared angry, restless, eager to put a stop to Drake's terrorizing. She could have been grateful, but old unease took over.

"No, you don't understand. I refuse to allow any man bully me into telling him my personal business."

His gaze narrowed. "Bully you?"

"I've already told you I don't want your help. So, you can stop pushing me. Now, if you'll excuse me, I'm going home."

She felt him back off, a wave of frustration and determination barely easing inside him. His emotions came on so strong and thick, that with her ability to pick up other's feelings, she struggled to remember his emotions didn't belong to her. Her shields failed on every level today. She couldn't block waves of hate coming from Drake or the turbulence emanating from Marcus and that worried her on a whole new level. Disappointed, she decided today would fall into the lessons learned category. She would get over it and start anew tomorrow with her defenses ready.

He reached into his suit jacket and brought out an expensive-looking silver pen and a sticky notepad. He wrote something on the pad and then ripped off the top sheet.

She smiled despite the tension lingering between them. "You carry sticky notes in your jacket?"

He returned her grin and shrugged. "Of course."

Of course. When she looked down at the note and saw telephone numbers, she asked, "What's this for?"

"My home and cell phone numbers. If that creep gets anywhere near you or calls and you're frightened, contact me."

What could he do if Drake called? Nothing. Not wishing to sound ungrateful, she tucked the note into her bag. "Thanks. I'll see you tomorrow."

After she climbed inside her car and locked the doors, she noticed he watched her leave the parking garage. Once on the road, she didn't feel safer.

She breathed deeply, trying to ride out waves of tension twisting her shoulder muscles into a knot. She could use a good massage right about now. Preferably from a tall, handsome, dark and not-so-dangerous man.

The man in her dreams.

She cracked the window on the car and took in the scent of moisture in the air. Puffy clouds lowered over the mountains, ready to unload rain onto the parched ground. As days eased into July and the weather grew warmer, trees and grass turned greener from recent heavy moisture.

When she reached Newcastle Road, she took a second to admire where she lived. Oak trees at least a hundred twenty years old lined the street. Victorian-era homes, some large, some modest, belonged to this neighborhood. Her house was a few down on the left. One of the smallest houses on the block, the Queen Anne design looked almost quaint and undemanding next to the Gothic monstrosity on one side and the larger Queen Anne on the other side. Last year she'd had it painted a fresh, light blue when the white exterior went dingy. When she pulled into the driveway, she was glad she installed an automatic garage door opener last winter onto the separate garage.

She kept her mind on pleasant thoughts when she left the garage by a side door and headed toward the house. Since the garage exit opened near the side of the home, she went for the door leading into the kitchen.

The white number ten envelope taped to the locked screen door made her stop cold.

Scrawled in black lettering, the warning on the envelope couldn't be any clearer. Her name, scribbled with haste in a handwriting she would recognize until the day she died.

She ripped it off the door and, without thinking, tore the envelope open. As she read the message, the words seemed to leap out at her. Their jagged edges and extreme forward slant suggested aggressiveness and hostility. Topsy-turvy, the up and down pattern of the words also said the person writing it harbored chaotic emotions and unstable personality.

Yes, it described this person beyond doubt.

Tara,
You thought I was still in Kansas when I called you. Didn't you?
Your beloved,
Drake

An ice-cold shiver ripped up her spine with jagged claws. All of a sudden, the air became too thick. Abhorrence lingered on the paper and envelope she clutched in her hands. She wanted to crumble the paper. Instead, she slipped it back into the envelope and jammed it into her purse. She might need this as evidence.

Evidence of what? That her lunatic ex-husband already tracked her down and could be nearby even now? Fear cascaded in a slow domino effect through her body and straight into her mind. She glanced around the area, well aware Drake could be close. She reached out with her mind and tried see if emotions other than her own lingered in the area. After several seconds, she detected no signs of Drake.

New dread threatened as she unlocked the door and rushed inside the house. She slammed the door, locked it and tossed her handbag on the kitchen nook table. While bright sun shown through the lemony curtains on the windows, the day seemed suddenly much dimmer.

Drake *would* do something. Not knowing what he planned bothered her more than anything. Clever and intelligent, the ex-soldier had muscle and mind to design a trap for her. Six years ago, she'd been a confident fool, so certain he could never hurt her again.

As she stripped off her suit jacket and laid it over the back of a chair, she contemplated her next move. She couldn't allow this maniac to ruin her life.

Anger brought hot tears to her eyes. She hated this. She stared at the torn envelope peeking out of her purse, and knew Drake would love how terror whipped into her like sharp teeth into exposed skin. An energy vampire, he would feed on her emotions, on her soul.

Scared spitless or not, she must stand up to him as she had back in Kansas.

Let today be the day.

* * * * *

Marcus walked into his apartment, his entire body keyed up and pulsating from the heavy workout he'd completed on the weight machines and treadmill in the apartment fitness center downstairs. A cold drink would be good right about now, but a shower would feel even better.

Tossing his clothes into the hamper in his closet, he thought about how Tara looked today. Vulnerable and uncertain. He never imagined her looking that way in a million years. Since he'd met her she gave out waves of competence and self-reliance he admired. How many other people with a physical quirk like hers could say the same?

He thought her one blue eye and one brown eye created the most beautiful gaze he'd never seen. She intrigued him all to hell.

"Fuck," he muttered as he glanced in the bathroom mirror.

Therein lay the problem.

From the first time he'd met her, he'd wanted to get her into bed.

Once in the shower, he tried to scrub away the image of Tara Crayton's large, frightened eyes out of his mind. She'd been scared shitless by that phone call, and during their conversation in the parking garage, he witnessed the fright lurking behind her casual façade.

Anger catapulted his blood pressure into the stratosphere when he thought about her ex-husband laying one hand on her. The thought of her skin bruised by a fist made Marcus want to call in a few favors and see if he could dig up the dirt on the sick bastard who'd dared to harm her. His current case didn't pertain in any way to investigating wife beaters. That didn't mean he couldn't watch out for her.

He had to.

Ignoring a woman in danger went against his honor. He refused to stand by and watch a female brutalized. He would do whatever he could to keep an eye on her. Worry drove him to work out extra hard earlier, and he knew his muscles would ache for the effort.

He never had the impression she hated men, but she was wary as hell. She didn't want a man to insist on taking care of her, and he couldn't blame her. Independent and gutsy, she didn't give in to self-pity or whining. Unstoppable, primitive male longing rose inside him.

Shit. If he didn't watch out, she'd think he was a fucking stalker himself. He would have to tread carefully and make sure she understood he would never hurt her or try to control her.

As lather slid down his body, he plunged his face into the spray. He'd deliberately ignored his ability to probe minds when it came to her. It went against his code of ethics and the Special Investigation Agency's policy to do mind probes without evidence it might pertain to the case at hand. Even with Tara's situation with her husband, he'd refused to drop his shields and enter her thoughts.

Fuck me, it's hard to keep away from dipping into her mind and seeing what's in that lovely head.

Forgetting a gut-level reaction to a beautiful woman would be easy if she hadn't crawled under his skin and stayed there the first day he met her. Two months did more than make him realize how attracted he was to her sweet smile and generous laugh. Witty and intelligent, she possessed genuine warmth that lightened his soul. Few women touched his depths and wormed straight into his mind like an insistent drug. His *real* work always kept him jumping, with the few dull moments in between rife with reports and his hobbies. Sure, he dated off and on, but many women didn't possess that special quality Tara had. He closed his eyes and recalled each womanly detail.

Oh yeah, her hair. He wanted to feel it against his fingertips. What would a metrosexual man call the striking color? He grinned. The beautiful shade reminded him of rosewood or maybe even burgundy, the richness a lush, radiant hue that would never fade from his memory. She usually wore her long, straight hair piled on her head, or pulled into a prim bun. Today she'd worn it down over her shoulders like a shimmering waterfall. Shit, he'd love to see it falling over her naked breasts. He wanted to pull her toward him and bury his face in the silky strands.

Not even her divine smile could hide her worry, and yet the sight of her made his libido roar. Each day her gentle powder-soft scent drove him nuts.

While she had curves in all the right places, he detected a fragility about her that concerned him. Her pale, oval face made him want to call her right now and demand more answers about the asshole who'd hurt her. He wondered if the little scar that bisected her right eyebrow was a result of a beating from her ex-husband. God, he hoped not.

Holding back his anger, he returned to remembering her when she smiled, when she didn't look as frightened as a doe.

He often caught himself turning toward her in their shared cubicle, wanting to touch her. *Face it, man. You want to do more than touch her.*

Kissing her wouldn't be enough. He wanted to fuck her in the most primal meaning of the word. Not some nice, delicate lovemaking session. Full-on wall-banger sex. She aroused some of the most incredible fantasies he'd ever experienced. *Jesus. I'm forty years old, and I'm acting as if I'm nineteen.*

Fantasizing about her would have to take care of his needs. He could take the pressure off the desire crawling through him.

As he wrapped his fist around his already erect cock, he imagined how it would feel to slide deep and hard through her wet, hot heat. He slammed his hand over the water shutoff. He leaned against the shower wall and closed his eyes. His balls tightened up close to his body. Permitting her image to form in his mind, he didn't allow a long, drawn-out fantasy. No. He needed to get off fast before he went nuts.

Tara lying spread-eagle on his bed, her lips wet and welcoming as he kissed her. As his hands roamed her cream and satin body, his tongue took hot possession of her mouth. She responded with a drugging intensity that drew his cock tighter and higher toward his stomach. He reached down and cupped his balls, imagining her long, slim hand taking and starting a much-needed motion. As their kiss grew hotter, he reached down and fingered her wet, plump slit. She'd be so creamy and aroused his touch would make her gasp. Heat splintered through his groin as he imagined finding her dripping wet pussy and anchoring his cock straight and true into the luscious heat. He groaned and his breath quickened as he pumped his cock with aggressive strokes. She would be so hot, so wet, so achingly beautiful. His breath rasped in his throat as he lengthened the movements, in his mind's eye driving his rigid flesh into supple flesh. In reality, his hand drew upward and downward with pumping movements.

She clutched at his arms, fingers sinking into his flesh as she tried to ride out the storm. Her breath puffed in his ear as she whispered nasty urgings.

Fuck me, she whispered with moaning, gasping need.

Her hips arched into his, starting a motion while he rode her with short, stabbing thrusts.

Oh shit, yes.

The buildup rose quickly. He masturbated his way to heaven, his legs trembling and his breathing coming hard. Seconds later he groaned, the sound harsh and hard with gut-wrenching, knee-melting ecstasy. Pulse after pulse of semen shot from his cock and he shuddered in supreme satisfaction. As he reached for the shower and turned the water on once again, he sighed.

His fantasies would have to do.

Chapter Three

ဆ

"Come in," Jason Forte said to Cecelia as she walked into his office and closed the door. "Thanks for coming here on short notice."

She looked shell-shocked, as if she expected him to do something drastic like fire her. When he walked into the center of the room, she followed. "Sure, Mr. Forte. Um…what can I do for you?"

"I have a project I need you to complete, but you can't tell anyone else about it. Especially not Tara."

Cecelia's eyebrows went up. "Oh?"

"You see, I'm afraid she's too cozy with Marcus."

Cecelia's eyes showed new curiosity, mixed with apprehension. She stayed just inside the door, and he realized he'd have to come closer. She sure the hell wouldn't.

I frighten her. Hmm. Too bad. Once this is over, though, she won't worry anymore.

"Uh, I don't know what you mean," she said.

"Do you find Marcus attractive, Cecelia?"

His direction change caused a false guiltless expression to come into her eyes. "He's all right. He's a geek, but I suppose if he relaxed he'd be okay. Why are you asking me that?"

"Because he's a part of the project. I need you to get to know him better, see why he's here at the company."

She smiled, one corner of her mouth quirking up in an attractive smile. "Even if I wanted to get to know him better, I don't see why you care if he's attracted to Tara."

Jason stuffed his hands into his pockets and strolled slowly toward her. "Come on, Cecelia. I know what kind of woman you are. I've been watching you for a long time. You're interested in me. You always have been. Wouldn't you like to have more power in this company? More prestige? I can give you all that and more."

With satisfaction, he noticed her eyelids drooping, her full lips opening until they made a small opening. He would taste her, let her know how it was with one kiss.

She shook her head. "No. You have me confused with some other woman in the word processing area. I'm not like that."

He laughed softly. "My dear, you're like other women in this building. You can be seduced. You can be had. And you will be."

Her mouth opened wider, indignation parting her lips. He closed his eyes a moment and, with one twist, he entered her mind.

She gasped, and took a step back. "What-what are you doing? It feels like…it feels…"

"Yes, Cecelia? Tell me what it feels like."

"Someone is inside my head."

"Oh, come on. That's ridiculous. No one can enter your mind." For a flash, he let her see his real eyes, his actual body, the one that could send the fiercest horror through a living soul.

She squeaked, one hand going to her mouth. Her chest heaved, and he felt her fear like a sweet, tasty treat in his mouth. Like sugar. Like intoxicating drink. Oh yes, he would have more of that. Feed on her until her yummy, delicious body was his.

"Mr. Forte, I don't think—"

"That's right. Don't think. Feel."

Before she could make a sound, his lips came down on hers. He didn't have to restrain her.

* * * * *

A nightmare formed in Tara's night. Darkness filled her house and the outside world didn't exist in this land of visions and hate. Restless and hot, she pushed the covers down and almost whipped the long nightshirt up over her head. No. She'd keep her nakedness for other dreams, for other more pleasant situations.

Anxiety trembled through her stomach and made her limbs tighten with tension. She had to escape to the street outside, to find shelter from his violence. As her dreams tumbled into an incomprehensible melting pot, she tossed and turned with agitation.

Drake stalked her from room to room, his maniacal laughter chasing the air. "Come out, come out, wherever you are."

The singsong quality of his voice bounced against her ears with painful intensity. "No. You can't make me. You can't." Drake's face materialized out of the gloom and she jerked in surprise and fear. "No."

"Yes, my darlin'. It's you and me now. No one can help you. Not your mother and father, not your sister and not your new boyfriend."

Shadows shifted until she realized she stood in a long, barely lit hallway with Drake on one end and her on the other.

"I don't have a boyfriend," she said in defense.

"You do. And when I find out who it is, I'm going to kill him."

He ran toward her. Fear froze the blood in her veins.

A loud jangling noise screamed through the darkness, and she slammed her hands over her ears rather than run.

In her heart, a litany rang out. Run. Run. Run.

She broke from the dream with a startled squeak.

Shrill and disturbing, her alarm clock demanded she wake. She slammed her hand over the snooze button. Glad to be back in reality and not the nightmare, she glanced at the curtains over her bedroom windows. Faint light shown through, enough to let her know the bright morning she expected had turned gloomy and bleak. She lay back down and rubbed a hand over her eyes.

Great. A dreary morning sky and a wearisome headache. That's all she needed.

Yesterday afternoon, huddled in her home and feeling vulnerable and watched, she'd contacted Ethel Allegra's office and discovered she couldn't get an appointment until Monday. When she'd called Bettina, the sweetie told her she could have the time off she needed to see to her affairs. After that, Tara spent a few hours calling home security companies and selecting three to visit her house and do quotes. Three of the highly recommended companies could see her on Saturday afternoon.

Despite her progress, falling asleep last night had been a bitch.

She didn't even have a sexual dream to satisfy her and wash Drake from her nightmares.

* * * * *

Marcus bolted out of his deep sleep. A rap song clunked against his eardrums.

"Son of a bitch," he snarled into the darkness of his bedroom. He groaned and reached for the bedside lamp. "Damn it."

He must have pushed the wrong music selector last night on his I-Doc communicator.

Light flooded the room, and he stumbled out of the bed toward the desk across the room.

"This better be good." He grabbed the palm-sized machine and frowned at the message launching across the screen. He pressed the button to mute the music.

A muscle worked in his jaw as Special Investigation Agency Division Six Director Ben Darrock's memo demanded attention.

Marcus,

Call me ASAP on your secure phone. It's extremely important. More information on current situation.

Ben

Marcus looked at the bedside clock. Six o'clock in the morning, and yet the bedroom curtains blocked most of the light. He fiddled with the I-Doc and grumbled as he tried to relay a confirmation message back to SIA. His big fingers slipped over the small keys and screaming music returned, this time a heavy metal song from fifteen or more years ago. While he liked heavy metal from back then, it grated on his sensitive ears. He quickly hit the mute button. Half tempted to lob the device out the nearest window, he gritted his teeth. After forcing a deep breath through his lungs, he managed to send the confirm message.

He glared at the multipurpose communications equipment. While SIA constantly came up with ingenious equipment for its agents, he felt like a dinosaur.

The I-Doc could send and receive email, page, be used as a secure cellular phone and do everything else minus walk the fucking dog.

He hated it. He wouldn't classify himself as technologically challenged, but he preferred the rush of hands-on dealing with problems. His Glock was a great conversation starter if an asshole didn't cooperate.

He shook his head, then rubbed his eyes. Time to call Ben and deal with whatever new info had materialized about public enemy Jason Forte.

He punched in Ben's number on the I-Doc and thought of Tara. Concern surged through him. He glanced at the clock. After he finished the call with Ben he might call her, early in the morning or not. Last night he'd barely found sleep worrying about her. Not even the intense erotic dream he'd experienced could remove lingering concern.

Fuck. And what a dream it had been.

The mystery woman had sucked him off so sweetly, so slowly he half expected to see cum on the sheets this morning.

"Ben Darrock," the deep Scottish voice said after three rings. "Division Six."

"Marcus here. Just got your message."

"Good morning. Sorry it came through early. I figured an interruption from the I-Doc would be less annoying than calling you by phone."

Marcus laughed. "It would've been if I hadn't set the music signal to rap by accident."

"Not your type of music?"

"No way."

Ben's soft laugh soothed his nerves a little. "I've got news on Jason Forte. Apparently, his activities aren't confined to embezzlement. We think he's involved in something darker. Our sources say some weird things about this guy. Stuff that is bloody well unbelievable."

"Only the FBI and the CIA think things are implausible. That's where we have an advantage."

"Yes, but this is edgy, next level stuff."

"Such as?"

Ben cleared his throat. "Try this on for size. Forte is into mind control that turns people into a type of zombie who do his bidding. Is that bizarre enough for you?"

Marcus shouldn't have been shell-shocked by the information, but in the many cases he'd handled for SIA, creation of zombies never came into the picture. "Yeah, I'd say that about caps it. Do these sources have any proof?"

"If they did, do you think we would've sent you in there?"

Marcus sighed and rubbed the back of his neck. "No."

"If anyone can discover what this Forte is doing, you can. I have faith."

"What if intelligence is right? What if he can do what the witnesses claim?"

Ben's sigh came over the line. "Then everyone in that company is in danger."

Uneasiness curled inside Marcus. He walked to his bedroom window and pulled back the curtains so he could look into the new day. "I've never picked up anything like that. This isn't good."

"No impressions?"

Marcus didn't want to lie. "No." He sighed. "In fact, I'm starting to wonder what is going on. I haven't gotten one damned impression since I started working there."

There, he'd said it. Now, if the sky fell he'd have to live with it.

Ben's voice edged with concern. "You didn't mention that in our last contact."

"I know. I should have said something right away. I figured I'd get some impressions and when I didn't..."

Why didn't he say something earlier? The question echoed in his head. He hated the niggling sensation in his psyche that itched. Complained. Told him that at forty he'd already washed up as a field agent.

Chased by annoying self-doubt, he said the one thing he could. "I guess I didn't want to believe it. I thought I could punch through the fog."

"Damn it, Marcus, if there's a problem, you should have backed out and let someone else take over."

Marcus felt heat rising into his face, but not from embarrassment. Nothing like pressure. Nothing like raw terror crawling into his gut when he thought of Tara subjected to Jason Forte's depravity. To the public at large Jason's psychic abilities would seem ludicrous. Yet the SIA knew and remained the last stand against paranormal threats to an unsuspecting population.

He scrubbed a hand over his hair-rough jaw. "I had to establish credibility first." He turned his back to the window and sparkling Denver lights winking in the distance as day broke over the horizon. "It took a while to convince people I really was a secretary."

Ben laughed. "Oh yeah? Reverse discrimination at work?"

"You could say that. Shit. Half the people in the office think I'm gay."

Ben laughed harder. "Very clever, Hyatt. Would you like to borrow my kilt, then?"

"You own a kilt?"

"Why are you surprised?"

"Well, just because you're a Scot doesn't mean you own a kilt."

Ben's accent roughened. "Aye, you have point there. But when I was younger I realized that a kilt is comfortable and seems a fair way to intrigue a woman."

Marcus snorted. "I suppose people are always asking you what Scots wear under their kilts?"

Ben cleared his throat. "Some have asked, but I never tell. They just have to find out on their own."

"I dunno. In my case, a kilt might not qualify for Friday dress-down day."

"Well, keep up the good fight."

"I don't know how good it is. If I don't get my abilities back soon—"

"Don't obsess. Maybe after this assignment you need a long vacation. You're tired, that's all."

Vacation, hell. He hadn't taken more than a day at a time in so long he couldn't remember. Becoming a top-rated and highly respected field agent took work. Now that he'd reached legendary status, he should be happy. So why didn't he feel like celebrating?

"Yeah, maybe I need to go out and get laid," Marcus said.

"You need more than that. Try at least a couple of weeks someplace hot and tropical."

Hot and wet. Oh yeah. All he needed was to sink into the hot, wet channel deep between Tara's legs.

"All right," Marcus said. "I'll take you up on the offer of a vacation when this case is over. Maybe I'm getting burned out."

A pause came over the line until Ben said, "Is there something else you're not telling me?"

Marcus knew better than to add his fascination with Tara into the mix. "No."

"Keep me up-to-date as soon as you get more information on what Jason is planning next. And Marcus, be careful."

Marcus snorted softly. "You know I won't."

"Don't try anything that gets you killed, understand?"

"You got it." He remembered something he should know before he went in the office today. "Hey, wait."

"Yeah?"

"Tell me…what the hell is a metrosexual?"

* * * * *

Drake lifted the receiver on the pay phone and dialed his parents' number. He hoped the old bastard would answer first. Old Jefferson Hollister. That's what everyone called the retired Marine.

God, he hoped his dad answered. The idea of talking to his mother felt unclean. After all, she'd tempted him with her flesh more than once. Tempted and wanted him to taste. The phone rang once, twice, three times.

A click and then a gravel-edged voice said, "Hello."

"Dad." Drake didn't know what else to say.

The pause went on so long, Drake wasn't sure if his old man would answer. Dad would slam the phone in his ear, as he had so many times before. Slam it and curse him to hell.

"Drake?"

Between odd relief and tremendous rancor, Drake swallowed hard. Maybe this time the old man would listen. Just this once. "Yep."

"You're out of prison." The old bastard's voice sounded deeper, rougher than the last time they'd spoken years ago. "Kendra told me."

Drake snorted and glanced around the lonely street corner. "Is she still fornicating around in Kansas City?"

A long pause again before Dad answered. "Son, let's not—"

"What, Dad? Get the truth out in the open?"

"All right. What's on your mind?"

Drake heaved a difficult breath, his throat tight, his limbs strung with high-wire tension. He felt he could leap from his skin and run screaming. Gnashing. Hitting.

Killing.

"Why are you talking to me now?" Drake leaned against the telephone booth's smeared glass. "You didn't talk to me in the last six years."

"I don't know why I'm talking to you."

His father's tone, lined with apathy, made him want to scream. "So what about Kendra. At least she came to see me. She came to visit her flesh and blood."

"We asked her not to. She defied us."

Drake threw his head back and laughed. "She's still living with you. She's fuckin' twenty-eight years old now."

"Yeah, she's livin' with us."

Drake snorted. "Son of a bitch."

"Watch your language." The old man's voice went rough and harsh. "There's no cause for it."

You talked like that all the time, you piece of shit.

Inhaling deeply, Drake left those particular words alone. "So you didn't kick Kendra out for defying you. Why?"

"She was punished."

Drake felt a sting somewhere deep in his bowels, as if someone had taken a red-hot poker and jabbed. Poor, poor Kendra. She might be a whore, she might be his dad's trinket, but Kendra had at least visited him in prison. He'd give her that.

"What did you do? You hurt her?"

The old bastard cleared his throat, and Drake imagined him sitting at his dark wood desk, swallowed by a mammoth leather chair in his big library. The library where he'd read the good book day after day, at least two hours a night.

"She paid. She made retribution to her mother and father for not honoring us."

So, the bastard still believed in Moses' commandments. Drake remembered, with vivid clarity, the man's razor-sharp voice lashing him nightly about the sins of the flesh. Mom would always be there, sitting dutiful and respectful of Dad as a man and the head of household. Her gingham dresses always tasteful, her smile never big and goofy like Kendra's, never disobeying. She'd been the best and worst mother he could imagine. A shudder slipped through him as he recalled his door opening at night those three times. Three times when he'd turned fifteen. She'd come to him and…

"You there?" the old man asked.

"Yeah, I'm here. How'd Kendra pay, Dad? What did you do?"

"She learned her lesson."

Drake laughed as anger flashed through him. He imagined the punishment his sister would suffer when Dad learned how many times Kendra had come to see him. "She visited me ten times. Did you know it was ten times?"

"Don't try and make it worse for her. I already knew. Ten times she visited you. Ten times I punished her." He cleared his throat. "'Keep close watch over a headstrong daughter, or she may give your enemies cause to gloat, making the talk of the town, a byword among the people, shaming you in the eyes of the world.'"

Fuck, his old man quoted the Bible again. And again, continuing right over Drake's thoughts.

"'Give her a bedroom without windows, a room that doesn't overlook the entrance. Do not let her display her beauty to any man, or sit gossiping in the women's quarters; for out of clothes comes the moth, and out of woman comes woman's wickedness. Better a man's wickedness than a woman's goodness; it is woman who brings shame and disgrace.'"

Drake loved it, and he laughed. "Ecclesiasticus 42."

"That's right. Very good."

His father's agreement felt like a balm. He soaked in the smidgen of approval.

Drake stared sightlessly into the bright sunlight outside the booth. He pictured his finely boned sister in her candy striper outfit—no, she'd be too old for that. Her waitress dress cut short up to her thin thighs.

Horse legs.

He remembered Dad calling her that to her face. Fat tears would run down her cheeks. Damn, wouldn't it be nice to see her humiliation erupt like a fresh wound.

"So you haven't changed much," Drake said.

"I'm thinner, have more wrinkles and less hair."

He waited in vain for his father to ask how he'd changed. No, Dad would never ask. He didn't give a fat dick.

Drake's fingers tightened on the plastic receiver. A mechanical voice asked for another coin to keep the call going, and as the money slipped into the slot, the metallic clink hurt his ears. He winced, his nerves raw and hot. He'd need something soon to remove the disturbed feeling, the restlessness.

"Then I'll tell you what I'm like, Dad. I'm everything you said I would be when I went into prison. I fuckin' was everything you said I was."

"Drake—"

"But I've also changed. You were right, Dad. I was a sinner. I got the Bible Mom sent me and read it from cover to cover. Over and over. Several times. Had a lot of time to think about what it meant over the years I stayed in that stinkin' hole. You know what? I found the Lord, Dad. I found the Lord."

A deep sigh echoed from his father. "Praise be." The old man's voice sounded strained. Almost...no, it couldn't be. Maybe the old shit was crying?

"Praise be, son. I knew if you read that Bible you'd see the truth. Everything you need to run your life is right there. You don't need any prison psychiatrist to know the devil worked in you." His father sighed once more. "Praise Jesus."

Drake laughed, the sound tinny in his ears. "Yeah, I got religion all right. Had it beat into me more than once by what I saw in there. What those other sinners tried to do to me."

"Come home, son. We'll commune together with the Lord."

"I'll come home, Dad. After I finish a few things here in Denver."

"What?" Dad sounded alarmed.

"I'm in Denver. What's the matter? Afraid I'll visit my wife while I'm here?"

"Your wife?" Caution ran through his dad's tone.

"Tara. Who else?"

"But she divorced you."

"She's still mine, Dad."

"No, she's not—"

"Under God's law she is. God's law overrules man's law."

A long pause followed, but Drake waited.

Finally, his father chuckled. He hadn't heard that crawling laugh in years. How he hated it. As much as he loathed it, he understood it now. Wanted that power for his own.

His dad quoted the Bible again. "'My son, attend to my wisdom and listen with care to my counsel, so that you may preserve discretion and your lips safeguard knowledge. For though the lips of an adulteress drip honey and her tongue is smoother than oil, yet in the end she is as bitter as wormwood, as sharp as a two-edged sword. Her feet tread the downward path towards death…'"

He heard it in the words. Father had given him understanding and permission at last. Satisfaction pierced him. *Yes. Yes.*

Dad continued. "'A man who loves his son will not spare the rod, and then in his old age he may have joy of him.'"

Elation spiked inside Drake as he realized he, too, could speak God's words at will.

He liked the Old Testament with a vengeance. Oh yes. He liked vengeance most of all.

"I've got to go, Dad."

"Drake, your mother wants to speak with you."

Before he could protest, his father handed the phone over.

"Hello, Drake." He hung between heaven and hell hearing his mother's familiar voice. Soft, yet edged with steel, her tone held a touch of Louisiana. She hadn't spoken to him once while he was in prison, and irritation rose in his gut. Damn her. Damn her to hell.

"Mother."

"Drake, it's…good to hear from you."

Sure, Mother. Sure. He didn't know what to say to her.

"Drake?"

"I'm here."

"You're coming home?"

"No. Not yet. I've got some business to finish here in Denver."

"Business? You're already working? Why that's good news."

"Yeah, I'm working." He smirked and watched a young girl ride by on a bicycle. Her white dress with yellow splotches reminded him of a dress Tara used to wear years ago. Used to drive him mad with a desire to fuck her.

Mother's voice went hard. "You're not getting into trouble already, are you? This business is legitimate?"

"Of course it's legitimate." He snarled the words. "When I get done here, I'll have Tara back and—"

"Tara?" Her voice rose sharply. "You're not taking up with her again, are you? She brought you down. She put you in that horrible prison. Of course, you got yourself into the mess, but it was with her help." Condemnation ran off her lips like a waterfall. "She isn't worthy of you."

"No, but she's still my wife, and I choose to keep her. Just like Dad chose to keep you."

"He did." Her voice held rusty agony. Like she might want to cry.

Hell, he'd never seen Dad or Mom cry. He remembered weeping as a kid, sobbing when his dad raised a hand to Mom. He shook his head and forced back the feelings. No, he couldn't. He wouldn't think about what Dad had done or how Mom had taken the beatings without making a fuckin' sound. How had she done that? When the pricks in prison had tried—shit, he'd turned on them so fast. They'd called him Animal. A fuckin' animal. He'd never forget the respect he earned from showing those ass-wipes he couldn't be butt-fucked or beaten.

He covered his eyes with his other hand and let the darkness in.

"Kendra's here," his mother said.

"Let me speak to her."

He heard his mother leave the phone, and whispered murmurings. A sharp sound, like a smack across the mouth. The old man still understood how to keep his family in line.

A few seconds passed, then a soft voice came over the phone. "Hi, Drake."

Soothing and cool, always in control, his younger sister's voice calmed him. He remembered how she'd looked when she visited him a month ago and learned he would leave prison early. Oh yeah. That good behavior certainly worked. Had people fooled. Except maybe Kendra. Her eyes had widened when he'd told her he would leave that hellhole prison in a month.

"Hey, sis. What's up?"

"Where are you, Drake?" Her voice trembled.

"Denver. Tara lives there, and I was just telling Dad that I'm going to get her back."

"No." The word came out sharp. "Please, Drake, don't do anything. You'll get sent back to prison."

He laughed. "You'd like that, wouldn't you? I think you enjoyed visiting me there, didn't you?"

"God no. No. It's horrible. Please don't do anything—"

"Give me that phone, girl." His dad's voice overran Kendra's. "Sorry, Drake."

His father said sorry. The word blazed across his mind in capital letters a mile high. His old man never apologized for anything. Surprised, he waited for the codger to speak.

Dad cleared his throat once more, that damned sound grating on Drake's nerves.

"Boy, I won't tell anyone what you plan to do. You hear? You sure you want Tara back? She wasn't worthy of you. And if she's been with other men, she's nothing better than a whore."

Whore. "Yeah. You got that right."

"I don't want to know what you're going to do."

"I'm not telling you. But when I have her, I'm bringing her back there with me. She's going to be mine. And she's going to do what I want. She's going to follow God's will."

Dad chuckled. "Good, son. Your Mother never liked her much, but maybe if Tara understands once and for all what it means to be a good wife...well..."

"I gotta go, Dad."

Before the old man could say another word, Drake hung up. A sharp rap on the glass startled him, and he swung around. A raggedy-looking woman with long graying hair and deep wrinkles glared at him from outside the booth.

He shoved open the door and brushed by the hag. He spit on the ground next to her feet and walked away.

* * * * *

By the time Tara reached the office, her headache turned into a throbbing menace. She headed into the employee lounge first thing and popped two aspirin.

Like clockwork, Marcus walked in. "Hey, good morning. I'm glad I caught you before work starts."

"Hi."

A wave of unexpected security and happiness stole over her as Marcus strode toward her, his grin welcoming. Today he wore a dark gray suit, but the plain white shirt and dull green tie did nothing to bring out the startling hue in his eyes or the olive tones in his skin.

"What's up?" she asked as she filled her mug with strong black coffee.

"Gross." He made a face. "How do you drink that stuff straight? That's why I bring coffee from home. I have some great chocolate java beans that are to die for."

He left the last sentence hanging with a higher inflection in his voice. She laughed softly. "Are you trying to sound stereotypically gay?"

He winked. "Hell, if everyone *thinks* I'm gay, what difference does it make?"

She eyed him skeptically and then took a sip of the hated coffee. Nice and dark and strong. As he predicted. She considered taking it intravenously if it would wake her up.

"I don't think you really care what anyone thinks," she said.

"I care what you think." He leaned in closer. "I looked up metrosexual on the internet this morning."

"And?"

His lips curved into a devilish smile. "I'm *not* metrosexual."

She sighed and rolled her gaze to the ceiling for a second. "You know, if you want to lose the metrosexual and gay tag you have to dress down a little. At the picnic last month you wore that island print silk shirt and khaki shorts. Too suave. You should have worn jeans and a ratty T-shirt. Something that spells totally masculine and ready to…um…pick up women." Her gaze cruised over him once more, impersonal and objective. "Your hair is definitely metrosexual. I'll bet if you let that hair down around your shoulders, women would go wild for you."

He laughed. "I don't let my hair down for just any woman."

His irreverence made her smile. "Okay, but I still say your hair is gorgeous. It's unique and not every man is brave enough to grow long hair when the style magazines say a guy should have his hair cut another way."

Instead of confirming or denying the statement, he grinned. "Help me."

"Help you?"

"Yeah. Come out to a mall with me on Saturday to pick out more masculine clothes."

Tara's mouth went dry, and she sipped her coffee. Anything to stall answering his surprising request. "You want me to assist you with picking out a wardrobe?"

"Sure."

"Why do you think I'm qualified?"

He wriggled his eyebrows. "You obviously know what it takes to dress a manly man."

Flabbergasted, she stared into the inky depths of her mug for a moment. "Anyone can help you with that."

He put down his mug and shrugged out of his suit jacket. He placed the jacket over the back of a chair. "If I'm going to be more masculine, I need tips."

She blinked, still taken off-guard by his request.

He moved closer, lowering his voice to a silky rumble. "Come on. You know you want to help me."

The warmth in his eyes cajoled her. "All right. Honestly, Marcus, why do you care whether anyone thinks you're gay or metrosexual? I thought you were more secure than that."

"Ah, that's where you're wrong. You don't know me as well as you think."

Disappointment edged into her consciousness. She didn't want to see him as self-doubting and geeky, but maybe his somewhat stereotypical pocket-protector mentality hid nothing at all.

"Okay, okay. I said I'd help and I will," she said.

He gave her a happy smile. "Thanks. I knew I could count on you. I'll pick you up. I'll include lunch in the deal."

She did need to get out more. Now that Drake threatened to make her life hell, she should refuse to let her ex determine the course of her life.

Marcus looked worried, and she clasped his biceps for a moment and squeezed. "It's a deal. It'll be fun."

Warmth filled his eyes, and he put his big hand over hers and pressed gently. "Great. I can't wait."

"Oh no. I forgot. I have security agencies coming over to talk about installing a system in my house."

He tilted his head slightly to the side, curiosity plane on his features. "It's good you're getting a system as soon as possible. What time are they stopping by Saturday?"

"Two, three and four o'clock."

"We'll make sure to be done by then. And I know a bit about security systems. If you want me to hang around during the appointments, I'd be happy to."

Curious, she asked, "How is it that you know about security systems?"

He shrugged, nonchalant. "I had one installed a couple of years back. Did a ton of research."

The lounge door popped open and Cecelia walked inside. Marcus and Tara jerked away from each other. Cecelia hesitated, eyes twinkling with mischief. For a weird second, Tara thought that Cecelia's gaze held interest in Marcus.

Marcus gave Cecelia a grin. "I've got work to do. I'll see you both later."

Cecelia stopped in front of him. She put one hand on her hip and tossed back her hair in a parody of a siren bent on seduction. She moistened her lips and sighed. "I'm sorry to see you go." She reached out and patted his chest. "I need to talk to you."

Marcus' eyes widened, then he grinned. Tara watched Cecelia with growing disapproval. What did the woman think she was doing? She'd never seen her this blatant with a come-on, even if she was teasing.

He didn't seem uncomfortable. "Sure. Stop by my cubicle."

Cecelia flicked a sideways look at Tara. "Alone. I need to see you alone."

"Well," he cleared his throat and said, "I've got a few moments now. But then I've got to get to work."

"No. After work."

Tara felt her blood pressure rise as she witnessed the strange situation. "Maybe I should go."

"No need," Cecelia said. "Meet me after work right here, Marcus. After everyone has left."

He lifted one eyebrow, then aimed a big smile at Cecelia. "It's a date."

He retrieved his jacket and mug and left the lounge.

Cecelia's eyebrows went up. "Well, well." After making her way to the coffee machine, the woman filled her mug. She retrieved half-and-half from the refrigerator and poured some in her coffee. "That was interesting."

"I'll say it was." Tara tried to keep her words even and she plastered on a fake smile. "I didn't know you were interested in Marcus."

Cecelia laughed softly, and when she turned her gaze toward Tara, an uneasy feeling flowed over Tara's body. Something had changed about Cecelia, as if her life force had been altered somehow. Tara didn't know how or why, but it disturbed her.

"I've turned over a new leaf," Cecelia said and left it at that. "But then, what I saw when I walked in here a few moments ago makes me think you're attracted to him."

Tara knew she could excuse herself and escape correcting the woman's assumptions.

Coward.

She'd learned after living with Drake that she couldn't avoid standing up for herself or it made it easy for others to put her down. "What makes you think that?"

Cecelia leaned against the counter. "Is it my imagination, or did I see you guys touching?"

"No. I mean, yes, you did see us touching. It was innocent. He wants me to help him update his wardrobe."

This time Cecelia's eyebrows really spiked upward. "What?"

"He wants help with his wardrobe. We're going shopping Saturday."

Cecelia put the half-and-half back in the refrigerator. "That's even more interesting. Do you think he's gay?"

Not understanding why the women in the office found the idea of him being gay so entertaining, Tara started for the doorway. "I don't know and don't care. It's none of my business."

Cecelia's meaningful air said it all. She shrugged. "Oh well. Can't say I didn't try to get to the truth. Are you coming to the potluck later today?"

"I brought the bean salad that's in the fridge."

"Okay, talk to you later."

Knowing Cecelia, it would be difficult for her to keep her mouth shut and in no time at all—

No, she wouldn't obsess over what people could say about her and Marcus. With a twinge, she realized she was obsessing over what Marcus and Cecelia would do after work. Then she hardened her feelings and put it out of her mind. If he had something going with Cecelia, that was his business. Unease niggled Tara's intuition. Was there something wrong with Cecelia, or was she imagining it? She shook her head and didn't try to decipher the truth. She needed to concentrate on outwitting Drake.

* * * * *

Marcus almost finished his work in the copier room that morning when Jason Forte walked by. Jason stopped and stared as if Marcus had grown a second cock for the entire world to see.

Shorter than Marcus by several inches, he still had broad shoulders and a smile most women seemed to find attractive. Esthetically, Marcus understood most women would find Forte's dynamic personality intriguing, but with the evidence against Forte at SIA, Marcus knew better than to trust the asshole.

The first time he met him, Forte's handshake had been cold, and Marcus felt like the executive tried to press into his mind. Marcus had experienced psychic attacks before on the job, so he understood what it felt like. With Forte, though, the invasive sensation hadn't lasted long enough to say for certain. Marcus had shored up his defenses and refused to allow Forte one inch inside his thoughts.

If Forte found out his real purpose here, solid human excrement could hit the proverbial oscillating device so quickly damage control wouldn't be an option.

Reading the guy's mind so far proved impossible. The few times he'd been close enough to Forte, other people milled around. He must approach Forte with caution.

Immediately Marcus checked his mental shield, visualizing a white light surrounding his body with protective aura energy. If Jason's psychic talents included mind control and manipulation, Marcus didn't plan on taking chances.

Marcus pushed the button on the copier to select quantity. "Good afternoon."

"Hi, Marcus." The man's smooth, deep voice possessed a quality women probably found irresistible and men found irritating.

Time to put on the right show. "How are you doing? Nice to see you again."

Forte looked at Marcus with a superior tilt to his nose and a smug twist to his mouth. One pale brow lifted, his mouth set in a tight line that showed barely hidden disgust or disdain. Arrogance rolled off the man. The CFO had blue eyes as mysterious as the jungle and just as perilous.

"Good to see you again." Jason's almost raspy voice sounded dry and hard. He turned away and headed out of the room without more small talk.

Marcus smiled faintly. Of course, the creep wouldn't lower himself. He might get some sort of germ off a person working in the lower sections of the company.

Marcus almost dropped his shield to tune into the man's frequency, but decided it wouldn't be a good idea. Not when he'd put up a shield to prevent—

Marcus turned off his desire to throttle the asshole and turned back to the copier. He'd barely returned to his copying when a strange tickling sensation touched the back of his neck. He gripped the side of the copier as sharp pain lanced through his right temple. An involuntary gasp left his throat.

Son-of-a-fuckin'-bitch.

Mind probe. Jason must be doing a mind probe.

Solidifying his psychic protection, Marcus closed his eyes and tried to keep steady. He locked his knees against weakness. Could this sensation be what witnesses reported? Anything else might be a serious medical condition, but Marcus knew better. A strange feathery sensation along his spine always signaled psychic connection, interference, or other supernatural occurrence. If it wasn't Jason trying to get into his head, who was?

You wanted a clue about what was happening. Well, here's evidence.

Another half-formed groan threatened to leave his lips. Pain sliced through his head.

Before he could move, Tara walked in holding an armful of folders. Her gaze narrowed in concern. Those different color eyes seemed more intense, direct and piercing than any other eyes he'd seen.

"Hey." She moved quickly into the room and put her folders down on a table near him. As she got closer, her soft scent soothed him somewhat. When she reached his side she touched his arm, a small brush of her fingers over his jacket sleeve. "Are you all right? I was walking by when I got this... When I saw you standing there."

He forced a grin around the queasy sensation making way into his stomach. God, he could feel her calming touch like the whisper of a ghost against his skin, even though two layers of clothes remained between them.

What would feel like if she touched him more intimately?

She leaned closer, her gaze searching. "Marcus? Come on, you're scaring me."

He blinked rapidly as the headache eased and his body stopped feeling like someone had plugged him into a low-voltage electrical socket. He half-expected his hair to stand on end and his suit jacket to smoke.

"Yeah, I'm great."

Worry inched over her delicate features. Even in the middle of feeling like hell, he appreciated her fragile beauty. Her nearness made him happy. *Damn it. No woman has a right to look so sweet and vulnerable. Especially when she's really so strong.*

"Was that Jason Forte I saw going down the hall?" she asked.

"In the flesh."

She eased back from him a little. "Jason does have that effect on some people."

"What effect?"

She shrugged, a semi-sheepish expression softening her face. "People get twitchy around someone with that kind of power. They think, 'This person could hurt my career'."

He couldn't argue with her logic. One thing bothered him, and he threw caution to the wind. "You've seen people react strangely to him?"

Her throat worked and she swallowed hard, the strength in her blue and brown gaze disconcerting. "Yes." She reached for her folders. "Are you finished? I need to get this done for Bettina before she skins me alive."

"Yeah. Fire away." After he removed his project from the copier and moved aside, she started work with her usual lockstep competence.

Okay, she didn't plan on answering him. He rephrased his question. "What reactions have you seen people have to Jason?"

Tara kept her attention on the copier. "It's hard to describe. I don't know."

The nausea in his stomach eased and he felt steadier on his feet. He stepped nearer to her and caught a soft whiff of her mouthwatering rose scent. *God, she smelled a- number-one fuckable.*

"Do people look nervous or scared?" he asked.

She darted a glance in his direction, but proceeded with work. "Sometimes."

"Ill?"

"Yes." That word came out stiff, as if she had to force it past her lips.

"What made you think I wasn't all right?"

She turned toward him, a cautious mixture of curiosity and mistrust darkening her expression. "You're always..." Her gaze roamed his face, then made an unmistakable quick assessment down his body. "Robust. You have a vigorous personality, even though you're trying awfully hard to cover it up."

Ah hell. The last thing he wanted was for her to think he possessed a hidden agenda.

Her gaze flitted over him, pausing on his chest before she met his gaze. Something mysterious ignited in her eyes and he felt the heat way down to his loins. His cock twitched. Maybe she was aware of him as a man and not a geek. He didn't know whether to be worried or excited.

"You're mentally strong, Marcus." Gentle and soft, her voice soothed. "I felt like—oh, this is ridiculous. You're going to think I'm nuts."

Good. Coax her into confession. Whatever it takes. "Nah. There's no way I'd ever think you were nuts. Unless you told me one day you were engaged to Jason Forte. Then I'd know you'd gone crazy."

She shuddered and wrinkled her nose. "No. I'm not the least interested in him that way."

"You're not like most women in the office? Women are always jabbering about how much they'd like to get to know him. They're drooling over the guy on a daily basis."

"No, I don't see the appeal."

Hallelujah. He almost showed her his relief. Instead, he caught himself in time to say, "Finish telling me what you were saying earlier."

Pink tinged her cheeks and as the copier stopped working, she turned toward it. "Your flame, your life force was diminished when I saw you a few moments ago."

A nagging sense permeated his thoughts. Maybe, just maybe she'd encountered this bizarre and debilitating sensation around Jason. Perhaps this woman had unseen depths he'd never imagined.

"That sounds New Age," he said.

Her lips tightened and he knew he'd said the wrong thing. Now she'd think he disapproved, and the last thing he wanted was for her to clam up. "I shouldn't have said anything."

"Hey, it's all right. I didn't mean to sound condescending. I meant it's unusual. How can you tell if someone's life force is diminished?"

She threw him an almost pained look. "Never mind. It's not important."

Caught between not wanting to push her too hard, and remembering he needed to investigate, he paused. She'd allowed her straight hair to flow down over her shoulders, and for a few seconds he wondered why she'd left her hair down two days in a row. Fragility showed in the delicate bones of her hands, the slim construction of her fingers and wrists. High heels brought her more in line with his height and gave her legs tempting curves.

No man should touch her with anything but tenderness. Heat melted in his stomach and he wanted to hold her like he wanted his next breath.

Damn it. He needed to learn subtly around her. What was it about her that made him say and do stupid things? Normally, when he wanted to obtain information from someone he could do it without the individual turning on him. He needed to watch the fumbling and stumbling.

"Thanks for caring about me," he said quietly.

She gathered papers and put them back in the folders. She stopped long enough to look at him. "Of course I care. You're a vital, energetic person. It was easy to tell something was wrong."

There. She'd given him a blanket explanation. A good cover-up for what she'd blurted a few moments earlier about life force. His intuition said he could discover more puzzle pieces inside her.

"You're being modest," he said. "I think there are a lot of depths you keep secret."

One russet brow twitched up. "What does that have to do with people reacting strangely to Jason?"

"Nothing. Except you're very perceptive. Does Jason have an odd effect on you?"

She held the files close to her chest like an armor breastplate. "I'm immune to him. He's…"

"What?"

Only the motorized purring of the copier sounded in the room. For a moment, he thought she wouldn't answer.

"He's charismatic, but false people don't stand a chance with me. I can't be brainwashed by handsome smiles." She sauntered toward the door. "He's charming, convincing and powerful. Some people are influenced by those things more readily than others. Greed and power create their own negative energy and some people are attracted to it. I'm naturally repelled." She cleared her throat. "Can we talk about this when we have lunch Saturday?"

"Of course."

She walked out, then made a step back into the room. Genuine concern crossed her face. "Do you feel all right now?"

Gratified more than he should be by her worry, he
"Yes, thanks."

She nodded and with quiet steps left.

Heat passed over him, and it had nothing to do with Ja
apparent mind probe and everything to do with Tara.

Make no mistake, his cubicle partner defined *hot*.

Keeping his libido in check around her proved difficu
he must. He couldn't afford the complication of a ph
relationship, even if she wanted to jump his bones. Cu
made him want to race out to her and demand an expla
about the life force she'd mentioned, but that would
pushing too far and she was already skittish. He need
trust and, so far, he thought he had it.

He acknowledged other complications. Jason had
down his mental shield without a whimper. Marcus' wh
gold light guard repelled most polluting influences, bu
proved he had heavy-duty powers that could cut t
defenses like a knife through flesh.

Marcus closed his eyes and took a deep breath, reple
the white shield that Jason had torn. He opened his eyes
refreshed.

His thoughts turned to Cecelia. When she'd come or
in the lounge earlier in the day, he'd been damned su
since she never paid him much attention before. Her a
annoyed him. He'd meet up with her and see what the
wanted.

Earlier, when he'd seen Tara's reaction to Cecelia's
Marcus had wondered if Tara was jealous.

Nah. That wasn't possible.

Chapter Four

&

For the first time in a long time, Marcus felt as gauche as a lumbering ape at a party for graceful antelope. The clatter of dishes and utensils filled the employee lounge as employees set up for the potluck. Bettina strode around the room giving orders on how to arrange the room. He'd applied muscle by moving chairs and positioning the extra long table he'd pulled out of the storage room. He'd removed his suit jacket and tie and rolled up his shirt sleeves. A few times, he'd noticed women in the department giving him curious looks. Maybe they didn't like his sudden transformation from uptight word processing clerk to casual furniture mover? Honestly, he didn't give a fuck.

What he did care about was that Tara hadn't shown up yet after disappearing a few minutes ago.

As Bettina passed by with a gelatin mold, he asked, "Have you seen Tara?"

She stopped, then frowned. "Come to think of it, no." She peered at him, her thick lashes framing eyes both inquisitive and teasing. "You could go look for her."

"No." He spoke a little sharply, then regretted it when Bettina's eyebrows went up. "I'm sure she's fine. She'll be here when she gets here."

"You're worried about her, aren't you? You're concerned about her ex-husband."

He'd learned long ago he couldn't fool Bettina. "Yeah, I am."

"I think she said she had some papers to deliver to another department, but maybe she had an errand to run on her lunch hour."

"She didn't say anything about missing the potluck?"

Now Bettina looked as anxious as he felt. "No." She sighed. "Well, if she doesn't show up shortly, one of us can go look for her."

He nodded, and Bettina continued to the table.

God, he'd become too wrapped up in Tara's state of affairs. He couldn't stop thinking about her. Determined to let it go, he headed for the refrigerator to retrieve the food he'd brought. A quick stop at the local grocery down the street this morning had solved his problem. He didn't have time to fix anything and he didn't want to. He also didn't think his version of low-carb, low-fat macaroni and cheese would have won any votes at this gathering. The table groaned under the weight of the monthly potluck dining experience.

"Son of a—" Marcus managed to cut himself off when he bumped into Cecelia on the way from the fridge to the long table.

His container of potato salad tittered in his grip.

"Oh, sorry," Cecelia said with a whispery intonation. She looked jumpy, like a whipped puppy anticipating another blow.

Weird. He couldn't remember seeing her like this before.

He smiled and said, "It's no big deal. You okay?"

"I'm fine."

Her words sounded almost sluggish, and he didn't believe her. A winsome, sad smile touched her lips. Lines had formed around her eyes and mouth, as if her vitality drained away by a long night battling emotions. Her eyes were rimmed with dark circles, their expression haunted. Curiosity made him drop the shield that kept too much information from bombarding him. As he allowed his senses to reach out for Cecelia, a smattering of impressions filtered into his mind.

He felt and saw her reactions as if he resided in Cecelia's body. She sat in an office, but the details of the room didn't come clear to him as he absorbed her chaotic physical and mental signals. Inside her thoughts, she screamed to get out, to leave the precarious situation. A man stood behind her and gripped her shoulders near her neck. He massaged the muscles with a pressure almost painful, his will pressing down on her like a lead weight around her neck. Down, down, her body slid further into the chair. She fought for restraint, for sanity.

The man whispered his desires into her mind. *Give your will to me. Do my bidding. Be my eyes and ears.*

Marcus jerked back from the smothering sensation.

Cecelia frowned. "Something wrong?"

Damn it. "No."

She put one hand on her hip, the pose at once flirtatious and defiant. "Right. I know what you're thinking."

He blinked. "What?"

"You're thinking we already have too many salads."

He glanced over at the table. "You're right." He grinned. "Way too many salads."

She giggled, and the girly sound made him wince. "Well, Mr. Forte is bringing the chicken, a special bought-it-in-a-bucket recipe. I'm sure it'll be great."

He chuckled. "No doubt."

She winked, and when he turned back to the food table, he could have sworn her gaze bored a hole in his back. He didn't know if the stare equated to a glare or if she was checking him out. His senses felt awash in skewed emotional turmoil he knew didn't belong to him. He put his salad and the serving fork on the table in time to see Tara enter. Relief washed away some of the apprehension.

Marcus caught her glance, and he gave her a reassuring smile. Her cool returning grin seemed tentative. She headed straight for the refrigerator and rummaged inside. He kept his distance, at once apprehensive that she might think he belonged with her ex-husband in the stalker category. He didn't want her to feel pressured to talk to him about her situation.

The room clamored now with the voices and movements of around forty people. He strengthened the white light around him, well aware the crowd could get to him if he allowed it.

Forte walked in with an entourage of people from the finance office. All of them carried a food dish, and Forte's container was heaped with fried chicken.

Marcus watched from a safe distance as Forte said hello to few people, mingling in with the crowd. Marcus kept to the back of the throng, not talking much to anyone as he assessed the atmosphere. The noise volume in the room threatened to unnerve him, but he forced back the featherlight prickles at the back of his neck that warned overload. He wanted to go somewhere quiet, but wouldn't be able to anytime soon. As long as Tara stayed here, so would he.

He watched Tara surreptitiously, certain if anyone looked at him they'd understand his true feelings. He tried not to hover and watch her every move, but fuck it—he couldn't stop wanting to protect her. Shit, if he didn't get a grip people would see through his pitiful veneer, and he'd be forced to acknowledge to himself what he couldn't admit in public. That her shining fall of dark hair and unusual eyes captivated, trapped him from the first moment he laid eyes upon her. It hadn't taken months or years to read her from cover to cover and learn all her shadows. From the first day he saw Tara, she'd trapped him.

A melting sensation started in his stomach. His libido went into riot. God, she was so pretty. She glowed with heath, from the vibrancy of her eyes, to the milky clarity of her fragile-looking skin. Marcus' desire to shelter her grew stronger. Yet he sensed genuine power inside her and it made him more than curious to explore.

"Everything okay?" Sugar asked, breaking him out of reverie with a jolt. "You look a little strange."

He recovered and smiled wryly. "You're just now noticing I look strange? I thought it was universally acknowledged."

Sugar's syrupy grin was sweet enough to give him a toothache. Her gaze jumped over his body with a swift assessment. He'd never noticed her checking him out him before, and it surprised the hell out of him. What had changed with Sugar and Cecelia?

A pretty pink stained Sugar's upper cheeks, and when he noted her low-cut, satiny blue dress, her flush deepened. She came closer, an uncharacteristic glint to her almond-shaped eyes. Guile and innocence wrapped in one package, and he didn't trust her. With swiftness born of desperation, he opened his mind to hers quickly.

A sweeping visual presentation streamed through him picture after picture, all of it static. One overt image came through clear as glass. She didn't like his attention to Tara, her jealousy stinging and potent.

She grasped his biceps, and the glint of her engagement ring caught his gaze for a millisecond. Flirtation filled her purring voice. "What are you thinking? You've got such a mysterious look about you today."

He almost snorted in disbelief. "Mysterious?"

Sugar's palm slid down to his forearm, her touch almost hot. "You always have that unapproachable look about you, but this is different." She practically leaned against his side. "What is it?"

He kept a smile in place as he moved away from her. "Your imagination. There's nothing mystifying about me. I'm hungry. Let's eat."

Her pout would be enticing if he liked that kind of thing in a woman. Familiarity like hers didn't surprise him much. In his forty years, a few other women had treated him like meat for hire. He wondered what her fiancé would think if he saw Sugar smoothing her fingers over a man's arm.

His gaze snapped up to find Tara glancing at them from across the room. Tara had a plate of food and she stood next to one of the computer techs, who gestured emphatically with one arm to make some point. Marcus didn't try and smile this time, but he saw something desperate in her eyes, as if she couldn't wait to either run from the tech or to leave the room.

He threw a thought Tara's way, unbidden and forbidden. *Let's see if she can catch this signal.*

Tara's gaze swept toward Marcus as an uncontrollable pull demanded she seek him out. Her heartbeat seemed to slow to a dull thud, thud, thud. Time had no meaning as everything around her melted under the force of his attention.

She heard a voice in her head and recognized Marcus' deep intonation. *Rescue me.*

Tara blinked, shocked at what she'd heard. She'd felt and experienced many paranormal oddities related to her abilities. Telepathic experiences came often to her.

Yet, hearing someone speak in her head, feeling as if someone targeted her specifically to hear him, had never happened before.

Did he have any idea that his thoughts had telegraphed to her? Not likely.

Beyond resisting, she excused herself from the computer guru's presence and wended through the tangle of coworkers. Nervous excitement stirred in her stomach. She wanted to be nearer to Marcus, and she couldn't deny it. Whether she'd liked it or not, nagging jealousy had marked her in the last few minutes as she'd covertly watched him talking with Sugar. She knew the emotion was counterproductive, and she wasn't proud of feeling this proprietary. God, she'd liked Marcus' attention and now that another woman seemed to have his undivided interest, Tara didn't care for it.

She'd never seen Sugar waylay a man like this. Tara wondered if Sugar had any idea the image she projected when she wore an engagement ring and yet flirted without remorse with Marcus.

"How are you guys?" she asked with a casual air as she came up to Sugar and Marcus.

Marcus' smile, warm and welcoming, went straight to her heart, and she felt her personal fleet of butterflies do pirouettes in pleasure. "Hi."

"Hi," she said simply, including Sugar in her greeting. "What's new, Sugar?"

Indifference and an icy boredom settled over the other woman's face. This wasn't the Sugar she remembered from a day ago. Her eyes owned a peculiar gleam, a fire at once cold and raging hot.

"Nothing much," Sugar said. "I was telling him how mysterious he is. It gets under a woman's skin." As abruptly as Sugar's jaded expression evolved, it disappeared. "What do you think?"

Caught without a good response, Tara glanced at Marcus. An amused sparkle entered his eyes, and then the answer flowed from Tara like water. "I like a man who is open with me. Mysterious can be dangerous. I don't need uncertainty in my life."

Sugar slipped her arm through his and leaned into him a bit. "Hear that? It takes a special kind of woman to appreciate you."

He kept Tara's gaze locked with his. "Yeah, I think it does."

Unwilling to play games, Tara decided she'd retreat. "I need to get more chicken. I'm starving."

She turned around and almost dumped her plate right onto Jason Forte's suit.

"Whoa," Jason said. "You okay?"

He sounded so sincere, his brow furrowed but eyes dancing with good humor.

"Sorry about that. Guess I'm clumsy today." She wanted to groan. Why did she feel it necessary to degrade herself to explain something of no consequence?

Unfortunately, Jason invited this type of behavior in herself and others, and it drove her crazy.

He winked. "Didn't know there was hooch in the punch."

Sugar giggled.

I never thought of her as vacuous, but maybe I was wrong.

Jason sauntered up to Sugar and put his hand on her shoulder, and she released her proprietary grip on Marcus.

"You've been slipping something bad into the bowl?" Jason asked Sugar.

Sugar's eyes widened in innocence, but her returning smile showed too much teeth. "Little ol' me?"

Jason's grin held a verisimilitude Tara never believed. She always thought of him as thorny, not someone a person could accurately know without making a pact with the devil first. Tara shuddered as Jason turned his all-knowing gaze to her.

Ew. The *ick* factor went way off the charts, and goose bumps hit her skin as his eyes toured her body. She saw Marcus frown and wondered if he noticed the way Jason surveyed her like a map.

"Can I talk to you a minute, Tara?" Marcus' welcome question practically made Tara jump for joy. Thank God.

"Sure."

"Oh, is this a private conversation?" Sugar asked with a little-girl-lost expression.

As Tara deposited her almost empty plate into a nearby trash bin, Marcus said, "Yes, it is."

Tara didn't wait to see Jason or Sugar's reaction to Marcus' statement. She followed him out of the room. Once she'd closed the lounge doorway, he looked around. "We need someplace private."

"We do?"

"Yeah. Come on."

He led the way toward an empty office down the hall. Curiosity made her follow, and caution made her want to ask a thousand questions first. He tried the door and then entered the windowless office and flicked on the light. Only a metal desk and some empty bookshelves occupied the room. She went inside with him, small frissons of alarm and excitement battling for supremacy inside her.

"Maybe Sugar is right," she said. "You're being mysterious. What kind of conversation requires this type of privacy?"

He turned toward her, seriousness in his eyes. "This is going to sound strange, but have you noticed something weird about Sugar and Cecelia today? Like they aren't quite themselves?"

She couldn't think how to answer at first. What had she expected him to ask? Certainly not this. "Well, come to think of it…"

"Go on." With his crossed arms and direct gaze, he projected strength and determination.

She rubbed her hands up and down her arms to start her blood moving. The short-sleeved cotton top she wore didn't compete well against the frigid office.

"Tara?"

His prompting made her answer, and she decided the truth would be better. "It seemed to me they are flirting with you. A lot. They don't usually do that."

One corner of his nicely carved mouth turned up in a quick burst of amusement. "You noticed, eh?"

She took a deep breath. "Well, it is pretty obvious flirting."

The glitter in his eyes held warmth. "Yeah, I was wondering about that myself. All of a sudden I'm not gay anymore."

She shrugged and rubbed her arms again. "I always thought you were nice-looking—"

When she realized what she said, she stopped cold and blushed.

"Thanks for the compliment. You've stroked my ego." His irreverent grin made her pulse pick up, and his nearness started a fresh wave of restlessness inside her.

"Well, you're certainly not an ugly man."

Good going. Just keep digging a deeper hole.

"Thanks again. Now, do you think they're joking with me, or there is something else weird going on?"

She frowned. "What else could it be but a joke? It's juvenile, but somehow it doesn't surprise me that they would think it was funny."

"You don't like them?"

"It's not that I don't like them, but I couldn't be close friends with either of them for quite a few reasons."

The brilliance in his eyes went deeper, darker and filled with a curious heat that generated an answering temperature inside her. "What about me? Do you consider me a good friend?"

She hadn't thought about it, but her answer came easily. "Of course."

Now his voice went lower, huskier. "Do you trust me?"

Worry pushed her awareness of his potent male presence to the side somewhat. "Yes. Why?"

He rotated his head and shoulders as if tired. "No special reason. I hoped that you knew you could trust me."

Behind his glasses, his stormy ocean eyes asked for capitulation, and she wanted to give it.

"I do trust you," she said.

"Good." He nodded and then headed for the door. "We'd better get back to the party or they're going to wonder where we've gone."

Heat filled her face again. And what we were doing.

* * * * *

Drake hated Tara.

The feeling grew within him minute by minute, night by night, and year by year. Soon she would understand what she'd done to him, and she would pay.

Darkness reached for him as he watched her small house from the opposite side of the tree-lined street. Murky tendrils reached into his mind and obliterated his momentary lucidity with blackness so profound he shivered. Nausea curled in his stomach. Hate inserted itself with insidious twists of its malaise deep into his mind and soul.

Not even a single light shown through a window. Vegetation rustled in a tentative breeze. Whispering of the trees urged him forward, beckoned him to cross the street and do what he wanted. Without interference, he could approach her quiet home and step inside. He could explore her mind through each room in the house. Her décor would tell him what he already knew. She owned the heart of a whore.

He imagined her walls painted colors painful to the eyes, and her bedroom would be lacy and frilly down to the last set of panties in her chest of drawers. She might try to hide her black heart with an innocent demeanor, but he knew her as few others could. With her flawless peach-hued skin and elegant nose, she portrayed herself as stately. He wanted to laugh. How could a woman with one brown eye and one blue eye be so damned haughty? That oddity alone should make her more self-conscious.

Instead she'd cut into his heart and ripped it out.

Yet he knew her true secret, the one that sliced her to the quick deeper and more tragically than anything in her life. He understood what motivated the bitch. Her sinful visions polluted her.

Hell, he knew better than anyone what evil worked in the deep souls of men and women.

Nothing he hated more than the wicked night. People used the darkness to perform perverse tasks abhorrent to him. They slept, they snored, they fornicated in the most horrible ways imaginable. Beasts resided inside the human mind, awaiting the nighttime to break free.

Oh, people claimed to be holy, to be without pride or other vices, but he saw through them into their hearts charred by the fires of hell. No, they needed help to remove the sins of the flesh and long-buried secrets.

He rubbed his hands together, wishing he'd brought gloves with him. *No. Her body and soul would feel so much more pliable and warm when he touched them with his bare skin.*

An old poem from somewhere in his childhood rang in his head. He spoke now and used it like a mantra. "'Sins and secrets shall not be kept. A young boy's thoughts must be cleansed...of all the nightmares he creates. Sins and secrets shall not be kept. All the night and all the day, a woman will be chaste and always clean.'" The words ran through his thoughts like insidious insects gnawing on his brain. "'The righteous shall inherit and all sin washed free from the earth. There is a utopia in the soil awaiting release. You must free it, son.'"

A breeze, tipped with unusual cold, brushed over his form. A shiver worked through his body from shoulders to shins. He thought about what he must do now. Right this minute.

He would purify her for the last time.

Chapter Five

෨

"I can't believe I'm doing this," Tara said as she traveled in Marcus' late-model gold Alterra toward one of the malls on Saturday.

Marcus grinned, cracking a cheeky, know-it-all-and-loving-it expression. "Yeah. Make me into the ultimate macho man."

He winked and then turned his attention back to the road when he came to a red light. One more light and they could turn into the huge mall.

"I make no promises," she said, glad she'd agreed to come with him. For a few hours, she could banish her ex-husband from her mind.

When Marcus picked her up on time at her house that morning, she'd been rife with doubts. She soothed her thoughts by remembering he was just a pal wanting wardrobe advice. He looked perfectly harmless. Nothing like the warrior she'd seen in her vision. He'd drawn back his long hair into the customary tieback and the glasses on his nose gave him that slightly large-eyed expression.

He pulled into a parking spot quite a ways from the entrance. The Saturday crowd filled the parking lots to the brim. He turned off the purring engine and unbuckled his seat belt. When he shifted his slacks-clad legs, hard thighs caught her attention. Her gaze snagged on those muscles, and a bolt of unexpected attraction made her stare. She wondered what it would feel like to touch his thighs and test their strength. Maybe he wasn't the stick-thin man he'd let everyone believe, and she couldn't hold back the accusation.

"You've been hiding, haven't you?" she asked.

Those dark brows popped up. "Hiding?" He slid his right arm onto the back of the seat, his fingers touching the head support behind her. "Explain."

She licked her lips and his gaze caught on the movement. "You've been hiding your physique under those slightly loose shirts and suits."

He shrugged, his mile rueful. "I need to work out more. Some people think I'm skinny."

"Uh-huh." Somehow, she didn't believe him. Well, maybe today she'd learn the truth.

"Come on. We've got work to do."

As they left the car and headed toward the mall entrance, Tara braced for the crowds. There would be mindless jostling, loud talking and the ever-present mental chatter she often picked up from numerous people whether she wanted to or not. In an expansive crowd, her shielding capabilities didn't always work well. She would have to labor hard to make sure her empathic sensibilities didn't overload.

As they entered a moderate-priced department store, she felt content and at ease at Marcus' side. They'd entered near the menswear side on the first floor, and she headed right toward the area she wanted.

Tagging along, his long legs eating up the floor, he didn't look too pleased about the journey. "What's first?"

"Something in lumberjack, I think." She stopped near a rack of shirts. She pulled out a size large red T-shirt. "This is perfect." She grabbed three more in white, dark green and navy blue. "There you go. Manly colors. What size jeans do you wear?"

After he told her, they trundled over to a few more racks, Tara snatching a couple pairs of jeans and handing them to him. "Better see if they'll even let you in the dressing room with that many items."

He looked green around the gills. "I suppose you want me to model them so you can approve?"

She crossed her arms and put on the appropriate haughty face. "Naturally. Now get your butt in that dressing room."

He saluted, a wide grin on his mouth. "Aye, aye, ma'am."

When he turned on his heel and swaggered to the dressing room area, her breath caught. Jeez, even in his slightly baggy clothes, she could see hints of a good body. Wide shoulders tapered to a narrow waist, trim hips and a world-class ass. He looked *fine* from this angle. Why hadn't she noticed before?

One of the salesgirls, a young Hispanic woman, intercepted Marcus on the way to the dressing room. From this distance, she couldn't hear what the woman said to him. Her cat-licking-cream expression said she liked what she saw. Figures. Animated and perky, the girl looked young enough to be his daughter. His eyes and smile screamed friendly and warm, but not flirtatious. Before he headed into the dressing room, he turned his gaze back to Tara and gave her an innocent smile. Her heart did a funny twist. *Holy javalina.*

Swift and dumfounding, a new emotion arose inside Tara. Her throat tightened, a hollow sensation entering her stomach. The feeling blossomed so fast it stunned her.

Annoyance at the Hispanic woman, and with herself, rose to the fore.

Oh no. It couldn't be. Not again.

I am jealous.

She inhaled and let out the tension, then turned away from the dressing room in mild disgust and distress. Jealousy had no place in her emotions. She shoved away the useless feeling ruthlessly. Okay, so she cared about him. Big deal. More complicated emotions wouldn't be tolerated in any shape or form.

It didn't take long for Marcus to leave the dressing room. He searched out Tara and she smiled at the same time he did. She walked toward him as the sales representative came up to him again.

Oh Lordy. The man did dress down nicely. Instead of leaving the T-shirt out, he'd tucked it into his jeans. His muscles flexed and bunched just right and he looked far too intriguing for words. People in the office might still think "gay" when they saw this. He needed something else that screamed masculine to the max.

His grin said he found this whole exercise amusing. "So what do you think?" He turned around with his arms slightly out to his sides. "Everything fits perfectly. Good guess on your part, Tara."

"It looks fantastic, sir." The young saleswoman's eyes sparkled, her admiration obvious. The girl almost drooled on his athletic shoes. "You'd look wonderful in a suit."

The sales clerk reached up and patted his shoulders, and Tara could have sworn the woman even squeezed a little. Tara gritted her teeth and reined in catty thoughts.

Marcus shrugged. "I've already got suits at home."

"But they're too large." The words came out of Tara's mouth before she could stop them. "I know you're trying to dress down, but if you had some suits that were the right size, well, it would look great."

Feeling a tad impulsive, Tara took a step toward him, yanked the T-shirt out of the waistband, and let it hang. "There. That's better."

The saleswoman frowned. "Umm...really it seems tidier tucked in."

When the woman tried to reach for his shirt if she planned to stuff it back into his jeans, he took a step back. "Wait, wait, ladies. I realize you can't keep your hands off me, but people are starting to stare."

A bit horrified, Tara looked around the area at the same time the saleswoman did. No one was paying any attention the tiny drama.

"No one cares," Tara said.

The woman's head bobbed in agreement. "Sir, I would never think of compromising a customer."

He wiggled his eyebrows in a ridiculous but endearing way and said, "Damn. And here I was looking forward to two beautiful women fighting over me."

The young sales representative arched her delicately plucked brows and crossed her arms. Her succulent lower lip stuck out a little. "Sir, I would never. But I can find you a suit I think you'll love."

"Great. That would be wonderful," he said.

Without sparing Tara a glance, the woman sashayed toward the Italian designer section.

"That was interesting," he said. "I'm not sure what it was, but it was interesting."

"I'm not even going to pretend I know what you're talking about."

His narrow-eyed expression took on a concentration she didn't expect. "If I didn't know better, I'd almost say you were jealous."

Shock made her mouth plop open and she glared as heat filled her face. "Jealous? Oh, give me a break."

"Well, you seemed to come on a bit like a lioness when she touched me."

"It's your imagination. But I think you need to keep the T-shirts out if you want them to be casual. They're not too baggy so you can get away with it."

His gaze still held speculation. "Okay. But more Italian stuff, eh?"

"Well, she's right. You do look great in it. If we got you some pants that fit and—"

"I do have pants that fit." He frowned and looked down at his jeans.

God, they really did fit him perfectly, outlining a trim waist, narrow hips and muscular legs.

"Yes, your jeans do, but those things you wear to work are a bit baggy."

One of his dark brows lifted in query, but before he could speak, the saleswoman came back.

"Here you are, sir. Three suits and silk shirts to match. Try them on."

Without argument, he went back to the dressing room. Again, the sales rep acted as if Tara didn't exist and went back to her counter. Tara tried to calm down. She felt jumpy, and she didn't know why. Add that to the acute embarrassment she'd felt when he said she was jealous and she wished the floor would open up and swallow her. Not many moments later and he stepped out of the dressing room.

Her throat clogged up and her breath stopped as she took in the sight of glorious male perfection. The sage green, short-sleeved fine-gauge silk knit shirt contoured well-developed muscles and smoothed down over his flat stomach. He hadn't tucked it in. The pants, a dark gray, fit him flawlessly. Even his clunky glasses couldn't make him look bad. He'd left off the suit jacket.

"These fit great," he said to the saleswoman as she smiled and batted her eyelashes.

"I always did know how to dress a man," the woman said, flicking a careless glance at Tara. "Some women have a talent for it and some women don't."

Heat burned Tara's face at the implication behind the sales rep's words.

As if I – why the little bitch.

Unreasonable anger clenched deep in Tara stomach, and she smiled with a hint of acid. "Marcus, it's clear you're in great hands here. I'll be down at the food court."

Yes, a good shot of double mocha latte should do the trick right about now.

She didn't give a rat's butt, in that moment, whether he accomplished what he'd set out to do or not. He could pick out his own clothes and didn't need her help. She walked away without another word.

"Tara, wait." She ignored him, and then she heard him say to the sales rep, "I'll be right back."

He caught up to her before she could leave the clothes racks. He clasped her upper arm gently, but forced her to stop. Stepping in front of her, he smiled, removed his glasses and slipped them into a pants pocket. Then he did something she never expected in a million and a half years.

He slipped his fingers into the hair at the back of her neck and pulled her against his body. Her hands came up on autopilot and touched his chest. The silk felt soft over steel-hardness. "Sweetheart, are you angry?"

Sweetheart? Had he lost his mind?

Before she could formulate a reasonable answer, his eyes blazed with an untamed anticipation she'd never seen in his face before. A combination of meltingly tender desire and heated excitement dominated his expression. She couldn't catch her breath in time to say anything.

He bent his head and kissed her.

Surprise held her immobile. His body, his lips...all felt furnace-warm against her. While his lips molded with soft attention, it wasn't a kiss designed to show minor affection. He plied and shaped, tasting her with raw intimacy and hot, drugging passion. A man kissed this way when he wanted to devour his lover. At turns soft, then hard, his mouth mated with hers so thoroughly, she trembled and couldn't get her breath.

Passion simmered inside her as well as dazed enjoyment. With one penetrating stroke, his tongue brushed over hers with a lightning-quick touch. Shivery excitement darted into her stomach and her nipples tightened into hard points.

He broke away.

Breathing a bit harder and reeling with sensual bliss, she stared up at him in amazement. She'd been kissed before, obviously, but nothing quite like this. Despite the fact the kiss couldn't have taken more than a few seconds, it ignited a riot of desire inside her. His touch, his gentleness, the restrained passion bubbled at the surface like a volcano. His gaze shimmered, passion-drugged and crackling with barely suppressed desire. Marcus also looked startled, like lightning had blasted down from a clear blue sky. She felt his self-control hanging by a tether, as if he'd like to do a hell of a lot more. He took a deep breath.

He winked and then a slow, seductive smile curved his mouth. "I won't be long."

With that simple statement, he released her. As she watched him with a combination of incredulousness and feverish excitement, she noticed the sales rep wore a frown about a mile and a half wide.

With an inappropriate sense of triumph, she headed to the food court without another glance.

She realized one other incredible thing. Marcus tasted and kissed precisely like her dream lover.

No. It couldn't be.

* * * * *

Marcus walked out to his car to put away the clothing purchases and thought about the kiss.

Yeah, he'd kissed *her* all right. It might have been quick, but he'd poured everything he felt into that moment.

Why? Knee-buckling lust.

Holy shit, but she'd tasted good. He'd savored her mint flavor, a sensation he wanted to linger over like fine wine or the mellowest whisky. He'd almost fell on his ass as he accepted something else. She kissed like the woman in his dreams.

No. The dream woman was a product of his imagination.

During the kiss he'd experienced a gamut of emotions he'd found only in his dreams with the mysterious woman. His rapid-fire heartbeat and fierce hunger for her almost brought him to his knees. He'd felt a soul-deep connection in that one kiss, a bond exhilarating and crackling with thrilling emotion.

Shaken, he kept walking. His brain felt blitzed by adrenaline. The last time he recalled feeling this hyper had been during Desert Storm in ninety-one.

He thought about the interesting exchange between the salesgirl and Tara.

He shouldn't have, and yet when Tara had stalked away from him in a huff, he'd taken her jealous display to heart. Sure, the salesgirl might be pretty, but he also had nearly twenty years on her and he didn't date women in their twenties now that he'd hit forty. The age difference seemed too much, and he didn't have things in common with them.

He knew ten different things he could do to Tara to make her confess that she had feelings for him. Kiss her softly, whisper suggestions in her ear and caress her from head to toe until she shivered. All of it would end, if he had anything to say about it, with Tara beneath him and his cock deep inside her.

Damn, those ideas sounded good.

Fuck me. I am so dead.

She hadn't kissed him back, but then he'd probably startled the hell out of her. And, when the warm, succulent taste of her lips had drawn him in, he could barely keep his hands from drawing her closer. The entire world disappeared in the short time their lips came together.

He dumped his numerous purchases into the car and headed back into the mall. His cock hardened at the thought of feeling her lips under his once more.

Fat chance, moron.

Not only was he lucky she hadn't told him to fuck off and die, he shouldn't kiss a woman with stalking issues. She didn't need his sex drive getting in her way, too. Top that off with her being an employee in the company he investigated, and it led right to trouble.

Never mind remembering how she felt cuddled in his arms, or the warmth of her tongue as he'd stroked once, deep and quick, into her mouth. He took several deep breaths and plowed his libido into submission. He couldn't walk into the mall with a raging hard-on.

Once in control and inside the mall, he traversed the hustle and bustle of the department store, then into the mall proper. At this time of day, the crowds started to build. He drew in a deep breath and pulled his mental shields up. He didn't want any stray thoughts, feelings, or bad vibes coming into his psyche from somewhere else.

The food court brimmed with individuals eating lunch.

All except for Tara.

His heart picked up speed as razor-sharp tension kicked into gear. He'd only been an SIA agent for over a year and a half. Before that, his military training assured lightning-fast attentiveness when he needed it. With his ears alert and eyes scanning for any sign of Tara, he surveyed the food court. The area held screaming babies, noisy toddlers and insolent teenagers. Most of the adults had semi-pained expressions on their shopping weary faces. Various food scents drifted to his nose. A cacophony of voices and harsh rock music filled his ears.

He zeroed in on Tara coming out of the ladies' room, and a deep breath of relief left his chest. He shouldn't have left her alone. Drake could show up any time.

Right then a tall, thin man stepped out of an alcove near the bathrooms and grabbed Tara's arm.

Instantly on alert for danger, Marcus almost broke into a run. He stalked toward them through the crowd, ready to rip the asshole a new one if he even thought of harming her—

Tara smiled and threw her arms around the neck of the skinny guy.

What that—?

Marcus slowed his walk. No way was this man Drake.

Tara pulled back from the man and started an animated conversation. The man was bone-thin, but he didn't have the pallor of the ill. His grin held a mouth full of very white teeth. His face was all sharp angles. Skinny dude saw Marcus first and grinned widely.

Tara turned around and spied Marcus. "There you are."

"Darling," the skinny dude said to her. His voice, a little high-pitched and effeminate, surprised Marcus. "Aren't you going to introduce the hunk?"

Hunk? Holy crap.

Tara must have seen Marcus' thunderstruck expression, because she laughed. Her eyes sparkled with genuine delight. "Benny, this is a friend from work, Marcus Hyatt. Marcus, meet my old buddy Benicio La Paglia."

Benny's black-eyed gaze swept over Marcus with clear interest, and discomfort went through Marcus. As far as he knew, he'd never been checked out by another man until now. He shook the much smaller man's hand and made proper salutations.

Benny held his hand longer than necessary. "So pleased to meet you, Marcus. I've heard loads about you."

"Really?"

She patted Benny on the shoulder. "I haven't talked about him that much."

Benny rolled his gaze to the ceiling. "Oh, please. You told me he was gay."

Marcus forced a smile at her. "Tara, you know that's not true. Why did you tell him that?"

She sighed heavily and frowned at Benny. "I didn't say he was gay, I said he *might* be. That was before I knew better."

The shit-eating grin on the other man's face made Marcus want to laugh. "Pity. Well, I mean if you're not gay, I hope you're considering being this sweet thing's boyfriend. She really does need a man."

Tara's cheeks turned pink, and Marcus felt his body react. His heartbeat picked up and his hands itched to touch her. His hormones couldn't take it. Right now, he wanted to toss her over his shoulder, take her home and fuck her until they both couldn't stand. Only great willpower kept him from tugging her away and heading back to the car.

Suddenly, Marcus realized Benny wore a shirt similar to one he'd bought.

"Gianni Rabbini," Marcus said out of the blue.

Benicio's mouth opened in a coo. "That's right. Lordy, lady, he has the fashion eye." The smaller man waggled his eyebrows. "You're a fashion hog, too?"

"Ah, no. That's why I'm here with her. I needed help."

Tara made a sound of disagreement. "Pooh. He was dressing so well everyone in the office thought he was gay."

Marcus almost squirmed in embarrassment. If the guys at SIA could see him now…

Benny frowned. "And what's wrong with that?"

The man's accusatory expression made Marcus want to bolt. "I don't like pretending to be something I'm not."

Boy, do you lie well.

He tried not to think about how Tara would feel if she knew his real identity.

"Get outta here," Benny said. "Well, I'd love to stay and talk, but Doug is waiting in the car."

Benny kissed Tara on the cheek and then gave her another warm hug. He glanced over at Marcus. "You take good care of my sweetie, you hear?"

Marcus nodded. "Count on it."

With a final wave, the man walked away.

"Wow," Marcus said.

An appreciative grin touched her mouth. "That he is. We used to work in word processing together but he didn't like the company. He said it creeped him out."

Alarm bells went off in his head. "Creeped him out?"

She shrugged. "He never explained. *Wouldn't* explain, as a matter of fact." She took his arm. "Come on. What kind of fast food are we interested in?"

He grimaced. "I'm not. Let's go to Giacomo's."

Her pretty eyes widened. "That's pricey, isn't it?"

"Yeah." He took her hand and held it firmly as he led her back toward the end of the mall. "It's worth every penny."

"It's a deal. But then we need to talk."

He heard trouble in those few words. "About what?"

"About why you kissed me."

* * * * *

"What is going on?" Tara asked Marcus.

When he looked up from his gelato dessert after a sumptuous penne pasta lunch, Tara realized she wouldn't pry answers out of him anytime soon. At least not about his devastating kiss.

"Nothing is going on." He lifted some dessert onto his spoon and held it toward her across the small table. "Have some gelato."

Husky and seductive, his resonant voice sent tremulous earthquakes straight into her stomach and between her legs. "But—"

The strawberry dessert slipped between her lips, cold and delicious. Marcus had left off his glasses and his smoldering eyes held mysteries overlaid with a heavy dose of sex. Was she imagining what she saw in those ocean-blue depths? He licked his lips as she swallowed, and the gesture struck deep into her primal needs.

The wild idea that he might be her dream lover spiraled back into her mind. Kissing him had felt incredibly familiar but at the same time it had felt so new. She shifted on the seat, uncomfortable. God, she had to crucify this restless, insatiable arousal. But how? Jump his bones and be done with it? Would one bout of bone-melting sex be enough to curb this crazy longing? Maybe sex with him wouldn't approach nuclear heat anyway.

Yeah. Right.

She knew deep down that making love with him would curl her toes and send her heart into overdrive.

Shock ran through her. She couldn't make love with Marcus. The strange situation with Drake and the time she'd spent around Marcus today must have turned her brains to oatmeal. Nothing else made sense.

On the way to the restaurant, he'd turned on the radio and flip-flopped a couple of times between a country station and a classic hard rock station. When he found a station that featured songs from the Eighties she smiled and decided she approved of his taste in music. Until recently she'd almost despaired of hearing Eighties music on the radio again. Now it seemed *de rigueur* for stations to play music from that decade. Only a few years ago smartass commentators on television had made wisecracks about big hair and Eighties music.

Throughout lunch, he'd remained quiet, as if contemplating the meaning of life. His monosyllabic statements worried her. Even the tiny Italian restaurant's sunny atmosphere and wonderful food aromas didn't light the gloomy atmosphere floating around the man across from her. Patrons all around them murmured low, as if they were in a library with a no talking sign.

A loud clap of thunder made her jump. She glanced out the large glass windows at the front and saw an enormous dark swirl of a thunderhead moving closer.

A tiny smile flicked over his lips, as if he understood her prickliness.

She broke down and tried again. "What's wrong? Are you angry?"

"What? No, of course not."

"You've been so quiet."

"That's a bad thing?"

"No, it's just…nothing. I'm sorry."

He held another bite of dessert out for her, and when she took it in her mouth this time, she made sure to hold his gaze. Maybe if she looked deep enough and long enough into those mysterious eyes she'd learn his secrets. Perhaps another vision would come to mind and explain what he was hiding. Instead sinuous heat pooled in her loins, daring her to ignore the ramifications. Trying to deny she found him attractive was futile. He did turn her on in many ways, and she didn't like it one bit.

"What are you thinking?" she asked.

"That this is the best damned gelato I've had in a long time."

He laughed softly, and she joined him. The tension broke.

Pushing him wouldn't produce results. Maybe if she started another line of conversation, things would ease back into the friendly, non-pressure mode she enjoyed with him at work.

"Tell me about your family," she said point-blank.

At first, she thought he might ignore this request, too. He stared at her a moment as if at a loss for words. When he finally answered, he cleared his throat first. "My family. They're an interesting piece of work."

She smiled. "Everyone's family is. I don't believe in the Waltons."

When he looked as if he didn't understand, she said, "You know. The television family that was on back in the Seventies. The one that always stuck together. The depression era—"

"Yeah, I know the program. My mother used to watch it faithfully when I was a kid. Maybe she was hoping if she watched long enough it would soak into the house somehow. You know, everyone would absorb the good family vibes and act appropriately."

"It didn't work?"

"Hell no."

Sarcasm lined his words. Okay, she'd hit on a nasty subject, apparently.

"My dad ran a small farm. Mom was a nurse. She's retired now. Both my parents have been retired for about ten years. I get along with Mom, but Dad…Dad is another animal all together. He's cold and enjoys mocking people."

"Oh." *Oh. That's great, Tara. Is that all you can say to him?*

"I've got two sisters and one brother." He put his spoon down and she eyed the rest of the gelato. As if he'd read her mind, he slid the bowl across the table toward her. "Go ahead. I'm full."

"Thanks." She dug into the dessert, only half sorry he'd abandoned it in favor of telling his family history.

Thunder growled in the distance, and when she glanced outside the clouds had turned a disturbing shade of greenish-black. Not a good sign.

"Are you the oldest?" she asked.

"I'm the second oldest. Elaine is forty-two. Clara is thirty-five and Joe is twenty-nine."

"So you're a sort of middle child."

"Do you believe in that birth order stuff?"

She shrugged and took another large spoonful of dessert. She allowed it to melt on her tongue before answering. "Yes and no. It depends on the family. For example, my family isn't what you'd call stable either. My mom is a homemaker and Dad was a mechanic at an auto dealership. Mom overprotected my older sister Josie and me, and Dad was detached. It took me a while to realize he wasn't ignoring me because of my different colored eyes, but because he didn't know how to show love. My family stuck by me during the craziness with Drake. Still, there are things about me they say they don't understand. Sometimes I have difficulty believing we're actually related with all the differences between our beliefs and personalities."

He nodded. "I've got one up on you. Elaine never married, and at first, my parents thought she was a lesbian. From the time she was a child she was afraid of men. They took her to several shrinks, and one time a psychologist accused my parents of sexually abusing her."

Shocked, she glanced up at him sharply, thoughts of dessert wiped clean away. "Oh my God."

"Exactly. That's what they thought. My parents would never have done anything like that and even Elaine said Mom and Dad didn't do anything to her. Through her teen years, she got rotten grades and when she barely graduated, she lived with my parents. She did odd jobs for years. I tried to convince Mom and Dad they should force her to go out on her own. They said she didn't earn enough."

"They enabled her," she said.

When his gaze returned to hers after scanning the room, she saw the relief there that she understood. "Yes."

She shook her head, her empathy for him growing by the moment. "Have you ever found out why she can't get it together?"

"In a sense, yes. Part of it is because she doesn't *want* to get it together. Some people never take responsibility for anything that happens in their lives."

"I can't argue with that. Drake's a good example of that type."

He waded up his napkin and put it on the table. He crumbled a straw wrapper lying next to his lemon-lime soda glass. "It wasn't until Elaine was thirty-seven and murdered a boyfriend that we found out who sexually abused her."

A knife turned deep in her stomach as the room filled with his tension-laced voice and a background of growing thunder. "Who?"

"My dad's brother. Uncle Joseph visited us a lot when we were kids. I never liked the guy, and I told my mother I didn't like him because he gave me the creeps. She said I had an overactive imagination." His lips twisted in a sarcastic smile. "She says that when she doesn't want to be bothered with my opinions and wants to escape reality."

"And your father?"

He shrugged. "He said I didn't know what the hell I was talking about. He was furious I'd even suggest it. Grounded me for a week."

"Oh Marcus. I'm so sorry."

Wind gusted against the trees outside and rattled the windows.

He took a sip of his soda and swallowed hard, frown lines forming between his dark brows. His mouth compressed into a hard line. "Yeah."

If she wanted to understand him better, she must know more. "You said your sister murdered someone?"

"Her boyfriend. It turned out she'd managed to pick up a physically abusive man, one of the first real boyfriends she'd ever had."

She put her face in her hands a minute. "Oh no."

"Oh yes. The first time he hit her, she took his shotgun and killed him point-blank. She didn't try to deny she did it. Her lawyer agued it was self-defense."

Stunned into silence, she waited for him to continue.

He didn't speak for a long moment, until rain lashed with fury against the building, wind swirling the moisture against the windows with vengeance. "Despite the evidence that he emotionally abused her and tried to beat her, she got ten years in prison. There's a chance she might get out in the next year or so on good behavior."

"Do you believe she did it in self-defense?"

"Yes and no. I think it's complicated."

"You haven't really decided what happened yet. You're processing it."

His gaze held a bewilderment she never expected to see in his strong, competent veneer. Seeing him this uncertain worried her on a fundamental level.

Finally, he answered. "I guess you could say that. Nothing is ever black and white, is it?"

"No." What could she say to him after *this* information? "Is that why you studied criminal justice?"

His eyes narrowed and he paused for a long time. "Yes and no. I was always interested in it. After I finished the degree, I thought about a law enforcement career. I decided I didn't want to chase criminals."

The waitress came to their table and cleared away their dishes. After the woman left, the silence settled into awkwardness. Tara sensed a more secretive nature inside him. He was holding back.

"How did the rest of your family handle what happened?" Tara asked. "How did you?"

"Mom and Dad were devastated, but they found Elaine the best lawyer they could. They blamed themselves, especially after I reminded them what I'd told them about Uncle Joseph." His mouth twisted in disgust. "I guess I was so angry I used it as a weapon." He glanced outside at the rain. "Not one of my finer moments."

She followed his example and watched as the thunderhead's intensity grew and rain pummeled the earth. "Do you blame your parents for Elaine's behavior? Everyone makes monumental mistakes, even those of us who follow our intuition regularly. There are no guarantees."

"I don't blame them as much as I blame Elaine. In the end, it was her choice to kill the man. It's been her choice all along how to react to what life throws her."

At that moment, Tara had an epiphany, and she felt as if she hadn't experienced one in a long time. Maybe Marcus attracted her because of their similar backgrounds. Modest-income families with major problems. What he'd said rang a bell of truth with her. She couldn't deny how she felt.

She nodded. "I have to agree. That's the way I look at life. What about your other siblings? What do they do?"

He leaned back in his chair, a pose more relaxed than expected for a man revealing significant family angst. "They think I'm being an asshole when I say the responsibility eventually rests back on Elaine."

"Oh." What could she say to that?

"Clara is married and a homemaker. She has three kids. Her husband is an executive with an insurance company. I love her to death, but she's a bit of a snob. My brother Joe is…" He grinned widely. "Joe is my buddy. He's a minor league baseball player in Wyoming. He's married and has two boys."

"What do your parents think of your job?"

He shrugged. "They understand it's my way of having a relaxed life. Word processing isn't a chore for me. I'd like to keep doing it. Dad went a bit weird when he first heard I wanted to lay low on my job and not take a management job or help him run the farm. He had to get over it, because I wasn't going to do the job he wanted."

She nodded, understanding the predicament. "Drake was like that. He kept telling me I should stay home and we should make babies. If I'd wanted to, that would have been fine. But that's not me."

He took out his wallet. "People's expectations can be a bitch. Hell, people judge me sometimes by my sister's behavior. As if I might turn out to be some sort of freaking serial killer."

"You don't deserve to be judged by what she did."

"Yeah, but people don't always think about that or care. They think violent behavior runs in the genes. Maybe it does, but you can be damned sure I'm not a criminal."

His adamant statement made her peer at him in curiosity. "Of course you aren't."

He stood slowly. "Let's see if we can make it through this damn storm."

Obviously, he tired of talking about his life. He'd opened up to her more than she would have expected, and it gave her a warm fuzzy.

Sure, that's what this heady, excited feeling in the pit of my stomach indicates. A warm fuzzy.

After they returned to the house, Tara watched Marcus quiz one security company after another. She felt grateful he'd volunteered to facilitate. He helped her select the best system for the least money. The company arranged to come out on Sunday afternoon to install the package for an additional fee. While she finished paperwork, Marcus excused himself to make a phone call. She thought about asking him whom he was calling, then nixed the idea. Maybe he called a girlfriend, but it wasn't any of her business. She wondered what type of woman attracted him—really turned on his pilot light.

I can.

She knew from his earlier reactions she'd turned on more than his pilot light. At the same time, a quick physical reaction didn't mean a deep or lasting attraction. She busied herself around the house and tried, fruitlessly, not to care.

* * * * *

Marcus scanned Tara's front yard and the surrounding area after he dialed the number of his contact at the security company. Standing on the porch while the rain turned gentle, he didn't feel bad about steering her toward Saturn Security. They would do an excellent job putting the security system in her house.

"Hank," Marcus said when his friend picked up the line. "Marcus here."

His buddy, a retired army colonel, gave a chuckle. "Hey, you old bastard, how are you?"

"Not old, but unquestionably a bastard."

Hank Tracer's returning laugh reassured Marcus. He could count on Hank. "So I take it you influenced our newest client to purchase our package?"

"I did."

"Thanks very much. You know we'll do a good job for her."

"Do an *excellent* job, Hank. She needs the extra protection."

He gave the former military police provost the story on Tara's situation.

"And you met her during a case?" Hank asked.

"I can't tell you."

"Right. How easily I forget. Then I take it there is another motivation here?"

Marcus grinned and continued examining the area for any signs of Drake. "She's special to me, all right? There, are you happy I admitted it?"

"Astonished is more like it. You're not staying with her?"

"I—" Marcus swallowed hard. "That isn't something she'd agree to."

"Uh-huh." The older man cleared his throat. "You know I'd do anything for you, Marcus."

Marcus didn't like that Hank still felt that beholden to him. "Come on, Hank. That's in the past."

"Doesn't matter to me." The man's voice went rough with emotion. "Tommy wouldn't be alive if it wasn't for you."

An ache centered in Marcus' heart when he thought about Hank's son Thomas Tracer. They'd served together in Desert Storm and almost died there, too.

"You've repaid me a thousand times over the years. I'm asking this favor as a friend. Not because I think you owe me anything."

"I know you're not, but its something I'll never forget. Besides, this way you can owe me one when the SIA is interested in more help from us."

"You got it." Marcus watched an old, beat-up black car maneuvering down the street, but as it went past him, he realized an old woman occupied the vehicle. "I take it the extra protection doesn't come cheap?"

"You know your money isn't any good with me."

Marcus smiled at his stubborn friend's insistence. "Just do it, Hank. Put it on my bill before I come down there and kick your sorry Army ass."

This time Hank's laugh came loud and long. "You must have a big thing for this girl."

A *big* thing was right.

Marcus grunted.

They ended the conversation on a jovial note with Marcus promising to give Tommy a call. He didn't spend much time thinking about Desert Storm or the horrible situation that had sent Tommy to a wheelchair, paralyzed from the waist down.

Right now, he continued to put Tara's well-being ahead of anyone else. The sexy, maddening woman inside the house needed him more.

Chapter Six

ஜ

Happy and satisfied with the outcome of her security plan, Tara turned a smile on Marcus as he reentered the house. "Thank you so much for helping me select a company. I owe you."

He shook his head and advanced toward her. "Forget about it."

He'd put his glasses back on long ago, and he looked so harmless she wanted to pinch his face like an aunt teasing a little boy.

Impulsively, she squeezed his arm. "Well, you didn't have to do this, so I appreciate it."

Grinning lopsidedly, he edged toward the front door. "I'd better get out of here. I've got a few things to do."

A shade of disappointment ran through her, but she schooled her voice into a carefree tone. "Sorry you have to go."

He'd touched the front doorknob when he stopped and turned toward her. "If you need anything else, call me. I mean that."

Gratitude and true friendship warmed her heart with a special glow, and she did one more impetuous thing. She slipped her arms around his neck and hugged his tall, strong body close.

A gentle, low chuckle left his throat. Husky and amused, it reverberated through her body. She pulled back and his gaze snagged hers. Instead of releasing her, he gazed deep into her eyes. Again, she felt the familiarity of his embrace, as if they'd done this many times before. The dream man popped into her psyche, tantalizing her with the possibility. What if he was her dream man?

She had to ask him another question, while she held him so near. "You never explained why you kissed me."

Chagrin passed over his face, as if he didn't want to remember the intimate encounter. "I thought it would be a good way to get the saleswoman to realize I wasn't interested in her."

She didn't know whether to be happy or pissed. "Oh, I see."

One thick eyebrow winged up. "Are you angry at me?"

"A little."

"Because I used you to drive off another woman, or that I kissed you at all?"

She remembered his warm, caressing lips tasting hers. Her gaze landed on that well-shaped, male mouth and her stomach tingled with unfulfilled needs. Oh yes. Not only had his kisses felt like her mystery man, they'd been more carnal, more incredible.

"Because you..." Her train of thought short-circuited as his gaze caressed her face, and he continued to hold her. "Because it was unexpected."

"You expect kisses to come with a warning?"

"No, of course not. I didn't think you'd *ever* kiss me. It's not... We're friends."

"Mmm."

His voice sounded throaty, a rough nuance that sent more arousal filtering into her body and tempting her to do something outrageous. A flush heated her face and she slid from his arms. Flustered, she allowed confusion and anxiety to course through her.

"It was very..." How did she explain what she'd felt when he kissed her without opening her heart to possible rejection? "Pleasant."

He frowned deeply. "Pleasant?"

Oops. Now she'd done it. She'd insulted his manhood, big time. She flapped her hands in a useless "oh well" gesture. "I didn't mean it that way. I meant it was a good way to get the saleswoman to lay off you. She did lay off, right?"

"Nope. She kept right on flirting until I left."

"Humph." Feeling a bit out of sorts, she said without thinking, "I guess the kiss wasn't realistic enough or intense enough."

His gaze turned dark, like the clouds continuing to storm into the late afternoon.

"Wasn't realistic enough?" He turned for the door. "Yeah, I guess from your response it was closer to being unpleasant."

She grabbed his arm and turned him about. "Don't get all huffy with me, Marcus Hyatt. You were playacting and I was so taken by surprise I didn't know how to react."

Smoldering heat gathered in his eyes when his fingers slid into the hair at the back of her neck and he tugged her against his body. "What's your reaction to this?"

Before she could protest, he covered her mouth with his.

Tara sagged against Marcus' strong body and clutched at his shirt. His mouth moved over hers with purpose, not with anger or desire to harm. His lips plundered and tasted with hungry attention. Her mind whirled as sensations battered her. The heat and hardness of powerfully muscled arms hugged her close, his warm male scent triggering long-buried sexual desires. His mouth coaxed and demanded in a passionate dance.

This time, though, she knew they didn't have an audience and it fueled a reckless need to burst free. Excitement gathered deep in her recesses. Every stroke of his lips upon hers, hungry and eager, made her body burn with need for fulfillment. Her breasts flattened to his chest as his arms pulled her nearer, slipping around her waist. His erection hardened against her stomach, like a man urgent and starving. Her clit burned with need to be stroked, her nipples taut.

He turned with her in his arms and pressed her against the closed front door. Startled but excited, she waited for his next move. He bent his knees so that her pussy lined up with the long length of his cock.

Oh my God.

Nothing else described the staggering desire that speared deep and hard into her as he rubbed his erection up and down her clitoral area. She moaned into his mouth as supernova desire slid through her veins.

Inflamed by his need she responded with equal fervor. Her arms slipped around his neck as she held on and opened to his embrace. Thrusting and stroking, his tongue caressed with a blatant invitation to the rest of her body. Tara felt his need echo inside her. Restless, she shifted in his arms, pressing her breasts tighter to him and her hips closer.

If he gets any harder, he'll burst the zipper right out of his jeans.

The knowledge ripped away her last bit of control.

His breathing quickened and he drew her closer yet, his steely muscle unyielding. He caressed her back, his touch languid and soothing. When she succumbed to his relentless touch, her tongue moved over his with a teasing massage, her hips writhing in an age-old cadence.

Marcus pulled back suddenly, and his breath rasped in his throat. His arms kept her manacled to him. His eyes shimmered with a wild desire so ferocious Tara didn't recognize the mild-mannered office mate she thought she knew well. She yearned to move forward with kisses and caresses. The fervor stunned her to the last fiber. She shivered, but not with cold.

Gently, slowly, he released her. The fire in his eyes remained, but now caution superimposed over his passion. His breathing came quickly, a sign of his continuing desire.

"I should go." His voice sounded deeper, huskier. "Now."

Staggered, she blinked at him wide-eyed and surprised. Her mind and heart wanted to speak, to say something profound or sexy, but she was speechless.

Less than a week ago, she'd never thought of this man as anything but her buddy. This minute he defined irresistible. Sexy. Disgustingly gorgeous.

Now she thought of him as all three.

"Good night," he said. "If you need anything, don't hesitate to call me, all right?"

Resonant and soft, his voice held a special gentleness that removed some embarrassment she felt over their embrace.

She moved away from him. "All right."

In less than a minute he opened her front door and left. She locked it behind him and almost went to the front windows to peek through the curtains. Instead, she leaned against the door in shock. It took her a full minute to regain some control. Rattled by their encounter, she eventually nuked a frozen dinner and ate in front of the television. She watched the news for a short while, then flipped channels trying to numb her mind with a sitcom. Nothing looked appetizing to watch, so she turned off the tube and decided reading might help her chase away the odd melancholy taking over her thoughts.

Silent and grim, the early evening threatened to bring a gloom to her home. Marcus had moved through her day, bringing her delight, laugher and novel emotions she'd rather not acknowledge. One thing she could be certain of, whether she liked it or not, she'd entered a new phase in her relationship with him. A dangerous, perhaps not so intelligent phase she should reconsider.

Later that evening the phone rang. The unexpected noise vaulted her out of the recliner in the living room where she sat reading a thriller. She snatched the cordless phone off the coffee table.

"Hello, Tara? Bettina here. How are you?"

Tara slapped her forehead. "Oh God, I'm sorry. I promised I'd update you, didn't I? Really, everything's fine. I'm sorry I didn't call earlier."

"No problem." There was a smile in Bettina's voice. "Did you have any luck with the security companies?"

She explained to Bettina about Marcus helping her select a company.

On impulse Tara asked, "What do you think of him, Bettina?"

"Marcus? He's a great man. And kinda cute, too. Why?"

"Ah, no reason."

"Uh-huh."

"No, really. I was...I was just curious."

Bettina's soft chuckle filled the airwaves. "I think he's got a thing for you."

"No, he doesn't."

Lie like a carpet, girl.

"After you tore out of here the other day, he went after you right away. He was that worried."

"But that doesn't mean it's anything more than friendship."

"Have it your way. Well, I'll see you on Monday then, okay?"

After they'd hung up, Tara sank back onto the couch and contemplated Marcus' real feelings. She tended to overanalyze relationships, and she wished she could stop the annoying trait. She closed her eyes and dreamed about his kisses, each texture, each movement, each taste. And promptly fell asleep in the chair smiling.

* * * * *

Marcus shoveled the Chinese takeout into his mouth without enthusiasm. He should have fixed something healthy, but the refrigerator needed filling and he didn't feel like stopping by the grocery store.

"So what," he said to the empty kitchen as he slumped in the dinette chair. "I'll do it tomorrow."

Glancing around the mundane apartment the SIA had picked out for him during this undercover operation, he realized the dingy gray walls needed a new coat of paint, and the threadbare blue corduroy material on the furniture looked awful. Located not far from work and a few minutes from Tara's house, the entire apartment complex fit the income of a low-level word processor. Of course, his SIA job paid significantly better, but he couldn't flaunt it and keep his cover intact. He missed his real apartment, a somewhat upscale bachelor pad with landscapes on the wall, a first-rate cappuccino and latte maker and a sound system that kicked ass.

Damned if this place didn't make him *feel* like his character. Although the apartment lacked pizzazz, it did portray Marcus the Nerd. Books lined the walls, his CD collection featured more classical when he preferred Eighties music and country. Marcus the Nerd liked complicated math and droll movies. Marcus the agent for SIA liked spontaneity, action movies and independent flicks.

He grinned. Marcus the Nerd liked predictable women in comfortable shoes.

Marcus the special agent liked women with spirit and a yen to wear fuck-me shoes.

In other words, women who loved hot sex.

Okay, so he hadn't seen Tara wearing stiletto heels, and he'd resisted the urge to rummage in her closet to see if she had a drop-to-your-knees sexy dress and shoes.

His biggest problem in the world wasn't pretending to be Marcus the Nerd. No, his monumental problem was discovering that Tara Crayton *could* wear both comfortable and fuck-me shoes on two different days and he'd still want to fuck her long and hard.

After that last kiss, he knew she liked hot sex.

Damn it, he felt out of control and out of sorts with Tara after the insane kiss they'd shared. Correction. *Two* psychedelic kisses. For the last ten minutes, he'd stared at the out-of-focus effect of an impressionist painting on the wall. Yeah, that described his state of mind since he'd wandered around for an hour trying to excavate his brain from the gutter.

He felt out-of-focus. Royally screwed.

His cock hardened. Maybe if he found another woman he could take to bed without guilt or emotion, he could remove Tara from his system.

Nope, that wouldn't happen anytime soon. He didn't fuck hookers for satisfaction. If he wanted to let off steam, his short-term solution meant jerking off. His cock didn't care how release came as long as it came.

He rubbed a hand over his face and heaved a sigh. Kissing her twice today was more than enough to give her ideas, and any grown man knew that meant danger straight ahead. It would be one thing if she didn't find him attractive, but she'd kissed him back without too much coaxing. The soft moans coming from Tara's throat and the way her body writhed indicated she'd enjoyed their embrace.

"What the hell was I thinking?" he asked.

The longer he remained with her, listened to her, got to know her as much more than a cubicle mate, the more he liked her. Hell, *like* was too mild a word. Try desired.

Fucking lusted.

Solutions ran around in his head like mice in a maze, but none of them fixed his immediate problem. He couldn't avoid Tara at work, and he worried her bastard ex-husband would show up and hurt her.

"Come on, Hyatt. You're a big boy. You can control which way your cock waves if you try hard enough."

Hard. Yeah, therein lay the problem.

His I-Doc rang, and he grunted. "Great. Now what?"

He snatched the device off his belt. He spoke his code name into the device when he saw the message blinking on the screen came from the research library at SIA.

"Twenty-four seven." He grinned sarcastically. "Always up and always ready."

"Now that's an exaggeration, don't you think?"

The female voice, a tad husky with a smoky nuance, never failed to stir him. Hell, it probably stimulated every male at SIA at one time or another. With just enough rust on it to make her age indeterminate, Dorcas Shannigan's voice held a seductive lilt. It reminded him of a female disc jockey's cajoling tone. Maybe listening to her voice would take away the pulse-pounding desire he'd developed for Tara.

"Dorky. What's cookin' in the kitchen?"

She chuckled and the sound purred. "I have some new information for you on Jason Forte I think you're going to want."

"You came through."

"But of course. What else do you expect when I sit around this big basement library all day researching dusty tomes and the internet?"

"You look up some of this stuff on the internet?"

"Of course."

"You should get out more."

She snorted. "Believe me, most men outside of the SIA wouldn't be interested in what I have to say. My mind is one big dictionary of ideas and notions."

He found it hard to believe men wouldn't be interested in her. Since he'd signed on with SIA he'd had numerous conversations with her by phone. They'd never met in person, and he heard no one else had seen her either. She preferred to keep her identity secret, and to his surprise, SIA went along with the idea.

She rushed onward. "I have my specialized occult resources that help me with this, too."

"Of course. Your very secretive, never-gonna-tell-you-cause-I'd-have-to-shoot-ya sources?"

"Phooey." She sniffed. "You know we don't shoot people for that anymore, Marcus."

"Damn, but I miss the old days."

Her sweet laugh, honey over velvet, stirred his loins in a purely male response he couldn't help. "Never mind how I get my information. You want the facts. First of all, you already know Jason Forte is a highly dangerous man."

His appetite returned a little and he swallowed another bite of beef. Marcus told her about the strange encounter with Jason at the copy machine, but he hesitated to reveal Tara's reaction to Jason. He couldn't confirm that what happened in the copier room with Tara proved that she knew more about Jason.

"It may be worse than you thought," Dorky said.

"Lay it on me."

"My sources tell me that Forte has the ability to bilocate. It's the capacity to show up in one place and another at the same time."

"I know what it is. I haven't seen a case in the SIA archives that deals with it. Are you sure he can do that?"

"A woman interviewed last night said she saw Jason Forte one day on the fourth floor of the Douglas Financial Group. When she took an elevator to the second floor and the doors opened, he was right there waiting for the elevator to open. She was so shocked, she fainted."

"Holy shit."

"Exactly."

"Wait a minute. Isn't that a doppelganger?"

"In some cultures, yes." She took a deep breath and he knew she would launch into a copious explanation. "In Europe and Britain doubles are known by a lot of different names such as wraith, fetch, waff, fye—"

"I get the picture."

"The Maori believe a double can't be distinguished from the real person unless it reveals itself by becoming foggy and people can see through it."

"Ben Darrock didn't mention bilocation as one of Jason's abilities."

"Like I said, this is new information."

"Isn't this double stuff a death omen?"

"Well," he heard pages rustling in the background, "on page 1001 of *Gautier's Encyclopedia of the Paranormal*, the author says bilocation isn't always a harbinger of death. It can be a conscious projection."

A creepy sensation ran up and down his spine. "This means his abilities are extraordinarily strong if he can do it at will."

"There's more. It's likely he can not only bilocate, but he may have mind control abilities. You've proved that from what happened to you in the copy room."

"It's a hell of a ticket to try and stop him if he can do all three things at will."

"After I told Ben about this, he asked me to call you directly."

"Yeah, he knows I'll listen to your beautiful voice a long time before I listen to his."

"Flattery will get you nowhere, Hyatt. Chocolate and champagne, maybe. Flattery, forget it."

"You're a hard woman to please, Miss Dorky."

"Who says I'm a Miss?"

Taken aback, he pushed aside his dinner. "You're married?"

"I'm not telling. You know I'm invisible all the time."

He gave an overstated sigh. "Yeah, right."

"Say, how's your love life? Any sweet young thing I know maneuvering after your butt?"

He pushed his chair back and carried his bowl to the sink. "Sweet young things, yes. But I'm *not* so sweet, and I'm sure as hell not young anymore. So saccharine and juvenile doesn't do it for me."

"Okay, how about old and wrinkly?"

Putting the phone into the crook between his neck and shoulder, he turned on the water and rinsed the bowl. "Are you saying you're interested in me?"

She huffed a sigh. "Surely you jest, twenty-four seven. My life is solitary and I don't plan on being a test dummy for agents with overinflated testosterone."

He groaned and opened the dishwasher. "Ouch! That hurt."

"Not likely. You have a heart ringed by steel, Marcus. Every good-looking agent in this mad place does. It's a necessary part of the job. It keeps you alive."

He put the bowl in the dishwasher and shut the door with a definitive click. Should he fake an injury or admit she knew the score? Maybe he would do neither. "You think I'm good-looking?"

"I know everything about you. That's a part of my job, too."

"So you're telling me you're not the standard-issue library grunt."

"I'm horrified you'd suggest it. There is nothing typical about me."

"Good. A woman with a healthy ego really turns me on."

"Down boy. Enough flirting. We've got work to do. There is something else that's very important. Are you having any significant difficulties with your mental shielding...your ability to protect yourself against psychic attack?"

He winced. Admitting it stung. "How did you know?"

She laughed softly. "I see and know all. You must be careful, Marcus. Attack could also come from quarters you least expect. Forte isn't the only danger you face."

Concern wiped away his jovial mood. "How do you know?"

"If Forte is working to convert people into these mindless drones, they may take on the talent to penetrate your mental barriers. It's hard to say what mental powers he may give them."

"Shit."

"Unfortunately, yes." She cleared her throat. "There is another thing you need to know."

"There's more?" he asked incredulously.

"Yes. Sexual activity can weaken your mental barriers. The more attracted you are to a woman, the more likely it will happen. Your attraction to the woman at your workplace could impede your investigation of Forte."

Startled, he couldn't speak.

"Marcus? Did you hear me?"

"Yeah, I heard you. How did you—" Fuck it all, he really didn't want to divulge this. "—how did you know about her?"

"I've got my ways. It's not important how I know. Just be careful."

He closed his eyes and sighed. "Yeah, right. Okay."

"I need to get busy now. I've got work to do."

His sense of humor returned. "People to see, places to go, and people to do."

With another trademark soft, super-sexy laugh, she said, "Sign off, Marcus."

"Night, Dorky. Pleasant dreams."

After he hung up, he realized that although he liked bantering with Dorky, it didn't mean anything special. When it came down to it, the only woman he wanted to get close and personal with he shouldn't get close to at all.

He made a firm resolution there and then, based on the new information from Dorky. While he was attracted to Tara, he couldn't indulge in a physical relationship.

* * * * *

Jangling and loud, the phone jarred Tara out of a deep sleep late Saturday night. Her heart pounded in her chest, and she bolted upright. She reached for the bedside lamp and switched it on, then grabbed the receiver.

"Hello." Her voice rasped, dry with sleep.

"Hey, darlin'."

Ice gripped her heart. She knew that voice anywhere.

Drake.

She hung up, unwilling to listen to whatever evil propaganda he planned to spew forth. The phone rang but this time she let it go. She sprang out of bed and headed for the hallway, flipping on lights. After turning on the lights in the living room, she hurried to the answering machine phone on the table near the dinette set. She switched on the mechanism and it picked up. After her short and cheerful message played, Drake's tone, laced with acid, came over the speaker.

"Darlin', I know you're in there. I know you're wishing I was there with you."

She took a deep breath and tried to remain calm. The mere sound of his voice filled her with unavoidable disgust and apprehension.

"You're afraid of me, aren't you? You should be. Because you need to find the Lord, and the Lord is vengeful." His accent, country in its colloquialisms, thickened. "And no pussy boyfriend is going to keep me from delivering you from sin."

Pussy boyfriend? Who was he talking about?

Part of her wanted to yank the phone out of the wall, but she knew she needed to record his voice in at least one message in case she needed it for evidence.

With horrified fascination, she listened.

"Or maybe you want to invite me in right now?" he asked. "Save me the trouble of making this difficult?"

Shivers darted along her skin and she rubbed her arms.

She needed help. She could call the police, but they couldn't do anything about a phone call. Then she remembered the vision of Marcus. When she had visualizations about people, they were never wrong. He might be a word processing clerk right now, but at one time he'd been a combat warrior of some kind. If he couldn't protect her, no one could.

Impulse sent her racing down the hall to her bedroom. She grabbed her purse from where she'd dumped it by the bedside table. She fumbled through the pockets until she found the sticky note with Marcus' phone numbers on it, then grabbed her cell phone from her purse at the same time. She punched in his home number and realized her hands shook. Another deep breath didn't seem to make a difference. Her entire insides quivered like gelatin.

Get control. Harness the fear.

Red digital numbers on her bedside clock said eleven o'clock. Marcus picked up the phone on the second ring, his voice clear and strong. He didn't sound like he'd been asleep.

"Hello?"

"Marcus." Even to her own ears, her voice sounded quivery, filled with rampant emotions so strong she couldn't contain them. "This is Tara."

"Hey." He sounded almost happy, then his voice deepened with undeniable worry. "Everything all right?"

"No. Drake called me and he's saying crazy things. I'm afraid he might be right outside my house."

"Are all your doors and windows locked?" His voice took on an immediate hard edge.

She looked up at her large bedroom window, thankful for the heavy honeycomb shade. "Of course."

"Stay right there. I'll be there in a few minutes."

Regret immediately overran some fear. "Maybe this isn't a good idea. I'm sorry I called. I mean, I shouldn't have imposed on you because Drake is playing games."

"He isn't playing games, Tara, and you know it."

She did know it, deep inside where her instincts lived.

"Don't hang up," he said. "I'm going out to the car now."

She heard him moving through his house and the quick jangling of keys. Just having him on the phone and hearing his husky voice gave her renewed calm. Her heartbeat eased and her breathing steadied. With this reassurance came the worry she'd overacted. Drake always did like to scare the crap out of her, and maybe that's all he meant to do now.

Still, prickling awareness said her ex-husband could be waiting outside. Even though she'd told Marcus the doors and windows were locked, she scurried around the house and made certain every lock was secure.

She heard an engine starting and the sound of a car pulling away at a quick pace. Reality sank in. "Marcus?"

"I'm here. Are you all right?" He sounded anxious.

"I'm checking the doors and windows again. Everything's locked. Maybe you shouldn't come over. If Drake is out there, he could hurt you."

"He can try."

His words, spoken in a completely indomitable tone, said if Drake tried, he'd fail.

Wow. In the midst of the fear lingering around the edges, a tiny, illicit thrill stirred in her stomach. A primitive wave of heat surrounded her. Marcus was willing to risk injury for her.

She'd never known a man willing to put his life on the line for her. The reaction it set up burned in her mind and body like wildfire, momentarily erasing apprehension and replacing it with inappropriate sexual arousal.

As he drove to her house, he kept her spirits uplifted with some stupid jokes he'd heard within recent months. She giggled, then realized she'd let her guard down with him more than any man she'd known since Drake. Disturbed, she tried to rein back her enthusiasm a little. She couldn't afford weakness.

"I'm driving up now," Marcus said.

"Marcus—"

But he'd already hung up. Fear renewed, tightening her muscles so much her jaw ached. She heard tires crunching in the driveway and rushed to a window overlooking the front yard. She recognized his car. As he left his vehicle, she kept watch, afraid she'd see Drake rushing out of the darkness, ready to attack. Despite Marcus' take-no-prisoners statement that Drake could try taking him out, part of her wondered if Marcus wasn't a smidgen too cocky. The world was populated with macho men who thought they could take on anything.

Marcus left his car and strode up the walk to the front door, his gaze vigilant and his mouth a firm line. He walked quickly toward her door, and in darkness obliterated somewhat by the porch light, she saw he wore a tank top and jeans.

When he rang the doorbell, she left her cell phone on the coffee table and headed for the small foyer. She rushed to snap on the light and the bulb went out with a pop. *Damn.*

Relief washed through her at the thought of him being here. She opened the door immediately and stepped back for him to come inside. She quickly relocked the door. As she turned back to him, she brushed against his tall body and took in his reassuring, masculine scent. He clasped her arms gently and her hands landed on his chest.

"Are you all right?" he asked, concern blazing in his piercing eyes and a frown grooving lines between his eyebrows.

"Yes." She clutched at his biceps, her vehemence transferring in her grip. "I'm sorry. I shouldn't have asked you to come here."

His gaze darted around the foyer and toward the living room, as if he searched for hidden enemies. "You already said that once."

"It's true."

His frown looked nothing like a geeky office boy. No siree. Marcus Hyatt had transformed into a reassuring, testosterone-filled presence. "Well, get that idea right out of your head now. I'm glad you called me."

"Did I wake you?"

He shook his head. "I'm a night owl." His mouth softened the slightest bit. "You're safe now." His fingers slipped over her arms until he cupped her face with one hand. "You're shaking."

A shiver worked over her body as the heat and caress from his fingers tantalized her senses.

"I am," she said breathlessly. "I don't know why."

"Damn it, that bastard has you scared out of your wits." His voice went rough and angry.

To her horror, unexpected tears welled in her eyes and threatened to spill over. Mortified by her weakness, she sniffed and took a deep breath. "I'm sorry. I don't mean to be—" She broke off abruptly, her voice quavering under the strain.

"It's all right." His voice, soft and rumbling, reassured her like nothing else.

He drew her close, tucking her head onto his shoulder, his fingers buried in her hair. His arm tightened around her back, and security and safety suddenly didn't seem so far away anymore. She slipped her arms around his waist, allowing his embrace to comfort and release the trepidation one second at a time.

She registered several things at once. All of them made her breath catch. She wore nothing but a long fuchsia nightshirt that reached to mid-thigh, and a pair of skimpy matching pink bikini panties. She'd been meaning for the last two weeks to buy another robe. Her last robe had gone beyond the call of duty and ripped up a side seam. She'd tossed it in the trash.

Marcus' big frame sheltered her with his strength. Tara's heart stuttered, skipped and then rammed into overdrive. Her belly fluttered with intoxicating need rivaling any feeling she'd encountered around him before. Cradled in muscular arms and pressed against his hard chest, her emotions whipped from one extreme to the other.

Watch out, Tara. Just because he's one hell of a nice guy, and he's come to your rescue, doesn't mean he feels something beyond ordinary compassion for a friend. Don't make this into anything more emotional or more physical than it is.

She could explain away these feelings as unadulterated appreciation for his willingness to help. Even the kisses they'd shared earlier in the day didn't mean anything extraordinary.

He eased her back and out of his arms. "Sit down and take it easy. We need to talk."

Feeling shell-shocked by what happened tonight, she settled onto the couch. She curled her legs to the side.

"I'll check the house," he said gruffly and stalked away from her.

Check the house? Her discomfort with the situation peaked. She'd already gone over the entire home. What more could he check? Tears of frustration and anger slid down her face. She quickly wiped them away.

A few moments later, he strode back into the room, that unconquerable gritty determination on his face. Her mouth popped open and she stared like the village idiot. Marcus might be forty years old, but he easily looked ten years younger.

A body-hugging navy blue tank top clung to his torso, lovingly embracing tight pecs and the ripple of a six-pack stomach. Chest hair peeked above the neckline and tantalized her. She didn't understand a woman who couldn't appreciate chest hair on a man.

His wide shoulders and long arms showed evidence of supreme physical strength. Jeans curved over his muscled, mile-long legs.

The man worked out big time, but his musculature said he could be mean in a fight rather than hampered by bulky power.

Thick strands of wavy hair gleamed with healthy shine and fell about his shoulders. Now his nose looked regal rather than thin, and the long line of his jaw softened by the hair tumbling around his face.

Everything Tara and the other women in the office once thought about Marcus Hyatt was blown away in one stunning revelation. He possessed that dangerous, take-me-or-leave-me edge few men could pull off without seeming ridiculous. Simply put, he oozed sex and sins and secrets. Earlier in the day at the mall, he'd looked yummy.

Tonight he made her mouth water, her heart pound, and everything feminine inside her take notice.

Oh God. I am in trouble now.

Chapter Seven

ଚ

Tara admitted it. The man in front of her was wildly exciting, rugged and damned mesmerizing.

Marcus frowned and stopped near the couch. He put his hands on his hips. "Something wrong?"

She swallowed hard. "No." Her voice cracked. "You…look different."

Damn, this was not a good time to become tongue-tied.

His lips parted in a bashful grin that sent a piercing sweet tug straight into her heart. "It's the lack of glasses. Sometimes my eyes can't take the contacts, so when I wear the glasses they make me look like a nerd."

Um, yeah.

She nodded, glad she didn't need glasses, and happy he'd misinterpreted her rapt attention. She almost launched into an impromptu statement about how handsome he looked, then common sense grabbed her by the throat.

Flabbergasted, she tried to forget that Marcus had gone from nerd to hunk in less than two days. If he became any more attractive, she'd need a drool bib.

He settled on the couch beside her, leaning toward her and clasping his big hands between his knees. "There's no sign of anyone outside but that doesn't mean he isn't out there."

"I should have known he was playing with me."

"How were you supposed to know?"

She shrugged. "Drake always played games. He's not a stupid man by any means. He was an army combat engineer and his secondary military occupational specialty was some sort of woo-woo secret stuff he never talked about. He went to jump school and passed most tests with flying colors. He may be a ruthless creep, but he's a smart, ruthless creep."

Discomforted by his nearness, she stood and wandered to the fireplace. She fingered one photograph on the mantel that showed her short, plump mother, and her tall, arrogant-looking father.

To her consternation, Marcus sidled up behind her. "Nice family."

Noncommittal and feeling a little numb, she didn't even smile. "Thanks. They're...interesting."

"Sounds like there's a story in there somewhere."

She snorted a soft laugh. "A soap opera might be a better description. Darrel and Alice have a way of making mountains move, though."

"You call them by their first names?"

"They prefer it."

"Uh-huh."

"You sound doubtful."

"Actually, I'm curious." He moved around until he stood on the opposite of the mantel, one hand braced on the dark wood. "Are you an only child?"

Surprised, her gaze snapped up to his. "No."

He stopped leaning on the mantel and waved at the photographs lining it. "There aren't any other pictures of people on the mantel. Just you and them. I'll also bet you don't make friends easily, and even when you do, you keep them at arm's length. Am I right?"

A hollow feeling rose in her stomach. No one had ever pinpointed her quite so quickly. Fear followed close behind. Sure, the reason she kept people at arm's length was so they couldn't discover her secrets. Yet this man, who didn't know her that well, had grabbed one of her secrets right out of the air.

Her apprehension heightened. "How did you know?"

She saw his muscled chest rise and fall as he inhaled deeply. Caution flickered in his eyes. "Because I pay attention. I'm a keen observer of people."

No, that didn't exactly answer her question, but his closed expression told her she wouldn't get more of an answer. She returned to the couch.

Tara pulled a pillow up over her lap. It served as a cover and something to cuddle for comfort. Marcus' casual pose at the mantel should have calmed her. Instead, her nerves remained hyperactive. Her fingers plucked at loose threads on the pillow sham. When she realized what she was doing, she stopped.

"Tell me about the phone call," he said as if he might be talking about the weather.

She pushed away the pillow and left the couch to head for the answering machine. "I can do more than that."

She played back tonight's partial message. "I'll screen my calls from now on."

"Damn." Marcus' voice laced with malice, and he walked toward her.

For one wild, scary moment his sudden action startled her. Danger and testosterone poured off him. The glare coming from his generally mild-mannered eyes intimidated.

When she gave an involuntary step back, his expression changed back to the at-ease man she knew. "Hey, what's wrong?"

A tremble jerked through her. "You— For a moment there you looked angry with me."

His brow furrowed as his glower returned. "Hell no." He reached up and brushed a caressing touch over her mussed hair. "No, I'm not angry with you. I'm pissed as hell at your ex-husband."

Relief poured through her and her legs felt like noodles. She'd already weathered tension strung taut as wire when she thought Drake might attempt to break in her house. The idea

Marcus could be angry with her, too, had driven her nervousness higher.

Marcus' frown deepened as he looked down at her. "Wait a minute. You thought I might hurt you?"

She nodded reluctantly, not eager to admit it.

"I told you before, Tara. I've never hurt a woman and I never will." When she still didn't say a word, his gaze grew thoughtful. "I can understand why you'd react that way. A ridiculed, physically abused human starts to have problems with trust. In your case, you don't trust men. I understand it."

Comfort eased into her. "Thanks. I get twitchy around men when they're..."

"Yeah?"

She sighed. "Drake is a very masculine guy. Tough."

"Brutal."

"Yes. And when you stalked toward me with that ready-to-eat-bear look it reminded me of his aggression. A little like when he was about ready to smack me one." Building momentum to the subject, she opened up and caught his direct gaze with hers. "Sometimes I didn't have a warning. Nothing but that look...that fierce stare that said I'd done or said something he didn't like and whammo—he cracked me across the face or the jaw."

A shiver slipped across her shoulders. She settled onto the couch once again. He followed and eased down beside her.

"Shit," he whispered. Tiny lines of anger and maybe even pain showed between his eyebrows again. "Just knowing what he did to you makes me want to kill him. Is that how you got the scar bisecting your eyebrow?"

"No. I got that from a car accident with my parents when I was a teenager."

Tension filled the air around him, and she knew he tried to hold back boiling anger at her ex-husband.

"You're getting the order of protection?" he asked.

"Yes."

"I don't think you should."

Surprise made her pause. Silence stretched out.

She cleared her throat. "Why do you think I don't need it? Everyone recommends it."

"Most of the time, it only works on people who never intend violence in the first place. You know that Drake is capable of violence." Marcus' frown held contemplation and heavy concern. "I know a lot of people say it's the best thing, but it can make things much worse."

Chaotic feelings danced through her. "God, I wish he'd gotten more years. Like life."

He didn't say anything, and she looked away from his intent scrutiny. A few moments passed before he put his arm on the back of the couch. His fingers, if he reached out, could almost touch her shoulder.

"A reasonable man would respond to the order of protection by realizing you're serious," he said. "The chance of that happening with Drake isn't good."

She shrugged and looked down at her clasped fingers, then back up at him. "Drake started out sounding reasonable, a good man, or I wouldn't have married him."

She heard her own words sound accusatory, and Marcus smiled. "Of course. If we love somebody we're less likely to see their faults, right?"

"Especially if they come packaged in deception."

"Was Drake one of those guys who needed excitement and seemed emotionally shallow?"

Her gaze on him sharpened. "You're describing him perfectly." She closed her eyes, and for an instant tears stung. "Sometimes I'm so ashamed."

She felt him slide closer to her. His arm slid around her shoulders, and he squeezed gently. "Why?" His voice turned soft and deeper. "What do you have to be ashamed of?"

She kept her eyes closed. "Because I should have seen it. I should have listened to my intuition. It told me early on something wasn't right with Drake, but I didn't listen."

His big palm smoothed over her arm, a protective gesture that soothed. "Yeah, you should have listened to your heart, to your intuition, instead of logic. But you can't keep beating yourself up over it."

She opened her eyes. "I can and I do."

One tear escaped, but before she could catch it, his other hand came up and he brushed it away with his thumb. His tender gesture, and the heat of his body, stirred more arousal inside her. He leaned closer, and his intoxicating scent tantalized her libido. Their eyes locked. His gaze melded with hers in a soft flicker, a gentle touch that deepened and heated. Under that look, she felt wanted and protected.

I must be losing it. Attaching more importance to what I'm seeing than he honestly means. I can't know what's behind that look.

Regardless, warmth spread over her face and down her throat. A sensual tugging stirred in her lower stomach, and her nipples tingled and went hard.

She'd never experienced pain and excitement mingled like this. Emotions welled up, and she blinked rapidly to fight more tears.

She turned in his grip so that she faced him. His arm dropped away, his palm sliding down the middle of her back in a gesture both erotic and comforting.

Her breath caught. "Thanks, Marcus. You're a great friend."

He nodded. "Good. I'm glad you feel that way. But I still advise against this order of protection."

"Drake will be arrested if he tries anything."

"Yeah, but that's just it. Chances are the order will set him off. And whenever he calls you and if he threatens, don't counter-threaten him, all right?"

"That could cause the escalation?"

"You got it."

Suspicion reared up. "How do you know all this?"

Something flashed in his eyes, uncertainty perhaps. "You saw the criminology degree on the wall."

"Were you a cop?"

"What?" He grinned. "No."

"But you wanted to be?"

"No."

"What were you before you came here, Marcus?"

He didn't miss a beat. "I worked with the Dracort Company for ten years as an administrator. Got burned out and came here. You know that. You heard about it the first day I started here."

True. She didn't believe him, but decided not to push the issue.

He brushed a finger over her nose in a sweet, odd gesture that made her tingle. She knew right then she would have to watch out for him. Marcus Hyatt did funny things to her heart.

Something elemental broke loose inside her. Tears assaulted her eyes again. One trickled down her face before she could stop it.

He did. His fingers brushed over her face and caught the errant moisture. Mortified at how weakly she'd reacted since Drake called her, she forced back the rest of her tears. "This is inexcusable."

"What is?"

"I swore up and down I wouldn't react this way to Drake no matter what happened. I've spent hours on the therapist's couch to avoid this sort of knee-jerk reaction."

"Fear because some asshole says he's outside your house is knee-jerk?" he asked incredulously.

She shook her head. "I want control of the situation. I've done what I can to stay safe."

"So what makes you think you're weak? You think tears are a sign of weakness?"

She closed her eyes against his scrutiny. "I learned it somewhere in my childhood, and Drake's reaction to my tears was definitely not sympathetic."

"Damn that son of a bitch. He really twisted you up, didn't he? Tara, when you cried he should have taken you in his arms and kissed you. Anything to show comfort. He was an A-number-one fucked-up-in-the-head-monster. Don't ever let his problems become your fault."

His lecture, spoken in a stern but quiet voice, did something to her she didn't expect. She started to relax, reassured by his affirmation.

"You're understandably afraid of this creep. There's no reason to put yourself down. Give yourself slack," he said.

For the first time since she'd received the news Drake had left prison, she felt renewed in spirit. "All right."

"Tell me about this situation with Drake."

She made a disparaging sound. "Where do I start?"

"How about at the beginning?"

Tara shifted on the couch, grabbing a pillow again and placing it over her lap. She leaned against the opposite arm of the couch, relishing the distance between them. Leaving space assured that her brain cells stayed online, and her libido didn't take over.

After drawing a settling breath, she said, "Drake and I met at Fort Leavenworth, Kansas. I'd moved from Albuquerque after secretarial college."

"You were born in New Mexico?"

"Yes. A small town not far from Albuquerque called San Pedro. Anyway, I got into the civil service system at the bottom rung and worked as a clerk in the education center on the post. I was there for a few years and received a couple of promotions. I dated occasionally, but nothing serious. Then I met Drake. He was a Sergeant and when I saw him, well, it was like love at first sight. I knew what I was getting in a way because I'd always been drawn to a certain look in a man."

When she realized what she'd said she glanced up from her pillow and straight at Marcus. His expression held nothing but curiosity, so she continued.

"He was tall, muscular and blond. Just my type at the time. A real beach boy expression, so easygoing most of the time. He had this underlying intensity, but I didn't think anything of it. We dated for two months before he proposed." She ran her fingers through her hair and her fingers tangled in the strands. She winced at the tiny pain.

"That's pretty quick."

"We weren't together more than four weeks of that time. He went out on some exercises for two of the weeks, then worked overtime on the other weeks."

She saw understanding in Marcus' eyes.

"I was really, really in love. At least with the man I thought he was. He was so sweet around my family and my few friends that no one suspected anything rotten in his personality."

He leaned forward, suddenly even more focused. He clasped his hands between his knees and stared intently at her. "That's interesting. Most men who are abusive show some sort of tendency toward it before the couple marries."

"Oh, he showed the tendency, all right. I just didn't recognize it for what it was. It seemed so incredibly impossible that he'd want to hurt me, that when he started working toward keeping me away from my friends, I didn't see it. Closer to the wedding he started criticizing me for insignificant things. Then he'd apologize right away and blame it on work pressures or the upcoming wedding stress. We were having a big wedding, so I spent considerable time getting ready for it. He said I was neglecting him—"

She stopped dead. Old pain took her breath as she recalled his first major outburst. "I remember it like it was yesterday.

Two days before the wedding, he got red in the face because we were arguing. We were standing in the kitchen and he threw this glass. He claimed he didn't pitch it deliberately in my direction, but the glass shattered on the floor in front of me and a piece of it hit me in the leg. The kicker was, he didn't act concerned about the fact that he'd hurt me. Here I was, standing there with this blood running down my leg and he didn't care."

Marcus' jaw clenched and she saw a muscle twitch there. "What happened then?"

"I should have gotten a clue. No man who loved me would think of throwing a glass at me. I guess I was too shocked and thought I'd overreacted. I apologized for taking so much time away from him and then everything was back to perfect through the wedding and into the honeymoon."

When silence grew steady and dark, a hole she couldn't hide in any longer, she continued her story. "He didn't start hitting me until after we'd been married five years. But he was consistently verbally cutting."

"You fought back, I hope?"

She shook her head. "Most of the time his verbal assaults were so damned indirect. He'd make a compliment sound like an insult in one breath. More than half the time I didn't have a good comeback for his idiotic statements."

Marcus' eyes, so passionate and intelligent, turned almost silvery in the low light from a single lamp on a nearby table. *You're picking up his emotions like they belong to you again.* Her barriers to his feelings felt thin. Not a good sign. She closed her eyes and envisioned a white light around herself. Instead of visualizing the white protective light spreading over her skin, the light covered only parts of her body and left plenty of room for Marcus' emotions to leak through.

Nope. Not good at all.

A little panicked that she couldn't block him, she allowed some of those emotions to leak into her.

Anger.

Concentrated yearning for something she couldn't name.

She shivered, realizing that he watched her without remorse, as if he, too, wanted to know her secrets. The idea frightened and thrilled her on a primitive level she didn't want to admit.

She inhaled deeply and let it out. "You're capable of verbally slicing a person to ribbons like that."

Surprise moved swiftly over his face. "What?"

"Remember last month? There was this woman in the office needling me about something insignificant."

Recognition dawned on his expressive face. "Yeah, I remember that."

"You very nicely and succinctly put her in her place. The difference is you wouldn't use it against a person out of meanness or spite. You were defending me."

"Damned straight," he said.

"Did I ever thank you?"

He smiled and the hardness left his eyes. Warmth flooded his face. "You bought me a couple of those awesome butterscotch cookies from the bakery around the corner. It was great."

She chuckled as she recalled him taking a bite, closing his eyes and tilting his head back in ecstasy. With a wild flash of heat and awareness, she wondered if he would look that hungry during a knee-melting bout of sex.

Oh God. Don't go there.

She rubbed the back of her neck as she felt her face go red. His eyes flared with acknowledgment, an accelerant that promised scorching sensual pleasure.

Her lips parted. His gaze landed on her mouth. Self-conscious panic fluttered inside her.

She nudged the pillow away, stood and went to the mantel. She stared at the photographs of her parents and sadness returned to her heart. "I can't believe my ego was so low that I let Drake get away with hurting me." She sighed. "During therapy I realized my parents' marriage influenced the way I reacted in my relationship with Drake."

Marcus stood and headed her way. Within a few steps, he stood in front of her, observing her parents' photograph. "They have a bad marriage?"

"Rocky. Let's say the verbal abuse runs both ways. They know how to cut each other up pretty badly."

"It's not physical, then?"

"No." She gave him a wan smile. "I knew when I was a kid that they weren't the epitome of a good marriage, but I guess some of it still affected me. During my relationship with Drake I reacted like an automaton. His verbal abuse seemed almost…natural."

Mortified, she covered her hands with her eyes again and said, "I was so damned blind."

She gave a mocking laugh. Tied up in knots, her emotions too chaotic, she felt her shield open.

"So you married at Fort Leavenworth and then stayed there? You didn't get transferred?" he asked.

"We stayed at Fort Leavenworth for a year and then received notice we'd transfer to Georgia in another year. Things started to get ugly. That's when his simple verbal artillery turned into something far more dangerous. I'd met other women who had abusive boyfriends and husbands, and I always thought they were ignorant for not leaving the situation. It was happening to me in my own home, but my stubborn pride wouldn't let me admit it. I felt like a failure when I realized I let it happen to me."

Sympathy and gentleness in his eyes melted her defenses, and this time she didn't keep back the tears. She looked away at the thick, gray carpeting, unnerved by the tenderness she saw in his face. A sob she couldn't control slipped from her throat.

He slipped his arms around her and brought her against his chest. Sanctuary enveloped her. Other feelings and sensations demanded attention. With the white light no longer protecting her, his powerful feelings penetrated her psyche.

Caring. An eager empathy that sliced into him as he took in her pain.

My God. He might be empathic, too.

Reassurance flowed from him, and she knew in that moment what she couldn't be certain about before. Marcus Hyatt was nothing like Drake.

As Marcus cupped the back of her head, she breathed in his unique, manly warm scent and it comforted and tantalized. Not only did he smell like heaven, his body represented protection. The hair peeking above the neckline of his tank top tickled her nose. Her hands pressed against rock-hard pectorals. He felt so good. His breath sucked in as she encircled his waist.

Marcus' arms tightened and she savored the delineated, powerful muscle that held her as tenderly as he might cradle a babe. His fingers explored her hair with brushes so featherlight she almost didn't feel his touch. Hot tears dried up in a heartbeat as she absorbed the soothing he offered. Wrapped in the glove of his care, she allowed her worry to drift away for a moment.

"I'm sorry," she murmured against his chest.

The stubble on his chin scratched her forehead when he moved. "For what?"

"For dragging you over here and then pouring out all this…this baggage."

He chuckled and the sultry, husky sound vibrated through her skin and down into her stomach. "You didn't drag me. I came over because I wanted to."

"Well, thank you. You're a great friend."

He stopped caressing her hair and allowed his hand to drift to her upper back. He rubbed gently. "You're more than welcome. As for the baggage, anyone who says they *don't* have any is lying. Of course, you know what this means, don't you?"

She lifted her head. His eyes held a unique sparkle, something drugging and sensual she didn't dare to interpret. She sounded a little breathless as she asked, "What?"

"You have to buy me some of those cookies again." He wiggled his eyebrows.

His silliness set off a giggle in her throat. She gurgled an unladylike snort and it started a belly laugh she couldn't control. Embarrassed, she buried her face in his chest and held on for dear life as uncontrollable mirth rocked her. He joined in, his quiet laughter more restrained, but genuine.

His hands coasted up and down her back, as if he still wanted to calm her. It had the opposite effect. As his big hands glided over her thin nightshirt, the heat pumped through her veins and the movement of hard muscle against softness started a chain reaction. Her nipples went tight and hard from the contact. He shifted his stance wider as his thighs parted. His groin brushed her belly. She inhaled on a small, startled gulp of air. *Very* hard arousal pressed her stomach. *Oh my God.*

Her friend was, without a doubt, becoming aroused. This had happened to them earlier today, and now they had on even less clothes. Well, she did, anyway.

Her tone came out sounding breathy. "Marcus."

"Mmmm?" His voice sounded husky against her ear.

She looked up at him and stopped short. He no longer looked cuddly, or even the nerdy Marcus she thought she knew from the office. His gaze held heart-shaking, smoldering fire. Friend or not, his body wanted hers. And whether *she* wanted to admit it or not, a stirring sent wildfire deep into her stomach. Muscles clenched between her legs and a deep ache centered there. Her breathing accelerated, excitement dancing with pinwheels over her skin.

Before she could move, he released her and stepped back. She couldn't stop the quick, covert glance downward. Oh yeah. She hadn't imagined things.

The man so many women at work thought was gay had an A-number one hard-on for her. Unfortunately what she meant to be unobtrusive didn't work, for her eyes lingered too long on the evidence.

A totally male grin parted his lips. "Uh, Tara? If you keep looking at me like that, I don't know what I'm going to do."

"Oh," she whispered, her throat dry and scratchy.

"It's getting late," he said as he turned away, breaking the spell that surrounded them.

She breathed a sigh of relief, unnerved by the powerful attraction. "Thanks for everything. I feel much better now."

"Great. We can talk more about the game plan tomorrow morning. I'll sleep on your couch tonight."

Startled, his statement took a second to penetrate. "What?"

"I've got a gym bag out in the car. I'll go get it."

"Marcus, this isn't necessary."

"You don't think I'm going to leave you alone before your security system is installed? If Drake saw me drive up and come in the house, he knows you're not alone. It'll probably deter him from trying anything."

A mild panic, laced with a sliver of gratefulness, worked its way into her mind. "You don't have to do this."

A finely sculpted representation of male animal, he looked daunting, dangerous as hell and unmovable. "No, I don't. But I want to. If Drake tries anything he's going to have to get through me first."

A picture of Marcus, all harmless and nerdy, popped back into her head, then was firmly quashed.

Another smile crossed his mouth. He walked slowly toward her until he stood so close her hormones clamored in serious appreciation. God, the man was sex on two legs. How could she have missed seeing it?

His voice dropped to a quiet but firm rumble. "Drake may have been in the army, Tara, but I was a Marine."

He winked and headed for the front door.

Chapter Eight

ഔ

Drake watched Tara's house, building hatred eating away at his control.

Get the fuck outta there, you piece of shit.

Wind battered the vehicle, tossing a loose branch and leaves over the hood. Thunder growled in the distance. Flashes of sheet lightning illuminated clouds to the east over the city.

The front door opened.

Darkness invaded his mind as he saw the man leave Tara's house. He adjusted the binoculars and zeroed in for a better look at the stranger, but couldn't see much. The front porch light had gone out. Drake could see the man was tall and powerfully built, with pussy-assed long hair that tossed in the breeze. A snort of indignation passed through his lips when he saw how pretty the hair made the man. Glossy and thick, his hair possessed a wave that curled it around the stranger's shoulders.

He sniffed. In prison, that shithead wouldn't have lasted a minute. As soon as the inmates would have seen that hair, they would have butt-fucked the guy into the next century. What kind of lame jerk-off wore long hair anyway? Only rock stars and pussies.

What a fuckhead.

The stranger rummaged in his car and brought out a gym-type bag. He reached inside the bag and retrieved a cell phone, then dropped the bag on the concrete driveway. He started to use the phone. Whatever the stranger said, he said it quickly, for he cleared the call within less than a minute. The man grabbed the gym bag and stalked back inside the house.

Suspicion burst inside. Anger exploded, burning rage down deep. His fingers clutched on the binoculars, and he barely harnessed a desire to leave this shit piece of car and tear the asshole from limb to limb. An itch started in his brain that he couldn't appease. Tara had picked up a boyfriend somewhere along the way. Wasn't *that* interesting?

The gym bag boy would be an easy takedown. *Shit, yeah. I'm still a soldier.*

Just because the establishment had put him in prison didn't mean they'd stripped him of his self. Sure, they'd discharged him from the army, taken his stripes and no one called him Sergeant anymore. That didn't mean he couldn't take charge like he always did before. When a snafu occurred and people refused to follow orders, he knew better than anyone how to shape them up.

Another wave of revulsion rolled up. If she hadn't angered him so much and forced his hand, they could be together right now.

And they would be again, very, very soon.

If he had to kill the long-haired pussy first to get to her, he would.

* * * * *

A dream came to Marcus. His mind filled with explosive carnal need as wet, tight pussy cocooned his cock in luscious heat. Drifting in a hazy, unclear world, he savored soft flesh yielding to his hardness. He took in her scent, a heady spice he couldn't identify but that stirred his desire into a frenzy. Losing control, he forgot everything but pleasure and her peppermint-flavored lips.

God yes. His dream woman always welcomed his touches, his kisses. Whenever he slid between the sheets and between her thighs, her body opened to him like a new flower, awaiting his first thrust. She never rejected his differences. Never pretended to understand his psychic abilities just to get him into bed. He felt her strength, her desire to please him and take him without reserve.

She begged.

She moaned.

Her breathing quickened.

As he powered into her, his thrusts rapid and unrelenting, he thought he couldn't make it another minute.

He drew back his hips and slammed forward, grunting with supreme satisfaction. A breathy female moan penetrated his headlong flight toward orgasm. He plunged his cock deep and hard into the woman.

"Please," the soft voice moaned beneath him. "Please."

He gave what she needed, rearing up on his palms and arching, using his thigh muscles to power deep into her slick pussy. Her pussy walls grasped him, clenching and releasing as an orgasm shuddered and shook through her entire body.

As burning, overwhelming ecstasy climbed into his loins, he fucked her with an intensity he'd never attempted before. It wouldn't be long now. Tension heightened, brought to a wavering peak by desire slamming like rocket fire into his cock. He plunged, gasps of breath accelerating with the pace of each unrelenting thrust.

He looked down at her and saw for the first time their color. One blue eye and one brown eye.

Something woke him violently from the dream, and his eyes flew open.

His heart hammered in his chest, and he shivered when recalled how she'd felt wrapped around his cock.

Then everything inside him went on code red.

A shadow made its way nearby the couch, and his muscles instantly tightened. His sleep-addled mind took a few seconds to register the slender form couldn't belong to Tara's ex-husband.

Tara opened the front window curtain a crack with her index finger and peered into the new day. He sighed in relief and his heartbeat slowed to normal.

He savored the thrust of her full breasts cushioned in a red racer-back tank top and the way her ass looked in navy chino shorts. She'd left her hair down, and he liked the way sun glinted over a few strands and sent red fire dancing over the surface. Pushing his fingers through her glorious hair last night had about sent him into premature ejaculation. Hell, last night when she'd nestled in his arms his cock didn't care if he wanted to play it cool or not. He'd sported an erection faster than a man could say cock-tease.

Damn it, he needed to stay cautious. When she'd called him with fear lacing her voice, protective instincts he didn't know he possessed had roared to instant life. Like a mission for SIA, keeping her safe became his single objective. He'd almost broken some major traffic laws driving over here. The thought of her at that asshole's mercy had propelled him toward her without a second thought. He could have called the police for her, but he didn't trust her safety to anyone else, and the police couldn't do anything about a simple phone call.

Staring at her now, his emotions rolled from elation to doom.

Elation because he loved being around her.

Doom because he couldn't afford to be horny as a dog, protect her and accomplish the case SIA required all at the same time. He'd vowed to keep his physical feelings for her down to a dull roar to keep his mental abilities honed. Damned if his body didn't give a flying fuck.

Yeah, he was going to hell for this one.

Then there was this morning's dream. Maybe his mind had taken the dream woman and made Tara fit the mold.

"Good morning," he said.

Tara started and swung around. She frowned deeply. "God, Marcus. You scared me again. What is it with you?"

He grinned and sat up. "Haven't had your morning coffee?"

Her features didn't relax. Instead, her gaze snagged on his bare chest. He'd taken off his tank top off during the night and tossed it at the bottom of the couch. She'd given him two pillows, sheets and a blanket. The sheet and blanket rode low on his hips, and he knew she saw his jeans lying at the end of the couch as well. When she licked her lips, his cock twitched.

Shit, he didn't need this crazy reaction to her. How could help it, though, when she stood there looking so hot?

"Did you get hot last night?" she asked.

A smile quirked his lips at the double entendre she'd made without even knowing it. "Yeah, I did."

"Sorry. I turned the air conditioner off. It gets cool in here sometimes."

Before his brain could kick in, his mouth said, "Maybe you need someone to keep you warm at night."

Silence dropped on the room like a death knell.

One beautiful blue eye and one beautiful brown eye widened in surprise. Her lips, rosy and parted, held a shocked oh.

Holy crap, Hyatt. Now you've done it. She's going to think you are a letch and kick you out on your ass.

Marcus jammed his fingers through his hair in frustration at his tactlessness. "Sorry. That was…uh…uncalled for."

She looked stunned, then she blinked and the surprise seemed to disappear. She grinned, and that sweet smile sent unwanted tendrils of coiling heat straight to his groin. *Shit on a stick.* No matter what she did anymore, it turned him harder than a railroad spike.

She started for the kitchen. "What would you like for breakfast?"

"Whatever you're having."

"Yogurt and fruit?"

He slipped out from under the blankets and reached for his jeans. As he shoved his legs into his jeans, he grimaced. Yogurt and fruit. Yippee yahoo. His body would devour it and need something more in less than two hours. When he didn't answer, she popped around the corner. Her glance did an unmistakable dip right to the unzipped and unbuttoned jeans. With another swoop, her gaze cruised up over his chest. Heat zinged through his veins.

Oh, okay, Sport. Did you ever think she finds you hideous? Maybe she thinks your ass is too skinny, your abs aren't flat enough and your chest is too hairy. You thought you turned her on, but maybe you didn't.

Suffering a pang of self-consciousness for the first time in a long time, he zipped his jeans hastily. "Why don't you go ahead and get your breakfast while I take a shower?"

She nodded but didn't say anything, a curious expression lingering on her pretty face that could be disappointment or even exasperation.

He grabbed his gym bag from the floor and headed down the hallway.

Tara watched his broad shoulders when he retreated. Jeans clung to his butt, cupping the taut curves of a fine male ass. Female appreciation coursed through her body with a long shiver she felt from her breasts all the way to her belly where heat coiled.

This sudden and awe-inspiring lust crawling its way into her mind and body had slapped her fast yesterday and she remained shocked to the root.

Last night he didn't hide the fact his testosterone went way off the scale. Even before he'd surprised her with his cocky announcement that he used to be a Marine, she knew in her heart if Drake showed up, Marcus could guard her. She'd slept like the dead. She'd awakened this morning after one heated erotic dream about her mystery man. He'd finally taken her, sliding deep inside her and thrusting strongly. When she'd awakened, she felt wet between the legs and aching, her vaginal walls pulsing as if she'd just experienced an orgasm.

She'd also taken time with her morning ritual. Sundays she didn't rush around, and she refused to make a huge alteration in her routine because Marcus slept on her couch.

She turned back to the kitchen and rummaged in the refrigerator for coffee. As she went through the motions of making the brew, she couldn't help visualizing his magnificent chest. Feeling his sculpted pecs under her hands had felt wonderful, but seeing his incredible chest was fabulous, too.

She leaned her arms on the counter and closed her eyes. Drawing in a deep breath, she remembered what he'd looked like lying on the couch with his eyes closed. In repose, his face showed genuine relaxation, no cares in the world. Stubble on his chin roughened his jawline and reminded her that a warrior lived inside him. His hair, unbound by the ponytail, tumbled in messy, sexy disarray. One tendril lay over his face, cutting a dark line. She tried to imagine him with a short buzz military haircut. She smiled. He'd look good completely bald or with hair down to the floor. Disgustingly thick, black lashes fanned down to shelter his eyes. The carnal shape of his mouth softened his strong jaw.

No, not softened.

Deceived. She knew deep in her heart, in the part of her that understood people too well, that his mouth might look vulnerable in sleep, but inside his heartbeat stayed steady, strong and unwilling to bend.

She didn't know if that made her feel better or worse.

Drake possessed too many of those qualities, especially when she first met him and admired the warrior façade too much.

When Marcus had awakened and sat up, her gaze had inventoried his incredible chest. Silky whirls of black hair fanned over his pectorals, down over his muscled stomach and thinned as it disappeared beneath the blanket. For a crazy second she'd been unable to say a word, stupefied by his male beauty.

No, he'd been way too striking and intimidating.

As the shower went on in the guest bedroom bathroom, she swallowed hard. No, no, no. She *wouldn't* imagine lathered soap sliding down that carved, heart-stopping body. Right. Telling herself she wouldn't think of him wet and naked had the opposite effect. She saw water trickling down his strong throat, past his pecs, over his stomach, over tight buns and thighs and over —

She wondered what his penis would look like. How well-endowed would he be? Yesterday and last night, when he'd pressed his hips against her and she'd felt his erection, she'd been too surprised at the time to wonder. Still, she shouldn't get hyped about his reaction. Many men responded to close contact with a woman's body and their penises went on autopilot.

She must remember the sultry look in his eyes hadn't meant anything extraordinary.

The sputtering coffeemaker jerked her away out of the fantasy.

Yep. Perfectly pathetic.

She couldn't moon over Marcus with the specter of Drake looming in the background.

Resolving to keep her cool, she hurried to set up the dining room for breakfast.

She put out silverware, then headed back into the kitchen. She realized yogurt wouldn't do it for her any more than it would fill up Marcus.

With a flurry of activity, she made scrambled eggs, toast and fruit in short order. She'd arranged the feast on the table when Marcus strode into the room, his wet hair tangling about his face and neck. He'd dressed in drab gray sweats that covered his appreciable attributes. A small piece of her felt disappointed.

She was pitiful all right.

"Wow, look at this," he said. "A great spread and a beautiful table."

She smiled with pleasure. The big dark oak table held eight people easily. The large turquoise blue placemats covered the table, and an antique-looking pewter candleholder graced the middle. "My parents gave me this table when they wanted a more modern dining set. It's antique."

He brushed his long fingers over the polished wood, the knotholes and scratches clear, but the integrity of artisanship evident. His fingers glided over the side of the table, and his caress along the wood made her stomach tingle. Oh yes. Give her a chance to discover what his hand would feel like against her naked skin. Pure sin and pure delight.

"I like it. And I like the looks of this breakfast. Juice and coffee, too. I thought you wanted yogurt."

"I did, then I realized I'm really hungry. And I don't think yogurt would fill you up anyway. You're too big."

As he slid into a chair across from her, one of his dark brows quirked. "Too big? Is that an insult?"

Heat tinged her cheeks. She shook her head and spooned eggs onto her plate. "Of course not. You're how tall?"

"Six-feet, three-inches."

"See, that's big. I would think a warrior would need a lot of food to keep going. I suppose half the guys you knew in the Marines would say this was a girly meal. The honey, anyway."

His gaze snapped up to hers, surprise written in those dynamic eyes. "Yeah. How did you guess?"

She cleared her throat. "I guessed that if U.S. Army men could make that statement about toast with honey, there's a good chance the Marines would, too."

His covert smile made her wonder what he was thinking. He glanced around the open area that included kitchen, dining set and the small living area. "I like this. Homey but it has a formal feel to it. Darker woods and none of that chrome and glass."

Pleasure slipped warm and satisfying into her heart. "I think it's mostly rebellion. My mother always liked the ultra-modern decorating schemes. If she'd warmed it up I would have felt comfortable. With her it's about efficiency. Stainless steel, black, gray and beige." She shuddered. "Yuck."

"You'd like my parents' house. They've got quite a few antiques passed down over a hundred and fifty years."

"Just what I'd expect for a farmhouse. Although you're not what I would expect of a farm boy."

"Yeah? What do farm boys look like?"

She shrugged. "I always visualize farm boys as big blonds."

He ladled scrambled eggs onto his plate. "Oh no. No stereotype in there."

"Come on, you know people think in stereotypes all the time. Superficially that's how we look at things until we can come to our own conclusions."

He buttered two pieces of toast and then squirted on honey.

When he lifted his gaze to her, he said, "Sometimes it's how we survive, right? We can't make it through battle if we don't think of the enemy as a faceless, nameless entity. Makes the killing a lot easier."

Ripples of unease started in her belly. She remembered her vision of him in desert khakis. "You mean when you were in the military you enjoyed killing people?"

He put down his toast and lines of consternation formed between his eyebrows. "Hell no. In war, if you personalize everything soon it'll tear you apart." When his gaze held hers, she saw the seriousness deep inside them. "I was in Desert Storm. Each war has casualties, and not just the physical ones. Your mind can get injured, too."

She almost asked him if he'd suffered from what he'd seen and did, but a lump grew in her throat instead. She shoved it down by pouring a cup of coffee from the insulated carafe and then taking a quick swallow. "What was your specialty in the military?"

He shrugged, as if his occupation had little significance. "Recon missions."

"Like a scout?"

His gaze scanned her, not the lighthearted man of moments ago. Questions burned in his eyes, too. "Occasionally. Other times we did hostage rescue."

What could she say to that? Instead, her mind wrapped around the idea he'd performed a perilous job. One wrong step and he might not be with her today. She tried swallowing another bite of egg but the lump wouldn't go away. Her heart thumped harder as she imagined, with a heavy heart, if he'd been killed during that war. One thought ruled everything.

Unconscionable.

A man as vibrant and strong as Marcus Hyatt not in this world? No, she couldn't bear to think about it.

"Was Drake in Desert Storm?" he asked.

"They never sent him, though some in his unit went."

Marcus took a bite of toast and chewed. A thoughtful look came over his face. After he swallowed, he said, "Did Drake spend a lot of time putting down other men?"

She took a sip of her coffee, eager for the caffeine to pep her up. "Drake was always insecure. He tried intimidation on everyone, including fellow soldiers in his unit. During the first year we were married, I saw him almost get into fistfights at two picnics."

"He picked fights?"

"Well, if he didn't pick them he always managed to be right in the middle of one. It's like he had bad karma following him. I suffered by association."

"You shouldn't have to suffer through anyone else's actions. Especially not that kind."

An ache centered in her gut, this one because of bad memories and not hunger. They ate in silence for a time, and she felt at ease in the quiet. Like most the men she'd met, he'd polished off his eggs and toast before she could.

She gestured at the platter in the center of the table. "Help yourself to seconds. I made plenty."

He gave her a cockeyed grin. "I thought you'd never ask."

As he ate his way through another helping and sipped his black coffee, she felt even more grateful for his help last night. "Thanks for staying last night. Most guys would have gone home."

He paused with his fork halfway to his mouth. "You really think that?"

"I know that."

He finished his bite of egg before he reached for his mug. He fumbled with the large blue mug's handle and stared at it with lingering concentration. She watched his absorption with an equally strange enthrallment she couldn't break.

When his gaze came up and locked with hers, the burning concentration stripped her core naked. "You thought after Drake threatened to hurt you that I would leave you? He could have waited until I left, then tried to break in. Any man who cared about you would never leave you unprotected."

Flustered, her mouth popped open and she couldn't say a word. He kept his stare on her like a sight on a target, and warmth spread straight up from her stomach into her torso and face. Arousal spiraled, working a languid trail throughout her body and straight into her heart as well.

He's found the way to flip my switch. All he has to do is get all protective and manly and my hormones do the happy dance.

"I imagine when a woman is abused both mentally and physically, after a while she starts to think a man could never care about her," he said.

Tears burned her eyes. Damn him for being so perceptive. She didn't like the sensation of openness, as if he could walk around in her head and pull out secrets any time he wished.

When she didn't reply, he asked, "What happened the last time you were with him? What exactly did he do?"

His questions hung in the air and she almost refused to reply. "Why do you want to know?"

"Because if I know how he operates it gives me a better idea of what we're dealing with."

"We? This isn't your battle, Marcus."

He moved his plate aside. "Hell, it was my problem from the time I heard about it the other day."

A quiet, mocking laugh slipped from her lips. "Do you always help people you hardly know?"

"Sometimes. In your case, I'm helping because I care about you. Do you always reject help when it's offered?"

Good point.

Dredging up the ugliest part of her history didn't appeal to her. She kept that part of her life buried deep and didn't dwell on what happened. She continued eating and stalled.

When she swallowed a last bite, she said, "It's a really long story, Marcus. I don't want to talk about it right now."

"Too painful?"

Is that what she felt? Pain? No. "Too shameful."

"I hope you don't mean your shame. Drake abused you because he's a bastard. Remember what I said earlier? That it wasn't your fault?"

She nodded. "I know that intellectually. I think of what happened and sometimes my mind reacts to it with shame rather than simple loathing for what he did."

Sympathy softened his eyes. "Everyone has done something they wish they hadn't. What he did to you shouldn't be something you're personally ashamed of."

"Maybe it shouldn't be." Her throat felt tight with unexpressed emotion. "But it is."

He didn't speak, but she saw curiosity deep in his eyes. He wanted to know what happened, not to mock her for weakness. She took a hint from him and pushed aside her plate.

She twirled a few strands of hair around her index finger. "It's like a broken record, you know? I have these doubts inside me running like a hamster in a cage, always talking to me about how messed up I was…am. I can't talk to you about what he did to me that final night. I don't want to feel the pain."

A revelation altered his expression, a genuine understanding igniting behind those inquiring eyes. "You think it's a stain you can't wipe out, and if you don't talk about it, then it won't exist."

She clenched her hands together on the table. "In essence, yes."

"Until it crops up in another corner of your life." He reached across the table and covered her hands with one of his own. "Damn it, Tara, you deserve a whole and happy life. You can't let him do this to you forever. It's clear he didn't need to come to town and threaten you. He still had a hold on you, even from prison."

Everything he said made sense, and he held considerable wisdom in that gorgeous, stubborn head.

"Give me more time to process, okay? Drake showing up on the scene threw my defenses out of kilter. It took a long time for me realize that I wasn't any of the things he said I was. Except maybe for the scared part. He once told me I reminded him of a petrified animal."

Anger flared in Marcus' eyes. "That's bullshit. You're one of the strongest women I've met."

Her throat felt too tight, too overflowing with emotions. Her heart beat too fast, her palms became damp with sweat at the remembrance of Drake's fists connecting with her face. She pulled her hands out from under Marcus' hold. She stood and took her empty plate with her to the sink where she rinsed it and put it in the dishwasher. He followed and she moved away from the sink to give him room. If she thought her awareness of him as a desirable man would disappear over breakfast, she was seriously wrong. His height, strength and unadulterated manliness penetrated her skin, her heart, her mind.

Had she ever met a man with this much power of personality? Drake, perhaps. The comparison scared her to death.

As he put his plate and utensils in the dishwasher, he said, "People often sabotage themselves on a daily basis. They usually have an excuse for not doing or not being what they want. There's always some obligation or emotion, or problem. I hope you never become one of those people. A person like that never truly lives."

She heard the message and understood it, and part of her wanted to smack him silly. Riled, she turned on him. "So now that you've psychoanalyzed me, Marcus Hyatt, why don't you tell me all your secrets?"

He smiled. "I don't have any secrets. There's nothing major in my life waiting to eat me alive from the inside out."

Sarcastic words didn't on average come to her swiftly, but this time she didn't have to wait for them. She snorted softly. "Mr. Perfect."

He crossed his arms. "Huh. Hardly. I've got plenty of faults. Ask my relatives."

She ignored his joviality. "Your military life didn't scar you? You must have seen and done some things you don't like thinking about? Am I right?" When his expression froze, triumph skated through her. "Ah-ha. I thought so."

"I'll tell you anything you want about my military life."

Startled, she saw nothing but a clear conscious and openness in his crystalline eyes. "Okay. Start by telling me about your first mission."

He sighed. "That's a really, really long story. Can I tell you later over dinner?"

Irrational anger worked into her like a splinter. "I see. It's all right for me to bare my soul, but not for you?"

Exasperation tightened his lips. "Of course not. I *will* tell you. But isn't the security company supposed to be here in a few minutes to set up the system? That's going to take a bit of time."

Feeling unreasonable, she opened her mouth and spoke before thinking. The one word came out contemptuous. "Yes."

Shaky and uncertain, hopeful and fearful, she couldn't believe her unsettled feelings around Marcus, how much she wanted to believe him. Her way of thinking about him changed since yesterday. He'd gone from a friendly office cubicle partner to a big, tough Marine with a core of tenderness. He stripped her emotions bare until she couldn't conceal her passions the way she habitually did. She felt out of her element.

I feel out of control. I feel...free.

Realization cut to the core. She sensed and saw Marcus' approval, sincerity and desire to help her. The ego she'd worked long and hard to restore was stronger than ever. She'd cried and laughed in his arms, and wanted to find pleasure there, too.

When he turned away from the sink, he stepped toward her. Involuntary reaction made her flinch and she edged back and bumped into the counter.

His eyes narrowed. "Let's get one thing straight. I'm not anything like your ex-husband. Got it? I don't hit women, I don't emotionally abuse women. Don't you understand by now, Tara?" The husky question, pitched low and intimate, caressed like a touch. Threads of deep response echoed inside her. "And you want to know why men probably aren't coming on to you in droves other than they are chickenshits?

Because they sense Drake still possesses you. His touch is like a brand they can smell. It's on your skin."

She gave an indignant little snort. "What? He does not." Frustrated with his simplistic and judgmental approach, she snapped at him. "I know myself a lot better than you do. Number one, I realized a long time ago that most men look right past me. There is always someone better-looking and more charismatic in the room than I am. And, I apparently have something stamped across my forehead in indelible ink that screams, 'Not an easy fuck. Stay away'."

Doubt entered his clear eyes. He leaned closer until he placed both hands on either side of her on the counter. She tensed. Not with fear, but with sweet longings. Arousal blossomed in her lower stomach. "Any man who doesn't want you is crazy. You're sensitive, smart and pretty as hell."

Her lips parted. She felt scattered, like an idiot who let things get out of hand and mixed up. He reached up and skimmed her cheek with a lingering caress. Her heartbeat threatened to pound through her chest.

Again, his deep eyes burned into hers. He'd neglected to shave, so day-old stubble gave him a rough and tumble aspect. His zippered sweatshirt was open down to mid-chest and revealed enough hairy chest and muscles to intrigue her femininity.

She put one hand on his chest to urge him away. "I don't think—"

His large hand covered hers and held it against his chest. She gazed at her trapped hand. His fingers completely encompassed hers. Power and assurance came from his touch.

"You don't think what?"

She couldn't tell him he made her nervous, flustered and intoxicated with want. "I don't think this...whatever this is we're doing is a good idea."

"Damn." He leaned closer as his gaze caressed her face. Low and a little rough, his voice touched her like a corporeal embrace. "You could tempt a saint to do things he shouldn't."

She couldn't stop the yearning swelling inside her. His musk scent, heady and rich, made her want him closer.

He reached up and cupped her face with his other hand. Mesmerized, she tried one last time to discourage them both from taking a dangerous step. "What are we doing?"

"I'm proving you are everything you think you're not. Maybe you need someone to wipe away Drake's touch."

Before she could protest or form words, his lips touched hers.

Chapter Nine

ஐ

With a deft twist, Marcus parted her lips. His tongue took possession, sweeping into Tara's mouth. A hot tingle darted into her belly and between her legs, and she moaned softly with pleasure.

He urged her to respond with a fervor that tossed caution aside. Her arms slid up around his neck and urged him closer. Relentless and feverish, passion slammed her hard. She wanted to crawl inside this man and discover his secrets until he begged her to put him out of his misery. The idea slipped through her arousal-fogged mind that she'd never experienced sexual desire so powerful or profound.

The scalding heat behind his kiss, drugging and fierce, made her forget who, what and where she was. Her hands gripped his shoulders, absorbing the gratifying sensation of hard muscles bunching and flexing under her exploration. An aching desire pulsed between her legs and made her nipples hard. He didn't just explore her with a single mind-bending kiss. He took one kiss. Another. A third, attacking her mouth at one angle and another until she quaked with pent-up passion. He drew her into a frenzy she couldn't resist, a desire to complete something absent inside her that she hadn't realized was missing in the first place.

Being taken by him would bring more than physical joy, it would fulfill a yearning in her soul for human intimacy. The connection that came from joining a man and woman. She moved, telling Marcus with her body how much she wanted and needed his touch, his attention.

His hands cupped her ass. She shivered against him as strong fingers kneaded her gently, pressing into her flesh with a demand that asked rather than took. Feverish and yearning, she felt the merciless ache deep inside her pussy turn to screaming demand as he bent slightly and lined up his full-on erection with her slit. His hips pressed hers back against the counter and then moved in a rhythm obviously designed to drive her straight off the edge of the earth. God, this is where they'd left off before. He knew she liked this—she could feel it. It gratified her to realize he noticed what she liked and intended to give her more.

As his hardness brushed continually over her clit, she thought she'd go mad. Up and down, back and forth, his cock pressed, brushed and tantalized until she panted into his mouth. She wanted to come so badly and she felt so close to bursting she knew it couldn't be much longer. Nothing mattered but the goal of screaming orgasm.

His hand came up and cupped her right breast, and she gasped into his mouth at the exquisite sensation. She wanted to do something wild and unspeakably forbidden with this man.

She tore her mouth from his, but his lips found her cheek, then slipped over to her ear. "You want to come, don't you? Tell me what you want."

His tender words, spoken in that liquid husky voice, made her quiver with unrestrained need.

She swallowed hard and answered, way beyond caring about self-control. "Yes. Yes, I want to come."

She gasped when he licked her earlobe, then gently bit it. A rough groan slipped from his lips and then his mouth trailed down her neck until he reached the sensitive skin between neck and shoulder.

"Oh my God," she whispered, unable to stop the ecstasy racing across her body. "Marcus."

"Yeah."

His soft confirmation that he'd heard Tara did nothing to stop him. He nibbled at her neck as his left hand pulled the racer-back tank top and bra down. He slipped the other side down to her waist, baring both of her breasts to his scrutiny.

His nostrils flared, his lips parting as his eyes dilated even farther. "God, save me."

She felt the cool air on her right nipple and a few seconds later, his hand cupped her naked breast in his gentle grip. She shivered, the heat of his hand both soothing and maddening.

Then, unexpectedly, he drew back and took her face in his hands. His gaze held the promise of lovemaking so heady she would burn up in the flames. "You are so beautiful, Tara. And don't ever let anyone tell you differently."

While he kissed her, his fingers brushed around her painfully aroused nipples. He tweaked them, the soft plucking motion sending her into a deep need that felt almost painful. He pressed his cock between her legs, his hardness nudging her sensitive clit while his fingers massaged her nipples. Tara writhed.

His tongue fucked her mouth, and the triple sensation of cock against clit, fingers manipulating her breasts, and his mouth making love to hers, threatened to pull an orgasm from her.

Soft whimpers left her throat, muffled by his mouth. Panting with desire, she struggled to hold back overwhelming emotions. She wanted to ask him so many things, know so much more about him. Another part of her wanted to scream at him to rip off her clothes and get inside her fast before she came without feeling his cock buried high up inside her. She gripped his waist, her hips moving in rhythm to his.

She quavered in delicious anticipation of what he might do next. Every sweet pluck on her nipples made her heartbeat quicken and her breathing accelerate.

She wanted his tongue there, laving and sucking deeply at her breasts. She wanted his mouth all over her body. She felt slick and hot between the legs and an orgasm bubbled out of reach, begging for fulfillment, screaming for an end.

Now.

The doorbell rang. She started, then a nervous laugh came from her throat as he stopped kissing her. His gaze blazed down at her.

"Shit," he whispered and gathered her close to murmur into her hair. "I'll bet that's the security company."

"Probably." Regret filled her voice, and the aching emptiness between her legs throbbed.

She'd never realized desire could literally hurt, but with the way she felt now she wanted to tell the security people to leave so she could take Marcus in her arms and screw him into the next century.

He drew back quickly and helped her rearrange her top and bra. "You'd better answer the door. With a hard-on like this…" He grinned, leaving her imagination to fill in the sentence.

She smiled, a dazed almost puffy feeling of happiness filling her head. She glanced down at his cock, which pressed against his sweats in a long, solid column. Hungry. Yeah, she knew the meaning of being hungry for sex. It beat in her blood, in her heart.

Dazed by what had happened between them, she moved away with her senses in riot and then rushed to open the door.

When the two men came in to install the system, she wondered for a wild moment if maybe what she'd been doing with Marcus showed on her face. She ran her hands through her hair and then greeted the men with a smile and a handshake.

Marcus returned to the living room a few minutes later looking composed, as if they hadn't almost made love right there in the kitchen. Marcus watched the installation bit by bit, and she felt more grateful than ever that he'd stayed with her last night and assisted in making certain the security system worked right. At the same time, her hormones wouldn't calm down. Standing within a few feet of him sent her thermostat into triple digits. She couldn't stop thinking about what they'd been doing before the security company arrived.

Would he want to continue when the security people left? The idea horrified her and stimulated at the same time. She'd wanted him with a hard, undeniable desire that called to her on each level of her being. Yet how could she trust raging physical needs that might have as much to do with fear as with anything deeper and lasting?

She couldn't be led around by her hormones as she had been with Drake. She refused to do it this way again.

Eventually, the men finished and she made certain she understood how the system operated.

Once the security people left, relief settled inside her. She walked back into the living room, then turned to face Marcus. "Thanks for helping out."

A twinge of renewed protectiveness made him say, "I don't feel comfortable leaving you alone. Even with the system in place."

Marcus watched her with a wary frown. Maybe she thought he wanted to stay with her to get in her pants. Did he? They'd been well on the way when the security people arrived. He'd lost total control with her hot, incredible lips under his and the sensation of her roused nipples under his fingers. God, those nipples. He'd been almost on the verge of leaning over and licking the hot berries.

Her breasts fit his large hands just right, not too large and not too small. Her nipples, a light rosy red, were large for her breasts and oh-so tempting. If he'd sucked on those tight, sweet buds he would have lost his mind. He'd have picked her up, sat her on the kitchen counter and fucked her, or he would have taken her standing up.

While the security people put in the system, he'd been able to keep his mind on his business. Right now, he didn't think he could take another minute of her nearness without his cock growing to painful proportions. Without him getting down on his knees and begging her to let him finish what they'd started earlier.

Cursing himself for creating a situation and making things complicated, he said, "Maybe we need space. What we did earlier…it wasn't a good idea."

There. He'd said the fatal words.

The crinkle in her brow, those unusual but beautiful eyes sad, almost made him wish he hadn't said it. Her somber mood stung his heart.

"Don't get me wrong." He stepped nearer. "What happened was incredible."

She nodded and clasped her hands together. "I haven't…I haven't felt so—" She stopped, a delicate pink hue touching her cheeks.

"Turned on?" he asked, hopeful.

A cheeky smile formed on that wide, sexy-as-hell mouth. "Yes. Okay, I'll admit it. The last few days I've come to realize that I'm attracted to you." She buried her face in her hands, as if embarrassed. "God, I can't believe I'm saying this."

Her shyness stirred his emotions. A deeper, more profound protectiveness broke loose. "You know I'm attracted to you, Tara. I think with everything that's going on in your life right now, we shouldn't get too wrapped up in each other."

Unexpectedly a wave of searing emotion hit him straight in the gut, and he wondered if the emotions came from her. Disappointment. She was disappointed in his nonchalance but wouldn't admit it. Then the emotion disappeared, as if she could shut it off like a faucet.

She nodded. "Of course. I need to take care of this situation with Drake."

He moved away before he could do something stupid like drag her into his arms, kiss her and say that everything would be all right. He knew he wouldn't want to stop until he'd buried his cock high inside her and witnessed her come apart in his arms. He wanted to confirm that she was the woman in his dreams. He had to escape now and save his sanity.

"Call me if anything out of the ordinary happens. Do you feel totally comfortable with running the system?"

She looked doubtful, but then wiped the wariness off her face in one blink. "Absolutely. Thanks again."

She didn't promise to call and that worried him, but he forced himself to walk away without looking back.

* * * * *

As Drake sat in his car and watched her home from a greater distance than usual, he lifted the powerful binoculars and scanned her quiet neighborhood. Watching her house was no longer an option.

From now on, he would have to plot from his base of operations. From there he could make plans to take out those who surrounded Tara. Then she would be his and his alone.

He'd seen the security van come and go and realized she'd taken electronic measures to keep him out. Granted he didn't have too much experience with security systems.

I'll implement Plan B. So, she has a long-haired watchdog and a security system. Bitch.

Heat rose in his body, as disrupting and fierce as the fires of hell. Time stretched out unbearably.

Shit. Fuck.

Bubbling fury rose into his system, biting like angry fire ants along his nerves. He started the car and turned back down the street away from her house. He went slow and easy, despite the hatred burning within like acid. No need to bring attention to himself. He drew in deep, steadying breaths. Irritation remained despite his efforts. Sweat beaded on his brow and he turned on the air conditioner. His right hand trembled and he felt his heartbeat try to steady. Another deep breath. Another.

Controlling his body became as paramount as managing her once again. For the pleasure would be ecstasy, an excruciating blend of pain, blood and sacrifice.

169

If he went to her, would she be reasonable? Would she comprehend her transgressions and that she must be cleansed? Any woman who hurt him the way Tara had deserved the punishment coming to her, but he would give her another chance. She had opportunity to redeem her ugly soul and bring her heart around to the salvation he could give her.

She would learn her lesson.

Tara's time would come soon.

* * * * *

As Tara drove into the parking structure at work Monday morning, she found her thoughts occupied by the events of the weekend. Drake's sinister call, the security system, shopping in the mall, the embrace of a man who set her on fire.

Marcus.

A man who made her feel more valued, respected and cared for than any other male she'd met.

His declaration rang in her memory. *We shouldn't get too wrapped up in each other.*

"Humph." She pulled into a spot on the bottom level of the multilevel garage. "I think it's a little late for me."

As hard as she tried to deny it, the weekend had changed her outlook on her cubicle buddy. Her self-effacing nerd had morphed into a kick-ass, gorgeous hunk of manhood. No, he hadn't morphed. She just didn't notice until now.

She'd been unobservant and stupid not to appreciate him more. She decided that even if he didn't want a sexual relationship, she didn't want their momentary insanity to ruin the friendship they'd built since he started working with the company.

Without Marcus by her side the rest of Sunday, she'd felt more vulnerable. She refused to give into edginess while she'd cleaned house, washed clothes and puttered around. Until evening came. Each small noise had made her skin prickle with goose bumps. Nerves ruled her until she didn't feel safe. She refused to call Marcus. The rest of the night, she'd watched two of her favorite DVDs, a romantic comedy and a musical.

That night she dreamed of shadows and strange creatures lurking in her peripheral vision at work. Her dream man stayed away.

Tara realized she sat in a parking space with the engine running, and she turned off the car. She needed to pay attention to the world around her instead of dreaming about Marcus' soul-stirring kisses. She couldn't blame Marcus for not wanting to get more involved, as much as it stung when he'd made his intention to stay clear obvious.

She stepped out of the car, taking note of the position of her vehicle. She'd parked quite a distance from the elevators, but didn't have much choice with the overload of cars today.

Jason Forte was holding a big meeting with corporate heads from an outpost company in Pueblo. The office would be hopping today. Good. Maybe the frenetic pace would keep her mind on work and off Marcus and her troubles with Drake.

As she walked toward the elevators, her narrow-heeled pumps clicked on the concrete flooring and echoed. She arrived at the elevators when a strange sensation overwhelmed her.

Someone watched her, the stare causing hairs on her arms to stand up. Her nerves tingled, aware of danger, harsh and unforgiving.

"Hello, Tara."

She started violently and as she whirled around, her heartbeat pounding.

Jason Forte stood not four feet behind her, his face as expressionless as a blank slate. "Sorry, I didn't mean to scare you."

Deep and rumbling, his voice stirred odd sensations inside her. She shivered, cold in the underground area.

"Hi, Jason." She forced lightness into her voice she didn't feel. "You showed up out of nowhere."

He shoved his hands in his pants. Today he wore his usual tailored suit, a cream concoction which went well with his champagne blond looks. She hadn't decided his true age, but she guessed he was somewhere around forty-five. He'd maintained an athletic carriage, yet the softness in his jawline reminded her that Marcus looked far more intriguing and attractive. She tried to conjure the same attraction other women seemed to feel for Jason's broad smile and movie-star good looks, but she couldn't.

He frowned and moved close enough she could smell his heavy cologne. "I'm sorry I startled you."

She often wondered if he ever smiled with genuine happiness or love. Whenever she saw him grin, it appeared plastic and insincere.

She managed a smile and turned to the elevators. "I'm fine. How are you today?"

"Well, I was hoping I would get a chance to talk to you."

A warning prickle made her stiffen in apprehension. "Oh?"

The elevator doors slid open and she stepped inside. When he followed her, he pushed the button to take them up to the third-floor offices. Their company occupied the first four floors of the fifteen-story skyscraper, with administration and word processing taking up the third level. His office resided on the fourth floor.

"I have some concerns about an employee and I'd like your opinion," he said.

His blue eyes glittered like a glacier ringed by a stormy sea. A chill went through her heart. He stepped closer. Her personal white force field shrank right along with it, as if it cowered under a strong energy.

When she took a whiff of his cloying aftershave or cologne, her senses literally swam and she leaned back against the elevator wall. Her white shield of protection faltered. Sure, she felt immune to Jason's charms, but this...whatever this was didn't feel like charm.

It felt…unsteady and filled with a barely toned-down malice.

Time crawled, stretching out like a cosmic rubber band. She didn't feel quite in control, the tension ready to snap.

"Listen to me." His voice sounded feathery and deep, potent with intent. "Marcus isn't what he appears and that concerns me."

Confused, she asked, "What do you mean?"

He shrugged. His jacket pulled a little across his broad shoulders. He slid his hand down the lapel in a grooming gesture. She blinked. Had he gotten closer? No, that was impossible. She hadn't even seen him move toward her.

"It's strange, don't you think, for a man to work in a secretarial pool?"

The antiquated idea made her temper rise. "Of course not. If Human Resources wishes to investigate something, it should be that only one woman works in the legal section."

His gaze glittered with unusual force. "I didn't mean to sound sexist."

Right.

A wave of emotion came at her, and she stopped it. Her white shield held, but his displeasure reached her. She felt touched by unseen hands and the creepy sensation worked up her spine with slow deliberation. Someone searched for a way past her defenses. Into her very soul.

"What is it that makes you think Marcus isn't genuine?" she asked.

"It's a feeling I have." Those cold eyes blinked once like an automaton. A crawling apprehension stepped forward and touched her with icicle hands. "You understand that sort of thing, don't you?"

She couldn't say she agreed with him or understood without opening a door where she didn't want to go.

"I know that he's a good, kind man." She held her oversized hobo purse to her waist like a wall.

"Maybe, but that's not what I'm saying. He isn't who he claims to be."

"Not to be disrespectful, Mr. Forte, but how do you know that?"

His expression stiffened, as if he didn't expect her to question his offhanded slander. "Like I said, I have feelings about people. And I think you're like that, too. But you try and hide it."

A wave of discomfort tightened her muscles and her heartbeat quickened. "I'm not hiding anything."

He started to step forward when the elevator jerked suddenly.

She let out a surprised yelp. His arms slipped around her just as the lights went out.

Before she could say a word, his mouth brushed over hers.

Chapter Ten

&

Startled, Tara stiffened in Jason's arms. The featherlight caress came and went so fast she wasn't sure it actually happened.

Her white light shifted, shrank and started to dissolve. Her mind shrieked in rebellion.

No. God no. What is he doing?

She jerked in his hold. "Oh my God."

"It's all right. You're safe."

"What's happening?"

"I'm sure it'll be all right in a moment."

He didn't sound the least concerned, and she made a quick decision. She strengthened her white light. As the white light thickened, a sudden pain erupted in her temple and she gasped.

A vision sucker-punched her.

In the vision, Jason let out a throaty laugh as he reached out and yanked her against him. He kissed her, mouth hot and greedy. Horrified and repulsed, she squirmed and pushed against steel-hard muscles.

He sucked the life from her with his baleful kiss. Drinking, drinking, he obliterated her thoughts and her soul until he absorbed her. Captured inside his mind, she looked down upon herself, an empty shell. Screaming, she writhed inside the dark place. She couldn't get free. Couldn't breathe. She'd become a zombie to do his bidding.

Her eyes snapped open. "No!"

"Hey, easy," he said. "I didn't know you were claustrophobic."

Her throat felt raw, her palms sweaty. "I'm not."

Darkness pressed in on all sides. Something predatory and insistent in his hold made her blood freeze. In the few times she'd been near him, she'd felt a strange, prickling sensation as if he tried to probe her mind. Despite her psychic abilities, she'd never encountered this with anyone, and now he held her in a forceful grip. That's why when she'd seen Marcus with him in the copier area she'd been so concerned about Marcus' physical state. What if Jason could harm people with his mind? It seemed too wild. Too crazy. Yet she must admit she'd seen far too many odd things in her life to dismiss it outright.

Pain touched her temple, and she struggled. "Mr. Forte, let me go."

With a jolt, the elevator started up and the lights flashed on. At the same time, Forte released her and stepped back. The elevator jolted and she stumbled, falling backwards at a strange angle. Her left ankle twisted painfully and she gasped.

He started to reach for her. Determined he wouldn't get the opportunity to touch her again, she pushed to her feet. "I'm fine."

Her ankle throbbed, and she knew she'd done some damage, even if only slight. She stepped back until she met the wall. Her knees shook and her breathing came much too fast. Although she looked away, she felt his keen gaze. The tingling, intruding feeling touched her mind. She shoved it away, daring to stare right at him for a full three seconds. Befuddled by the strange vision of him kissing her and turning her into a zombie, she couldn't think straight.

"That was quite a spill you took," he said.

She plastered on a smile and nodded. "I'm fine."

His grin spread in a tight line over his face. "When we talk next, we won't be interrupted. In fact, would you like to have lunch with me today?"

She stumbled into an excuse. "I can't. I'm having lunch with Marcus."

His eyes showed his dislike for the idea even as his mouth fixed into that plasticized grin. "I advise against it."

The elevator opened and Marcus stood right there, as if he'd been waiting for her. His gaze snapped to Jason with a hard glare, then back to her. When Marcus looked into her eyes, she felt a strong wave of relief and happiness. She left the elevator and tried not to limp. Marcus took her arm.

"What happened?" Marcus asked. "The elevator was stopped."

She shook her head. "I don't know, but thank God it started again. The lights went out, too."

Jason flipped open his cell phone. "I'll get the report turned in about the elevator. I'll take the stairs the rest of the way." He walked off without another word.

Marcus' gaze held extreme worry as he smoothed his hand down her arm. "Now that he's gone, tell me what really happened."

She shook her head. "The elevator simply stopped and the lights went out."

"Tara," his voice held a warning tone. "You're shaking. Don't tell me nothing happened."

Her entire body vibrated gently, and her nerves strung tight. She kept her voice steady. "I'm sure it's a breakdown."

His expression said he didn't believe her. "We need to talk later."

An idea came to her. "Do you have time at lunch?"

He nodded. "Of course."

As his attention caressed her face, his nearness caused a bittersweet longing to well inside her. She wanted more. More touches, more kisses. She wanted to throw herself into his arms and tell him what occurred in the elevator. But he wouldn't believe her. No sane individual would.

Then she remembered his strange questions the day she'd seen Jason walk out of the copier room and she found Marcus pale and shaky. Could Marcus understand her apprehension around Jason? How could she explain what happened with coherence when *she* couldn't understand it herself?

God, she hated this sense of unreality, this knowledge her whole world rotated at a crazy angle she couldn't control. First Drake, then her attraction for Marcus, now the weird vibes and vision of Jason.

Her ankle throbbed. Her shields malfunctioned, and dread slid up her body and nestled in her stomach with sickening concentration. She couldn't afford this. Somehow, she must rebuild her mental shield or the bombardment of heavy emotions from others would wear her down to a nub. She'd be babbling like an idiot before long.

"I'd better get to work. I've got that appointment with the lawyer today and I need to finish today's work before then," she said.

As she walked, he moved along beside her. "Tara, you're limping." His gentle clasp on her shoulder brought her to a halt. His gorgeous eyes deepened, anger mixing with concern in their deep depths. "You're hurt and it happened in that elevator."

"I told you, I'm all right. The elevator thing scared me but it's no big deal."

"Yeah, right. That's why you look like you're about ready to fall on your face and you're limping."

"You're imagining it." Her head felt about two sizes too big for her body, and as she took another step and faltered, Marcus scooped her up in his arms. "Hey!"

"Be still."

"Be still? Why you... I..."

Words failed her.

His grim expression didn't alter as he walked straight into the office for all to see, her clasped securely in his arms. More emotions poured from him into her, further incapacitating her ability to argue. She felt far more than attraction, she sensed a deep care and anxiety for her well-being. Gratified, she let the delicious knowledge warm her. She slipped her arms around his neck.

Questions followed from every side.

"Uh, Marcus. This is causing a stir," she said.

"So what?" With a grumble, he continued through the cubicles toward the employee lounge.

Cecelia and Sugar trotted along behind them, peppering them with questions, while others stood up and looked over their cubicle walls to stare.

"What happened?" Cecelia asked.

"Is she all right?" Sugar asked.

"The elevator freaked out and almost dropped a couple of stories. I'd say that's enough to scare the crap out of anyone." Marcus marched on. "Mr. Forte is calling in for repairs."

"Oh my God," Cecelia's hand went to her mouth. "Where is she hurt? Shall we call an ambulance?"

Alarmed by the rapidly spiraling situation, Tara improvised and smiled to allay fears. "No, no. Please don't do that. I sprained my ankle a bit, that's all. Marcus is taking me to the lounge for the first aid kit. I'll get an elastic bandage and I'll be fine."

This time she felt hilarity coming from him. Good. At least his sense of humor hadn't disappeared entirely under his serious mien. Embarrassed by all the attention, she also intercepted a few more emotions hurtling her way. Two women glared at her over their partitions, jealousy and dislike in their cold eyes and tight mouths. They thought she did this for attention. Nothing like a herd of resentful, narcissist women to make a working environment acidic.

When he nudged the employee lounge door open with his foot, she was relieved to see no one else there. "Please put me down."

He settled her on the couch. "Stay put and I'll get the first aid kit."

"Yes, sir," she said testily. "I could have walked."

He opened a closet near the sink and brought out the kit. "You've got a sprained ankle. There's no reason to make it worse, is there?"

She didn't want to listen to logic. She hung her head a minute and wondered what the other women in the office thought of Marcus carrying her.

"I can't believe you'd care what a few women think," he said.

The man seemed to be plucking her thoughts right out of her head.

She rubbed her hands over her cheeks, heat still radiating across her face. "I shouldn't care, but people probably think I'm some sort of weakling. Or that I'm playing at the fainting helpless woman to get your attention."

He sat down next to her, his nearness soothing and thrilling all at one time. He sat with his legs spread wide, and she gulped when her glance landed on his crotch.

Get your mind out of the gutter.

"We know the truth. That's all that matters." His voice turned husky, soft. He winked. "Besides, I like carrying you."

Melting heat poured into her belly at his admission. She blurted out the truth. "I like being in your arms."

Accessing, his hot gaze seemed to penetrate to her soul. The idea that he could read her mind flitted through her psyche once more, but she waylaid it. He opened the kit.

"Lift your leg and prop it over my thighs."

She did. When he cupped her knee with one big, warm hand, she started.

His grin was cheeky. "I'm not going to hurt you."

"I know that." Her clipped words sounded cross.

Aching awareness worked up her spine as his warm palm eased up her calf to the back of her knee in a long, lingering caress. Then his hand roved with deliberate attention down to her ankle. She blinked in surprise and looked at him.

He pressed on the delicate bones of her small ankle. "Any pain?"

"No."

"Good." The molten heat in his eyes sent a wildfire flash of arousal through her stomach. "Rotate your ankle."

With her shoe now hanging from her toes and her leg propped up on his hard, muscular thighs, Tara felt somewhere between nervous and wanting his bold exploration and glances to continue. She did as he said and her shoe fell off and clattered to the floor. She ignored it and so did he.

"It doesn't really hurt," she said. "It might be sore later, but it's no big deal."

He frowned. "Did Jason touch you?"

A strange question, but she answered. "Yes."

His gaze intensified, daring her to look away. Anger grew in his eyes. "How did he touch you?" When she refused to answer, he whispered, "Damn it."

The growl in his voice made her stare at him in surprise. "That's a little extreme a reaction, don't you think?"

"No. There's more to this guy than meets the eye."

"That's what he said about you." His hand moved, his fingers slid over her instep with a tickling caress that made her flinch and giggle. "Marcus, stop. That tickles."

A devouring gaze erased the gloominess in his gaze. Heat from his thigh muscles seeped through her hose. Her short-sleeved white linen blouse and blue skirt felt too warm. Sensual awareness dared her to move way.

He removed the elastic bandage from the first aid kit and worked slowly to bind her ankle. Her senses tuned into Marcus with acute mental and physical bonds. Her nipples tightened and a rush of moisture between her legs made her want to squirm. God, he gave off enough pheromones to start his own factory.

His body was so big and comforting, but the way his large hands caressed as they worked made her ache with the need for fulfillment. When he finished she thought she might die from the heavy-duty desire pulsating throughout her body.

When he paused, his gaze fell on her breasts for a moment and she realized her nipples poked at her thin bra and blouse for the world to see. She could claim to be cold, but she knew differently. Her breath constricted as his palm cupped over her knee again. His eyes held a longing she couldn't ignore.

"How does that feel?" he asked.

"Wonderful."

His slow grin melted her. "I meant the bandage."

She couldn't suppress a small smile. "I know. You were very gentle. Thank you."

His smile faded until his gaze shimmered with an undeniable edge of danger and challenge. He smelled so good and his attentiveness made her restless and needy for more.

His arm went onto the back of the couch and he leaned in closer. "Damn it, Tara, I—"

The door snapped open and his hand clamped down on her knee. Bettina came in, worry clear in her gaze. "I heard what happened in the elevator. Someone said you twisted your ankle?"

Tara pulled her leg away from his grip and off the cradle of his thighs. Embarrassment burned in her face. "It's really no big deal. I stumbled."

Bettina strode the rest of the way into the room, command written over her features. "What exactly happened in there?"

Tara gave the shortened, less dramatic version that left out Jason holding her. Irritation and frustration made her speak sharply. "Like I said, it was no big deal. I wish people would stop making more out of it than it was."

Bettina crossed her arms. "Take it easy. We're just concerned."

Rubbing her forehead, Tara stood and tottered. Bettina took her arm. Marcus reached for her shoe and knelt down to slip it over her foot. Even that tiny contact from him sent a frisson of heat straight to Tara's pussy. She almost clenched her teeth in frustration.

"I need to get to work." Tara moved toward the door with barely a limp.

Eager to escape, Tara went straight for her cubicle. Bettina went to her own office and Marcus followed Tara. Cecelia and Sugar pounced, though, before they could reach safety.

Sugar's wide-eyed gaze pinpointed Marcus. "That was so heroic."

His expression held a distinct aw-shucks air to it. "Thanks, but I wasn't trying to be heroic."

Cecelia batted her eyelashes at him. "That's the point."

Not caring to watch her office friends flirting, Tara slipped into her cubicle and started working. Moments later, her cubicle mate sat behind his desk. To her surprise, he didn't try to strike up a conversation. He clacked away at his computer with his usual fast keystrokes, a soothing and regular sound.

Time moved quickly and she managed to accomplish her daily workload before noon.

"Lunch?" Marcus said when noon came around.

She nodded, a flutter of anticipation and trepidation mixing inside her as she reached for her handbag and followed him out of the cubicle. They wandered to a small, popular restaurant in the lower lobby frequented by people in offices nearby.

Few things comforted her more than soup. Since her encounter with Jason, she felt cold all the way to the bone. As she tasted the potato and leek soup, Marcus chewed on taco salad.

She worried about his silence until she couldn't stand it any longer. She put down her fork. "Is something on your mind?"

His head snapped up. He'd been glaring at his salad bowl like it might jump up and bite him. "Yeah. I know more happened in the elevator."

She made a snap decision. If she wanted answers, she'd have to give him answers.

"Okay." She glanced around, then lowered her voice. "When we got in the elevator, he told me you aren't who you say you are."

Neither surprise nor shock showed on his even-cut features. "Did he say why?"

"He alluded that you were hiding something. That you don't want to reveal who you really are. Why would he say that, Marcus?"

He shoved aside his salad plate, then took a sip of his cola. His eyes almost seemed to darken, their clear depths as eternally deep as an ocean, filled with secrets. "Beats me. I don't have anything to hide."

Intuition told her he lied, and that bruised her confidence in him. God, she didn't want to believe it, but her instincts screamed that he withheld something vitally important.

When she didn't speak, his frown deepened. "You believe him."

"I think there's something you aren't telling me about your past, yes. If it isn't bad, then tell me what it is."

He leaned forward, his voice quiet and reassuring. "You know I'd never do anything to hurt you, right?"

"Of course." She knew that down to the marrow in her bones. "But whatever you're hiding makes me wary. How can I trust a man who is obviously hiding something so big a major officer in the company is willing to risk telling me about it because he's concerned?"

His annoyance turned to a scoff, the curl in his lips indignant. "Tara, with everything we've been through the last few days, you're going to believe a man you don't know over me?" Frustration mirrored in his eyes. "Haven't you ever known anyone you feel down deep in your soul you can trust without thinking about it?"

She nodded. "Yes. Not many people, but yes."

"You *know* me, despite any secrets you think I'm holding." His large frame crowded her at the tiny table. He covered one of her hands with his. Heat shot straight from her fingers to her stomach, arousal spreading with licking, tantalizing flames. "That's the way I feel about you. Your integrity and your honesty tell me I can trust you."

She couldn't meet his eyes, afraid of the vulnerability he might see in her. She looked down at her plate and relished the warmth of his fingers. He pressed gently.

"That's wonderful, Marcus. I just don't know…"

"Then tell me. Do you trust me, or do you trust Jason Forte?"

Her head snapped up. "I don't know what his motivations were for asking me questions about you."

"What did he ask?"

"We didn't get that far before the elevator jerked and I stumbled."

His eyes sharpened. "You said earlier he touched you."

"He pulled me into his arms to keep me from falling."

His nose twitched and he scowled. "Then what?"

"He acted like the proverbial knight in shining armor trying to comfort me."

Marcus' gaze turned harder and less receptive, a flame igniting inside that stroked her sensitivities like a physical touch. "There's more. You're holding back."

She inhaled deeply. "It was nothing. He… I think when it was dark in the elevator that he sort of kissed me."

"What?" The sharp syllable rasped from his lips. His jaw tightened, and she saw anger returning to his eyes. "Son of a bitch. He 'sort of' kissed you?"

"It was just a light brushing, and I'm not even sure it was that. I was stunned by the elevator coming to such an abrupt stop."

Hot emotion filled his eyes. "Did you welcome his kiss?"

Jolted into indignation, she said, "Of course not."

A desolate ache started in her heart. Tara felt his ire and a wave of jealousy coming from him that surprised and gratified her somewhat. Could he be a little possessive?

He took his hand from hers, crumpled his napkin and tossed it in his empty salad bowl.

Maybe she should open her already faltering shield. If she did, she could discover what he buried beneath his often mild-mannered attitude. Something didn't add up.

With a deep breath, she envisioned allowing her white light to dissolve until nothing stood between them to mask emotions. Risk came with the action. Other people's thoughts and feelings could intrude. She'd have to take the gamble.

"I don't trust his motivations any more than I believe you're totally honest with me, Marcus. The truth lies somewhere in between." She leaned closer to him and allowed the sensual thoughts she experienced around him to flow back toward him. The shield operated two ways. When she let things in, she couldn't keep her own emotions a secret. "Wouldn't you agree?"

He blinked, his attention centering on her mouth. "What can I do to prove to you that you don't have to doubt me?"

"I know you care about me or you wouldn't have tried to protect me from Drake. You've been wonderful, Marcus."

His gaze caressed her face. Feathery-light excitement danced over her skin, as if he'd touched her somewhere forbidden with a tantalizing brush of a finger tip. "*Try* to protect you against Drake? I *will* protect you. Don't ever doubt that."

I'm going to melt right here.

He hadn't finished confessing. "I do care about you. Very much."

How could she resist the sincerity she felt flowing from him like a river? Yes, she perceived his protectiveness and knew he meant it one hundred percent. It blew her away. She took another risk and opened up even more. She drew nearer as a forceful yearning formed inside her to understand him.

The heat coming from him almost made her gasp. A tormenting arousal pushed outward to her. He wanted her with a violence that would have knocked her off her feet if she'd been standing. He cared acutely about her and she turned him on.

Amazed, she stayed mute for a moment before saying, "I'm pretty lucky to have a guy like you looking out for me, you know that?"

A smile erased his grim expression. Satisfaction came from him and poured into her. The feeling warmed and teased her with promises. "Why is that?"

"Well, despite the fact you're hiding something from me I also can feel that you're trustworthy in every other way."

Looking a tad stunned, he put his hand over hers again. If anyone bothered to see, Tara knew people would believe they were lovers. "Okay, I guess I can live with that assessment."

She caught a glance at her watch. "My appointment is in less than an hour. I have to get moving."

She drew her hands away, reluctant to leave the tenderness flowing between them.

"Do you mind telling me which lawyer you're visiting and where it is?"

She knew why he asked. If anything odd happened to her between work and the lawyer's office, he'd know where to start looking. Dread snaked over her body. God, she didn't want to think of it like that, but what choice did she have?

"Ethel Allegra is two blocks from here at the law firm of Allegra and Boucher."

"I know where that is. Be careful, please. Keep your eyes and ears peeled and if anything strange happens call me on my cell phone right away."

"And what could you do? You'd be to far away to help me if anything strange did happen, Marcus."

His eyes narrowed, reviewing at the same time they continued scrutinizing with sensual observation. Had she ever met a man so capable of throwing her off-guard and leaving her shaky with need? No, never.

"Oh, believe me, I could do something to help very quickly," he said.

The cockiness in his voice made her stare at him hard. "Such as?"

Before he could answer, the server brought their check. Marcus said he'd get lunch this time and before they left the table she closed her eyes a second and put up her shields once again. Outside the restaurant, the atrium area teemed with people, yet she felt as if she existed alone in this world with him.

He did trust her, but not as much as she would like. Now she wondered what she could do to earn his confidence. His eyes held that fiery concentration she couldn't resist. If she didn't cut and run now, his caring would make her want to yield and agree with whatever he wanted her to do. Drake had handled her that way for years, and though Marcus was twice the man of Drake, she couldn't afford to let Marcus push her agenda one way or the other. Any decisions she made would be because she wanted to do them.

She smiled. "Thank you for being so understanding and for all you've done. I don't know how I'm ever going to repay you."

His gaze forayed over her face, down her neck and over her breasts in a quick but unrestrained once-over. "I can think of at least one way."

Her breath caught. Did he mean—?

"You can buy me one of those great cookies for dessert before you go."

He winked.

* * * * *

"An order of protection can be filed," Ethel Allegra said to Tara as she leaned on her desk and smiled. She tipped her large blue mug to her lips and took a sip of coffee. "We'll set it up for tomorrow at the latest if we can get a time with the judge. Everything is going to work out fine."

Mrs. Allegra—calling her Ethel wouldn't seem right—possessed the kind of presence that screamed competent. Over six feet tall, the lawyer had some extra weight around the middle. With her tailored, together style, no one would disregard her. Her platinum blonde hair was scraped back into a tight bun and her makeup was subtle and professional on her square-jawed, but nicely sculpted face. Her engagement and wedding ring, a six-carat pink diamond, glittered on her long-fingered hand.

Brunhilde.

That's what her name ought to be. For Drake's dangerous, caustic personality, Tara knew she'd need a woman like this. Mrs. Allegra's demeanor, dour and imposing, would scare off many men in court.

Tara wanted to believe what Ethel said, and her confident smile inspired trust. While the offices of Allegra and Boucher verged on plush, Mrs. Allegra refused to charge her anything. As Bettina had said, Mrs. Allegra wouldn't take payment for helping a woman being stalked.

"Mrs. Allegra, I can't tell you how much I appreciate this. I...the rates for some of the other lawyers—"

"No problem. I'm glad Bettina referred you."

The tall lawyer stood and came around the desk as Tara stood. "I'll contact you later today to see if we have a court date and when it will be. In the meantime, be careful."

Tara shook her hand and moments later, she headed out of the office and down to the multilevel parking garage. She glanced at her watch. Her consultation with the law firm had taken the afternoon, and unusual exhaustion crept into her body. Flopping into bed with a good book sounded comforting. She made her way quickly to her car and headed back to the office. She could finish one more hour of work before quitting time.

She didn't savor the idea of sitting in a courtroom soon, but she had to stop Drake. Her life wouldn't be dictated by a madman's actions. She took a steadying breath, aware her heart beat faster and her neck muscles tightened with tension. Even thinking about the man drove her blood pressure up more than late afternoon traffic.

This can't be good for my health. Maybe if I dream about my mystery lover tonight, that'll take the tension away.

Oh yes. A nice bed session with her dream lover would erase what ailed her.

Marcus' smiling face popped into her thoughts. But no. A dream lover didn't come with emotional entanglements. A dream lover didn't keep secrets from her.

Troubled by the events of the morning, she mulled over Jason Forte's strange actions and the intriguing lunch she'd experienced with Marcus. Two men with secrets. Two men who wanted something from her.

As she slid into a parking space on the lowest level of her office building, she made sure her white light barrier surrounded her with mental safety. Glancing around the parking area with caution, she stepped out of her car. She'd no sooner locked the car than she heard a strange noise behind her. She flinched and whirled about.

Chapter Eleven

∞

Drake stood not thirty feet from her, his posture insolent.

Yawning fear roared up and demanded notice.

He grinned and hooked his thumbs in the belt loops of his jeans. "Hey there. I thought I'd never catch up with you."

Tara always thought Drake's smile hid the sins of ages, a charming grin overlaid by a hunger to injure, to despise in the most dangerous way a man could hate a woman. Anyone who didn't know him would think him harmless, or at the least an upstanding guy. He radiated the charisma necessary to bilk old people out of money and fuck unsuspecting women blinded by his military uniform and the honor it implied but didn't guarantee.

His ordinary looks made him easy to ignore on first glance. With his dirty blond hair styled like a new military recruit and boyish features, he appeared younger than his years. His five-foot-eight frame held a wiry strength that could kill. All those years ago she hadn't understood that his sharp aqua green eyes held not mystery, but a calculating, amoral determination to dominate.

If she'd only known from the beginning.

Should have. Would have. None of that helped her now.

Five seconds of screaming panic raced through her, then she hardened her resolve.

"Drake," she said simply, keeping her voice even and unemotional.

"Gee, I thought you'd be *unhappy* to see me." His voice sounded the same, a mellow production laced with a fine, cutting edge.

Her throat wanted to close, emotions she hadn't felt in a long time crawling around inside her like worms putting down root. Anger, malice, a desire to make her pay.

Oh, no, no, no. *They are his emotions. Not mine.*

She'd always experienced his raw and penetrating emotions, and they caught her off-guard like a punch to the belly and scraped away her defenses. He'd been so damn good at it. Nothing had changed.

Time to find a way to transition away from this threat before it blew up in her face.

He walked toward her, his casual saunter saying he expected her to stay put. She held her ground.

"Stop right here," she said. "Don't come any closer."

He ignored her. She moved away at a rapid pace, her steps firm and confident, keys positioned in her right hand to use as a weapon in case he tried something. She refused to let him intimidate her more. *She refused.*

He grabbed her upper arm. Instantly she sprang into action, yanking away from him. She readied to scream, to slice and stab at his face with her keys if necessary.

"Touch me again, and I swear—"

"Whoa, whoa!" Hands out in supplication, he continued a mocking smile. "I mean you no harm."

"Then stay away from me." She backed toward the elevators.

With the attitude of a man approaching a frightened creature, he stepped toward her. "What are you gonna do? I don't think you'll do anything, Tara. You know why? Because you don't have the courage. Never had it and never will. But you have to see the error of your ways. You need to be cleansed."

Cleansed? What the hell was the lunatic talking about?

He grinned. "'When you see a comely woman among the prisoners and are attracted to her, you may take her as your wife.'"

"What?"

"It's in the Bible, Tara. When we're rejoined, you'll read the Holy Book every day and learn its rules."

He'd gone around the bend for certain. He'd always hated his parents' ultra-conservative religious rants.

Boiling resentment almost made her step close enough to get in his face. But no, that would be stupid and dangerous. "Your intimidation and threats won't work. Leave me alone, Drake."

"How can I leave you when I've found you again?" He spread his hands in petition. "You think those years in prison made me forget what we had? Admit it. You missed me. We always belonged together. Sure, you needed to be taught a lesson once in a while, but we were perfect together. We'll renew our vows, darlin' and then you'll understand you belong to me."

Ice resided in his soul, and it penetrated deep into hers like shards of glass. Her body resisted the sensation, but her earlier openness with Marcus left a fracture open so that Drake's emotions ran into her freely. She didn't have time to rebuild the splinter and concentrate on keeping him out of her head.

She'd experienced his brand of hate so often it became an indelible stain on her psyche where it festered and lived. As he glared, his gaze gleaming with dark intentions, she knew no amount of reasoning would tame the revolting beast gnawing at the last of his humanity.

He latched on to her arm and started to pull her toward him. Tara used a blocking motion that caused him to lose his grip for a second. He twisted and jammed her back against a car with a lightning move. As his weight squished her, she uttered a gasp of pain and protest. She shoved the long key into his ribs with a grunt of fury.

"Shit!" He jumped back. "Bitch! You fucking bitch!"

He stalked toward her and everything crawled into a weird slow motion. Her limbs felt thick, her heart pounding in dull, painful thuds as memories of another beating surged into her mind. That beating had almost killed her.

"Stop!" a deep, familiar voice commanded from nearby. "You lay a hand on her again, and I'll break every fucking bone in your body."

Hope raced through Tara's body at the rough, authoritative sound in Marcus' voice. She saw him coming to her rescue from near the elevators. When Drake charged her again, Marcus broke into a run. She darted away, her heart ramming into her throat. Adrenaline spiked and she pushed her limbs into quick action.

Marcus' powerful arm looped around Drake's neck, and brought the bastard to a halt.

Marcus' face twisted into a combat-hardened warrior. His lips held a sneer of contempt. Much larger than Drake, he possessed an advantage.

Marcus barely seemed to break a sweat. "I said, if you come near her, or speak to her again, you'll wish you'd never been born. She's under my protection."

Under my protection.

Primitive female instincts reacted to Marcus' statement. A feral bolt of excitement leapt to action inside her at Marcus' possessive words. Whether she wanted it or not, the sight of him kicking Drake's ass turned her on.

Drake strangled, his hands going up to the grip cutting off his air. "Son of a—"

To her surprise, Drake suddenly sagged in Marcus' hold. Marcus tossed him away, and Drake landed in a heap near the wheel of another vehicle. Coughing and groaning, his eyes flashing with loathing, Drake struggled to his feet and then trotted off toward the exit.

"I don't think…I don't think that will be the last I see of him," she said and wrapped her arms around her upper body and quivered in reaction.

Marcus turned to her, his expression filled with anger. He started toward her, and released from the terror, she met him halfway. When he gathered her close, she looped her arms around his neck and held on tight, her keys still gripped in her fingers. Her heart pounded a relentless tune. His fingers speared into her hair, caressing with touches that brought comfort and safety. She buried her face in his shoulder and snuggled into his embrace.

"Are you okay?" he asked. "Are you hurt?"

"No. He wanted to hurt me. He might have if you hadn't come along." She pulled back a little to look into his face. "Perfect timing."

He brushed away a tendril of her long hair as it fell into her face. He kept his other arm looped around her waist as if he feared she'd escape. "Yeah, perfect timing." To her surprise, she felt his body tremble. Tenderness swept into his eyes. "Damn it, Tara."

"What's wrong?"

He laughed without humor. "When I saw him holding you, I wanted to rip his fucking head off and feed it to him. If he'd harmed you—" He shook his head and wouldn't finish.

"I'm fine. How did you happen to be here just in time?"

"Something told me to come down here."

"Something?"

His gaze went distant, and he looked over her head into space. "A feeling. We should call the police."

He took out his cell phone and reported the attack to the police.

Despite the adrenaline spiking her system, she no longer felt one hundred percent stable on her feet. Her ankle throbbed.

As if he could read her mind, he reached out and cupped her face. He leaned forward and pressed a light kiss to her forehead. "What's wrong?"

"My ankle hurts."

"Lean against me and take the pressure off."

She drew in a breath of his aftershave and nestled her nose into his neck. God, it felt good to have a man hold her with nothing but tenderness and protection. She'd never felt such emotions with any man but him. Not even when she'd fancied herself in love with Drake. She didn't like violence, but Marcus had showed his strength and willingness to defend, and the aphrodisiac ran hotly in her blood. Warm arousal taunted her breasts and pussy. A strange way to feel after surviving an attack, she knew, but she couldn't seem to quell the reaction.

She allowed Marcus' emotions to enter her. Affection and anger ran in circles inside him.

Quiet surrounded them and chased away fear. "That was some headlock you put on Drake. Where did you learn that?"

"The military."

"Oh. Of course."

"You weren't doing too badly for yourself. You were about ready to put the bastard's eye out. The keys were a good idea."

"He's so strong my self-defense training didn't do much. The way he appeared like that so quickly, he had to be watching me or following me. Damn it."

He kissed her forehead and sighed. "I can teach you some other defensive drills. I guarantee you could take down a man larger than yourself with some of the tricks I know."

Tears crept into her eyes, and she wanted to swear and brush them away. "Isn't that the point of self-defense? Being able to react to surprise attacks? When you think about it, it wasn't even much of a surprise. I had warning."

Those frown lines appeared between his eyebrows. "You're being too hard on yourself. You did damned well."

"I hope that jab to the ribs left a hole in him. I should have aimed first for his eyes." She gave a sarcastic smile. "Or better yet, his nuts."

Marcus snorted a laugh. "Don't berate yourself." Silence fell over their cocoon for a few moments until he said, "You know he's going to keep trying to get to you."

Part of her wished he hadn't been blunt about that fact. "I know."

"You can't be alone anymore. At least not until he's arrested."

"And you're volunteering for the duty?"

"Damn right."

When she gazed into his eyes, a heated, possessive look took over his expression. A tingle started in her belly. How could she have ever, *ever* thought of him as nerdy?

"Thank you for coming to my rescue. It sounds cheesy, but you've become a real knight in shining armor."

A devilish grin caught his lips. "You're one helluva woman. Have I ever told you that?"

"No, but thank you. I'm feeling kind of useless right about now."

"Drake doesn't have a hold on you. Don't ever let him make you think you're not worth it. Because you *are* worth a man's love."

The word love on his lips caused a sweet tremor to pass through her. She knew her emotions must show plainly. "Thank you, Marcus."

Not long after, a police car came down the ramp and proceeded in their direction. Nerves made Tara's stomach cramp.

God, Tara, you are being such a wimp. Buck up.

When the officers exited the vehicle, she knew what she had to do. She must press charges against Drake. After the police officers took the report, they said Drake would be charged with assault and domestic violence.

"I suppose I'd better call Mrs. Allegra and let her know about this," Tara said.

Marcus shook his head. "An order of protection isn't going to help much. I told you that. Like I said, it will only escalate his behavior."

She didn't want to believe him, but down deep she wondered if he might be right. "I don't know…"

Marcus gripped her shoulder lightly and looked deeply into her eyes. "Do you trust me?"

She did trust him. With her life. "Yes."

"Then call Mrs. Allegra and forget the order of protection."

She sighed and nodded, willing to believe that he knew what he was talking about. She stood with Marcus in the cold garage and tried to hold onto a feeling of security while it lasted.

* * * * *

After work, Marcus followed Tara's vehicle down her street, aware Drake could come out of nowhere to cause more havoc. A sadistic creep like Drake wouldn't give up easily and that worried Marcus.

When they pulled up at her house, Marcus exited his vehicle swiftly and made sure he stayed right beside her when she left her car.

He put his hand on the small of her back and kept a keen eye on their surroundings as they went into the house. Wind teased at their bodies and demanded attention. As they stepped into the house, a few raindrops splattered the house.

"Great. Rain again," she said. "I don't know whether to be happy or not."

"Be happy. It looks good on you."

She turned a weak, but appreciative smile onto him. "You too."

Damn, but the susceptibility he sensed within her caught him off-guard. She might be a tough woman, but she'd been bruised and battered today and deserved a feeling of security. They agreed to tell only Bettina what had happened in the parking garage.

"I'm checking the perimeter. Stay inside and keep the security system engaged," he said.

She smiled, tossed her purse on the couch and peeled off her trench coat. "That sounds like something from the military."

Feeling edgy, his battle-savvy training online, he said, "It is."

A worried frown touched her lips. God, he couldn't spend this much time thinking about her lips and remain sane the next second, the next minute, or the next day. Everything about her screamed soft and vulnerable, from her dark hair to the concern in her eyes.

Temptation pulled him closer, and he drew in her scent with heady enjoyment. She intoxicated him, drove him to do and say things he shouldn't. How did she entangle him in her web? Maybe from the first day he'd seen her in the cubicle at work he'd been a goner. Elemental requirements stirred like a deep, dark beast inside him. He'd shoved away the chaotic needs her presence generated until recently. Now those feelings refused denial. He knew what he must do.

"We need to talk," he said.

The worry in her eyes deepened to a tiny alarm. "About what?"

He opened his mind to her thoughts and felt anxiety that grew from a shock to the system. She hid tension and dread, but he experienced it fluttering inside her like the wings of a terrified bird.

"Give me a few moments and then we'll take all the time we need," he said.

Reaching out for her would be so easy. When he'd drawn her into his arms in the parking garage it had been automatic.

He'd wanted nothing more than to cradle her close and assure himself Drake hadn't harmed her.

He stepped outside and toured the grounds around the house. Wind rustled the trees into a sibilant whisper. Clouds scuttled across the sun. A dog barked a few houses down, but after letting out a few sharp yips, it shut up. He sensed no threat.

He'd made up his mind to contact Ben Darrock and explain the situation. Ben might not like it, but at this point, he couldn't afford to leave Tara here alone. Hell, this would make things more difficult. Trying to run an investigation into Jason Forte's weird activities and protect Tara from a crazed ex wouldn't be easy.

He put in a call to Ben. Ben answered his secure number on the second ring.

He explained the entire situation to Ben. "I'm staying with her."

A pause made Marcus wonder if Ben planned to object. If Ben nixed the idea, what could he do?

For Tara he would break the rules and even defy his direct supervisor. The realization stunned him.

Holy shit, I've got it bad.

"Is her situation unrelated to the Jason Forte case?" Ben asked.

Marcus hesitated, but only for a second. "Completely unrelated. But there's something strange going on. The way she responded to Forte tells me she knows he's not the average, normal Joe Blow on the street."

"You think she's in league with him?"

"No. God no."

"Are you saying she can read people the way you do? That she's psychic?"

Marcus rubbed the tight muscles at the back of his neck. "That's what I'm beginning to think. At the very least she's sensitive and knows something is wrong but isn't certain what it is. I know this isn't standard operating procedure, and I shouldn't get myself involved with her problems, but she's a sitting duck if I don't help her."

"She has self-defense training and a security system?"

Ah hell. Here it comes. A flat out order not to get involved. "Correct."

"Then why do you feel you need to protect her?"

"She may be a tough woman, but I'm a tougher agent."

"Ah, is that what it is?" Ben's voice held amusement. "Are you sure you're not getting in over your head?"

Affronted, Marcus said, "You doubt my skills?"

"Not at all. The problem comes when an agent allows personal feelings like affection or sexual attraction to mar his judgment. Dorky filled me in. She said that your mental shields may deteriorate if you allow your connection with Tara to grow closer."

Oh yeah. No doubt about it. Sexual attraction figured into the equation. Nevertheless, he would not abandon Tara. "I can handle it."

A long silence made Marcus nervous. Ben cleared his throat. "I trust your instincts. If this affects your ability to continue your pursuit of Jason Forte, we're in trouble. A man's desire to protect a woman can send him on journeys he shouldn't take."

Needing to defend his position, he continued. "She did a good job with Drake in the parking garage up to a point, then the asshole's physical strength overwhelmed her. If I hadn't showed up, there is a good chance she would have been severely injured or killed. I'm going to show her some more defense moves."

"Then I suggest you take advantage of the situation," Ben said.

Marcus wasn't sure he'd heard Ben right. "What?"

"There's more than one thing going on here. She needs protection from this Drake character, and she might know more about Jason Forte than you realize. Use your special mental talents to discover what is going on in her head. If she does know something about Jason, you'll find out."

Uh-huh. Not the answer he'd expected, but a good one.

When Marcus didn't speak, Ben said, "I don't have any problem with you staying with Tara and discovering what she knows. She could be valuable to the investigation."

Providence must be with him. He'd expected Ben to display his legendary resolve to stay hard-line on case protocol. Maybe he didn't know the Scot as well as he thought.

Relief filled Marcus after Ben signed off. He entered the house with a new sense of purpose. After making sure the security system operated properly, he took off his suit jacket and hung it in the hall closet. A coat hung there along with a couple of ball caps, a visor and a scarf. The ball caps all said something about Wintyler Museum. Perhaps she'd visited there? Suddenly he wanted to do more than protect and hold her, he wanted to know more secrets. He wanted to feel the essence that made Tara alive, absorb that energy into himself and explore her.

She wandered into the living room wearing a short-sleeved polo shirt. Navy blue shorts clung to her curved butt and showed off her long, elegant legs in a way he'd never seen before. Athletic shoes covered her feet. She looked good enough to eat. Literally.

He snapped out of it when she smiled, a pink tinge dusting her cheeks. She'd caught him ogling her breasts like a pimply pubescent boy who'd just realized he liked girls for the first time.

"Why don't you take a load off?" He caught a whiff of something delicious cooking in the kitchen. "That smells like dinner."

"It's pot roast in the slow cooker."

"My favorite."

One of her elegant brows lifted. "Can you stay for dinner?"

"Of course." He walked toward her and kept his mind open. "You didn't think I was going to leave you here alone, did you?"

She sighed. "I thought you'd insist on staying."

"I do."

When he stood near, her pupils dilated and he felt a jump in her pulse rate. Pleasure moved through him. God, he could forget dinner, forget the investigation, forget the fact he probed her mind for answers without her knowing it. Instead, he'd lay her down on the couch and explore her body the way he would have to investigate her mind. Protective instincts roared inside him, demanding he do everything in his power to keep her safe. If that meant moving into her house, he'd do it.

He cupped her shoulders. "You've had a rough day, and I'm not leaving you alone."

Her gaze grew soft. "I don't think I want you to leave. This whole thing with Drake…"

Marcus gently brushed his hands upward until he cradled her face. "He's never going to hurt you again."

A small furrow dented the skin between her eyebrows. "This is dangerous."

"What is?"

"If Drake tries something again, you could be hurt." She slipped away from his touch. "This situation with him isn't your problem."

"I'm making it my problem."

She frowned and then turned and headed for the kitchen. "What's my next move?"

"How about opening a bottle of wine to go with dinner?"

She reached for a merlot in the small wine bottle stand on the counter. "That's not what I meant."

As he rolled up his sleeves and gathered utensils to set the table, he threw her a glance. "I know. I thought it might get your mind off what happened today."

"Another clever idea."

"Thanks."

She set out two wineglasses and used a wine bottle opener to remove the cork on the wine. Every movement seemed orchestrated with smoothness and precision.

He didn't feel clever. Instead, he felt like the biggest buffoon in the world around her grace and beauty. Some people, even those under tremendous pressure, radiated staggering confidence. She was filled with dignity, good nature and sincerity. If anything, her qualities added to his out-of-this-world sexual attraction.

They decided to add a salad to the meal. While he chopped tomatoes and mushrooms, he noted how simple she'd kept her home. The heavy salad bowls in terra cotta and green, the plain handles on the stainless steel utensils. A single glance around the kitchen confirmed things he'd wondered about her for weeks. Though tasteful, her home held a sense of transition, as if she didn't expect to stay here forever.

Soon they settled at the table and ate.

Unexpectedly she asked, "You're going to say I need full-time protection, aren't you?"

She'd caught him flat-footed, but he didn't lie. "Yes."

She moved her food around on her plate with her fork. The small wrought iron chandelier above the table threw soft light on her face. "Having someone underfoot twenty-four hours a day... I don't know..."

Determined to bolster her self-belief, he said, "You can handle anything but a man's unrelenting violence."

She laughed softly. "You have a great deal of confidence in someone who couldn't keep her assailant away. If it hadn't been for you, I don't know what I would have done."

He didn't want to think about it too deeply. "Drake has serious mental issues and reasoning with him isn't an option. Don't allow his insanity to feed insecurities."

A faraway look came into her eyes. "I'd almost forgotten what my marriage did to me." She sipped wine. "Correction. What I allowed it to do to me. I can't bear the thought of Drake controlling me that way again."

"You've created a good life. You're not the woman you were when you married him."

A long, tempting length of her hair fell over her cheek as she glared at her plate. "Funny you should describe it that way. I think, from the beginning, he was terrified of my power."

He sensed more meaning behind her words, but he didn't want to force an explanation out of her. "All weak men are afraid of secure women. Many do anything they can to stop a female from being independent."

Tears shimmered in her eyes. In that moment, he thought her brown and blue eyes the prettiest he'd seen, even if they filled with unwelcome sadness. Desire rode him. Any man who couldn't cherish Tara for the intelligent, creative woman inside her didn't deserve her love.

Love.

Now there was a word he couldn't afford to invest in right now. Desire. Concern. Friendship. He felt all those for her. He thrust aside thoughts of deeper feelings for the time being.

He finished his pot roast and shoved aside his plate. "Unless you order me out of your house, I'm your shadow. I *am* your protection."

Tara slowly stood and gathered their plates. "As I said before, you could get hurt. I don't think I could take that."

"And remember what I told you?" He stood and helped her bring the dishes into the kitchen. "I won't abandon you when you need help."

As they stacked the dirty dishes in the dishwasher, the companionable silence stretched. After they'd cleaned up the kitchen and dining area in relative quiet, Tara started to refill their glasses. Her hand shook and she slopped some wine over the side of her glass.

"Whoa," he said softly as he took a napkin and wiped up the dribble.

Embarrassed, she put the wine bottle down on the table and engaged the crystal stopper. "I can't seem to get a grip. I still feel jumpy."

"Come on. Let's go into the living room. You need to decompress, and I have some questions for you."

Marcus' declaration didn't ease her tension. Since the attack she'd felt wired, her appetite mostly nonexistent, and some of her muscles ached. Wineglass in hand, she walked with him into the living room and sank down on the couch, realizing that her attraction to him also made life more difficult. She stared into her wine. Jumbled thoughts threatened to take over any sense of calm. Coming down from danger left her teetering on a wobbly pedestal.

"Hey."

She started as Marcus' deep, soothing voice came from behind her. When he walked around the side of the couch, she couldn't help but admire him. This man had already given her so much she couldn't repay. On top of his sincere caring, passion boiled right below the surface.

His hair stayed pulled back, and the long angles of his face looked harsher. His eyes, though, held an infinite gentleness she couldn't escape. He'd rolled up the sleeves on his white shirt to the elbows. He looked sophisticated and nothing like the snarling, ready-to-kick-ass man from the car garage.

How could she reconcile this civilized man with the savage tendencies she knew lay beneath the surface? That sort of deception started her descent into hell with Drake years ago.

"Hey back at you," she said nervously.

He sank onto the couch beside her. "You all right?"

With a plethora of emotions vying for attention, she didn't want them to spill over. If they escaped, she'd become a one-woman pity party. "No. I don't think so."

He propped one knee on the cushion and an arm along the back of the couch. "Do you want to talk about it?"

His open stance, not crowded or demanding, made her relax. "Part of me does."

He learned forward slightly. "Then let that part speak first. The part that doesn't want to talk now can speak later."

"Okay." She cleared her throat, then took a small sip of wine. "What happened earlier today is repeating over and over in my head."

"Trauma will do that to a person. It'll take some time to ease. You need to talk about it now before it becomes too ingrained inside you."

The wineglass felt too heavy and she placed it on the coffee table. "I've read about the effects of trauma on a person's psyche and physical well-being. I don't have time for violence to spill across my mind twenty-four hours a day. I need to be ready for Drake's next move."

Unlike many men she'd known, including her father and Drake, Marcus truly listened. The serious cast in his eyes proved it. It gave her comfort even in the middle of extreme dismay.

"Violence marked you a long time ago. You can't escape it, drown it, or hide from it. Otherwise you become a statistic year after year — one of those people who lives on medication to drown their pain," he said.

She glanced at her wineglass. "Do you think that's what I'm doing now?"

"Of course not."

Quiet enfolded them for a short time before he spoke again. "What major thing set Drake off in the past? What made him come unglued the most?"

Alarm bells sounded inside her. How could she tell him? If she did, he may turn away from her forever, believing she'd lost her mind.

"It's not important. As you said, Drake has problems with rationality. We can't change that."

He placed his wine on the table next to hers and leaned forward, his eyes intent. "Yes, but if I'm going to understand how his mind works, knowing what set him off might help."

Suspicion niggled at her. Uncertain, she asked, "Why does it matter?"

Frustration crowded into his eyes. "Knowing will make it easier to help you."

"No. I can't."

Impatience made those mobile, intriguing lips tighten. "You can't, or you won't?"

What could she say without sounding moronic?

She waited, and the irritation left his eyes. "Why don't we talk about something else and get your mind off Drake?"

Relieved, she nodded and leaned her head back on the couch.

"What do you think of Jason?" he asked. "Honestly."

He seemed interested in maligning Jason, and while she couldn't say she blamed him, his mysterious vendetta worried her.

She closed her eyes and tried to relax. "He's a very unusual man."

"In what way?"

She smiled. "Why are you so interested?"

"I think he's a dangerous man."

"Two dangerous men in my life? I don't think I can stand the excitement. Are you sure it isn't three dangerous men?"

He ignored her question and continued. "Tell me what you know about him."

She clasped her hands together over her stomach. "He gets under my skin, and I don't think it has anything to do with being a chief financial officer in the company. He has an arrogance that makes me uncomfortable. Sometimes he radiates hostility. I've seen him push people around with verbal barbs. He's immune to everyone else's retaliation from what I can tell."

"How?"

"No matter what he does, he's never reprimanded by the higher-ups. I think there were complaints about him to personnel for sexual harassment and other charges and nothing ever happens to him."

"He made you more than uncomfortable during the trip in the elevator, didn't he?"

"Yes. That day when he was with you in the copier room was bizarre. Jason is an all-around strange man, but I couldn't tell you why other than he's a jerk."

His penetrating gaze wouldn't let her go. "I think it's more than that. When he gets near you, does it seem like he's trying to read your mind?" When she didn't answer, he asked, "You can feel people's intentions, their fears, their emotions, can't you?"

She couldn't have been more startled if he'd cracked her over the head with a frying pan. How did he know that? Fear tightened her throat.

"No." She couldn't go down this path where he knew she had psychic abilities. She wouldn't.

Afraid, she stood and walked away, not certain where she planned to go or what she'd do. She balked like a lamb, a creature knowing its own slaughter came soon.

He caught up to her outside her bedroom and clasped her upper arm gently. She swung around.

"Please don't run from this," he said.

She shivered, so aware of the big hand gently encircling her arm that she couldn't think straight. While she didn't fear his touch, it reminded her too much of how Drake had snagged her arm in the parking garage. She pulled away from Marcus.

He must have sensed her unease, because he said, "I'm not Drake. Whatever made him go off on you isn't going to do the same to me."

"What I can do affects people differently. I can't conceal it forever, no matter what I do. But I can hide it from as many people as I can for as long as I can."

He drew close enough to kiss.

"Tell me," he said in a low, soothing voice.

His nearness, so potent and rich on her senses, made her body heat with a clench of desire. "I don't think that should be my first priority. What I do need to know is how to defend myself against Drake."

"Let's work off some tension, then. We can push the furniture around in the living room, and I can show you some moves."

Show me some moves, eh?

Oh, yeah. She could well imagine what types of moves he could show a woman. The thought made her body yearn for his nearness to continue, even though she knew it would wrestle away her control.

He frowned. "Wait a minute. How's your ankle feel? Maybe we shouldn't be doing this."

She shook her head. "It's hardly sore. Let's do it."

She was ready to give in to whatever came next.

Chapter Twelve

ଋ

Tara went to her bedroom to change into sweats. The whole time she switched clothing, a heady sense of anticipation simmered in her blood. Butterflies did pirouettes in her stomach. She could fool herself all she wanted. Gathering new self-defense moves would be a good thing, but her motivations had as much to do with wanting his touch as it did learning new tricks. Their conversation had unnerved her, and she'd rejoiced when he'd steered them in another direction. She couldn't afford to let him know about her psychic abilities. Down that path lay mistrust and discomfort. She wouldn't reveal herself to anyone that way again.

When she returned to the living room, her throat about closed up because he looked delicious enough to eat. He'd obviously retrieved his gym bag from the car. He'd peeled off his shirt, and he wore nothing but blue jogging shorts, socks and athletic shoes. She felt like she'd never seen his naked chest before. Tight, developed sinew outlined his shoulders and his impressive arms. She loved the way dark hair feathered over his pectorals and defined six-pack stomach. That thatch of hair trailed into the waistband of his shorts and made her wonder once more what his cock would look like.

Her face flushed.

And his legs. Oh, his legs. Long and well-developed, they looked like they could run for miles or deliver a powerhouse kick. She allowed her glance to wander downward, her curiosity about what he looked like completely naked threatening to derail her concentration. She'd seen men with powerful upper bodies with incredibly skinny legs, but his muscled thighs and calves, covered with a dusting of hair, turned her on.

Remembering her vision of him that one day in the employee lounge, she realized this Marcus fit that picture of a tough, go-get-'em Marine. Perhaps he harbored as many secrets as she did. Determined to find out, Tara decided that while they worked on defense moves, she would open her mind to him again and see what she could detect.

"Something wrong?" he asked.

Apparently, he didn't know that his blatant masculinity had the power to make her mouth water, her breathing to come faster and her heart to beat frantically.

"Nothing. Let's get started."

"We won't do any of the harder moves until we can pick up a mat or something. We don't want to get hurt."

She smiled. "I like how you say that. We."

He grinned back. "Of course. I know with the right instruction you could do some major damage to me."

One of her eyebrows winged up, and she put her hands on her hips. "The right instruction. I've had some instruction already, remember?"

He winked. "Yeah, I remember."

He started walking around her, making a big circle. Stalking her, trying to intimidate.

"This isn't going to work, Hyatt."

He laughed, the sound throaty and sexy. "Oh yeah. It is. Think of me as the bad guy."

"That's going to be hard to do."

He made a growl in his throat and came at her. Defenses up, she readied for his attack.

He stopped before he'd taken two quick steps. "See, you're ready."

She laughed, her breath coming hard from the scare. "You jerk."

His grin said he didn't take offense. "That's right. Think of me as the jerk. I'm here to do bodily harm, and you've got only a few seconds to respond. What do you do?"

She tensed as he came closer. "Kick your ass."

A low chuckle left his throat, and his eyes betrayed him with a humorous sparkle. "That's more like it."

He charged and she sidestepped. He whirled and reached for her, but she dashed away.

He followed her. "You've got nowhere to go. Do you surrender?"

"No."

"That's my girl."

The patronizing tone made her mad. "I'm not your girl."

His eyes narrowed and his mouth curved into a feral grin. "Work with me here. Remember, I'm a scumbucket. A guy who will catcall one moment, then try to pinch your ass the next."

She stopped edging away from him. "I'm not trying to get away from guys like that. I'm trying to defend myself against Drake. He does a hell of a lot more than catcall and pinch ass."

Marcus nodded. "So what? My method is working. It's making you mad."

Madder that he was right, she frowned. "You're a pest."

"I'm worse than that. I've got a mean streak, and I wanna eat you alive."

His eyes, normally such a kind blue, turned impassioned and mimicked deadly intent or the desire for hard, hot sex.

She couldn't be certain which.

Immediately her heart took up the beat, her body heating. Before she could tap into his thoughts, he charged. She ducked away, throwing her leg out so that he'd trip over it. Instead, he dodged her trick and came at her once more. Mercy wasn't on his list, because he countered her with lightning-fast actions blocking everything she tried.

She could tell he tempered his strength, but during one of her attempts to trip him, he swung out too quickly and cracked her one in the shoulder. Pain vaulted into the joint and she staggered.

"Shit." He moved toward her. "Are you all right? I didn't mean—"

"Come on," she said with vehemence and backed away from him, unwilling to let up the fight. "Is that all you've got?"

His eyes narrowed and determination flashed through his expression. "Hell no."

"Then give it to me."

Blatant male appreciation flooded his eyes. "Oh, I could give it to you all right."

She tried to trip him and he reversed the action, her feet shooting out from under her. Before she could fall, he jerked her against him, hard chest against soft breasts. Her hands clutched at his shoulders and his muscles quivered. Without taking time to think, she allowed her fingers to trace down until they touched his chest.

Hair tickled her fingers and she couldn't help a sharp inhalation. "Marcus."

"Yeah?"

"You're…" She swallowed hard. "Fast."

"You could do it, too, if someone trained you."

If someone trained you.

Another vision of what he might mean popped into her head. In her mind's eye, she imagined him kissing her, and she took another deep breath to return a little sanity. His eyes blazed down on her, his nostrils flaring with the effort and maybe something else.

"Isn't that what you're doing now?" she asked.

"This is just the beginning."

"You're quicker than I am. Stronger."

He nodded. "That's why you have to be cleverer."

He released her and they returned to defensive positions. Her heart pounded a relentless beat, her pulse fluttering as she prepared for his next sally. He sprung toward her, and she flitted away, her lightning-fast move sending him crashing into the couch and falling onto his ass with a grunt.

Triumph made her celebrate. She pumped one fist in the air. "Yeah!"

She laughed, the sound bursting out of her throat on a high-pitched giggle she couldn't control.

He sat, legs spread out in defeat. His lips twitched as if he might start laughing with her. "Damn, that was good. Think you can do that again?"

She crossed her arms. "Of course."

"Sure you can."

The doubt in his voice set her off. "I could have hurt you."

"You could have, but it would have taken more force."

Once more they fought, their actions tempered by his restrained strength.

On one rally, he came up behind her. His arm slipped around her upper chest, and he thrust a muscled thigh between her legs to throw her off balance. She squirmed involuntarily. One hand slipped over her stomach and pressed her tight against him. His hand felt so big and warm. When he slipped his hand into her sweats and palmed her naked stomach, she writhed in his hold.

"Marcus, what are you doing? This isn't on the menu."

"Are you sure? Does it make you mad? Make you want to fight?"

No. It makes me want you.

His breath rasped in her ear as he nosed her hair aside and whispered, "What are you going to do now?"

Now would be the time to open her mind to his and see what secrets lay inside his thoughts. She allowed her white and gold shield to drop.

Visions slipped into her with lightning speed, and she gasped from the impact of their clarity. A blinding white light filled her head before she saw Marcus 's desires in full color and experienced what he wanted from his point of view. All sensations rushed together and formed a reality she couldn't ignore. A bolt of heat filled his cock as he mentally reviewed everything he wanted to do to her. His thoughts filled her head.

In his mind, he turned her to face him. Tara was naked, warm and willing in his embrace. Marcus kissed her, experienced the softness, the texture of her lips under his. His tongue plunged inside her mouth and devoured with hot strokes. She tasted fresh, delicious, hungry. Her nipples hardened against his fingers. She squirmed against him, restless and eager.

Unable to wait, he slipped his fingers between her legs and found wet pussy lips. Tara's breath caught as he probed and manipulated, her hot cream moistening his fingers. He dropped to his knees and immediately parted her. Her clit looked stiff and swollen. He breathed deep and sighed as her musky scent made his cock lengthen and harden. His tongue brushed over that tiny pearl, and she jerked and moaned. He smiled as he savored the sound, taking it inside him.

Primitive male need demanded he stake a claim, do anything to show her that she was his. Another lick made her twitch and sigh, her fingers burrowing into his hair. Yes, yes. He wanted this as if he demanded food and water to live. Her taste spurred him on. With long, devouring licks, he claimed her. Her deliciousness made him dizzy and he enveloped her clit in his mouth and sucked, flicking his tongue over her flesh at the same time.

He jerked away from her and the connection broke. She whirled around to look at him. His gaze trapped hers, stunned. His chest heaved up and down with each breath, his hands clutched at his sides as if he feared reaching for her.

Did he know what she'd done? That she'd invaded his fantasies without his permission? Could he somehow feel it?

Shame and extreme excitement warred inside her for a place. What she'd experienced went beyond anything she could have imagined. Her breathing still sluiced through her parted lips in amazement and the exertion of their mock battle.

Shaken by his thoughts, another part of Tara fiercely enjoyed his need to possess her in some small way. She wanted everything he showed her with excruciating detail. Her body reacted to his visional desires, a deep throbbing centering high inside her. She wanted Marcus' cock to brand her with raging heat and hardness that would breach her wide and deep.

She ached. God, how much she wanted him to—

"What was that?" he asked. "What did you do?"

Oh no, no. How could she explain it to him without giving away everything?

"I didn't do anything."

He frowned. "Don't lie to me."

His harsh words took her off-guard, and she stumbled to answer. "I don't know what you're talking about."

"I think you do. It felt like someone was reaching around inside my head looking for answers."

How could he know what she'd felt? With mind snooping, she'd never had anyone realize what she'd done.

Dawning understanding took over his face. "So that's how you knew what Jason Forte was doing that day in the copier room when I felt so damned weak."

She shook her head. "I don't know what you mean."

Marcus advanced and she edged toward the hallway. "Yes, you do. You can sometimes venture into people's minds."

A cold shiver passed through her body. At first, she didn't know whether to panic or to abandon fear. She could keep on denying it, but she knew him well enough to recognize his intelligence. He would never relent until he knew the truth. A shaking started in the pit of her stomach as the unwanted panic arrived. She started down the hallway and he caught up with her, grasping her shoulders and turning her around.

"Wait."

She pulled out of his grip. "You've got the prize, Marcus. You guessed my big, bad secret."

"Don't run from me. Please," he said, his eyes filled with a need to comprehend more.

A lump grew in her throat. "Why do you care?"

He sighed and exasperation crossed his face. "Because I care about you. I wasn't showing you the defensive moves to hurt you or humiliate you. I want you to be safe."

"I know that."

"Then why are you afraid to admit that you can see into my mind?"

Fear rose as she dared look deep into his eyes. A wave of compassion came from him and Tara knew he wouldn't berate her for her empathic and telepathic talent. Relief fought with the tension in her muscles.

Uncertain where to start, she said, "Since I was a child I've had visions of things to come. From the time I could talk, I drove my parents nuts because I could predict things that would happen and sometimes I had telepathic abilities. They wanted me to keep quiet about the strange things I saw and felt."

He gently gripped her shoulders again. "What kinds of strange things?"

"I can sometimes feel people's emotions and know their intent beforehand. Bullies had a hard time with me because I could always predict what they planned before they could get the upper hand."

As his fingers smoothed over her arms, sweet tremors of excitement tingled in her stomach. She couldn't contain the reaction, her heart starting a new and frantic beat. "You believe me?"

He tucked a strand of hair behind her ear, and when he spoke, his voice held tenderness. "I believe you. More than you know. I think I could teach you a little about empaths."

Passion entered his eyes, a hot and hungry look that drew her closer to him.

"How could you teach me more?" she asked, confused.

"I know a lot about extrasensory perception."

Surprised and somehow relieved, she smiled. "Then you don't think I'm crazy for admitting that I know things about people because I can...because I can sometimes read their intentions?"

"Of course not." He dipped down and whispered in her ear. "I'm not going to hurt you. Feel what I feel, take me into you. Know who I really am." His hands slipped up her shoulders, over her neck. She shivered lightly. He cupped her face with both hands. "Tell me how it is. Make me understand. You saw my fantasy, didn't you?"

Heat burned her face. "Yes."

As his eyes drifted closed, she felt a nudge in her brain, as if he wanted inside to see her dreams and desires. Her eyelids fluttered closed in response.

"Oh my God," she whispered. "You can...you can see into other's minds, too."

A swift, stomach-melting wave of pleasure quickened her breath. Liquid and sensual, the feeling of him inside her head made her quake. She'd done this to people many times in the past, before Drake had beaten the idea out of her. Shaken to the core, she waited in breathless anticipation for what Marcus would do next.

His warm breath tickled her earlobe and caused quivers to roll up her spine. Overpowering desire reached for her, body and soul. She knew in a stunning instant that his longing for her reached a zenith he couldn't ignore.

As he probed her mind, she let him see her dreams in one overwhelming flood. He became the man who made love to her each night with mouth, tongue and cock.

He released her and sprang back. "Shit." Marcus' chest rose and fell rapidly, his hands clenched at his sides. "You're the one in my dreams." He swallowed hard. "I dream about a woman at night. In the dreams we never finished making love, until the other night."

Tara placed her palms on her burning cheeks. Recognition flooded her. "How? How did we find each other in our dreams?"

"I don't know. Maybe because we've got a strong friendship? Because we've been trying to deny that we want each other?"

"How long have you had the dreams?"

"Since I started working at Douglas Financial Group."

She nodded, astonishment striking her silent. She swallowed hard and managed to say, "That's when I started having the dreams. The day you first came to work."

The implication stunned her, and she could tell from the amazement in his eyes that he was, too. A few seconds later, his flabbergasted expression altered significantly.

A feral heat filled his eyes, and for one moment old wounds opened. Fear rushed in to surprise her, and she backed up to the wall. He might be gentle and considerate, a good man on all fronts, but the craving she saw in his eyes, his body, his movements spoke a thousand words. Words of hunger, and a desire to conquer the way men had conquered from the time of the cave. His hands came down on either side of her, a cage she couldn't escape. His naked chest thrilled and scared her at the same time.

"Don't," he said softly. "Please don't be afraid of me."

He leaned down and placed a soft kiss to her neck. Pleasure shivered through her. She craved him the way she'd never longed for a man before.

"I would do anything for you, don't you know that?" he asked.

His declaration set her blood on fire.

His warm lips traced silken nibbles across the side of her neck. Quaking with unmet wishes, she savored his touch. Her fingers slipped through the cool satin of his hair as the leather cord he'd used to tie it back fell open and away. He moaned as his hands traced her small rib cage and then slid down to her ass. As he squeezed and cupped her, she pulled back far enough to look into his eyes.

What she saw sealed her fate.

Hot, unfettered, giving desire.

This man would protect her with his life. He would give Tara his body and perhaps his heart.

Joy replaced hesitation as she tugged him down into a deep, drugging kiss. Wine flavored his breath, a heady aphrodisiac to her already inflamed senses. Without pause, his tongue plunged into her mouth with persistent strokes. She met and matched each taste, coaxing until her tongue slipped into his mouth and consumed him.

It started with a mild foray into her mind, but then he entered her thoughts like a tender brush of fingers against skin. His visualization of what they could do and be together.

And, oh God. *What* they could do together.

Tara witnessed their lovemaking like a movie unfolding on a screen. Only this time she showed him what she would like, what she could envisage.

Marcus pressed kisses to her neck, and she reacted fiercely, needing his touch as a body needs water. Sweet, soft and lingering, he made love to her skin. A shiver coasted over her as he licked the hollow of her neck, sampling her like a gourmet meal set out for his enjoyment. His hands cupped her breasts, balancing their weight in his hands with reverence. His fingers tormented as he circled round and round without touching the puckered tips.

The barrier of her clothing couldn't stop him from driving her insane. Down and down his hands drifted lower until they cupped her hips. Marcus pressed against her and his cock grew harder and thicker against her belly. She cried out softly as her pussy tightened with a voracious need to have him inside. His touch drifted over her body with a tenderness that unraveled her one unbearable step at a time.

If he didn't thrust inside her soon, she would die from the ache.

She pulled back, gasping for breath. His arms stayed tight around her.

"Did you see it?" he asked hoarsely. "Did you feel it?"

"Yes."

An unrepentant smile touched his mouth. "Do you want it?"

She closed her eyes and tipped her head back. "Yes."

He shook his head. "God, I shouldn't do this. But I can't...stop."

Reality overcame the fantasy as Marcus cupped her breasts and measured her in his palms. Through the sweats and bra, the insistent brush of his fingers over her nipples generated an arousal that screamed for release. She writhed under the touch.

"Shit, these are so sweet," he whispered with low insistence.

His hands traced her body with relentless fervor and searched out her secrets. She wanted him with a deep craving that clawed at restraint. His breathing came fast, and she knew he'd lost it.

Longing gathered deeper inside her, more potent and untamed than any force she could imagine. Desires racked Tara and asked for completion. Without remorse. Without hesitation.

She heard it in his mind as he echoed her wants.

His mind whispered to hers. *Now. Now. Now.*

Yes.

The time for slow loving would come later.

She reached up, drew her sweatshirt over her head and tossed it away. She tore at the front clasp on her bra and it fell open. The bra fell onto the floor.

Animal passion flared in his eyes. "Oh yeah."

Potency spilled into her veins, as searing as the sun and filled with pleasure. No man before Marcus had given her so much and made her wish to give more.

She pulled off her shoes and tossed them aside. She stripped away her socks and sweatpants, then straightened. Only her black bikini panties kept her from being naked.

Tara started to reach for the waistline of the panties, but he caught her hands and kept them still. "No. Let me do it."

She expected him to take them off immediately. He brought her against him and the rough, soft combination of his chest hair teased her nakedness. His fingers slipped into the panties, then tightened on her ass. She groaned as skin moved over skin, his hands slightly callused. Moisture dampened her panties. She shivered and rubbed her hands over his hard pectorals. His nipples tightened beneath her touch.

"God, honey," he rasped against her collarbone, "if you keep that up, I'm going to have to fuck you right here, right now."

His guttural words set her off. She slipped her hands up to his head and dug her fingers into his hair. His nostrils flared and his eyes dilated. In the shadowy hall, his eyes glittered almost black.

"Then do it," she said with equal candor.

A husky laugh left Marcus' throat. Tara clutched at his shoulders as he kissed his way down her neck, teasing her with his tongue. He traced her collarbone with tentative fingers, as if he feared he might hurt her. Then his palms slid down, down until he clasped her slender ribs and his mouth paused over her nipples, not touching but waiting. She hung by a tether so thin she knew it wouldn't take much to break.

He blew on one nipple and it went pebble hard. His tongue feathered over the tip and she moaned softly.

He covered her nipple with his lips and sucked. She gasped and quavered in his arms. "Yes. Oh yes."

He clasped her other nipple between thumb and finger. As he pinched and plucked one nipple, he sucked with warm, hard pulls on the other. He switched breasts, keeping one under the relentless torture of his lips and tongue, and the other pleasured under the rhythmic attention of his fingers. He sucked and licked and stroked for so long, Tara considered screaming at him to stop. The pleasure came too high, too amazing to bear.

As lightning sensation pulsated out from her breast and centered down low in her belly, a tight ache throbbed in her pussy. Soft gasps and moans came from her throat without pause, her pleasure so demanding she had to give it voice.

Tara wanted Marcus with a screaming lust that tore at her insides and demanded immediate, unequivocal action. If she couldn't have him right now she would die.

Lack of shame pressed her to admit it. "Please, Marcus. I've got to have you now. Please."

He groaned. "I've got to get a condom, honey."

"No. I'm on the Pill."

He made a sound of relief. "Oh shit, yes."

He growled softly and ripped her panties off her ass.

"God, Marcus."

"Mmm." His pleasure came like a purr against her flesh.

She shoved his shorts and briefs down his ass to his thighs. Her fingers slipped around his cock to test his length and breadth. He was big and incredibly hard. While she clamped her fist around him, he shuddered against her.

"That's it. I can't take it anymore." He hissed in a breath and reached between her legs to find soaked folds.

He explored and touched with a gentleness that sent shivers over her skin and a hard throbbing between her legs. Whimpers left her throat as he strummed over her clit.

He pressed, rubbed and teased quickly, and as her body shook with a rising conflagration, he taunted her with arousing words. "That's it. Come on, take it."

She shook her head, half frightened of the intensity.

"Come." His voice commanded, forceful and thick with desire. "Come on, honey, give in to it."

But she couldn't. Too excited, she gasped for breath, her body shaking and shivering uncontrollably.

Before she could entertain one more thought, Marcus lifted her up against the wall, his fingers digging into her ass as he held her aloft with astonishing strength. His cock probed between her legs, and as the head penetrated her, she let out a small gasp of delight.

"You want it here? Now?" he asked.

"Yes. God yes."

Her fingers dug into his shoulders and held on for dear life. She twined her legs around his waist. Broad and unbelievably hard, his cock pushed through her folds relentlessly. Slick and hot, her body opened to him, and with a steady plunge, he took her, ramming to the hilt with a grunt of male contentment.

She squirmed on the thick intrusion as she realized she'd never had a cock this large inside her before. It felt…it felt…

Amazing.

Thoughts fled. She became an altogether physical being, incapable of anything but staggering pleasure.

His breath rasped in his throat, his chest rising and falling rapidly. "Fuck, yeah."

He sounded like a barely leashed jungle cat, his voice rough with emotion.

This was the sex, the heated passion she'd longed for all her life and never experienced. Until now.

"I can't do this slowly. Not this time," he said against her neck.

"Then don't."

Her voice didn't sound like her own. It belonged to a woman possessed by a screaming, demanding passion she couldn't escape.

He pressed deeper. He had one more inch to give her. She moaned and then he drew back and thrust forward, throwing his weight into it. She cried out, moaning with exquisite pleasure as hard, thick cock speared her to the core and touched her cervix. Her body yielded to his possession, her pussy swollen and so incredibly wet. She ached for the thrusts she knew would come.

As his flesh dragged along her pussy walls, he caressed her high up inside. His hips churned and the motion caused his cock to rub a place deep within her no man had reached before. She whimpered and her head fell back against the wall, exposing her throat. He buried his mouth in the flesh beneath her ear.

"Oh God, God," she whispered without remorse as he continued the stirring motion of his hips.

She wouldn't last long. Already her pussy rippled, the contractions starting with gentle pulsing.

Repeatedly he rubbed and stroked with a steady but slow rhythm. He asked, "Can you feel that?"

"Can I feel it?" She gasped and squirmed, shimmying as she tried to pump harder. His fingers gripped her ass so tight she could barely move. "Yes, oh yes."

A stabbing thrust caused her to cry out. As his mouth came down on hers and his tongue took possession, he started thrusting heavily, his cock jamming deep. She gripped his shoulders and held on for dear life as the stunning sensation of his cock drilling her made continuous moans part her lips. Every aroused sense came to one hot, surging crescendo that couldn't be contained a moment longer. Her moans deepened, quickening as her climax started. Her pussy rippled around his cock as he thrust, pulled back, thrust again.

She wouldn't last another stroke.

The burn rose, the exquisite ecstasy only one more moment away —

He thrust hard.

She screamed into his mouth as she detonated, her hips surging violently. At the apex, she shivered, in the moment, inside her senses with total abandon. She wanted to weep with happiness.

Her surrender freed him, and with one last powerful lunge, he threw back his head and roared his pure sound of male animal. Marcus' fingers dug into her butt cheeks as he ground his hips against hers, pumping his cum with hot spurts deep inside her. Panting for breath, he buried his face in her hair. She expected him to release her, but instead his hips shifted, and she realized he was still hard. His cock caressing her deep inside sent new streamers of excitement tingling inside her, and she clutched at his shoulders in stunned reaction.

"Oh God," she said with a gasp as her head fell back. "That feels so good."

To her surprise, he drew back and thrust once more, and again. She moaned as over aroused tissues responded.

"I've got a little left for you," he said with smug male satisfaction that made her smile.

"I can feel that."

"Mmm."

He pumped a steady motion that made her delirious with sensation. Floating in a world of continuous pleasure, she couldn't stop the soft moans that left her throat.

Back and forth he stroked, swiveling his hips, his cadence maddening. The rhythm took her up, her body reaching for another collision with ecstasy. Sweet agony hovered just out of reach, and her fingers tightened on his shoulders as she groaned.

"Let it come." He quickened his strokes, rubbing and pressing deep inside in a way that urged her to move with him in a search for completion. "Let it take you."

She writhed and whimpered as sensitive tissues tightened and released. Her muscles shivered around his cock. Sobbing in sheer delight, she hit the zenith, a supernova of light and beauty. Aftershocks quivered along each nerve, her body weak from the most spectacular orgasms she'd ever experienced.

Easing down from bone-melting delight, she opened her eyes and stared without seeing. He pulled back until she couldn't avoid looking into the passion still smoldering in his eyes. Through the dazed, happy feeling in her head, she saw concern blossom there as well.

Slowly he inched from her and gently lowered her feet to the floor. He pushed her hair back from her face and kissed her forehead. "God, that was wonderful. Are you all right? Did I—"

"Stop worrying." She grinned and brushed her index finger along his jawline. "I've never felt better in my life."

A boyish grin parted his lips. "Me either. Woman, you are hot."

Happy embarrassment flushed her face. How could she even think of being disconcerted when she'd just had the wildest sex of her life? Her mind still open to his thoughts, she caught something that made her blush deepen. Erotic thoughts tumbled through his mind, despite the fact they'd gone at it like teenagers. His hands drifted over her lightly, as if he wanted to search out new secrets within and without. His palms skimmed over the sides of her breasts, and she gasped as her nipples tingled to renewed life.

Trembling with a giddy lightness of being, she looked into his eyes. She wouldn't have this night any other way.

"I can't believe it. I mean, we were...it all happened so fast," she said.

He moved back from her and hitched up his briefs and shorts. "Not having regrets, I hope?"

"No. Not a one."

"Good," he said as his voice went raw and smoky. "Because this night isn't over. I want you again."

She didn't hesitate. Tara reached for him and banished thoughts of the next hour or the next day, or the consequences of passion unleashed.

He lifted her into his arms.

Chapter Thirteen

ॐ

Marcus laid Tara on the king-size bed in her room. He'd broken his vow to keep his hands off her, and unleashed a terrible craving consuming him from the inside out.

The consequences could bring his mental barriers crashing down. Drive him to the edge.

Fuck, Hyatt, who are you kidding? She's driven you over it.

Instead, he knew nothing but craving. Longing to bring them together in a deeper, lasting union. His conscience said they should think about Drake and the problems he'd caused and would cause. Marcus couldn't. Simply couldn't think about anyone or anything but the woman lying on the bed.

He'd never completely opened his mind and feelings during sex before. It scared him. Conquering fear didn't come new to him, but this went beyond the usual. Opening his mind to her probing, to the incredible realization that she could also read minds, sent him into an ecstasy he couldn't contain.

Her soft, naked form lay across the bed like a prize for a king's bounty. As the day darkened into evening, the shadows grew longer. Her eyes opened and she cast a smile at him, and he knew he wouldn't retreat. Relationships during a case could be messy, a violation of his personal code. Yet she'd turned him and swayed his defenses from the first day he'd met her. Tonight he'd discover her secrets one by one until her walls crumbled.

He couldn't move, couldn't speak as he observed her lying quietly waiting for what would come next.

She was perfect. Her slender shoulders, her long arms, the rounded breasts crested with tight, rosy nipples begging for his touch, his mouth. Just that quickly, his cock went spike hard.

Dark pussy hair shielding her most private treasures. He wanted to spend more time touching that hair, threading his fingers through it until he sank his fingers and cock into the tight, hot channel. Long, pretty legs led to her narrow feet.

For a crazy moment time halted, and he enjoyed overwhelming peace.

"Marcus?" Her voice drifted softly to his ears. "Is something wrong?"

Her gentle query broke his trance. "No. I'm standing here contemplating the meaning of the universe and how damned beautiful you are."

A smile played with her mouth. "Thank you."

He'd never met a woman he liked to please more than Tara. Seeing her smile, hearing her laugh brought light to his soul. He panicked when he thought of the day he'd leave her, when he couldn't hear her voice each day or see the fine-boned structure of her face and smell her subtle but intoxicating scent. He'd miss the way her full breasts pressed his chest, the way her thighs tightened around his hips as he thrust inside her wet, tight channel. Oh yeah. He'd fucking miss all of it.

Unable to wait any longer, he stripped off his shoes, socks and the remainder of his clothes, tossing them to the floor without a second thought. When he climbed onto the comforter next to her, he tugged her into his arms. Her hair tickled his fingers as he brushed it away from her face. When she let the straight, silky strands fall loose, she looked free. He wondered if tonight he could bring her a new escape. One they created only with their bodies. His cock demanded quick release, but for her he would hold out.

Her arms looped around his neck, and he gave up thinking. Sliding into a purely physical world, he kissed her. Her lips cushioned his, parting enough to tempt. He took the invitation and thrust into her mouth, eager to explore. He devoured, tasting deep, using his lips and tongue to show the strength of his need. She caressed his shoulders, testing the muscles. Marcus shifted her so he could explore her smooth back and the cock-pleasing curve of her sweet ass. God, her skin was so soft and delicate, he worried about hurting her. Yet when he'd fucked her up against the wall, the roughness of the act seemed to turn her on as much as it did him. He cupped her butt and squeezed, urging her against his hips. Pushing one thigh between her legs, he pressed her pussy. She undulated against his leg, and their combined moisture bathed his skin.

Her tongue teased his and pleasure made his belly tighten and his cock wild to fuck hard and deep. He wanted her under him, her legs spread like a woman with no inhibitions or worries. He wanted her the way she'd been in the hallway, out of control and beseeching.

He broke the kiss, breathing coming hard. Before he lost his tenuous thread of control, he would make sure orgasm rocked her.

After rearranging pillows so he could lean against the headboard, he spread his legs and urged her so she sat with her back to his chest. He curled his arms around her in a hug, pressing a kiss to the top of her head. A sweet, delight filled sigh left her throat and he smiled. God, he loved holding her, making her feel pleasure mentally and physically.

His palms drifted over her arms from shoulder to wrist until he lifted one of her small hands and pressed kisses to it.

Her content sigh filled the room. "Marcus, what are we doing?"

While he understood her real meaning, he didn't acknowledge it. He tipped her neck to the side and kissed the hot pulse he found there. "Enjoying. Taking. Giving."

He licked a path up to her ear, and when he breathed into the small shape, he reached up and cupped her breasts. Soft and plump and round, they filled his hands just right. Her warm skin drove him crazy, but he kept his grip loose so not to hurt her. With a squirm, she moved closer until her butt pressed his cock.

He couldn't keep a groan from escaping his lips or a rough suggestion. "Do you want me to touch your nipples?"

"Yes."

He clasped her nipples and tugged, then listened as she groaned and gasped.

Then he took a risk. Some women didn't like dirty talk, but desire rode him hard and he said it anyway. "You want to get fucked?"

"Oh yes."

Her unhesitant answer made a low growl of gratification leave his throat. Oh yeah, he would fuck her. When he couldn't take it anymore and she asked him to take her. Only then.

She shivered and put her hands over his, urging him into motion. His fingers closed over her nipples and squeezed gently. She gasped and shimmied. He loved the texture of her hot, hard little nipples drawing up tight. Swirling his fingers around the very tips, he let them stab at his fingers, as if they reached for him. His cock surged and throbbed with a relentless beat until he thought he would burst here and now. Breathing harder, he hoped he could maintain control a while longer.

As he drew his fingertips from base to tip over her nipple, he licked her earlobe and then fluttered his tongue inside. Another soft exhalation left Tara. He moved to her other side, tasting the area between her shoulder and neck while he massaged her nipples. Pulling, tugging, pressing, he manipulated her tender flesh until her breathy sighs and whimpers came nonstop. Fueled by remorseless desire, he kept at her, wanting Tara's full surrender.

He didn't think about letting her into his mind, and suddenly she was there, showing him what she wanted, needed. His body jerked at the shock, as her pleasure filtered into him through the mind channel they'd created.

Her nipples stung a little with his constant touch, but the burn ignited a heat already raging in her lower stomach. She wanted his hands there, touching, exploring. When he accommodated, reading her requirements, she quaked with an overwhelming delight. She parted her thighs. His hands retreated from her breasts, sliding with hot palms down over her flat stomach, down until he pressed her thighs further apart. Oh, oh, yes. Then he did something she didn't expect, and the fire inside her rose with anticipation.

He urged her, his voice soft. "Ease up a bit."

She did as he said, and when he clasped her butt cheeks and pulled them apart, she quivered on the edge of excitement, wanting to ask him what he planned.

She didn't, and then his voice came again. "I'm going to put my cock up against your ass, so you can feel how hard I am. How much I want you."

Husky with passion, his statement sent her longing higher. "Yes."

She eased down until the broad width and length of his cock was nestled between her butt cheeks. It felt good. Better than incredible. A wicked thought flitted through her, a thought so hot a blush covered her face. She wanted him there later. In her ass. She'd never thought about it much before, never desired the act before she met him. Now she wanted to get fucked in the ass for the first time.

Then his touch removed all of her thoughts and tumbled her into another world filled with unending excitement.

Using index finger and thumb, he pressed apart her labia and exposed her clit. She felt cool air, then the hot touch of his middle finger as he tapped her clit. She groaned as lightning flickered over her senses. Teasing her with gentle rubs, he smoothed moisture over her clit, circling the highly sensitive flesh with steady pressure. Repeatedly he rubbed her, and the sensations became too much. She clutched at his thighs, knowing her fingernails bit into him a little. As her excitement rose, he stopped fingering her clit. She moaned with disappointment. Seconds later, she gasped in delight as he grasped her clit and tugged. The combination of feelings, his fingers manipulating first clit, then cunt, his cock between her butt cheeks, made her exhilaration skyrocket.

He tortured until she thought she would scream, and her arousal became desperate, her cries earthy as she reached for the ultimate. She felt the wetness on her thighs, aware her pussy wept with arousal.

Then, slowly, he inserted two fingers deep, deep into her aching center. Her hips surged upward with the pleasure, a low groan leaving her throat. He tugged gently on her clit and then withdrew his fingers partway. He plunged his fingers deep, then moved out so he could pluck and stroke the tiny pleasure center. Repeatedly he teased, as he fucked her with his fingers, then tormented her clit. Fire threatened her sanity, and she wanted to cry out for him to do it. To take her.

He broke their mind link with a gasp, his heart pounding frantically as he absorbed how his touch affected her.

He removed his touch from her pussy, and a single, agonized word tore from her lips. "No."

"Easy." His voice went raw and shaky with desire. "There's so much more I want to do to you. I want to lick you, stick my tongue inside you."

Oh my God. Yes, I want that. But she wanted climax more. She must have one orgasm to burst free, to release the energy that seemed to be building with intolerable pressure. "I can't take any more."

Tara knew her plea sounded desperate, and she was. She throbbed deep inside her pussy. She suffered a blinding need to feel his solid, long cock penetrating hard and deep. When he'd slipped into her mind, she let him see everything she felt, feel it down to his roots, to his skin and bones. Encompassed in his warm embrace, his mouth and hands taking her to new ecstasies, Tara longed for a vanquishing thrust to end the agony.

"Then take me." His voice, untamed with desire, brushed over her already inflamed senses. "Show me what you want."

She complied. She lifted up and he clasped her waist to steady her. She eased down over his cock, inhaling sharply as the broad head breached her pussy. Down, down, she sheathed him until the base of his cock sealed her, until the length and width filled and stretched her deliciously.

"Yes," she whispered at the exquisite sensation.

She tightened her pussy over his cock, and he pressed upward with a groan. "Shit, sweetheart. God, that feels good."

A gentle laugh escaped her, and it turned quickly to an exclamation of pleasure as he pinched her left nipple gently, and with his other hand, returned to finger her clit. She started a pace of tightening and releasing her pussy muscles over his cock, and the heat rose higher. Nothing in her lifetime prepared her for this moment where no rules were listed, nothing was limited, and pure emotion caught her up and wouldn't let go. This man meant so much to her, gave her so many things she couldn't begin to repay. Marcus washed away Drake's nasty memory and touch and replaced it with delight beyond her dreams. The music of their bodies, moving in perfect rhythm, delighted her at the deepest level, leaving her shaken, excited and eager.

"That's it," he whispered. "Squeeze me deep inside."

She did, until the cadence made the ache unbearable.

"I can't stand it," she said, breathless as the pleasure rose.

"You can," he said, his voice hot in her ear. He gripped her nipple and plucked. He smoothed his finger over her hard, highly sensitive clit. "You're giving it to me now." His breathing came harsh and hot against her neck. "I'm going to fuck you until I shoot this load inside you."

His words, rough and uninhibited, stirred more arousal in her overheated body.

He switched to her other breast, tugging with insistent rhythm as he increased the stroke over her clit. He moved his hips just enough, a tiny increment that rubbed the thick head of his cock against a spot high up inside her.

He swiveled his hips and another gasp left her throat. "Oh."

Marcus couldn't thrust, but he could shift inside her with those infinitesimal brushes of cock along her inner walls. He'd found the angle and a few more movements made the friction agonizing.

Another twitch of his hips, and the pressure coalesced and couldn't be contained.

She let go. Simply released in one flood of screaming tissues, pulsing muscles and agonizing bliss. A sound left her throat, a high-pitched groan as her pussy rippled over his cock. Her whole body quaked, heart racing, breathing rapid as a soul-stealing climax shot through her. Her groan subsided into delighted whimpers.

When she stopped shivering, he lifted her off his cock and she came to her knees. He moved behind her and with a spearing thrust, he pushed, parting her walls and lodging deep. She couldn't help a gasp of excitement. His arms came around her as he hunched over Tara and took her with sharp digs, each movement punctuated by a grunt.

He sounded like a beast, his moans and heavy breathing wildly stimulating. From this angle, he hit the special spot inside her with every deep plunge. He fucked with ruthless speed, his hips banging against her, his cock jackhammering, his balls bumping her clit.

With one gasp, a strangled, agonized groan, he jammed deep. His entire body shivered, and she felt hot cum spurting inside her. When his climax released him, he pulled away from her and drew her into his arms. Wordlessly they cuddled, his embrace tight as their breathing calmed. Floating on a sea of happiness, Tara forgot the bad things in her world and concentrated on the way his skin felt hot and how his heart thudded in her ear. She would live in this moment and let the past and future take care of themselves for now.

* * * * *

Darkness grew into daylight, and as Marcus opened his eyes, he groaned softly. No, he didn't want the night to be over. Memories of their wild sexual escapades made him smile. Shit, he couldn't remember the last time he felt this good. Tara lay on her stomach, one hand resting on her pillow, the gentle curves of her face serene in sleep. He couldn't help it. He rolled on his right side and traced his palm over her back. Silken skin felt warm under his touch, and he followed the hill of her buttocks and enjoyed those damn sweet cheeks. With an evil grin, he reached between her parted thighs and traced her labia.

As warm moisture made his fingers slick, he hummed in satisfaction. "Yeah."

He couldn't seem to get enough of her. While he'd fallen asleep with her in his arms last night, they'd awakened after midnight and talked for a while longer before falling asleep again. Now he felt energized, ready to take on anything and anyone. Another taste of her body would be what he needed to start the day.

Tara awakened, awash in glorious sensation. She felt Marcus' fingers between her legs, rubbing gently, then inserting two deep into her pussy. With a gasp, she parted her legs farther and enjoyed the steady push and pull as Marcus slid two big fingers in and out of her drenched channel. She arched a little, wanting more forbidden things than they could do right now —

"You want me here." He slipped his wet fingers upward between her ass cheeks, tickling her small, tight hole. God, there he went again, reading her mind. She groaned and writhed against his fingers.

She wiggled, the feathery sensation maddening. "God, Marcus. Yes."

"Say it. Tell me what you want."

Tara kept her eyes closed and her voice low as he continued to massage her anus with gentle, maddening touches. "I want us to have… I want anal sex. I've never done it before." She swallowed hard, the sensation of his fingers toying with her forbidden places making her bolder. "Have you ever taken a woman there before?"

"One woman. A long time ago. She was…older. She taught me how to do it so it won't hurt the woman. We can take care of one thing right now, though." His husky voice went low with need. "Roll over."

She did as told. Hot and aroused, his eyes told her everything she needed to know. His need was great, his desire plentiful. Marcus' cock stood rigid and ready to give her the immense pleasure she'd experienced last night.

He slipped his arms around her, then reached between her legs to touch her clit. She moaned in delight. He pushed his other hand under her ass and squeezed. She tilted slightly her left side to give him easy access. Without warning, he latched onto one nipple and began to suck. She stuffed her fingers through his hair and held him to her breast as he suckled.

Wildfire craving made her close her eyes and shudder all over. He stopped kneading her ass and tasting her breast for a moment. He dipped one middle finger into her pussy to gather moisture, then drew it back to her anus. He worked the wetness into the hole repetitively until he could ease his finger into the small entrance.

Exquisite sensation made her wriggle as he slowly thrust his finger up her anus. He used his other hand to finger her clit. Electric pleasure caused her to cry out as he thrust his finger in and out of her anus. The drag and push roused nerve endings she never knew she had, and the continual stimulus of her clit drove her to move her hips, seeking more.

"Like it?" he asked.

She didn't open her eyes to see his expression. She felt so good she could barely answer him. "Yes."

His mouth covered her breast and he swirled his tongue over her hard nipple while finger-fucking her ass and pleasuring her clit. As he took her to the highest pinnacle, her body responded with mounting pulsations. It didn't take long. Her arousal rose too quickly to wait, and the sensation of his finger plundering her nether hole brought her new excitement. Frantic for release, she tightened her muscles rigid as ecstasy beckoned. Heat. Excitement. Passion pushing forward without remorse. Her heart raced as he drove her to a helpless bliss, a melding of body and mind that brought more pleasure than she could have guessed. He pushed two fingers slowly into her pussy, and the exquisite sensation took a match to her escalating joy.

A high wail left her throat, and climax took her. Her pussy clenched over the fingers he moved in and out of her channel, and he continued the motion of his finger in her anus. She quivered through the last waves of delight.

As she came down slowly, she said with a dry throat, "That was wonderful."

He whispered against her hair, his voice so full of tenderness, her heart ached. "You're incredible. I've never seen anything more beautiful than watching you come."

Such a simple thing to say, but it made her emotions swell with a tender joy. She knew she was in trouble, because no man in the past had made her feel desirable the way Marcus did now. Never again did she need to hide, to conceal her true core with a mask of protection.

"You all right?" he asked when she didn't speak.

"I was just thinking."

"Is that a good thing or a bad thing?"

"In this case, a good thing." *Go ahead, confess to him.* "I was thinking how you make me feel. That I don't have to hide anything from you. Now that we know we can read each other's minds...well, what else is there?"

"I never thought I'd say this, but I'm glad you can read my mind. Then you'll know that I'm not like Drake and never will be."

"No, you're not." Tara took the plunge. "But you're still hiding something from me, aren't you?"

His cock lengthened against her thigh, a blade demanding attention. Marcus left the bed before she could make more than one tentative stroke across that hot brand.

"Don't go away," he said as he entered the bathroom.

Tara stretched out on the bed with a sigh. Damn. He hadn't answered her because she hit too close to the truth. She could choose to be angry, or she could give into the moment and forget the misgivings that could take over a woman's self-possession.

She tried not to analyze how she'd managed such stupendous fortune all of a sudden. Maybe she'd been building good karma in her life far away from Drake. Now he'd come to try and destroy that peace. Her time with Marcus remained as a tiny island of paradise amid growing troubles.

No, she wouldn't let Drake intrude on what she now had with Marcus. That part of her life would be separate, incorruptible by the destruction that followed Drake everywhere.

Marcus returned to the room, his stride confident male animal. His cock, in the light of day, defined pure beauty. Yet there was nothing feminine about his physical being. Long and thick, his masculine prowess invited her touch. When he came alongside the bed, she rose on her hands and knees and crawled across the big bed toward him.

"You're gorgeous, Marcus." She breathed the words, admiring and awed.

She knew infatuated women saw their men in a perfect light, but nothing about him was ordinary. As she cataloged his attributes, she saw his perfection as individual but like no other man she could imagine.

His build said he worked hard, his sinew bold and defined, his lines hard and without remorse. Broad shoulders, carved-to-perfection arms, corded muscles in his thighs and calves. His chest made her long to touch, to explore the delineation of his pectorals, the crisp hair over his nipples, his hard stomach. His strength made her feel safe, alive and cared for. Tara sat on the edge of the bed and he stood in front of her. What happened between them last night and this morning emboldened her.

She started to reach for his cock, but stopped. Old memories flooded back of another time, another awful place.

He clasped her head and tilted her gaze up to his. Thick, dark lashes framed the bluest, most clear eyes. In them, she saw concern and something she could almost mistake for love. The hard cut of his jaw was covered with stubble, and he looked dangerous, a far cry from an office nerd.

"What's wrong?" he asked. "I'd like you to touch me. I want your hands and your mouth, your tongue on me."

His words, raw with sex, made an answering stir of arousal return to her body.

Only moments ago, she'd marveled at how safe he made her feel. Now…

He frowned, then his expression softened. "You don't like to give head?"

She sighed and clasped his wrists. "Drake is the only man I experienced it with."

He pushed his fingers through her hair. "And you didn't like it."

"Not with him. He gagged me with his penis." Embarrassment managed to creep around her new attitude toward sex. "He'd shove his cock down my throat so far it was uncomfortable."

Anger hardened his eyes. "Jesus, honey." He brushed hair back from her face. "You don't have to do anything you don't want."

She glanced at his cock, which had softened a little during their pause. "I want to make you feel fantastic."

"You already have." His voice turned husky. "More than any other woman."

His acknowledgement and patience stirred tender feelings. Possessiveness rose up inside her. She reached out and brushed her index finger down his cock. A shiver coursed through him.

She took a plunge. "How many women have you made love to?"

Her bold question didn't make him flinch. "Six."

Six. Not as many as she imagined.

He smiled and sat on the bed beside her. "One was the older woman I mentioned earlier. I was a virgin until I was nineteen."

Surprise made her say, "Really?"

He nodded, his grin wide. "I was a tall, gawky kid. Girls didn't find me too interesting. I was too wrapped up in sports and played soccer and ran track. Then in my second year of college, I met this woman, Georgina. She was a senior and in my advanced chemistry class. She was actually sort of plain, but the more I got to know her the more I realized we had a lot in common. Her intellect turned me on. We slept together on our fourth date."

When she pondered the information, he asked, "What about you? How many men have been privileged enough to see this beautiful body?"

"Two. A couple of years before I met Drake I dated this man at work. I liked him a lot more than he liked me." She shrugged as dispassionately as she could. "It was a big deal to me at the time, because I was totally in love with him. He decided to go back to his old girlfriend." She smiled remorsefully. "I understand now that what I felt for him wasn't so much love as a need to belong to someone. So when I met Drake, I thought my feelings for him were real."

Marcus drew her into his arms and held her tight. "Of course they were real at the moment. Hey, I thought I was in love with the older woman who initiated me into sex. She left me for an older man. A much older guy of thirty."

She drew back to look at him, and the warmth and laugher in his sparkling gaze made her heart thud faster. It would be so easy to fall for him. So damned easy.

"Come on," he said. "We've got to get ready for work."

Chapter Fourteen

ഔ

Tara looked out at the city scenery going past the window of Marcus' car. He kept his eyes on the road. She'd sensed hyper vigilance in him since they left her house.

She'd called Ethel Allegra to let her know she wouldn't need the order of protection. Ethel's disappointment was palpable, but Tara trusted Marcus' opinion enough to believe him when he said it would make the situation worse to actually have the order of protection.

She thought back, instead, to her time with Marcus this morning. Rituals like taking a shower, getting dressed and making tea took on a new significance with Marcus in the house. Sadness threatened to overwhelm the warm and fuzzy feelings she'd experienced waking up in Marcus' arms this morning.

"All right?" Marcus asked, breaking her out of the reverie.

She smiled with effort. "Yes. I want things back to normal. I want peace, quiet and no excitement."

He glanced at her and grinned. "No excitement. Are you sure about that? I thought last night was exciting."

Did she hear need in his voice? She liked his eager tone. "Okay, that type of exhilaration is good. Very good."

He laughed softly. "Glad to hear it."

She swallowed hard, too caught up in conflicting feelings. A thousand thoughts ran around in her head. She felt like she had so much more to tell him, to reveal. Another part of her balked at showing him so much.

"Everything is happening so fast between us, Marcus. I don't know what to think."

He nodded as the car drew closer to their workplace. "It boggles the mind. Look, how do you want to handle our relationship in the office?"

She worried the leather strap on her purse and caressed the brass buckle on one end. "Good question. I think people already have a good idea what's going on."

"Then we'll keep it as low-key as possible. We want to be professional anyway."

"Of course. Besides, until this is all over with Drake, we can't really... We can't plan anything permanent between us."

The words slipped from her before she could stop them. She winced and glanced at him. His face had gone hard and cool. She shouldn't have used that notorious word *permanent.* Men tended to freak when they thought you wanted commitment or anything equal to it.

"You're right. We can't talk about permanent now." Marcus' detached tone sent a shaft of pain right through her heart.

She'd done it. She'd caused herself hurt by prompting his answer, by letting him know she felt something deep and lasting.

What she felt for him would stay in her heart for a long time, no matter what they did with the relationship. How could she ever forget a man this warm, this caring? Drake had ripped her to shreds with his condescension, with his highhanded, so-called intellectual statements about her desires, her feelings. He'd taken sharing and turned it into heartache.

"You know I'd never do that to you?" Marcus said, his brow creasing with a frown.

"You read my mind again." She couldn't keep the dismay out of her voice.

"A little. The feelings. Not the words."

Having him crawl around in her mind when they had sex didn't seem bad, but she didn't know if she liked the idea he could read her thoughts at will.

They didn't talk until they reached the parking garage, and then about inconsequential things.

As Tara walked into the office with Marcus by her side, she noticed the attention swinging in their direction. People probably speculated about why she'd come in late today with Marcus, but she couldn't help what they thought. They also had to know about Drake's attack on her in the parking lot.

Cecelia and Sugar stood by Sugar's cubicle deep in conversation, and when Tara aimed a smile their direction, Sugar frowned and turned away. Stung and angry, Tara kept moving. Great. What had she done to deserve this sudden disregard?

Once in the cubicle, she wrote on a piece of paper, *What is up with Sugar and Cecelia? Did you see how they looked at me?* She handed the paper to Marcus. His brows rose as he read it. After he sat at his desk, he wrote a note back. *It's grade school time. They're playing games, and we're passing notes back and forth.* She read his note and then wrote, *I think they're jealous because of the attention you're paying me. They can tell we're together.* Marcus read her note and smiled. He wrote, *What is there for them to be jealous of?* She finished off with, *You, silly. You. They see you as a hunk now that they know you aren't gay. They don't understand how a woman like me could get a man like you.* Marcus read her piece, then had to tear off a new piece of paper to write his note. *They're mindless worker drones. Don't pay attention to them. Besides, you're a terrific, smart, beautiful woman. I'm lucky to have you.*

Sweet pleasure flooded her. The man made her crazy with his gentleness, his strength, his steadfast refusal to leave her vulnerable to Drake. If he didn't stop being so reliable and gorgeous and beyond sexy, she'd—

Oh no. No. She couldn't fall in love with him. *But your heart already cares for him a great deal. A lot more than friends.*

She would have written him a note back, but he winked, picked up a stack of files, and left the cubicle.

* * * * *

The phone rang around eleven at Tara's desk, and she turned her attention away from a document to answer.

"Tara?" The female voice sounded vaguely familiar, soft and almost frightened.

"Yes, this is Tara."

"It's Kendra. Drake's sister."

A million emotions erupted inside Tara. Pure resentment arose first. "How did you find this number?"

"I...uh...Dad doesn't know this, but I have a friend on the police department. I met him through my waitress work. I explained that I wanted to warn you about Drake being released from prison. So my friend dug up your number."

Great. So much for trying to stay hidden. A wild thought raced through Tara's head. Was Drake's sister in league with him?

"After Drake called us the other day, I was worried about what he was planning." The woman's quavering voice held regret and pain. Kendra always sounded beaten down, her reserves in danger of shredding.

Stunned by the development, Tara almost couldn't speak. She swiveled her chair and noted Marcus wasn't in the office.

"Tara? Are you there?"

"Yes. I'm not sure I want to talk to you."

"I understand." Kendra's voice warbled. "I know what I did to you can't be erased. What happened was... What I did was horrible."

"I'm not likely to forget it any time soon." Tara's throat tightened with unwelcome pain. "I'm not sure I want to forget it."

"I'm not asking you to."

"Then why are you calling me? Do you know what Drake's been doing to me?"

"Stalking you?"

Tara's insides tumbled with nerves. "Yes."

"He was talking crazy when he called us."

"You could be helping him. I shouldn't talk with you."

"Please don't hang up. I swear I'm not working with him to hurt you. I wanted to warn you about what he said. He spouted a lot of Bible passages to Dad and a couple to Mom and me." She laughed without humor. "Made Dad happy."

Tara closed her eyes and tilted her head back. "I can imagine it would."

"I thought about calling you before Drake got out of prison. To warn you he might come after you I used to visit him while he was in prison. We still live close to Fort Leavenworth."

Antagonism returned to slow boil. "What stopped you from calling?"

For the first time, Kendra's voice held derision. "Would it have made a difference?"

Tara considered it. She heaved a sigh. "Probably not."

"After Drake started talking crazy, I thought I should tell you. And, to do something else. Something I should have done a long time ago."

Tara couldn't speak, her throat was tight. She opened her eyes and stared at the partition wall with the calendar, the Irish castle scenery beckoning to her to escape. Escape this conversation, this office, this world.

Kendra stretched the silence, and Tara wondered if the girl changed her mind. Finally, Kendra spoke. "What I did back then, when Drake—when he beat you—it was wrong. I just...I'm working on getting my head straight, you know? When I didn't speak up for you that last time and didn't tell the courts what I knew about my brother..." A sob broke from the woman's throat. "I wanted to tell someone. Anyone. I was a coward, Tara. I held back because my Dad would have done things. Horrible things to me or Mom."

Tara could well imagine. What she knew about the retired military officer made her shiver. Shocked by the conversation,

Tara almost couldn't choke words past her throat. "Do you still live with your parents?"

"Yes."

Words came easily, then. "Damn it. Why haven't you left there? You have to get out of that house if you want to ever live."

"Mom and Dad wouldn't understand. They'd find a way to get me back."

One thing she knew about Kendra was that her family didn't change. They mired deeper into their twisted lives year by year. "And? You're old enough to be on your own."

Kendra sighed. "I know."

Kendra's disjointed speech patterns, not quite stuttering, but never self-assured, reminded Tara of Kendra's fragility. On the other hand, the woman had put up with untold miseries all her life. Maybe she wasn't as weak as Tara believed.

Kendra spoke with a firmer voice. "All those years back, I should have done something to stop Drake."

Tara rolled her chair back under the desk. She stared at her computer screen and the cursor blinking in the document. "You couldn't stop him. I should have left him sooner. That was my fault. I could have been out of the situation long before it came to such a horrible end."

"But in the end, after he…after he hurt you so badly, I should have stood up for you. I mean, it wasn't so hard at first back when Drake was just bad-mouthing you and Mom was being so nasty around you. But Dad got tired of my lip those last weeks before Drake beat you to a pulp. Dad hit me again and again. I couldn't go to work for days and the diner almost fired me for not showing up. I told them I had the flu, but you know those people. They don't give a crap about things like that. They didn't believe me. My Dad went down there and spoke up for me, and I kept my job."

Annoyed with the woman's rambling, Tara interjected her frustration. "Kendra, it's been over six years since all that happened. There isn't anything you can do to repair that. You can do something for yourself now."

"Why should you care what happens to me?"

Tara wanted to scream. "You've got to move out of that house. Your mother and father will keep their foot on your neck until hell freezes over. They're twisted, just like your brother. And if you don't get out of there, you will be twisted, too."

Kendra laughed softly, a fake sound. "I already am. I already am, Tara."

"You can change. Everyone can change if they want to badly enough."

Silence dropped down between them until Tara heard a wretched sob slip from Kendra's lips. She could visualize the woman's trembling hands, her pale cheeks devoid of makeup, and her long, straggly blonde hair tangled and in need of a cut. Six years ago, Kendra's thin, petite frame would bow under any stress or threat. She probably looked no different now.

Tara loosened her grip on the receiver as a dull ache moved through her wrist. "Kendra, you know I'm right. There are shelters for battered women."

"You didn't go to one."

"I was confused and frightened and didn't think straight. I should have gone to my family. They would have taken me in. You don't have family you can rely on. That's why you need a shelter."

"Mom and Dad aren't home now but they should be soon. I can't leave right away."

"Then do it soon. Before they destroy you for the last time." Tremors ran through Tara as distaste, anger, fear and pity warred inside her.

"Can you...can you forgive me for not helping you that last time?"

Tears stung Tara's eyes, and she sucked in a breath. "I don't know."

"Okay. I can live with that." Sadness laced Kendra's voice. "Oh no. They're coming. Mom and Dad are coming home, and I'm not dressed to work. I need to hang up."

Kendra hung up off without another word.

Tara placed the receiver in the cradle and hung her head with her eyes closed for a full thirty seconds as she absorbed the disturbing conversation. Tara's fingers shook as she released the receiver. What did Kendra hope to accomplish by calling? Until Kendra turned on her six years ago, Tara considered the young woman her only true friend in the family. A bright spot in the Hollister house of horrors. She'd thought that ray of light included Drake until he came unraveled and her dreams exploded along with his violent nature.

"Tara?" Marcus' quiet voice startled her.

He squatted down beside her chair and put his hand on her forearm. His quiet strength comforted her.

"Hi," she said.

"What's wrong? Are you all right?"

"I'm good." Then she laughed sarcastically. "No, I'm not." She dropped her voice to conspiracy level. "Drake's sister called."

"What?"

"Just what I said. I'll tell you about it later. We can't right now."

He nodded, but looked like he'd rather pursue it this minute. "All right. Later."

* * * * *

Marcus didn't make it too far down the hall when Cecelia came toward him from the opposite direction. She moved in a way no one could mistake for anything but sex on high heels. By the time she reached him, her perfume assaulted his senses, and he tried not to wrinkle his nose in distaste. She stopped so near to him, he took a step back. He stood his ground. His glance snagged on the top she wore, a low-cut lacy thing barely professional enough for the office. Her generous-sized breasts filled out the top with no problem. Her hair was tossed about her head in a messy style. Wrapped in that outfit and that aroma, she could slay a few hundred hungry men with one ravenous look. By the sly glance she gave him, she knew her effect on males.

Cecelia's skirt, a dark navy blue that contrasted with the red top, hugged her well-curved hips. Any man with blood in his veins should appreciate Cecelia's high-toned sexual energy. Nothing, though, stirred in his body. His cock didn't care.

She placed her hands on her hips. A little taller than Tara and wearing high spiked heels, she didn't have to look up far to see into his eyes.

"Marcus, I always wondered what it would be like."

"What?"

She inched closer, and he stayed put. What the hell was she doing?

"To take a taste of you."

"Uh, Cecelia, I'm not—"

"I know. You're not interested. But you would be if Tara wasn't here. You're not fooling anyone." Her fingers drifted over his polo shirt until she cupped one of his pecs. The friction against his nipple caused it to rise up. Her smile exploded in her eyes and formed on her lips.

Okay. Involuntary reaction. Any sort of pressure against his chest might cause this.

He gently plucked her hand off his chest. "I'm not interested."

She kept her fingers tangled with his, then edged nearer. "Are you sure?"

He wiggled his hand free. "Yeah, I'm sure. Even if I was, this isn't the time or place to do this."

She winked. "Oh, come on. The time and place hasn't stopped you from coming on to Tara at work."

Son of a bitch.

"Look, I'm supposed to be on the way to see Jason Forte right now."

"Jason." She almost hummed the word.

A flicker passed through her expression, uneasiness at odds with her earlier bravado. Damn it, he didn't have time for this, but the change in her personality, the edginess didn't feel right.

Curiosity made him ask, "You've changed. What's happened to you in the last week?"

She didn't blink. "I learned who I really am."

"Who are you?"

"Cecelia in the raw. Not cooked. Not tossed with dressing." She flipped her hair over her shoulder and stuck her chest out. "What you see today will be me from now on. The old Cecelia is dead and buried."

Her weird wording gave him pause. "Really? Why—?"

"It's not important." Cecelia's grin simmered with sensuality. "Are you sleeping with her?"

"Who?"

"Tara."

He kept a straight face. "Even if I was, I wouldn't tell."

She grinned and plastered her lithe body to his. Her scent slammed him, earthy and intoxicating. A quaver went through his system. She wrapped her arms around his neck, and before he could blink, she planted one on his lips.

A wave of dizziness hit him like a two-by-four between the eyes. *Holy—what the hell is happening?* She parted his lips and stroked her tongue deeply inside. She grasped his crotch and stroked his cock and balls. He jerked and pulled back. She dove for his neck like a vampire, a tiny growl ushering from her throat. She planted two kisses under his jaw. He yanked away from her hot, searching mouth and set her away from him.

"Stop it. I don't want this," he said weakly.

His voice trembled. Shit, he could sit down in the hall right now his legs felt so much like fucking spaghetti.

He had to get away from her. Now.

"I'm not doing this," he said. "Not now. Not ever."

He headed for the stairwell. As he ascended the stairs, he held on to the railing in case his shaky legs decided to collapse.

Jesus, Hyatt, what the fuck happened?

His shields obviously failed. Other times he'd been around Cecelia, he'd never noticed his white and gold barriers failing.

Damned if he knew what happened, but the unreliability of his barriers in recent days disturbed him to the core. He'd call Dorky and get a handle on what might be happening before it was too late. He needed advice, and he needed it fast.

* * * * *

The day continued fast-paced until three. Tara needed a caffeine injection and some liquid to wash down the trail mix she'd brought from home. She headed for the employee lounge. She passed Cecelia's empty workspace. No sign of Sugar in her work area, either. Perhaps they'd left to plot more ridiculous high-school antics. She hoped to talk to them at some point and see if they would explain their sudden enmity toward her.

She yawned until her jaw cracked. Maybe sexual antics with Marcus last night had taken away from her rest. She didn't care. Being with him, making love with him came before petty concerns like sleep. She grinned. She was certifiable.

Before she reached the lounge, she heard a giggle and a soft moan. She rounded the corner and stopped in her tracks.

Cecelia stood near the stairwell, her arms wrapped around Marcus' neck, and her lips pressed against his. Marcus wasn't holding on to Cecelia, but it didn't look like he was resisting that much.

Tara thought her heart would stop.

She quickly moved back around the corner and leaned against the wall. She closed her eyes and the sight of Marcus kissing Cecelia ran through her head in an ugly replay.

She heard Marcus say something, then Cecelia's low murmur. God, she didn't want them to know she'd seen or heard them. Her jaw ached as she clenched her teeth together. She opened her eyes and stared blankly at the wall across from her. Pain seared her. Marcus was kissing Cecelia. She couldn't compute it, didn't want to take in reality. The man she'd given her body to, and yes…her heart, stood in the hallway kissing another woman.

Betrayed again.

Tears threatened, stinging her eyes. No. She wouldn't do this. She would cut this relationship off at the knees before she fell for him the rest of the way.

Oh, who are you kidding? Damage is already done. You love him.

No. Not anymore.

She heard Cecelia's voice, but couldn't put together the words. Marcus' low voice uttered a few more words, then she heard the slam of the stairwell door. Cecelia's footsteps clinked against the flooring.

Time to make an appearance. She took a deep breath to steady her skittering pulse. Her heart continued to thump an anxious beat.

She turned the corner. Cecelia headed right toward her. With each step, Cecelia's full breasts jiggled in a bra that didn't support well, and her hips swayed in the clingy skirt. Her curls tumbled about her shoulders in wild disarray. She looked dressed to kill, to devour man with power and purpose.

How could any man resist?

Tara almost sneered. Any faithful man could resist. Faithful? Marcus had never said anything about an exclusive relationship. Old unease tore at her insides. She wanted to kick self-consciousness out the door, but it stared her in the face like a haunt bent on acquiring attention with rattling chains and unearthly moans.

Tara affixed a smile, but internal spite made her want to bitch-slap Cecelia into the next century. "Hi Cecelia."

"Hey."

The chill had come off Cecelia's face since earlier in the day. No matter. From this point forward, nothing would be affable between them, even if Cecelia confessed.

Cecelia stopped in front of her, spike heels on her pointy pumps clicking as she stopped. "I thought you'd be hard at work."

"I need coffee. Where have you been?"

Cecelia winked. "Enjoying some quality time with Marcus."

"Oh?"

Cecelia put a slim hand on Tara's shoulder and squeezed. "Darling, there's something I need to tell you about Marcus."

"I don't have time to talk about him right now."

"This is important."

"I'm sure it is, but—"

"No buts about it, darlin'." Cecelia's eyes sparkled with a sinister gleam. She kept her grip on Tara's shoulders, her touch tightening. "He's not faithful. You don't want him around you. You should see what he did in the hallway a moment ago. In fact, I'm going to report him."

Anger shuddered through Tara in a great wave, but she couldn't say whether she was pissed at him or at Cecelia.

She stepped out of the other woman's grip. "Report him for what?"

"Inappropriate behavior that jeopardizes the stableness of the workplace."

"What? What type of behavior?"

Cecelia chuckled. "As people used to say when we were kids, that's for me to know and you to find out."

Tara's blood pressure spiked. "What's happened to you, Cecelia? I can tell you've changed in a matter of days. Earlier you didn't want to give me the time of day, and neither did Sugar. Now you're talking to me. What's happening?"

"Nothing's changed about me." Cecelia tapped her on the shoulder. "Now you, that's another matter. I think it's you that's changed. I've seen how you look at Marcus. There's a lot of gossip going on about you guys and what you've been doing after work. People see you leave together and then — well, what happens is anyone's guess — but I've got a bet with Sugar you've been sleeping with him. It's in the glow on your face."

Tara wanted to escape the accusation. She stayed. "If I was sleeping with him, what I do outside this building isn't anyone's concern. It's my private life. What Marcus does outside work isn't anyone's business."

Cecelia grinned and walked away.

Blindly, her heart aching, Tara turned and headed for the employee lounge.

She opened the door and froze.

She couldn't scream. Fear didn't factor into her immediate reaction.

The horrific tableau refused to register. Her mind didn't want to register what she saw in front of her.

Then, one shattering thought sprung from her mind and hurtled outward.

Marcus. God, Marcus where are you? Help me.

* * * * *

Marcus made his way to Forte's office with his thoughts running amok like jackrabbits. The encounter in the hallway with Cecelia disturbed him on a deep gut level. Why the hell had she jumped him in the hallway where anyone could have seen them? In any case, his shakiness didn't make sense. He could have overpowered her any time he wanted. It wasn't like she was dangerous. Angry at his reaction, he walked faster.

No. This is more. Unnatural.

His unease came from recognizing something anomalous moving within Cecelia. It didn't feel right, damn it. It felt viscous and dark and beyond redemption. Sweat beaded on his forehead.

A worker from another office walked by him in the hallway, and as he murmured a greeting, he noticed the man gave him a weird look.

Shit. Cecelia's well-painted lips had coasted over him several times.

He searched for the men's restroom and ducked inside. Lucky for him, the bathroom was a one-holer. He locked the door and stared into the mirror. She'd managed to land three distinguishable red marks on his face. One on his left cheek, one right above his shirt and on his chin. No wonder the guy in the hallway had eyeballed him strangely. Damn it, he didn't need this. First Sugar acted as if she wanted to worm into his pants and now Cecelia had grabbed his package and stuck her tongue down his throat.

He ripped toilet paper off a roll and dabbed at sweat and the evidence of Cecelia's kisses. Drawing in a deep breath, he checked the status of his mental shields and found them punctured. He replenished his mental shields, but it took far longer than it should have. Frustration made him tighten up, and he opened his eyes.

A glaring truth hit him. Dorky had warned him that sex could degrade his mental shields. He'd jeopardized the case by having sex with Tara. He'd allowed his powerful feelings for her to degrade his abilities.

Good going, Hyatt.

He'd never screwed up so royally. Angry with himself, he straightened his clothes and left the restroom. While he walked, he thought over his options. If he stopped having sex with Tara, he'd hurt her. She'd wonder why he'd gone cold. He could tell her about the case…

No. He couldn't do that, either.

Possibilities tumbled through his head. Maybe the problem with his mental shields had as much to do with Jason Forte as it did sex with Tara. Something strange was going on with Cecelia and Sugar.

Marcus walked into Jason's outer office. Xenia, the secretary, sat at her desk typing with incredible speed on her computer. Marcus blinked, astounded by how fast her fingers moved. She must be typing over one hundred words per minute. She stopped and swiveled her chair to look at him. A weird shiver went through Marcus as she eyed him from head to toe. Her glacial green eyes, straight fall of shoulder-length inky black hair and skinny body reminded him of a woman from a horror film. What was it with the women around here today?

"Marcus." Her voice purred a deep and sultry sound. "Mr. Forte is expecting you."

Intuition made him pause. When Bettina told him to make copies of the documents for Jason, he assumed Xenia had extra work to do and the copying job flowed into word processing. It happened sometimes.

Marcus stepped closer to her desk and smiled. "How could he be expecting me?"

Jason stepped out of his office. "There you are. Come in."

Marcus' military training had honed his instincts to a fine edge. Maybe he could obtain some information from this creep today if he worked things right. Improvise and infiltrate.

Marcus nodded politely. "Good afternoon, Mr. Forte."

Marcus entered Jason's office and hoped he didn't fail this small mission for the day.

"Come in, Hyatt. I've got another meeting in thirty minutes with the president."

Jason returned to his desk, then gestured for Marcus to sit in the chair across the desk from him.

Marcus placed the documents Bettina had asked him to copy and deliver to Jason on the desk. "The copying you asked for."

"Good. But that's not why I wanted to see you."

Marcus leaned back in his chair and sprawled in easy comfort. "I guess it's a good thing I happened to stop by then, isn't it?"

If Jason thought his attitude sucked, he didn't indicate it. "I have serious issues to discuss today with both Bettina and Human Resources. Recommendations."

Fine tension drew Marcus' muscles tight. He flexed his fingers and shifted his legs. "And what has that got to do with me?"

Jason shoved one big hand through his thick crop of blond hair. "It has everything to do with you."

Great. This sounded royal fucking serious. What did this dickhead have up his sleeve?

Easing back into his chair, Marcus pushed his glasses farther up his nose and linked his fingers together in his lap. He could act the confused, artless metrosexual with ease. "I don't understand."

"You know that word processing doesn't come under my department, but I have a vested interest in this company running smoothly."

Come on, shit face. Spill it.

"Sounds reasonable."

Jason stood with a swift movement, then put his hands behind his back. He treaded the carpet with deliberate, almost heavy steps. "People in word processing say your relationship with Tara Crayton isn't professional."

Marcus held on to his cool demeanor with effort. "We're very good friends. Is there a policy against that?"

Jason stopped pacing and glared at Marcus. Something beyond pure idiocy drove this man and Marcus knew it. Had Jason uncovered his purpose for being at Douglas Financial Group? How?

"Please don't think because I'm cordial this isn't serious." Jason resumed pacing. "Last month the president asked me to be on a special task force to deal with sexual harassment in the workplace."

Marcus didn't speak, unwilling to sound eager or disinterested.

Jason cleared his throat. "Your behavior with Cecelia in the hallway, and your obvious relationship with Tara Crayton put your job in jeopardy."

Cecelia didn't have enough time to call up to this office and make an accusation. No way.

Marcus kept a poker face. "Cecelia?"

Jason turned on his heel like a soldier and stared at Marcus, pinpointing him like a heat-seeking missile. "You know what I'm talking about. Denying it won't help you. Cecelia will testify."

Marcus allowed a smile to touch his lips for about three seconds. "Testify. You make this sound like a trial. What you have is a person making a false accusation. If Cecelia said I did anything inappropriate with her, she's lying."

Jason sneered. "I know what you do behind closed doors with Tara."

You fucking bastard.

"What has my relationship with Tara got to do with Cecelia?"

Muscles moved in Jason's square jaw. He looked like a fashion model with his over trendy blue silk shirt and expensive matching blue tie. Mixed with the slick sheen of his dark gray suit, Jason must have spent a hefty sum on his clothing. His eyes seemed to spark with underlying fire, an abyss widening second after second in the man's eyes. Cold dread raced over Marcus' skin. No. He couldn't give into apprehension around this slimy creep. *Stay on target. Work through it. Understand what Jason wants.*

"I don't see what the problem is," Marcus said.

Jason leaned both palms on the desk and glared. "It's obvious. If you molested either Cecelia or Tara—"

"I didn't do anything to Cecelia. In fact, she kissed me. If she's angry because I wasn't interested in her—"

"Because you're with Tara."

"Because I'm plain not interested in Cecelia."

Jason didn't change posture or his battery-acid expression. "I'm concerned for the safety of women in this company. I won't allow them to be intimidated."

Marcus wanted to laugh his ass off, but he kept a straight face. "Of course you wouldn't. Neither would I."

Jason practically snorted disbelief. "Right. All this will be reported to Bettina, Human Resources and the president. We'll decide what action to take from there."

Excellent. Brilliant. His dick would end up in a meat grinder because Cecelia and Jason had something up their sleeves. Guessing at Jason's true motivation came easily. If he was kicked out of the company, Marcus couldn't investigate, couldn't influence Tara, or protect her while she was at work. Why would Jason be after Tara? Perhaps he wasn't targeting her specifically, but all women at this company.

He closed his eyes for a second and let his shields down so he could see into Jason's twisted mind.

It took maybe two seconds for Marcus to realize he'd made another big mistake. Jason's evil reached out for him like an inky well. Marcus' eyes snapped open. As a horrible feeling swallowed him, murky and ancient, he shivered. Jason's glare went from human to hellish, his eyes turning coal black with red rims sparking fire. Marcus didn't have a chance to slam his shields closed before his throat tightened and his air supply disappeared. Panic grabbed Marcus, and his heart sped up. He stood, and before he could make one step, the world went black.

Chapter Fifteen

ह०

Tara opened her mouth, but no sound came out at first. Perhaps Sugar's eyes, wide open and never blinking, told Tara speaking wouldn't matter. Her heart slammed in her chest as she observed Sugar's motionless body. Inside that immobile shell, her friend used to reside. Not a close friend, but a woman she'd worked with day after day, joked with and felt she knew as well as she could.

She found her voice though she knew the woman wouldn't answer. "Sugar?"

Propped in sitting position against the cabinets, Sugar sat with legs sprawled out, arms akimbo and limp. Sugar's body screamed of death. Maybe not quick, peaceful death, but death nonetheless.

"Oh God. Oh God." Tara forced her legs into action and rushed to the body.

Sugar's skin looked almost rubbery, white, lifeless. She felt even colder. A quick check for pulse and breathing confirmed worst suspicions. Sugar had passed beyond help. Ice worked insidiously up Tara's spine. She thought about closing Sugar's eyelids, but couldn't bear to touch her again. Tara bolted to the phone hanging on the wall by the cabinets. She dialed 911 and reported what happened, then hung up and dialed Bettina's extension. Her hand trembled as she spoke to Bettina.

"My God." Bettina's voice shook. "Do you know what happened?"

"No. She's…she's just laying here. I found her like this." Tears welled up, and her voice broke. "Can you come down here?"

"Of course."

Tara waited, frozen with dread and the feeling Sugar's demise heralded the beginning of an evil far more terrible.

More than an hour and a half later, Tara watched as paramedics rolled the gurney with Sugar's body out the employee lounge door. A gaggle of horrified employees, including Cecelia, stood around the lounge murmuring in low voices. If the paramedics had given the police indication of why Sugar died, Tara didn't hear the answer. Maybe she didn't want to know. Two uniform police officers and one detective strolled around the lounge questioning people. They'd already quizzed her extensively, and in the back of her mind she realized they cataloged her as someone to watch. As if she might have killed Sugar.

Murder?

But who? How?

Bettina finished talking with one of the officers and returned to Tara's side. "That's it, then. They're almost done."

"Do they...do they know what happened to her?"

Bettina shook her head. "They haven't said. Maybe it was a stroke or heart attack."

Tara shuddered. Her body and soul felt frozen. She didn't know what to say or think.

She couldn't remove the sight of Sugar's immobile features from her mind. Perhaps the image would remain burned into her mind forever.

Bettina put her arm around Tara's shoulders and squeezed. "We should get you out of here. Come to my office. I've got some nice chamomile tea."

Another woman from word processing ran down the hall and toward the group, her expression shocked and scared. "Something weird is going on. Marcus dropped like a fly in Mr. Forte's office."

Tara's thoughts froze into immobility. She could barely get one word out. "What?"

The woman babbled. "Mr. Forte's secretary said another group of paramedics have taken him to the hospital."

"What happened?" Tara managed to say.

The woman shrugged. "Guess he passed out."

Tara looked at Bettina, and Bettina whispered, "This is insane. What is going on around here?"

Tara almost choked on her next words. "Is he...?"

"He's alive, but they don't know what's wrong with him," the other woman said.

"What hospital are they taking Marcus to?" Tara asked, already moving down the hallway.

Her heart pounded in her chest, her mouth dry, her eyes brimming with tears.

"Denver General," the woman said as Tara continued walking.

Blood rushed in Tara's ears, an ache deep in her body. Her breath shortened as she walked faster and faster. She knew one thing. She must get to Marcus quickly.

"Something's terribly wrong, Bettina. What happened to Sugar and Marcus is connected."

"How?" Bettina asked.

"I don't know, but it is." Tara walked as if dragon's fire followed her.

Bettina raced after her. "I'll drive."

* * * * *

A twenty-four-hours news channel reported the latest alarming statistics on crime as Tara watched. She sighed and leaned back in the hard vinyl chair in the hospital waiting room. They learned nothing about Marcus other than he was alive, and a glimmer of hope rose in Tara's heart. At the same time, she wanted to scream, to release from this icy prison around her emotions and heart. She couldn't think. Couldn't feel anything but stony silence and shock. One elderly woman and a haggard young blond man in a chartreuse jogging suit occupied the room with them. Considering the large size of the hospital, Tara wondered why more people didn't occupy the room.

Her thoughts ran around in chaos from one insignificant thing to another until pressure threatened to detonate. How could she hope to stop this terror lodging so deep inside her psyche she could hardly swallow? Her mouth felt like desert, and tears threatened.

When did I become so weak? Marcus is fine. He'll be all right.

All that matters is Marcus. Her heart ached. God, she didn't think she could take it if anything happened to him.

No. Too incomprehensible, too harsh in the light of day. *No. No. No.*

Bettina sat beside her, face grim as she flipped through a magazine.

She glanced over at Tara and pressed Tara's arm. "I think I could use some coffee. They actually have a coffee cart down the way. They make excellent lattes."

Tara smiled, even if it made her face feel brittle and her emotions uneven. "You're kidding. I thought all they had in these places were machines with tiny paper cups of nasty sludge."

Bettina grinned and closed the magazine. She placed it on the small table between them. "Not anymore. Come on, let's get some."

"No. I'll stay here."

"Would you like me to bring you something? You look like you could use refreshment."

"Yes. Okay." She reached for her purse by her feet.

Bettina held up one hand. "It's on me. What'll you have?""

"A fully leaded mocha latte. The works."

"Whipped cream?"

"On second thought, hold the cream."

Bettina nodded and started to walk away.

"Wait," Tara said.

Bettina turned.

Tara couldn't help but smile at her supervisor. "Thanks so much for being here. A lot of supervisors wouldn't have cared this much."

Bettina returned and sat in the chair beside her. Her wrinkled face belied the youthful vigor shining from her eyes.

"I don't believe supervisors have to be unfeeling. Some of my colleagues may think otherwise, but that's never the way I've seen it."

"That's because you're human and kind."

Bettina laughed softly. "Some of my colleagues aren't sympathetic and they don't give damn about what happens in the long run. They're in this for themselves. I kind of think of Marcus like a son. He's a good man. He's going to be all right."

Tara nodded. "Do you know what Marcus was doing in Jason's office?"

"He delivered copy work he'd done. Jason Forte's secretary said he looked and sounded fine when he went in the office. No sign of illness."

Tara pondered the information. She recalled the incident when she'd walked into the copy room and Jason Forte had just been there. Marcus had looked bad and he'd admitted to her that Jason bugged him in a major way.

She couldn't tell Bettina that, though.

"I'll be right back, dear." Bettina gave Tara that serene smile and stood. She walked away.

The young man coughed, then leaned forward and put his head in his hands. What happened to bring him here? Her mind raced to the old woman's scenario. What or who was she waiting for? She looked so patient and calm. God, what she wouldn't give for some relief from her nagging doubts. Not even high-test mocha coffee would make her feel better. Not until she saw Marcus, talked to Marcus—

"Miss Crayton?"

She turned at the quiet masculine voice. A middle-aged doctor with receding curly brown hair and a kind smile stood at one entrance.

She popped up and met him as he came into the room. "I'm Tara Crayton."

"You're a friend of Marcus Hyatt?"

"Yes. Is he all right?" Anxiety made her voice go higher than she intended.

The doctor's calm voice washed over her like a soothing balm. "He should be fine. We can't find any sign of skull or brain injury, stroke, heart attack, aneurism or other disease. Right now it is a mystery. His vital signs are strong."

What he said should make sense. Instead, it bothered her. "Are you saying he's in a coma and you don't know why?"

"He doesn't really fall under the criteria of coma. He does respond to certain stimuli that a person in a coma wouldn't. But that doesn't mean that he's entirely out of the woods. When he wakes, we'll want to run some tests to see why this happened to him."

Okay, she could take that for now. At least the doctor hadn't told her worse news. The fact his unconscious state baffled the doctor bothered her almost as much as dire news.

"You can see him any time you want." He gave her instructions on where he'd been moved. "He has a private room on orthopedics because that's the only place we had a bed for him. I'll check on him later."

"Thank you."

She stayed in the waiting area until Bettina returned. She explained what the doctor said and asked if Bettina wished to go with her. "It's okay, dear. You go ahead and visit him. I'm going to sit here, relax and sip my coffee."

Bettina's support made her affection for the older woman grow. She hugged her, careful not to dump either of their coffees. "Thank you so much, Bettina."

"For what?"

"For supporting Marcus and me."

Bettina smiled. "I can't halt the course of true love. Go on now."

Tara's cheeks heated as she walked away. So, the woman thought something romantic was going on between her and Marcus. Were they that transparent?

As she made her way down the hall and to the elevator, an ugly memory flashed in her mind. Cecelia kissing Marcus...Marcus kissing Cecelia.

She wanted to hate him for it, but she couldn't. She took the elevator up, and had plenty of time to ponder. She could give him a chance to explain. But what explanation could he have for kissing Cecelia in the hallway at work? Kissing her at all, for that matter?

Unless, what Tara had seen wasn't anything less than what she'd witnessed. Marcus getting it on with one of her fellow workers. No, she didn't want that. Refused to pay attention to it while he lay unconscious and unable to defend himself. When he woke up, then she would ask him.

She found his room and eased the door open on quiet hinges. Overriding apprehension almost halted her at the doorway until she forced one foot in front of the other. She crossed to the bed and stood at his left side. He looked defenseless for the first time since she'd met him, and it crushed her to see him in the light blue hospital gown. Automatically she reached for his left hand and squeezed it. His fingers felt warm and it gave her some relief. Mental pain seared her. She couldn't stand this, wanted to run far away from the agony of seeing him defenseless and yet knowing she would sit by his side as long as it took for him to wake.

Dark circles marred the skin under his eyes, but otherwise his handsome features showed infinite peace. In repose, he managed indestructibility. She rubbed his fingers gently. Then she did something brave, something deep from the heart with no shame.

The railing on his bed was down on her side, so she leaned into the bed to come closer. After releasing his hand, she whispered close to his ear. "Marcus, can you hear me? I'm right here. Whatever is keeping you inside there, you're safe now. Open your eyes. Open your eyes for me."

Hesitating, she reached up and touched his face with reverence. Stubble along his jawline prickled against her skin. Pressure built in her chest, a deep ache that demanded release. Why keep it in any longer? No one could see her, and the stress of it ate her alive from the inside out. Her breath hitched and tears came, spilling over her cheeks. She closed her eyes and took several deep breaths. She didn't want to lose control, but the valve broke.

Her fingers caressed his again and she squeezed his hand. "Please, Marcus, please be all right. Just come back to me, and I'll kiss you. I'll forget everything I saw."

"Mmm. That feels good. Don't stop."

She gasped, and her eyes popped open. "Marcus." She brought his hand to her cheek, then kissed his fingers. "Marcus."

His eyes looked blurry, but his smile broke wide and sincere. "That's my name. Did I hear something about a kiss?"

With his dark hair tousled around his head and without his glasses, he looked sleepy and sexy. Happiness propelled her to lean over, and still clutching his fingers, she placed her lips over his. His other hand came up and slipped to the back of her head. He pulled her closer, his kiss deep and claiming as his tongue possessed her mouth.

A quiver of heat and wanting passed through her frame. She ached for more, to take him to bed and stamp her ownership on his body and heart. Tears trailed down her cheeks, and when she pulled back from him, he wiped one away with his fingers.

"What's this? Why are you crying?" he asked, his gaze concerned.

"How do you feel?"

"I feel great."

"No headache? Nothing?"

"Nothing. Don't worry. I'm ready to run a marathon."

When he tried to sit up, she pushed him back with a gentle palm on his chest. "You're not going anywhere, Marine."

He groaned. "How long was I out of it?"

"About three hours."

He scrubbed at his chin. "Damn, that's longest time it's taken me to recover."

"From what?"

Amusement left his eyes. "Passing out."

"You pass out often?"

"No."

"Then what caused it? The doctor couldn't come up with a reason. They want to do tests."

He shook his head. "No tests. What's wrong won't show up on any scan they have."

"Marcus, you have to let them find out what is wrong."

He reached up to caress her cheek in a light touch that sent shivers of warmth through her. "I'm telling you that if they test me, nothing will come up wrong."

"Why?"

He shook his head. "I can't tell you right now."

"You can't tell me." Frustration made her voice strident. She dropped his hand. "Damn it, Marcus."

"What's wrong?"

She flinched away in anger. "You scared the crap out of me by falling over in Forte's office, and you have the gall to ask me what's wrong?"

A crooked smile touched his mouth. "I'm sorry, but I'm so damned happy to be alive that I'm having a great time right now. Kissing you. Being close to you."

His words, husky and soft, melted some of her defenses.

"You're trying to flatter me so I won't be angry," she said.

He winked. "Sounds like a reasonable plan."

She'd forgotten the coffee on the bedside table. She moved away and picked the drink up for a deep sip. The hot drink didn't warm the cold, hard facts. "I can't believe you're so nonchalant about this."

Concern replaced humor in is eyes and mouth. "I'm actually pissed this happened. Falling on my face in the middle of Forte's office was one of the worst things I could do."

She shook her head. "Don't be embarrassed."

"It's not embarrassment, believe me."

"What happened? Do you remember?"

"Forte was haranguing me, and when I stood up, I passed out cold."

Nothing in his expression altered, but intuition told her Marcus held back information. She wanted to blurt that he lied, and her trust in him would never return. Never? Perhaps not that long, but seeing him kissing another woman started a chain reaction of uncertainty she couldn't shake.

She took another long sip of coffee, then placed the cup back on the bedside table. She kept her voice slow and forced calmness she didn't feel. "Did you feel ill anytime today? Do you think you're coming down with something?"

"No. I'm sure I'm not."

"Then what is it?"

He reached for her hand, and rather than draw it back, she allowed him to encompass it in his big fingers. The heat in his touch reassured her in a small way.

"You were worried about me?" he asked, humor touching his voice.

She glared. "What a question to ask. Of course I was."

"But you're also angry with me." His voice softened and went deep and tender. The sound whispered over her nerve endings, a gentle breeze that curbed her irritation. She didn't want to talk about seeing him kissing another woman, at least not right now.

He kept his fingers laced with hers, his grip firm but not too tight. His gaze intensified, wrapping around her as he searched her face. She gasped as she felt his mind brush against hers. "Tell me what else has happened. I know something has."

Her voice cracked, her throat dry. "Sugar is dead."

His eyes widened. "What?"

"I found her dead in the employee lounge."

He cursed, long and hard. "What the hell happened?"

She shook her head and didn't speak at first. In halting tones, she managed to tell him what she'd seen and did. As she gave the blow-by-blow account, his eyes flashed.

"Shit. Shit," he whispered. "I'm sorry you had to see that."

"So am I." She slipped her hand from his.

Marcus' face went hard, his eyes reflecting deep thought. "It must be connected."

Confusion pulled her to ask, "What is connected?"

He gazed intently into her eyes. "Do you trust me?"

Oh, that was a good question. Did she really? After watching him kiss Cecelia in the hallway? Worrying about him and trusting him didn't fall together immediately. "I don't know if I can."

"Why? I know you trusted me before. What's changed that?"

She heaved a breath, bracing for what he might say after she dropped the bomb. "I realize we never said anything about having an exclusive relationship together."

He tipped his head slightly to the side. "No, we haven't."

"I'll have to admit that when I saw you kissing Cecelia in the hallway today, it blew that notion of exclusivity all to hell."

His mouth popped open and major surprise flickered in his eyes. He rubbed his hands over his face. "Damn it. Tara, I wasn't kissing her. She was kissing me. Both she and Sugar have been acting weird lately. Cecelia came on to me. Both of them have been flirting with me, and they never have before. I wondered if they'd set it up between them just to see if they could get me to take a bite."

She tilted her head up and looked down at him over her nose. "And you did."

"No, I didn't." He reached for her hands again, but she crossed her arms. Silence dropped between them as he contemplated her. "That's what this is about. You think I'm into other women? I'm flattered if you're jealous—"

"Don't be, Marcus. I'm feeling a little mortified because I let my emotions get…"

"Yeah?"

"I let myself care too much. That stops right here and now. I can't do casual relationships." She shook her head. "Look, I'm not explaining this well. Let's drop it for right now. Getting back to what you said before, how is Forte involved in Sugar's death?"

Hesitation tightened his expression into a mask. "I'm not one hundred percent certain."

She didn't know what to say, surprised by the lack of conviction in his voice. "You have a feeling about Forte, I know you do. You think he somehow murdered her."

"Yeah. But I can't say how or why."

"You mean you won't."

Regret flickered in his eyes. He jammed his hands through his hair. "I have to be certain first."

She paced across the room, putting distance between them "You asked me to trust you, but you're not willing to give me the same consideration."

"Tara—"

"No, don't." She put up a hand. "Let's talk about something else."

A muscle jumped in his jaw, his eyes filled with regret and exasperation. "All right. But we *will* talk about what's happening between us, Tara. I'm not leaving it like this."

She looked at the floor. She couldn't remember feeling this torn in a long time. An ache started behind her eyes. *No. No, I won't cry again. Then he'll really know how much I care. How deeply I feel for him.*

He started to speak, but the doctor walked in and interrupted. Obviously startled that Marcus had awakened, he examined Marcus and told him what tests they wanted to run. He would need to stay overnight.

"I can't stay overnight," Marcus said.

"We need to find out why you fainted, Mr. Hyatt. This could be serious," the doctor said.

Tara stepped forward. "Please, Marcus. Stay and have the tests."

"But you can't be left alone at the house. You need protection."

"I'll be fine."

"You won't be fine if Drake knows you're alone."

"The security system will keep me safe."

Marcus' voice rose and frustration etched his face. "What about when you leave work? What about while you're getting out of your car? This guy is serious, Tara. Very serious."

The doctor's attention swiveled back and forth between them. "Would someone like to clue me in?"

"My ex-husband is threatening me. Marcus is staying with me as a bodyguard."

The doctor nodded. "I see." He looked back at Marcus. "Well, Mr. Hyatt, if we don't make sure what it is we are dealing with here, you might not be able to protect her at all."

Marcus closed his eyes. "All right. I'll stay."

Uncertainty and some fear made her ask, "I could stay here with him."

The doctor nodded. "We'll arrange to have a cot brought in."

Marcus smiled. "Thanks. I know I'd feel a hell of a lot better. When can we do these tests?"

While the doctor explained, worry ate a hole through Tara, and her heart tripped over at the sight of Marcus' handsome face. Whether she liked it or not, he'd worked his way into her heart. Whether she wanted it to or not, even his interest in another woman couldn't wipe away her growing feelings.

After the doctor left, she reached for her coffee and took a large swallow.

"Are you okay?" Marcus asked.

"Of course." A weak smile flickered over her lips. "Why wouldn't I be? I'm not the one in a hospital bed."

"You look uptight. I hate seeing you like this."

She took another sip and wished the caffeine would kick into gear.

When she glanced at him, a gentle smile touched his mouth. She wanted to lean over and kiss him, to remove every uncertainty from their lives with the erotic touch of mouth against mouth.

A flame answered in his eyes, his gaze intense with heat. Desire spiked hot in her belly.

He adjusted the bed controls until he sat up. Vitality glowed in his face. "Even if you are mad at me, I'm not going to sacrifice your safety. If you never touch me again, that's your choice. But I'm not letting Drake hurt you. I've got your back, Tara, and I'm not giving up on you."

* * * * *

"He doesn't want to let me out of his sight, Bettina," Tara said as the two went down to the hospital cafeteria for dinner later.

Bettina patted her on the back. "Of course he doesn't want to, not with Drake skulking around out there somewhere."

As they walked into the dining hall lounge, Tara's stomach growled. "I didn't think I was hungry."

"It's getting late. Lunch was a long time ago."

A few people stood in the cafeteria line, and voices chatted in the background. Whoever designed the cafeteria had gone to great pains to make it cheerful, to remove the expected sterility. Artificial plants and flowers graced corners, and light blue and green walls added color and cheer. Food scents touched Tara's nose, and her stomach growled again.

She laughed softly. "Okay, that's it. It's a hamburger for me. I'm starved."

Bettina licked her lips. "Sounds delicious."

Tara inched along with the rest of the line, not knowing what to say. She switched gears. "There may be some more tests for him tomorrow. I'm torn. I want to stay with him, and yet work can't be neglected."

Bettina shook her head. "Don't you worry about work. He's your good friend. He's more important."

"I've had too much time off as it is."

"I'll take care of it." She reached for a tray and didn't say anything more as they selected food.

They settled at a table for two far in the back away from the crowd. A little time passed before Tara let out a weary sigh. Her lower back ached, her eyes itched and her neck was stiff with tension.

"Something wrong?" Bettina asked. "Besides what's already happened, I mean."

Where did she begin and how much did she tell? "It's too weird. You'd never believe me."

Bettina's gaze concentrated on her, discerning eyes clear and probing. "Try me. You'd be surprised what I believe. Despite what some of the other employees think, I can be open-minded."

Bettina's grin reassured Tara. "Of course you can."

"Tell me what is going on." Bettina put her fork down and stared at Tara, once more the stern supervisor.

"I can't." Tara smiled halfheartedly. "Not with you looking at me like I'm a recalcitrant employee you caught slacking off."

Bettina laughed. "Sorry. Look, whatever is bothering you, I'm not going to give you a hard time about it. You've been through a shock a couple times over today. A friend is dead and a man you care about fell sick. That would rattle anyone."

Tara's throat tightened up and although she ate her hamburger, it felt like a ball of lead resided in her belly. "I'm not sure where to start."

"Start anywhere." Bettina grasped her fork and sifted through her meal.

"Marcus and I...especially Marcus, think what happened to him today is connected to what happened to Sugar."

Bettina's fork stopped halfway to her mouth. "What?"

"Just what I said. He thinks that Jason Forte had something to do with Sugar's death."

As soon as the words came out of her mouth, Tara felt like she'd betrayed Marcus. But, she had to tell someone, and the only other person she trusted was Bettina.

Bettina chewed thoughtfully. After she swallowed, she put her fork down. "Under normal circumstances, I'd say that was crazy but I've had my suspicions about Forte for a long time. So what I'm about to tell you probably sounds nuttier."

Tension made Tara's shoulders ache. She shifted in the hard plastic chair. "I find that hard to believe."

Just as she found it hard to believe she'd started the conversation in this direction.

Bettina's expression turned grim. "I've wondered about Jason since the day he started work here. It's strange, but I started off thinking of him as a fairly reasonable man." She took another bite and chewed slowly, leaving Tara hanging on the tension. "I've never trusted him, though. Something isn't right about him, but I couldn't tell you what."

"How do you feel when you're around him?"

Bettina glanced up from her dinner, her eyes sharply penetrating. "Now that's a question. I've got good sense when it comes to people. I trust my intuition. Now the question is do you trust yours?"

"Most of the time. It serves me well."

"Then you don't feel comfortable around Jason, either, do you?"

Could she dump her secret thoughts onto Bettina when she couldn't tell Marcus? Maybe Bettina's sympathetic ear would make the difference.

"No. Neither does Marcus."

"A perceptive man, your Marcus."

Your Marcus.

Tara twisted the paper napkin in her lap.

"I might as well tell you what happened while you were in visiting Marcus," Bettina said. "My trusty cell phone—hate the thing—rang and it was Jason checking up on Marcus. The concerned executive, you know. Anyway, he's told Human Resources about Marcus and they're going to investigate his involvement with Sugar, Cecelia and you."

Anger boiled up from Tara's insides. From what Marcus said about his conversation with Jason, she shouldn't be surprised. "Why?"

"He's accusing Marcus of sexually harassing the three of you."

Tara realized her fingernails dug into her palms, and she flinched. She looked down at her half-full plate of food, then shoved it away. Her stomach protested that she'd eaten.

"That's ridiculous. He isn't sexually harassing me. We have a—"

She cut herself off, and Bettina smiled. "You have a mutual relationship with no coercion involved. Don't worry, dear, you don't need to hide your feelings for Marcus around me. Did I say I frowned on relationships between coworkers?"

"Do you?"

"Not at all."

Relief flooded Tara. "Good. But this garbage about him sexually harassing Sugar and Cecelia is crazy."

"I agree. Marcus isn't that kind of man. Period. He's too smart for those girls, and I've never seen any sign that he was interested in them. Now you, that's a whole different story. I've seen the way he looks at you. Hungry. Protective."

What could Tara say to that? "That's why I know he wouldn't have anything to do with them."

"Jason will tell Human Resources about his suspicions. They'll probably interview Cecelia and you."

Tara pushed her chair away from the table. Chills slid over her skin, and she rubbed her arms. "Do you think they'll frown on my relationship with Marcus?"

"I know Amanda Cortez very well. She's an honest woman. I don't think she'll take Jason's accusations at face value. She'll investigate on her own."

"Good. At least there's that."

Bettina's eyes softened. "Don't worry, dear. Things will be all right."

"How can you be sure?"

"I'm an optimist." She grinned.

Tara couldn't resist the smile, and she reciprocated. "It's a little hard for me to feel positive right now."

"I know. I don't blame you. You have enough worries on your plate."

Tara traced her finger through the condensation on her water glass. "If Jason says that Marcus was harassing Cecelia and Sugar, the police might think Marcus murdered Sugar."

Bettina pondered, her gaze glued to the table in front of her. "I suppose it's possible. We don't even know the cause of death yet. There weren't any visible wounds on her body. None that I could see, anyway."

Tara moaned softly and covered her eyes. "This is so insane. I can't believe all this is happening to me and around me."

A sardonic tilt touched the older woman's mouth. "Life has a way of getting complicated and then getting more complicated. Roll with the punches and keep fighting."

Renewed strength filled Tara. "You know I will."

"If you're finished, maybe we should check on Marcus."

"Good idea."

Tara left with a new respect for Bettina, and knew she'd discovered a friendship she could rely upon. Heaviness weighed on her thoughts, but she could handle it one step at a time.

Chapter Sixteen

ॐ

"It's good to be home," Tara said as they walked in the door of her house.

After Marcus stayed in the hospital an additional day and they performed more medical tests, they'd discovered nothing wrong. Just as he'd predicted.

He headed toward the bedroom, his grin irreverent. "Mind if I get a shower?"

"Go ahead."

While he showered, she started making soup and sandwiches for them. They'd arrived home around noon.

Once the food was ready, they consumed it in record time. Then they took naps to ward off exhaustion. When they woke up the day had turned bleak and dark clouds ushered in an early dusk. They decided go outside with glasses of tea and enjoy the last sunlight.

"I can't stop seeing Sugar's face," Tara said to Marcus as they walked into the backyard. "She looked shell-shocked."

"Frightened?" Marcus asked.

"Yes."

She glanced at Marcus as he settled on the lawn chair, and she nestled into the lounge couch. Fluffy cushions made her sigh with comfort. He didn't look so comfortable, though. In fact, the touch of annoyance she'd sensed coming from him all afternoon worried her. What killed Sugar? Until the police or medical examiner answered that question, Tara knew she wouldn't feel safe again.

She sighed. No, she didn't feel safe before, and now Sugar's death made it worse. That's why she wanted to sit out here before the storm burst upon them in the last breath of daylight. In this haven, she'd find temporary respite.

Still, Marcus' morose mood surprised her. What was happening inside that handsome head?

"Are you okay?" she asked.

He'd leaned his head back against the chaise, and this angle she couldn't see his face clearly anymore.

"I'm fine."

"You've been quiet."

He shifted, putting the glass down on the concrete patio. Muscles rippled under his T-shirt and the shorts he wore revealed his extraordinary legs. God, she loved the way his hard body moved. All animal. All male. Her body reacted to his as if she'd only just met him. A chemical response that said an eligible male crossed her path.

"Nothing's wrong."

She sipped her drink. "Right. That's why you look like a bear about to eat someone's head off."

He frowned, then his eyes warmed. "Come here."

His gentle command worked on her heart, and she put her glass on the small table in front of her and left the couch.

She sat on his lounge chair and faced him. A teasing grin wiped away worry on his face and replaced it with devilish intention.

Heat slithered through her lower stomach as he reached up and cupped her face. "I didn't want you away from me."

She gazed into his eyes and saw messages there. "You want to be near me because of what happened with Sugar. You don't think her death was natural."

Solemnly, he nodded. "I don't want you in the same room with Jason Forte. There's something wrong with him. I don't know what, but it's fucking powerful."

Despite his strong words, his touch on her face stayed gentle. His fingers slipped down over her neck, and she shivered with longing. When his touch reached the V-neck of her short-sleeved top, she covered his hand and held it there. His touch felt so strong, so protective, he intoxicated her.

Even his caresses couldn't obliterate her next thought. "Something was wrong with Sugar before. Cecelia is out of her head now. They were fine until right after I heard about Drake getting out of prison."

"I noticed."

"You think Sugar's death was…?" She couldn't speak it. If she did, the horrible possibility became too real.

"Murder."

The word hung there, a talisman, a harbinger of further death.

She shook her head and kept his hand on her chest. Drawing comfort from the simple touch. "How? She looked…depleted. I can't even believe it was the same woman I knew a week ago."

"I know it's going to take some time to forget."

His voice held strain, as if he tried to hold back strong emotion and almost failed.

"What do you think actually happened to her, Marcus?"

Clouds hovered in his eyes. His big body coiled with fine-edged tension. "It wasn't accidental, but the police won't find signs of foul play."

"How do you know?"

"A feeling I have."

"Intuition."

"Something like that."

Why didn't she believe him? Yes, she knew as well as anyone the legitimacy of psychic ability. Still…

"Like psychic abilities?" she asked. "Like what we have between us?"

"Less than that, but more than intuition."

Her skepticism held. "You're not telling me everything, Marcus. Not by far. We can communicate telepathically—"

"You think I can read minds well enough to tell what's going on with people like Jason Forte. Well, I don't. What I do have is this amazing connection with you. You feel it between us all the time."

Marcus skimmed his hand up her back and his touch drew her near. Light faded into night, and the deepening shadows threw his face into mystery.

As his hands roamed, learning her secrets as if he'd never touched her before, Tara shivered on the fine edge of ecstasy. If she wanted to remain sane, she couldn't touch him. Feeling his skin, his energy beneath her fingers would destroy composure. She'd forget who she was and where she was.

He pulled her closer and before she could take a breath, she sprawled across his chest. His mouth closed over hers, warm and searching.

She arched into his embrace, turned on by the power in his arms, the solid feel of his chest. Her fingers spread across his chest, the other hand brushing the rough stubble on his jaw. He groaned into her mouth as their kiss exploded. His tongue plunged inside her mouth and mated with hers. Drugged by the pleasure, she took his kiss and deepened it, giving into desire. He cupped her breast and his thumb circled over her nipple with a maddening stroke. She shivered delicately, so excited she couldn't suppress a happy whimper.

He broke off the kiss, his chest heaving with each breath. His eyes burned into hers. He leaned in, took her earlobe between his teeth and worried it with his tongue. Spirals of tight, hot desire coiled in her stomach. His breath puffed in her ear. Fine tremors coursed over her skin.

He slipped his hand into the back of her shorts to cup her ass. His fingers probed the crease, tickling her anus with featherlike touches. Her pussy wept, wanting him inside her with a fierce ache.

"Let me see inside you," he whispered hoarsely.

As easy as that, he popped into her mind. Like the first night they'd made love, she felt him there, touching her thoughts.

I know what you want.

She sucked in a deep breath. *You do?*

Mmmm. Yes.

He rolled them onto their sides on the wide lounge chair. His palm swept down over her belly until he could slide his hand down the front of her shorts.

"Open to me, baby," he said hoarsely.

Excited and wanting him so much, she propped her leg up to give him access. He found her creamy wet.

"Oh yeah." He breathed out the words, his sigh deep satisfaction. "So ready."

A shudder passed through her body, hard and swift as he slipped one finger deep into her and stroked. Another finger joined the search, plunging in and out with steady but gentle pressure.

As he covered her mouth with his, she quaked under his onslaught. His fingers felt so good, so right rubbing insistently. Breathing hard, she allowed the exhilaration to capture her. His fingers slipped out but he rubbed over her clit. His touch teased, strummed. She moaned as the excitement became almost unbearable.

He released her, and she whispered a protest. "Marcus."

"Easy." He released her and moved back. "Lay back on the chair."

She did as he asked. He eased her sandals off, then drew her shorts and panties down her legs. He pressed her legs upward until her feet lay flat on the chaise, her pussy open and vulnerable. She shook with fine tremors of desire, knowing what he planned next and wanting it so much she ached. He scooted back. His fingers slid over the back of her thigh and a tremor shot through her.

"You're so beautiful." He let her thighs rest over his forearms and leaned in. He took a deep breath as he stared at her folds. "Jesus, you smell good."

His throaty declaration made her pussy weep. Desperation drove her to say, "Lick me."

"With pleasure, baby."

He leaned in and stroked her pussy with one long sweep of his tongue.

She jerked in delight, her gasp loud. "Oh yes."

With enthusiasm, his tongue traced one fold and then the other. She could hardly stand the pleasure as he drove his tongue into her. She whimpered as Marcus maneuvered his hand until he could caress her clit with his thumb. He worked her with passionate intent, every thrust of his tongue and brush of his thumb threatening to send her into orgasm. She shook, panted, begged. Then he slowly slipped two fingers deep into her pussy and thrust. She held back a sharp cry and lifted her hips to bring him deeper.

Tara thought she would lose her mind because the pleasure was so great. With gentle, maddening caresses, he tongued her clit, his fingers working deep into her pussy with stroke after stroke. He pressed upward and found a spot high within her. She did cry out then, a tiny exclamation of pure bliss as he brushed that area, his fingers manipulating as his tongue continued its relentless movements.

She couldn't take any more.

She couldn't make it…couldn't claim the final summit. He thrust his fingers faster. His lips closed over her clit and sucked hard.

Panting harshly, she moaned and writhed in his grip. He sucked harder. Her eyes sprung open as climax seized her. Shivering, she accepted the soul-deep pleasure as orgasm sparked and ignited. Rocked by breathless pleasure, her head fell back.

"That was beautiful." His voice, husky with continued desire, whispered. Marcus slowly slipped his fingers from her. "We're out in the open. Hope your neighbors don't peek over the fence."

She laughed softly. "I didn't think of that." Raw with lingering desire, she slipped away from him and removed her top and bra.

"God," he whispered. "You're so sexy. So damned gorgeous."

"You can barely see me."

"I know your nipples are hard, and your breasts are ready to be sucked. I know how your heart beats faster."

"Then take me."

Completing their union was all she cared about, all she drank and breathed at this moment. He stripped naked, then lay back on the double lounge. Needing him inside her with an ache she could no longer stand, she straddled Marcus.

She drew in a sharp, pleasure-filled breath as he gripped her hips, tilted his hips upward and worked his iron-hard cock into her wet passage with a deep, sharp plunge straight to the womb. *Hot, thick.* He felt incredible.

Could her neighbors hear them? The mere thought made her squirm, skewering on his cock with excitement.

Marcus writhed under her tight, hot embrace. He couldn't resist the wild and sinuous movement, the steady rhythm as she rode him. He could barely see the color of her eyes in the waning light, but he could feel. Smooth, liquid, mind-blowing pleasure eased into his body with each movement of her hips. He matched her, thrusting, taking. Shit, he'd never felt anything more erotic than her soft, tight cavern embracing his cock in hot wetness. Seconds blended into forever, as she took him like a rider on a steed, a woman without inhibition, without regrets.

Breaths coming fast and hard, he caressed her body with mindless, carnal hunger.

Pagan and forbidden, she took him like an Amazon, demanding all he could give her.

He palmed her hips and savored their gentle curves, cupped her breasts and enjoyed the texture of bead-hard nipples against his fingers. *Yes, oh God, yes.* He wanted to give her the wildest, most incredible orgasm she'd experienced.

"Come on, baby," he whispered. "Don't hold back."

Even as her soft exclamations grew a little louder, he felt her body tighten around his. Pumping hard, he speared her high and deep. Her hair tossed about her head as she took him fiercely. She leaned down and kissed him, and as her mouth sealed to his, he thrust his tongue deep. He cupped her butt, squeezing and anchoring as he thrust harder and pushed her to the limit. Her body started to tremble, and she screamed into his mouth as her pussy flexed and shivered around his cock. He tasted her pleasure, took it in and let himself go.

He drove into her with one, two, three hard thrusts. With a harsh growl, he came. Hot cum shot from him, tossing him into a gut-wrenching ecstasy as all his muscles clenched and shivered.

As they relaxed, Marcus inhaled the animal aroma of their sex. He'd always wanted to protect her, and now they'd taken their relationship beyond friendship, he couldn't shake this primitive need to claim her as his. If any man challenged him for her, he would fight. If Drake tried to harm her, all rules were off.

He gathered her closer and kissed her forehead, listening to her soft breathing and the contented sigh that parted her lips.

* * * * *

Tara fielded calls that night, one from Bettina and another from a concerned acquaintance at the office. When the phone rang a third time, she grabbed it.

"Hi, Tara." Drake's cold, deep voice came over the line. "I think you've been a bad girl. You fucked him again, didn't you?"

She reacted. "That's none of your concern now, Drake."

"Of course it is. You're my wife."

"Ex-wife."

"Not for long. We'll be married again."

"Drake—"

"You shouldn't play games with a man, Tara. You never did understand what it's like. A man lusts in his heart for a woman, and she's the cause of all his troubles. If I'd never met you, I wouldn't have spent six years in prison." He laughed. "But you're really my good luck charm. I wouldn't have found the Lord without you."

She wanted to hang up, but the cool, calculating tone in his voice kept her rooted to the spot in sickening fascination. "If you've found God, Drake, then you know He doesn't want you and me to be together."

His voice remained deadly calm. "You're wrong."

She shivered. "Drake, please—"

She stopped as Marcus walked into the room, his hair wet and slicked back from a shower, his T-shirt and jeans-clad body looking healthy and capable. He frowned deeply, and when he locked gazes with her, he shook his head.

Hang up.

The words rang in her head.

Don't talk to him.

She knew better, but she'd broken the rules, and now she paid for it.

"Your pretty boy is with you all the time, isn't he?" Drake's animosity crackled through the line. "He's a sin against God, as you are. I can save you, Tara. You could walk out of that house right now. Walk out of there and let me show you the way to salvation."

Anger plowed into her like a truck gone wild. "No."

"Your life depends on what you do in the next few days."

His words echoed in her head, demanding a retort. Her fingers clutched the receiver tightly as she spit out words. "I'm never going back to you. You're insane."

Marcus grasped her upper arm gently. His brow creased as he frowned, and he shook his head. He wanted her to shut up, but she couldn't stop, couldn't back off the need to put Drake in his place.

"Why can't you let go?" she asked, her voice breaking.

"Because you're mine. We took vows and those vows are sacred before God. You broke the vows by disobeying me."

"I never vowed to obey you. Never."

"That was my mistake. I should have demanded you say the vow. I helped you to ignore your duty as my wife."

"You sick asshole," she hissed. "This isn't ancient history. Woman are equals, and you can be damn sure I—"

"Shut up!"

His biting words worked. Shocked into silence, she waited.

A cold breeze seemed to cover her heart. She could almost feel the freezing hatred coming over the phone.

"You'll regret disobeying me, like you regretted it the last night we were together," he said.

She wanted to scream and kick and cry. She shook with growing rage. "The only person who is going to regret anything is you."

Marcus took the phone from her and put it back in the cradle. "Enough."

She glared at him, her mouth open in pure fury. "Damn it, Marcus. Why did you do that?"

He put his hands on his hips, and his voice came low and calm. "Because you were making it worse. Escalating. You should have hung up the minute you realized it was him. Next time—"

"No." Clipped and hard, the word shot from her as resentment came to a boil. "Don't you dare tell me what to do. I won't have another man pushing me around, treating me like a second-class citizen."

His lips parted, but nothing came out. Hard and cool, his gaze held resolve and impatience. "You know me better than that. You know I'm not like Drake."

She stalked the room, gazing everywhere but seeing nothing but red frustration. "If you're not like him, then you can't tell me what to do and you won't take the phone away from me when I'm talking. I don't care if it's Jack the Ripper on the other end of the line."

She didn't look at Marcus, but she could sense the heat of his own growing disenchantment rising. "You're tired. You need some rest."

She couldn't stop the tide. She turned on him. "I'm angry at Drake because he's spouting religious rhetoric in my face that's full of crap. But I'm also pissed because you're manhandling the situation. Little ol' Tara can't take care of herself. She needs big, strong word processing nerd to keep her safe. I don't think you're that much different than Drake. You want to control me, too, just in a different way."

She knew she'd done it now. His eyes flashed with internal fire, his mouth tight and his lips a straight line. The predator in Marcus came through, and seeing that hardness directed toward her startled Tara.

He took a step forward, then another. She flinched but held her ground. For a horrible second Drake's face seem to superimpose over Marcus' handsome visage. A shiver worked up her spine.

Marcus' gaze softened. She almost forgot her ire under the other emotion she saw burning in his eyes. Damn him for reminding her of what he'd done for her, the wonderful times they'd shared.

She didn't want to remember. "No, Marcus. Don't come any closer."

Hurt flashed through his eyes. "You know me. I would never hurt you. I'm trying to help."

Tears welled up, and more irritation poured into her wounds. She didn't want to cry and suffer humiliation from losing control. Her throat tightened so much she couldn't speak.

"Tara, you knew better than to engage him in conversation. I understand that you're so angry you couldn't resist. I wanted to stop it from getting worse."

She breathed deeply to ease the shivering deep inside and couldn't do it. She marched past him and headed down the hallway, half afraid he would follow her. She reached the bedroom, went inside and slammed the door. She locked it.

Lying down on the bed, she allowed the floodgates to open. Tears started slowly, then flowed freely. Shamed now that she'd lost control, her sobs came harder, and her heart wanted to crack in two.

* * * * *

Marcus flipped channels with the remote, but nothing interested him, not even a sports channel.

"Shit. You fucked up, Hyatt." He clicked the off button and the TV went blank. "And your brain is rotting."

He scrubbed his hands over his face and groaned. After Tara had gone into her room and didn't come out, he almost knocked on the door and demanded she let him in. No. That would have added fuel to an already raging firestorm. She didn't need any more stimuli, any additional demands.

Instead, he sat on the couch and pondered how screwed up this case had become. She was more than a "case", of course. He'd long ago lost objectivity or professionalism when it came to her. She'd invaded parts of him, worked so deep into his heart he knew he'd never get her out.

Did he want her out of his life? Could he bear the thought of leaving her alone to fight Drake?

Oh shit.

His gut told him the answer. He was on the verge of saying something he'd never said to another woman.

I love you.

It scared him shitless. Firefights in nasty places around the world, he could take. Facing down mind manipulators like Jason Forte, he could handle.

Telling Tara his deepest feelings for her made sweat pop out on his forehead. He didn't want to think about it too long or too hard.

He ran over the conversation earlier with Ben on his I-Doc when he reported to SIA. Ben was alarmed by the incident in Forte's office, and he didn't leave anything vague in his concerns.

Maybe you should pull out of this assignment. We'll send in someone whose barriers are working on a higher level for now.

He'd wanted to curse, but Marcus also understood Ben's stance. He'd argued right back. *Who else will you get on short notice? We can't afford more time elapsing while a new person is established. I can still do this.*

He must prove to himself that he could complete this assignment.

Ben's other questions echoed in his ears. *What about Tara? Can you protect her and battle Jason Forte?*

God, he had to protect her. It was his number one priority, bar none.

Ben relented, but required Marcus to drop the case if anything more happened on a physiological level that he couldn't handle. Marcus agreed.

Worried about Tara, he headed down the hallway to her room. When he reached it, he knocked softly.

"Tara?"

He didn't get an answer, and when he tried the door it was locked. Before he could turn away, she opened the door.

Red-rimmed and puffy, her eyes betrayed her state. Despair lurked in her eyes, and he reached out for her. To his surprise, she came into his arms without hesitation and melted against him. God, she felt so right in his arms. So good. He wanted to hold her, caress her until she forgot anger and felt only the hot, elemental requirement of his body inside hers. Heat rose on his skin like a fever.

He tangled his fingers in her hair and then tilted her head back so he could look into her extraordinary eyes. "It's going to be all right. You don't need to worry. I'm not going anywhere."

Tears trickled down her face. "You can't make it all better. I think when I…when I was yelling at you for no good reason that's what I realized. No one can help me."

He could see that anguish rode her hard. He felt it in her rigid muscles as he kept his arms around her waist. "You're not alone. I'm committed to your safety."

She nodded. Sadness ringed her being, and he felt it in his soul.

"I didn't mean what I said earlier." She smoothed her palms over his forearms, up his biceps and stopped at his shoulders. He shivered under her warm touch, his body forgetting harsh words and longing for the wet, hot softness between her legs.

"And I'm sorry I pushed you. I wasn't giving you any slack. You've been on overload the last few days. I understand that."

"No, I should have listened to you. I really do know better than to enrage Drake and now I've made it worse."

"Yeah, you probably have," he said and kept his smile.

She answered with a sweet, genuine grin. Man, he loved it when she beamed like that. It made him feel taller, stronger. He could fuckin' do anything if she cared about him.

She laughed, then sniffed and wiped away an errant tear. "I'm so sorry. I don't want to fight. I wasn't thinking. I'm so tired of this cat and mouse thing, and now Jason Forte is accusing you of sexual harassment."

"It's all right. It doesn't matter."

As he held her, his body hardened, wanting to hold her forever. It didn't matter what Forte and Cecelia plotted, or that he couldn't tell Tara about his agent status. He cradled her head to his shoulder, drew in her intoxicating warmth and scent. She felt so damn right in his arms.

"Marcus? Aren't you worried?"

He kissed her forehead. "Yeah, I'm worried. About you."

"Why?"

"You know why. Drake. Your job. If you lost your job because of me—"

She pulled back and covered his mouth with her fingers. "Shhh. I don't think it's me who would lose my job."

"Maybe you're right. Come on. Let's talk strategy. We need to think about how to survive whatever Drake, Jason and Cecelia have up their sleeves."

Marcus looked so damned handsome. Snug T-shirt strained over his muscular chest and down over his stomach. She longed to reach out, to feel those hard planes and the heat beneath them. His mouth, strong and yet sensual, tempted her almost beyond endurance. She was enticed to taste him, throw caution away and devour him until they made love long and hard.

"God, you're beautiful." His husky declaration sent heat racing throughout her body.

She couldn't speak, but she didn't need to. Her heart must have shown in her eyes. Warmth surrounded her as his gaze caressed with a loving attention she'd never seen in a man's eyes before.

His hot attention made her squirm, but not with discomfort. She wanted him to look at her like this for the rest of her life. As if he'd discovered something wonderful and new every time he saw her. As if she meant more to him than anything else on earth. She ached with wanting it, and it scared her to death. Because if she wanted these things, it meant she cared far more than friendship, beyond lust.

"I was thinking that I'm one lucky woman."

"Why is that?"

"Because I have some of the greatest friends in the world. Bettina...you."

His hands trailed to her upper shoulders. "Is that what you think I am? Just your friend?"

She lifted one brow. "You are, aren't you?"

A sexy smile warmed his mouth, and her heart tripped over itself. "I'll always be your friend, Tara."

Friend.

Well, there she had it. He wanted to be friends, perhaps an occasional bed partner. Once her situation with Drake was resolved, there would be no reason for him to remain with her. Guarding her body. Guarding her safety.

God, what she wouldn't give to make this a permanent arrangement.

The realization stuck in her throat. Her eyes teared up. *Oh no, no, no.*

"What's wrong?" he asked softly, the husky nuance in his throat sending a skitter of arousal over her skin.

"Nothing."

He frowned and his grip on her shoulders tightened a little. "I can see it in your eyes, honey. Don't try to hide it from me." Passion simmered, dangerous and deep, in his ocean-depth eyes.

"Speak to me. Tell me what's going on in that gorgeous head of yours."

She smiled. "Flattery will get you nowhere this time, Hyatt."

His hands roamed down her arms until they latched onto her hips. His fingers caressed her skin through the lightweight cotton until they slipped under the leg of the shorts and caressed her upper thigh. Heat burst in her lower stomach as arousal spiked furnace-high in her libido. How could this man turn her to mush with a simple touch, with a few well-placed words? He made her nuts with passion, and it took almost nothing to drive her within inches of climbing on top of him and fucking him right here.

"You're making me nuts, Tara." His voice rasped, deep and needy with desire. "I want to stick this cock high up inside you. I want to fuck you so hard and long you'll never want another man. You're mine."

Possession burned in his eyes, and the excitement inside her started to diminish. No. This felt too much like ownership, like losing control of everything she'd gained since Drake went to prison.

She pulled back, slipping from his arms. "I can't do that."

"What?" His gaze still sparked with desire. "What's wrong?"

"I can't do this...this possession thing." Fear made her speak fast. "A man doesn't own me. You can't own me, Marcus."

"What?" He looked confused.

Tears stung her eyes, and it felt like a ball of lead had settled in her chest. She couldn't take this. "Maybe this isn't a good idea. I'm tired anyway. I'm going to bed."

She turned and left, heading down the hallway to the bedroom. She closed the bedroom door and locked it.

God, how did she do it? How did she get herself into these emotional messes? Sinking down onto the bed, she sighed with misery. Lying back, she closed her eyes. Tears leaked through. Marcus didn't knock on the door, and sometime later she heard the dishwasher go on and other movement around the kitchen. Good. Maybe he wouldn't knock on her door and beg her to come out. No, Marcus would leave her to stew in her own juice. Tears flowed down her face, and she curled into a ball and let them come.

Chapter Seventeen

🔊

Frustration ate away at Marcus the next day as he watched Tara grab her keys and her purse from the couch. "I'm taking you to work and dropping you off."

"Are you sure you want to do that?" Her voice was cool.

She'd avoided eye contact with him all morning, and it drove him nuts. He clasped her arm and gently turned her around to face him. "Can you stop and look at me a minute?"

She sighed and locked gazes with him. Dark circles marred her mysterious and beautiful eyes.

"You look tired," he said.

"I didn't sleep well."

"I didn't either. I missed you next to me." A smile dashed over his lips. "The guestroom bed was cold and lonely."

He moved nearer and inhaled her intoxicating scent. He wanted to bury his face in her hair and his cock inside her heat. Hell, who was he kidding? Her smile, her beautiful, unusual eyes, her musical laugh...it would haunt him forever. A lump formed in his throat and he swallowed hard.

"No matter what you think of me, there's one thing that's true," he said.

She waited.

He trailed his fingers up her arms and cupped her face. He half expected her to pull away, but instead her eyes widened, warmed.

"Even if you hate my guts, Tara, you can always count on me. If you need me for anything, don't hesitate to call. If you're afraid, call me and I'll be there for you."

She reached up and clasped his wrists, her eyes liquid and soft. Maybe there was hope yet. God, her mouth look so fuckin' delicious.

He almost leaned forward to kiss her, but he had a feeling she'd balk. He released her. "Come on. We don't want you to be late."

* * * * *

Drake watched the street traffic roll by, his insides churning as he dialed his family's number. After one ring, Kendra picked up.

"Drake." Her voice sounded pliant, as it always did. The way a woman's voice should sound.

Not harsh. Not defiant like Tara's.

He'd soon remedy that.

"Kendra." He purred the word certain she could feel it across her skin. A tingle started low in his gut.

It shocked him. He'd never felt sexual toward his sister. He smirked. There was always a first time for everything.

"What do you want?" she asked.

He gazed locked on the dirty street outside the telephone booth. Streetwalkers dominated one side of the avenue, minor drug dealers on the other. He didn't care. They didn't frighten him, and when he'd walked past them, they'd parted away from him like the Red Sea. They knew death walking when they saw it. Plus, his Lord God the Almighty gave him a shield and protected him from his enemies.

"I want to talk to Mother and Father," he said.

"They're not here. They're at a church function."

"Why aren't you?"

"Because I'm sick."

She sounded vaguely defiant this time, and it ground in his gut like glass. "Yeah, right."

"Really. Something with my stomach."

"Father always made you go to church, even when those bitch cramps of yours doubled you over. What's changed?"

A pitiful laugh slipped from her throat. "He didn't have much choice. I was throwing up." A long pause filtered over the line until she said, "Why do you want to talk to Mom and Dad?"

"I want to let them know what I have planned."

Kendra's voice grew stronger. "What? What are you gonna do, Drake?"

"'Every vow by which a widow or a divorced woman has bound herself is valid... The husband can confirm or repudiate any vow or any oath by which a woman binds herself to mortification.'"

"What?"

"It's from the Bible, dear sister. Tara bound herself to me. She'll come back to me or be punished by the Lord."

"You mean…"

"I mean, she'll love me again. She'll do my bidding."

"Drake, don't do anything." Her voice turned to a whiny whimper, grating on his nerves like a nail file over bare skin. "Please don't hurt Tara."

"'You set my foot on my enemies' necks, and I wipe out those who hate me. They cry, but there is no one to save them; they cry to the Lord, but he does not answer. I shall beat them as fine as dust before the wind, like mud in the streets I shall trample them. You set me free from the people who challenge me, and make me master of nations.'" He paused for breath. "Psalms 18."

She sucked in a harsh breath. "No, Drake."

"It'll be in the papers."

"What will?"

"Her long-haired boyfriend is going to die. I need to rescue her from him."

"She doesn't need you anymore Drake. Why can't you leave her alone?"

He made his voice high-pitched. "'Why can't you leave her alone?'" He threw back his head and laughed. "You're a bitch, just like Tara. I'm surprised Father hasn't beat you into submission yet."

"He never beat it into you." Her voice warbled. "Or did he?"

"What do you mean?"

"You never believed in Daddy's God, Drake. Not the one he uses to hurt Momma and me. The one he used to damage you."

"What the shit are you talking about?" he growled out the question.

"You always said his God was crap, Drake. What made you change? What made you believe in Daddy's vengeful God?"

Fire burned in his soul, and he wanted to reach through the phone and hurt her. Maybe when he had Tara, he would go after Kendra and show her what it meant to cower under a man's wrath. If she thought Father could hurt her, she didn't know the meaning of pain.

He glared out at the busy street. "I'm going to tell him what you said."

"No, Drake," she gasped. "No."

He loved the fright in her voice. "Tell Father and Mother I plan to make headlines. Then I'm going to come back there and make headlines again."

He heard her sob before he hung up.

* * * * *

As she sat in Bettina's office, waiting for Human Resources manager Amanda Cortez and Bettina to come in, Tara fiddled with the leather strap on her handbag. She wished she were anywhere else. A long, cool sip of water would do right now. So would a vacation. A cruise ship somewhere isolated.

She wanted to forget her fractured relationship with Marcus. When he'd dropped her off at the parking garage elevator, she left the car with a curt goodbye. He'd waited until she was in the elevator before pulling away. Earlier, when he'd said he'd be there for her no matter what, she'd almost pulled his head down and kissed him. She'd almost traced the chiseled line of his nose and jaw. In green T-shirt and worn jeans, he'd set her heart pumping. Dressed or naked, the man stole her breath. He'd spoken so softly and gently to her this morning, when he could have been cold. After all, she'd come down on him hard last night more than once.

Dread of possession lingered inside her, despite his reassurances. No, she couldn't let him claim her as Drake had many years ago with romantic promises that became blatant lies.

Weariness dogged her. She closed her eyes and sighed. Tired. So tired. She rubbed the back of her neck.

The door popped open and startled her.

She turned in her chair, expecting to see Bettina and Amanda. Instead, Forte and Amanda entered. Tara's heart started a dull thud, thud, thud. Heat, then cold flashed over her skin. Nausea touched her stomach, then retreated.

What's wrong with me?

She stood. "Mr. Forte, Amanda. I thought Bettina would be joining us."

Forte smiled, oily and self-assured. "We told her we needed to talk with you alone."

Amanda smiled, her gaze steady. She always wore her suits with style and confidence, her boyish, short-cropped black hair wavy against her head and her caramel skin and blue eyes a startling contrast. Long-limbed and lithe, she reminded Tara of a feline.

She put out her hand and Tara shook it. Amanda's fingers gripped hers hard and her ring dug into her fingers under Amanda's too tight grip.

"Please sit down," Amanda said without further greeting.

Unusual. Unusual and icy. Tara's stomach flipped, then flopped and she sank into one of the chairs in front of Bettina's desk. Amanda sat in Bettina's chair, and Forte stood slightly behind Tara and to the side. She glanced at him curiosity. *What the hell did he have up his sleeve this time?* Amanda had considerable cheek commandeering Bettina's desk.

"We know things have been rough for you lately," Amanda said as she sat forward and leaned on Bettina's desk.

"It hasn't exactly been the greatest week," Tara said.

"We're not going to play games here," Amanda said.

I'll just bet.

Forte spoke up, his voice hard-edged. "We know you have a relationship with Hyatt."

Oh-oh. Here comes the bull layered on thick.

"And?" Tara asked.

"And we know he's tried more than once to seduce Cecelia and Sugar. In fact, we told our suspicions to the police. Who knows if they'll be visiting him soon?"

Tara wanted to reach across the desk and smack the Human Resources manager. Amanda's eyes sparked a second, an odd fire deep in the center. Tara blinked, and the heat in the woman's eyes dimmed and flickered.

Tara crossed her arms. "Marcus had nothing to do with Sugar's death."

"How can you be certain?" Forte asked.

Tara felt him draw nearer, coming up behind her chair. "Because he has no motive, and he's not that kind of man."

Amanda's smile turned icicle cold. "It doesn't matter anymore. With him out of the way, we don't have to worry about interference."

"Interference?" A prickle of warning touched Tara's lower spine. Anxiety quickened her heart beat. "He's not interfering with anything you're doing. I'm not sure why you're telling me all this."

Amanda shrugged. "Because we wanted to do something."

Pinned by Amanda's chilly stare, fresh panic threatened to overwhelm Tara's ability to protest the ridiculous conversation.

"We want you to be a part of our family," Forte's raspy voice said behind her. "And that can't happen if an agent from the SIA is lurking around."

Amanda pushed her chair back and propped her ankles on the desk. "Marcus was very savvy, until Jason pulled some information out of his mind the other day."

Confusion tried to overwhelm Tara's thoughts. Whatever these two plotted, she refused to participate. If she had to leave the room without finishing the bizarre conversation, she would.

She started to stand, but Jason clasped her shoulders and held her in the chair. "We're not finished. Not until you understand that your darling Marcus has deceived you."

She glared at Amanda, then shrugged out from under Forte's grasp. She turned in her chair enough to look at Forte. "I don't know what you're talking about."

"The SIA," Amanda said. "Marcus is an agent for the SIA."

"What is SIA?" Tara asked.

Forte laughed, and the oily sound slithered down her spine. "Special Investigations Agency. A branch of the government that works against subversive paranormals and other terrorists."

Forte's heat seemed to radiate off him and touch her. A queasy, unnerving sensation rose up from her stomach and into her head.

"He's not a word processor, Tara. He's a very dangerous man who needed to be brought down," Amanda said.

God, they were certifiable, the offspring of some wild nightmare about an invasion of pod people. That had to be the explanation. Any moment Tara would wake from a horrible dream.

Tara tried to turn, but Forte's hands clamped on her shoulders again and forced her to turn toward Amanda. Lacerating pain seared her shoulders, and a tight, breathless gasp slipped from her throat. She couldn't find one bit of air as agony froze her lungs. She stared in mute horror at Amanda and the woman's hellish smile.

"Why?" Tara managed to force from her throat.

"Because Jason has plans for us all. And you'll be a part of it. Marcus isn't going to get in the way anymore. We're making sure of that."

"We?" Tara quivered as the pain in her shoulders increased. Stunned, she couldn't pull her thoughts together.

"Quiet!" Jason transferred his grip to her head.

Defiance reared up and with a burst of strength, she reared out of his grip and stood up. She swung toward him. "Get your hands off me!"

Molten with anger, his eyes literally glowed red. "You will obey."

Wrong words. She'd had enough of men, even ones with fiery eyes from a nightmare, telling her how to run her life. Rage gathered with screaming intensity. Her whole body shook and her muscles tightened with pain. How could he have broken through her white barriers so easily?

He put his hand out, and Tara felt him cut through the final barrier of her white light protection. His influence poured over her senses and her will. She struggled as her heart pounded, her breathing coming fast. How would she get out of this one? How?

"No. I'm not going to obey you." She managed to grit the words through her teeth.

Must escape. Must not let him —

She started toward the door. He grabbed her arms and pain sliced through her body in one vicious rip.

She gasped and a whimper slipped through her lips. "No."

She closed her eyes, drew the white light down from the top of her head and tried to bring it over the rest of her body. Her protection stopped halfway as another force shoved it back.

No. No. Please no.

She squirmed in his hold. "Let me go!" Useless, stupid words. "It was you that hurt Sugar, wasn't it? And Marcus."

He chuckled, and as she dared look into those red eyes, the world started to drop away. She felt dizzy, then Forte's arms came around her. Tara heard Amanda's laugh, husky and deep, in the background.

"Let me inside you, Tara," Forte said before his lips came down on hers.

* * * * *

Marcus watched Tara leave the parking garage elevator that evening, her walk confident. His nerves stayed taut, ready for any contingency. He hated not being with Tara and hated not protecting her.

He made the decision as he saw her luminous smile. When he took her home, he'd tell her everything. If it meant going against SIA rules, so be it. Her life meant more to him then keeping her in the dark.

"Hey," she said as she slid into the car and tossed a smile his way.

"Hi." He responded to her warm expression. "You're in a good mood."

"Of course. It's a beautiful day. Let's go home and celebrate."

He peered at her. "That's a big contrast from this morning. What happened?"

"I'll tell you when we get home." Wicked intent moved through her eyes.

She licked her lips and his groin tightened. He started the car and pulled out of the parking structure. They'd pulled onto the highway when her fingers clasped his thigh.

He jerked in surprise. She explored. His cock swelled to attention. "Um…maybe we should wait for that until we get to your house."

She licked her lips, her eyes smoldering. Instead of answering, she rubbed his denim-clad cock with firm strokes.

Holy shit. What a transformation. She'd gone from cold to a sexual siren in one day flat.

He sucked in a breath as she continued her gentle assault. His cock didn't care that they sailed down the highway. It wanted completion. Soon, when he got her home, he could sink deep into her liquid depths.

He put one hand over hers and tried to restrain her touch. "Honey, I'll come in my pants if you keep doing that. I'd rather come inside you."

She slipped her hand away from his cock and down his thigh to his knee. She lingered a minute before retreating.

"What's changed?" he asked into the silence. "This morning you couldn't wait to get away from me. I thought you were angry."

"I was. Things have changed. Tremendously."

"Like what?"

"I'll tell you when we're in the house."

She wanted to tease him. Whatever the case, it worked. His cock stayed like granite all the way to her home.

Once they reached her house, he glanced around the area. No sign of Drake skulking around outside, but that didn't mean anything. The man obviously watched the house from time to time.

He locked the door, and once inside activated the security system. She dropped her purse on the coffee table, then eased off her pumps and left them lying in the middle of the floor. Her hips swayed, her body in tune with a song he couldn't hear. Dying to know what brought on this new woman, he followed her.

"They made an announcement today that Sugar died of natural causes. No homicide," she said.

Marcus frowned as she unbuttoned her blouse. "Natural causes? What's natural for a young woman?"

She shrugged, and her lack of concern disturbed him. "You're off the hook, then. Forte and the others can't make up some stupid story saying you did it. They can't add it to your list of crimes."

"I've accumulated a list now?"

"According to Jason, yes."

He smirked. "When did you start calling him Jason?"

Her enigmatic smile sent shivers of misgiving up his spine. "As of today."

Jealousy hit him square in the gut like an explosive round. He sucked in a breath and watched her walk down the hall, discarding her clothes without a care in the world.

She paused long enough to strip off her pantyhose and toss them over her shoulder at him like a grenade. He caught them, then threw them on the couch. She unzipped her skirt and it slid to the floor. She walked out of it. A moment later her blouse fell, too.

Son-of-a-fuckin'-bitch.

She'd worn utilitarian white panties, and her white bra wouldn't win awards for sexiness. No, it was the way her hips moved, her body enticed, her scent intoxicated. Grinding desire ached in his loins. Need roared through him like a mountain lion and mingled with the jealousy. He felt hot, possessive and ready to take whatever she wanted to give. He would wipe her mind clean of that Forte bastard no matter what it took.

Marcus followed her like a lamb, fascinated as first her bra and then her panties came off. Like breadcrumbs her clothing items drew him to a...a what? A bout of hot sex? A slaughter? Something about her actions seemed uncharacteristic. Too bold. Too calculating. He didn't have a problem with her choosing to be sexually uninhibited. He wanted her wild beneath him, on top of him, up against a wall. Wherever she wanted to be. But this felt...off.

She turned, and he gawked as if he'd never seen her flesh before. Under the dim bedroom lighting, her skin held a golden hue. His mouth watered as her high, rounded breasts enticed. He wanted to reach out and taste those nipples. He wanted to cup the small rib cage and waist, coast over the smooth, curvy hips and flat stomach. Exploring those beautiful, well-muscled legs and tasting her hot cream would be... God save him. His jeans restricted his cock painfully, and he almost reached down and undid the button and zipper.

She smiled, hands on her hips, and then he saw it. A fire-bright storm of red light in her eyes.

Holy shit.

He snatched her to him, and her body collided with his. She grunted softly, but his rough movement didn't erase that eerie smile from her lips.

"Tara, what happened today?"

Confusion creased her brow, and she stared almost sightlessly at his chest.

"Tara, did you meet with Forte or Cecelia?"

"Cecelia wasn't at work. She called in sick. I saw Forte and Amanda. They..."

"They what?"

Bewilderment filled her eyes. "I-I don't remember."

Her hands came up to caress his chest, and the intimate touch aroused him even more. She rubbed his nipples. He reached for her hands. Pinning them against his chest, he halted her exploration.

"Honey, tell me what happened during the meeting."

Innocence left her eyes, and she glared at him. "I'm not your honey. When you decided you wanted to tell me what to do, to possess me, you lost the privilege to call me honey."

Mercurial, her eyes danced from teasing to hard with contempt. Forte had gotten to her. She was acting as freaky as Cecelia. The son-of-a-freakin'-devil-whore had touched Tara. Rage built in Marcus' system like a hot wire. Guilt burst inside him at the same time. He shouldn't have let her go to work today. Fear followed like a sucker punch.

"Did Forte touch you? Did he kiss you or…" Marcus gritted his teeth and swallowed hard. "Did he try and have sex with you?"

She blinked slowly, as if she hadn't quite heard him. "I don't… No, I don't think so."

"You don't think so."

"Why are you asking me all these questions?"

"Because," Marcus almost growled. "Because number one, if that fucking devil spawn so much as touched you, I am going to strip his hide, marinate it and cure it in the sun. But if he did more—"

He couldn't finish, the fury and the nausea rising inside him like lava trying to escape a volcano.

She frowned, and he saw confusion and fear dance in her gaze. She couldn't remember. Oh hell, she couldn't remember.

She shivered, then comprehension started to come over her. The slightly dazed expression slipped from her eyes. "Marcus?"

"What is it?"

"I went into Bettina's office and Amanda and Forte were there, and they were trying to tell me bad things about you, and I didn't believe them."

He caressed her naked shoulders. "That's good, honey. What else happened?"

"I felt weird around them because it didn't feel right what they were saying, and then I was disoriented and Forte kissed me."

Shaking with anger, Marcus tried to regulate his breathing. "What else did he do, Tara?"

Now wide-eyed, with an edge of panic in her eyes, she shook her head. "I don't remember anything until just now." She glanced down at her body. "How did I get home?"

"You don't remember the rest of the day? Or coming down to the parking garage?"

"No."

"Damn it."

"What?" she asked, apprehension written into her eyes.

"Obviously Forte wanted to turn you into a walking zombie, sort of like he did with Sugar and Cecelia. But it doesn't seem to be sticking with you, thank God."

She shivered.

He swallowed hard, and his cock twitched as he realized what he must do.

The only cure to erase Forte's touch was to fuck Tara blind.

"Mother-fuckin'-hell-son-of-a-bitch!" he growled.

What choice did he have?

He drew his T-shirt over his head and let it fall, then started unzipping his jeans.

Chapter Eighteen

ဆ

Tara started at Marcus' vile curse and blinked up at him. She floated in a fog, her gaze unfocused, her body feeling light as down. His outburst frightened her.

Tears sprung to her eyes. "Don't curse at me!"

His eyes held a golden fire, a heat she'd never seen in them before as he raked her body with a thorough once-over. His bare chest, muscled and so damned sexy, made her swallow hard. A hot trickle of moisture gathered between her legs. Her pussy ached. She licked her lips. *Oh yes. Yes.* She wanted that hard cock in her now. She couldn't wait to fuck like a bunny. Needing him, wanting him so much she could die, she almost reached out.

Then reason returned.

He didn't want her because he loved her. In a flash, she remembered something Jason had said. Marcus was this so-called SIA agent. A betrayer to her heart and trust. Like Drake.

Renewed fury assaulted her. "You lied to me. Jason said you're some sort of agent."

Marcus cursed again. "It doesn't matter right now. I'll tell you all about it later."

"You've been lying all this time."

He'd cursed at her, grabbed her arm and glared like she'd committed some huge crime. Just like the few times she'd tried something outrageous to seduce Drake. When she allowed her true self to come out, Drake had always discounted her and claimed her needs resembled perversion.

"You're just like him," she said.

His eyes flashed, and for a moment she saw Drake in his eyes. His ability to hurt. To maim.

No. No man would do that to her again.

"No!" She reached for a big hardback on the bedside table and launched it at his head. "No!"

He batted the book away with his forearm. "Calm down, Tara."

"Calm down? Calm down? You're running after me like a beast, and I should calm down?"

She threw another book at him. With a lightning-fast move, powerful arms crushed her breath and they fell to the bed in a tangle of arms and legs.

He pinned her beneath his weight. "Tara, honey, listen to me."

She wriggled under him, half tempted to rip out his eyes with a careful slash of her fingernails. Heat enveloped her, a fever she couldn't stop. God, he was so strong, she could barely move. If he wanted to kill her, he could snap her neck in a second.

Tears poured down her cheeks. Self-reproach skewered her like a knife. How had she gotten herself into this situation again? How?

His gaze softened as she twitched under his restraint. "Listen to me, sweetheart. Don't cry. It's going to be all right. You know I'd never hurt you."

The tenderness in his voice stopped her struggles. Breathing hard, she gazed into the meltingly warm, passionate entreaty in his eyes.

"Something happened when you were in the office with Forte and Amanda today. The same thing that possesses Cecelia possesses you. That's why Cecelia kissed me. The only way to cure you is to have a connection with someone you care about." He swallowed hard, and he lowered his head to brush his lips over her forehead. "And I think you still care about me, don't you?"

Her heart pounded, her breath still came hard. Tears swept over her again, but she held them back. "How did he do this? Did he... God, did he rape me?"

Marcus brushed a kiss over her forehead again. "I don't think so sweetheart, but we can't be sure until your memory comes clear. And it won't as long as his taint stays with you. I'll be damned if I let him possess you forever, you hear? I'll be damned if I let him take you away from me."

She shifted and absorbed the heady, welcoming sensation of his hard body pressed along hers. Sensual need for Marcus overwhelmed anger.

"Trust me?" he said, gaze tender and pleading, voice hoarse with emotion.

His hands pinned her wrists above her head, and one hard thigh pressed up between her legs. The pressure against her pussy and clit made her gasp. She ached down there, her clit throbbing with new need. She wanted him to stroke her, lick her, feed that big cock into her until she forgot everything else. Tara knew one thing and one thing only. Sex.

She moved a little and the hair on his chest caressed her breasts. *Oh it feels so good.* She inhaled sharply. She moved against that hard thigh and the pressure on her clit was exquisite. Nothing else mattered but sex.

Sex.

He grunted as she writhed under him.

"Marcus."

"Listen to me, Tara. I'm not a rapist. I'm not going to force anything on you. But you have to understand what's happening. I don't know everything that Jason did to you, but we're going to take care of it. I'll protect you. I'm not letting you out of my sight. Do you understand?

Panting, she couldn't stand the torment anymore. "Yes. Yes, I understand. Just do something."

Blazing with a need so hot she felt seared by it, she sobbed.

His gaze roamed her face. "What do you want me to do? Say it. I need you to say it."

Again, she pushed up, this time not eager to escape, but to feel his hard body. She didn't hesitate to let raw words command her. "Fuck me. Please fuck me before I die."

Her guttural demand set him off, and with a low growl, he kissed her.

All impressions flooded her with agonizing intensity. Warmth of the room, the gentle fading light spilling over their bodies from the window, their hearts beating frantically. Desire culminated in a burst. He released her hands and kissed her again, his tongue torturing repeatedly in a mock of slow sex. He slid his other thigh between hers and pressed his cock to her mound. She gasped into his mouth and rubbed against him like a cat. It felt so good. She twined her arms around his neck and pulled him closer. A moan slipped from Marcus, and he took the kiss to another level. His tongue swept inside for one deep, hot stroke.

She yanked her mouth away from his. "Now. I can't wait. I can't."

His gaze filled with fire and want. "Yes."

He pulled away from her long enough to yank off his jeans and briefs. She got one glimpse of his cock, hard and so big. He panted, a flush high on his cheeks. He lowered his hips between her thighs and thrust. She cried out at the first hot slide.

Breathless, she moved her hips. Deep inside, his cock head caressed, and the thick, hot length stretched her pussy, filled her to the womb. "Please. I'm going to die if you don't —"

He growled low in his throat and thrust hard. She whimpered in pleasure. She'd never felt so good. He knew what she needed.

Oh God, please.

He nailed her.

His hips jammed against hers, a strong rutting motion.

His mouth came down over hers, tongue thrusting deep as he showed her how desperate he'd become.

Light and heat mingled, building. A flash of lightning brightened the room, and thunder rolled. Rain poured down. Wind battered the window as his hips pounded against her relentlessly.

Every powerful shove sent her to a new plateau. Her nails scraped over his shoulders as she held on for dear life. Panting, shaking, she reached for the pinnacle.

Her senses combined with only the storm and the wildness in their joining meaning anything to her. She'd never been more alive, more giving, more taking, more needed. Her pussy tightened, rippled and orgasm slammed her.

She shrieked into the night, the loud scream almost animalistic.

"Yeah," he groaned against her throat. "Oh shit, yeah."

She tightened and released over the hard cock plunging into her. She thought she'd never stop coming as he pushed her into a mindless pleasure with no ending.

His hips never stopped moving, the motion prolonging climax and sending her straight toward another explosion.

Moaning, she clutched at his hair, his shoulders, his back. His hands slid under her ass as he powered into her with increasing force, his male grunts and groans drawing her into frenzy so wild she lost all thought. His panting breath, his hot hands, the relentless rub of his chest over her breasts.

Thunder rumbled.

She came in a violent explosion. "Marcus!"

He growled into her neck and his body went rigid. Another growl and then yet another issued from his lips as he shot hot seed inside her again and again.

Shuddering against each other, they stayed locked together. He rolled to his side and held her tight, keeping her hips anchored against his.

"I'm not letting you go," he whispered fiercely. "I'm not." She started to cry and he kissed her nose and lips. "Don't cry. I'm not going to let anything happen to you."

She couldn't stop the tears, and he crooned to her gently, whispering how much he needed her. His cock hardened inside her and his hips moved. Slow and steady, he fucked her, the motion slick and hot and so different than their last frantic joining. Gentleness dominated his touch as he pulled out of Tara and urged her to turn over on her stomach. He parted her thighs and thrust deep inside her from behind. He stirred his hips against her, thrusting with long, slow, deep penetrations.

This time the sex seemed made of tenderness, of love itself. She sighed with happiness.

God, how much she loved him.

The words tightened in her throat, the knowledge threatening to spill from her lips.

I love you, Marcus. I love you so much.

Marcus felt Tara relax under him, as he eased in and out of her. Tonight he'd give her whatever she needed, do whatever it took to rid her of Forte's taint. The first orgasm should have split him in two and exhausted him so much he'd be down for the count. Instead, the way she'd writhed under him, screamed, shuddered…it all made him want her more. Making her come again and again was his only goal tonight.

As her hips moved, he gripped her waist and anchored her closer. He slowed her motion. Drawing out the pleasure would be better. His heart banged against his ribs, his breathing came harder as arousal started to peak. He drew back, wanting this time to last.

He leaned over her, and slipped his fingers between her pussy lips to find her clit. Drenched, her folds yielded to his touch and parted. When he manipulated her clit, she gasped.

"Yes," she whispered, arching her back. "Again."

Happiness penetrated the animal impulses driving him, and he laughed softly. "Again."

He inched in and out and established a slow rhythm. She whimpered, quivered. He pressed his nose against her back and drew in her sweet, hot scent. Sex permeated the air, and he absorbed the musky aroma, relished it. As he continued the steady cadence, she panted, appeals tumbling from her lips. Still, he wouldn't speed up.

Triumphant, enjoying her helpless murmurs, he refused to pick up speed. Instead, he continued to ease in and out.

Tara thought she would die.

She'd never felt more intensely, felt more clearly than right this moment. Her heart pounded, her breath rasped. She shuddered as her pussy ached and tingled and muscles deep inside clenched on his cock. If he didn't move faster, didn't fuck her out of her mind right now, she would go insane.

For a fine pinpoint in time, she heard her own heart pounding frenetically, her breath gasping and her moans of finely strung pleasure.

It had never been better than this. Never would be quite the same way again. It was right there.

Hovering.

Fulfillment.

Then she heard Marcus whisper in her mind. *Come for me.*

Oh God. Yes.

She gasped, her pussy clamped down on his cock, and she let go. She reared back, forcing his cock deep into her as a hoarse cry left her throat.

Searing ecstasy pulsated inside her, and sent rushing heat up through her chest and face. She couldn't stop the groans, the gasps for breath as he held the searing, rigid length of cock deep inside.

He kissed her back, and murmured to her. "God, you're beautiful. So sexy."

He pulled out, and gently turned her over. He lay down beside her and drew her into his arms As Marcus kissed her, his hands explored with rising passion. Happiness flowed through and around her. As if electricity charged the air, his touch tingled.

He inched his way along her body as if she was a delicacy. His tongue explored her neck, his lips tasted her ears. All the while, his fingers manipulated her nipples, tugging and plucking and his lips followed. She writhed in growing arousal. She couldn't believe it.

"I want you again," he said.

"Mmm…good."

He swept his tongue over one nipple, then tugged the sensitive flesh into his mouth. She grabbed his head and held him there. His fingers slid over her other nipple, and with a strong, steady motion, he pulled and caressed.

He moved back from his feast to say, "Be right back."

He returned with his cock sheathed in a condom and a bottle of lube. "Tilt your hips up."

She did, and he placed two pillows under her hips. A wicked grin played about his mouth. "Close your eyes."

As she closed her eyes, excitement filled her blood as she realized what he planned. Arousal drove her despite the orgasms she'd experienced. She heard him open the bottle of lube, and she licked her lips.

Two fingers wet with lube teased between her butt cheeks. She moaned softly. A few seconds later those wet fingers touched her anus. He probed gently with one finger and tickled.

She let loose a small laugh and wiggled. "Oh God. Marcus."

He continued his gentle massage of the area. "Does this feel good?"

"Yes. More."

He teased until she felt her tight entrance easing around the steady, light pressure.

"Play with your breasts," he said hoarsely. "Play with them."

She'd never touched her own breasts before during sex, but it seemed like the most natural thing to do.

"Look at me," he rasped.

Wild with a need to please him, she opened her eyes and stared boldly into his gaze as she tweaked her nipples. Then, unable to take the lusty, intense look in his eyes, she closed her eyes again and continued to pluck at her sensitive flesh. Quivers darted out from her aroused breasts to center deep in her belly. She couldn't believe the excitement. As it grew, she became oblivious to all but their breathing, the soft sounds they made.

Inch by tantalizing inch, he thrust one finger up her tight back hole. She moaned softly. Back and forth, he worked his finger in and out. Her clit ached, and she reached down and eased her middle finger over the small, hardening flesh.

"Oh yeah," he said, his voice harsh with desire.

He eased his finger out and replaced it with two. As two fingers worked slowly in and out of her passage, she fingered her clit faster.

Her panting escalated as anticipation rose. She couldn't quite reach the pinnacle. Frustrated, wanting more than anything to come, she begged him.

"Marcus, please."

"Easy. Easy." He drew his fingers from her, and then whispered gently, "Tell me if you want me to stop."

She opened her eyes and caught the infinite gentleness in his gaze. He'd never hurt her, and she'd been insane to think otherwise.

"Don't stop." She closed her eyes again.

With slow easing, and gentle testing, he worked three fingers into her. He pumped, working his slick fingers, fucking her ass with an insistent but tender rhythm that brushed nerve endings and served to stretch her passage. After what seemed an eternity of blissful sensations, he pulled out his fingers.

"Now?" he asked.

"Yes."

As his cock teased her anus, she tried to relax, exhilaration brewing inside her. She couldn't imagine, in that one minute, how she could take his whole cock up her ass. He guided the tip of his cock to her and pressed.

Seconds later, his cock thrust slowly and gently into her anus. She whimpered as her passage stretched around his thick length.

"Okay?" he asked.

"Yes. More."

A soft laugh left his throat. "Oh shit. Yes, ma'am."

His raw curse inflamed her, and as he pressed another firm inch inside, she arched upward to help his cause.

It felt different.

Tight.

Illicit.

He worked the tip back and forth, thrusting only a small bit in and out, in and out. This friction felt different, exciting, and she wanted more.

She massaged her clit and teased her nipples, loving the sensation of cock easing back and forth with small advances into her anus. Delicious friction threatened to make her writhe, an orgasm quivering on the edge. In this lust-drenched, heady world, she could disregard the storm outside, forget her own name.

"That's it, honey. Play with those nipples and clit. You're driving me crazy."

Sounding out of his mind with lust, he coached her. With gliding pushes, he eased back and forth into her. Suddenly, with a wrenching breath of ecstasy, she realized his entire cock moved deeply into her anus. She rubbed her clit harder, and his pace became deep, then shallow. His hips rocked as he moved inside her nerve-rich passage. She felt the heat climbing.

Yes. Yes. Yes. Yes.

His hips thrust faster, groans now issuing nonstop from his throat. "You're so tight. So fuckin' tight."

She couldn't keep quiet any longer as the pleasure drew her into the stratosphere, heaven on the horizon. "Marcus. Oh God, Marcus!"

Orgasm gripped her as she contracted and released over his cock in earthshaking spasms that stole her breath. She sobbed, her breath shaky with pants as she allowed the climax to rip her from the earth and join the heavens. Marcus continued to thrust and when she opened her eyes, she saw the passion-glazed evidence in his eyes that he wouldn't last long.

He pushed deep and erupted into climatic tremors. A growl ripped from his chest. He shook, he panted, his eyes opening to lock with hers. He collapsed upon her slowly, and drew her into his embrace.

Chapter Nineteen

❧

"Does Tara seem normal this morning?" Dorky asked over Marcus' I-Doc the next morning.

He leaned against the kitchen counter and looked at the clouds hanging over the Colorado mountains. "She's not awake yet. That's one of the reasons I'm making this call at oh-dark-thirty."

Telling Dorky that he'd had sex with Tara to remove Forte's influence hadn't been easy for Marcus. Sexual relationships weren't for general consumption—his private life was private. This time, though, his physical relationship with Tara couldn't be separated from the case. Even if Tara hadn't been influenced by Forte, Marcus would have wanted her in his bed anyway.

"Right." Dorky sounded sheepish, a rarity for her. "Well, you've inoculated her for the time being. Probably. Forte is obviously one of the most potent beings from the Shadow Realm that we've encountered. You've got strong psychic shields and it sounds like Tara does as well, but they don't hold up long under this bastard's sway."

"Any suggestions? Other than the fact I've got to figure out how to kick his Realm ass back into the other dimension without getting knocked unconscious like I did the last time? And has anyone at SIA decided what Forte really is? Does he have a classification?"

"Like I said before, he is a combination of several nasty elements. He bilocates, but he probably doesn't do it often because it would cause suspicion. He can dominate weak minds. Even strong minds like what you and Tara possess, he can manipulate or weaken. That could be what happened to Sugar and Cecelia. It would explain why they both started coming on to you and why Cecelia's kiss made you feel weak. Maybe Sugar's mind and body couldn't take the strain Forte put on her and that's why she died."

"Fuck." The curse slipped from his lips easily. Anger pulsed inside him like a live thing.

"And he's not a weredemon?"

"Apparently not. There's a good chance the human body everyone sees is Forte's ability to cloak himself in human form. I doubt he can possess different bodies like a weredemon."

"At least that's a relief."

"Let's just say he's a new species of Shadow Realm nasty we haven't seen before." He heard computer keys tapping. "Okay, here's what I suggest. Do you still have your electrical converter sword?"

He rubbed the back of his neck. "Yeah, but they sure as hell aren't going to let me walk in with a sword under one arm."

"Right." She sighed. "Well, what about your particle energy weapon? Works as well."

"As long innocent people aren't in the same room with Forte when the weapon goes off."

"Sounds like it's still the only choice. It's easier to smuggle into the building, too."

"Piece of cake. Except I don't like Tara being in the same building with the bastard. He's already influenced her once."

"What choice do you have?"

He stayed silent. His ego had taken a battering on this assignment, and he didn't like it.

"Let go of your ego, big, bad Marine," she said. "Forte is unprecedented. The SIA knows you're capable of protecting yourself against most foes we've come across from the Shadow Realm. No one is going to think less of you."

"Maybe not. But I'll know. Are you a mind reader, Dorky?"

"Of course not. I know you. You have significant success at SIA in taking down bad critters."

"Before they get a hit in on me, yeah. Not after they've kicked my ass once."

She huffed. "Men."

He laughed, and it felt good. He could count on her to ease his ego at the same time she told him to get over himself.

"It must be nice," she said.

"What?"

"To be a woman like Tara and have your protection, Marcus." Her words, soft and appreciative, took him by surprise. "Someday…"

"Someday what?"

"Nothing. I'm saying they broke the mold with you."

"That was probably a good thing."

Her warm chuckle filled the line. "Yes, a good thing. Now get out there and get this case wrapped up before Ben Darrock barbeques your butt."

He broke into a big smile. "Yes, ma'am."

"That's better."

"And Marcus?"

"Yeah?"

"Be careful."

"Roger that."

"You know, I've always hated that saying. Don't people ever say ten-four anymore? Or just plain Roger? Where did this *that* come from?"

"Leave it to you to care."

"Brat."

"Ten-four, okay?"

He hung up and smiled. Someday that woman would meet her match, and she wouldn't know what hit her.

Sheet lightning flickered in the pewter clouds, and he marveled at the bizarre weather. Rainstorms sometimes lasted all night and into the morning hours here in Colorado, but not often. It was almost as if something weird disturbed the air, an aberration.

He had to put an end to Forte's plans, whatever they might be.

He went back to bed, slipping off his sweatpants and cuddling up to Tara's naked body. She nestled against him, and without waking her up, he held her tight.

At five-thirty the alarm jolted them awake. Tara jumped in the shower after kissing the life out of him. The phone rang again, and Bettina's slightly rough-edged voice came over the line.

"They've fired you," she said.

He moved into the living room and sank down on the couch. "What?"

He didn't know why he sounded surprised.

Bettina's regret filled sigh came over the line. "I'm telling you this over the phone because they said they don't want you to come back."

He snorted. "You've got to be kidding?"

"They said you're a security risk."

Considering what he knew about disgruntled employees going postal, not letting a man take his medicine in person was a good way to *start* a security risk. But Amanda didn't necessarily know that, and he didn't think she cared now. From what Tara had said, Amanda was under Forte's power.

"I'm sorry, Marcus. You know this isn't the way I'd choose to do this."

He laughed, amazed he could find any humor left. "Would you have fired me at all?"

"No." The syllable came out firmly. "You're the best word processing employee I have, outside of Tara. I know you didn't do any of the things Forte is accusing you of doing."

"Other than involvement with Tara."

"Big deal. I know you love her and you're trying to protect her against her ex."

You love her.

Strong words. Words with a hell of a lot of power.

Before he could deny or confirm her assertion, she continued. "I'm going to protest this ridiculous scheme to fire you."

"Don't."

"What?"

"Try and stay away from Forte and Amanda today."

"Why?"

He rubbed at the tension building at the back of his neck again. "Do you trust me, Bettina?"

Here I go again asking a woman to trust me.

"Yes."

"Make excuses not to see them. Do whatever you have to."

"Marcus, what is going on? I know there's something odd about Forte—"

"You can do me another favor, too. I won't ask for it again."

"What is it?"

"I want to come in and get my personal items. Tell the receptionist at the front that it's all right for me to be there so they don't call security."

"Marcus, I don't like the sound of this."

A muscle in his jaw throbbed and tension tightened across his temples. "Please, do as I ask. I'm not going to hurt anyone, you know that."

"All right. You'll come in with Tara, then?"

"Yes."

After he hung up, he headed back to the bedroom. Tara was laying underwear out on the already made bed. He devoured the view of her smooth, bare back and delicious butt.

"Don't move," he said softly.

She glanced over her shoulder and gave him a devilish smile. "Why?"

"Because there's a dangerous creature coming up behind you."

"And he wants a clear path to attack?"

"Exactly."

Tara watched him stride forward. Nature had made the most gorgeous man she'd ever seen with a bare chest and wearing sweats. The way he looked at her, like a big jungle cat stalking a tasty morsel, made her body ache with desire.

Marcus wrapped his hands around her waist and pulled her back against him. His heat enveloped her as he nuzzled aside her hair so he could kiss her ear.

"God, you smell good," he said.

"Who was on the phone?"

"Bettina." He told her about the conversation.

Alarmed, she tried to turn in his arms, but he kept her still. "No, honey. Let's forget what's ahead for a moment."

His cock pushed against his sweats and nestled along her backside. Last night he'd taken her higher and hotter than ever before, and right now she felt renewed heat building between them.

Don't worry. His words echoed in her mind. His hands moved, sliding up to cup her breasts and tug on her nipples.

She gasped. "Marcus." She had to ask him something she'd meaning to discuss for some time. "Marcus, we've never talked about how we can sometimes read each other's minds and why we dreamed about each other."

"The dream part is easy. We were trying to hide how attracted we were to each other. I know I was trying to hold back what I felt. As for reading minds, I've always had strong telepathy, but only randomly."

Somehow, she knew he continued to deceive her. Her mind felt mushy from last night and the effects Forte had on her. She couldn't even remember everything Forte had said about Marcus. "Well, you know about my psychic abilities."

He kissed her neck. "So you see it's no big deal between us."

She stiffened in his arms. "No big deal that we make love in our dreams?"

"It's extraordinary that we found each other like this, and our talents with telepathy meshed. I don't believe we can explain everything in this life. Sometimes we wing it."

He kissed the other side of her neck, his palm brushing down over her belly. The heat rose inside her as her pussy tingled.

"Marcus…"

"Mmm…I know. We've got to get ready for work. This won't take long."

"Oh?"

"Uh-huh."

"Are you proposing a quickie, Mr. Hyatt?"

"Oh yeah." His husky words, laced with harsh desire, sent her libido into the stratosphere.

She quivered as his hands explored, his mouth trailing over her ear, then to the back of her neck, across to her other ear.

He zeroed in on the moistening folds between her legs and drew the wetness up and over her clit. He pinched her nipple at the same time, and she gasped at the exquisite sensations. Mapping her body, he plied her clit and tugged her nipple until she hung on a fine precipice, ready to fall.

He eased his sweatpants down and off. A second later, his cock probed against her labia. With a steady, deep push, he took her. A moan left her throat. With gentle, giving thrusts, he worked her aroused pussy while his touch kept busy on her nipple and clit.

He tortured her through dozens of long, slow thrusts until she leaned forward and placed her hands on the bed, opening herself like a plea.

With a moan of need, he slammed into her once, and she came unglued. Orgasm splintered her into pinpoints of sweet, hot, rushing joy. Marcus growled and held her tight as he thrust hard one last time and flooded her with his cum.

Panting, he stayed deep inside her. "Damn, if that isn't the way to start a morning."

She smiled. "I agree. Marcus?"

"Yes."

"We're going to be late if we keep this up."

"It's okay. They hate me anyway. This will give them another excuse to malign my name."

Anger for his situation filled her again. "How could they? This is crazy."

He shook his head. "Shit happens."

She frowned. "You're very laid-back about it."

"I can't afford to be anything else at this point."

"You're not fighting for your job?"

"No. Right now I'm more concerned with making my full-time job protecting you."

Warmth and aching tenderness filled her heart. She didn't know what to say.

He pressed a line of kisses over her shoulder. "First Drake is after you, and now Forte is playing some weird mind games with you."

"I'm worried. I don't understand any of it. I was acting like a slut—"

"No." He slipped from Tara and turned her around. "You were influenced by something psychic. The same mind control that affected Cecelia and Sugar."

She slipped her arms around his waist and looked up at him. "I know. And it scares me because we don't know why."

"I'll find out why."

Tara remembered the cryptic statement Forte had made yesterday, and it nagged at her. She'd forgotten it in the sexual haze from last night. "Marcus, what is the SIA?"

He twitched, and she saw the slightest flash of uncertainty in those eyes before he schooled his expression. "SIA? I don't know."

"He said you were a part of it."

"He's a nut. I don't know what he's talking about."

She didn't believe him, but decided to put aside the mistrust for the moment. Maybe, just maybe, if Marcus chose not to tell her about the SIA, he had a good reason. She had to keep believing in him. His stalwart body brought her the deepest pleasure, but his faithful friendship meant even more. She could give him the benefit of the doubt.

She almost confessed. Almost revealed those critical words. *I love you.*

But she couldn't. She wouldn't risk saying it when things with Drake and Forte stayed unresolved. She didn't know whether she dared say those three scary words ever. That last time she'd said them had sent her down a frightening and painful path.

He swatted her butt. "Now we need another shower."

She smiled. "Whose fault is that?"

"Mine. All mine."

* * * * *

Marcus headed toward the cubicle with Tara, absorbing the strange looks he received. He nodded and smiled at a few people, and some of them gave him a thumbs-up, a smile, or made some sympathetic noises. Others ignored him. None of that mattered. Eliminating Forte from this world became his first objective. Correction. Tara safe and happy mattered more to him than his own life. His gut ached at the thought of any harm coming to her.

He'd known, way before he'd pushed deep into her soft body this morning that he loved her. Way before Bettina said it for him.

Once this bullshit with Forte finished, he'd arrange Drake's disappearance. He knew SIA friends who'd help him. Zane Spinella and T.J. Calhoun to be exact. He didn't plan to kill the bastard. Committing murder in cold blood didn't come into the equation. Other equally effective methods would ram Marcus' message home.

Stay away from Tara or die.

Marcus' gut twisted. After he eliminated Forte, he'd tell Tara about the SIA. When she discovered his true occupation, he'd be *persona non grata*. The thought hurt like hell, but he clamped down tumultuous emotion. Distraction would get him killed.

They entered the cubicle, and Tara helped him gather his few personal items. The phone on her desk rang, and she answered it.

"Yes. Yes, he's here." She held the phone up. A frown tightened her expression. "It's Jason Forte."

It didn't surprise him the bastard knew he was here. The receptionist at the front desk might have warned Forte, even though Bettina said he could enter.

What difference did it make? He needed to see the man anyway. Marcus took the phone from Tara. "Yes, Mr. Forte."

He felt the heat over the phone, a sulfur scent filling his nostrils. The man on the other side of the line came from the Shadow Realm, but maybe he had a second residence in hell.

"Hyatt, you need to come to my office immediately."

Marcus smirked. "I'm fired. I know. I got the message."

"Come up here now."

Marcus couldn't resist pushing the asshole an increment further. "Why should I? As kids will say, you ain't the boss of me."

Tara stared at him, her eyebrows going up. He smiled, then looked away.

Heat simmered through the telephone line. "Bring your company identification with you, Hyatt."

In a tip-of-the-hat to Dorky's advice about the particle weapon, he said sarcastically, "Roger that."

He hung up the phone.

"What was that all about?" Tara asked.

"I've got business with the ex-boss. He wants me to turn in my company identification."

Placing her hands on her hips, she looked around the cubicle. "If you're done, I'll go with you."

He drew close to her, well aware the intimate distance would come in full view if anyone cared to look. He whispered into her ear. "No. I won't be long. Whatever you do, don't come up there. Even if you get a call from Forte or his secretary or Amanda."

"Marcus—"

"Do this for me. Do not go up there." He swallowed hard. "It's dangerous."

She pulled back and stared into his eyes, frowning deeply. "Marcus, does this have something to do with the SIA? You're scaring me."

He brushed his fingers over her cheek, savoring the softness. He kissed her on the forehead. "Promise me."

She hesitated for so long, he thought she might refuse. Her gaze softened with a deep tenderness that made his chest ache.

"All right," she finally said.

He left with the knowledge he'd have to take Tara with him when he left the building. She would probably lose her job after today anyway, but he wouldn't let her come back here alone where Drake could harm her.

* * * * *

Tara clacked away on her computer, her unsteady typing speed frustrating her. She recalled the pleading look in Marcus' eyes when he'd told her not to come up to Forte's office. Curiosity tormented her and played havoc with concentration. Twice she'd screwed up documents, and twice she'd redone them while she waited for him to return. She glanced at her watch. Fifteen minutes passed since he'd left. Was that all?

She typed a few more minutes before the tension wouldn't bear it. She needed to move and she needed coffee. She left the cubicle and headed for the employee lounge. Once there, she filled her mug to the top and took a deep sip. It was bitter, but she didn't care.

She headed for the closed doorway when she heard the noises. A strange continuous *pop-pop* sound she hadn't heard since she'd lived on a military base. She tensed and listened, mug frozen halfway to her mouth. Each muscle locked as she the sounds repeated.

Again the distinctive *pop-pop-pop*. Nausea filled her stomach, and she put her mug down on a table. Tara understood what her brain should have told her a few seconds earlier. She heard women scream and men shouting and realization cemented into one horrifying thought. Automatic weapon fire.

She knew, in the deepest regions of instinct. Fear seared her like a burning poker. "Drake."

* * * * *

Marcus entered Forte's evil den, as he'd started to think of it in the last few minutes. Forte kept him waiting in the outer office with the secretary. Marcus kept his eyes closed as he sat on the hard leather couch. He called forth his reserves, building the white and gold protective light around his body. Once inside Forte's office, he'd move fast.

Finally, Forte's door opened and Amanda walked out, her body sinuous and sleek as she moved. She didn't even look at Marcus as she left. Very odd, but it didn't shock him. Maybe after Forte died, his grip on Amanda, Cecelia and, no doubt, Forte's secretary would disappear.

Marcus walked into Forte's office, his identification badge and a little surprise tucked into his hand.

Forte stood behind his desk. Good. Perfect. This would be a piece of cake. Then he saw Bettina standing next to Forte.

Shit. Hell. Fuck. Damn.

There weren't enough expletives in usage to cover this.

Improvise.

He said hello to both of them, but stayed close enough to the door. His fingers tightened over the badge and the credit card-sized particle energy weapon. Damn it to hell, a gun would have done the temporary job. He could have shot Forte and asked questions later. Explaining to Bettina, the cops and anyone else would have to come later.

"You look startled, Hyatt." Forte's gaze cruised over Marcus. "And your attire is inappropriate for office wear."

Marcus wore his hair loose, a T-shirt, jeans and hadn't bothered to wear his fake glasses. Marcus immediately felt a push at his mind, this one softer and less intrusive than he would have expected for Forte. *What the hell?*

"What do you want, Forte?" He didn't bother to keep his voice polite. "All I'm here to do is turn my badge in, though I see Human Resources walked out the door."

"Bettina will take it from you."

Again, he felt a push against his brain.

Marcus. The voice whispered in his head, and he recognized it. His gaze flicked to Bettina. She nodded. *Do whatever you're going to do. I don't know how much longer I can hold him back.*

That's when he saw the sweat beading on Bettina's upper lip and along her hairline.

Bettina's mind reading ability tripped up Marcus. *How are you...? Who are you, Bettina?*

Someone sent here to search out Forte and force him back into the Shadow Realm.

Addled, Marcus wrapped his mind around the concept. *Are you like him?*

In none of the bad ways.

Good, because if you were —

I know. You're going to finish him off, aren't you?

He wouldn't say.

When he didn't answer, she said, *Don't worry about me. Just do it. Do it now.*

He didn't take time to answer her telepathically or ask questions. With a flick of his wrist, he tossed the identification badge and the razor-thin particle energy weapon onto Forte's desk.

Forte glanced at the silvery card lying on the desk with the badge. A low-pitched whine filled the room.

Marcus had a second to look at Bettina. She cleared her throat and said, "This is where I leave."

She blinked out. Disappeared.

Forte's stunned expression propelled Marcus out of the office at a dead run. He slammed the door and heard Forte's bellow echo off the walls with excruciating terror. His secretary put her hands over her ears, her expression horrified and shocked.

A slicing sound split the air. Blinding white light streamed from around the cracks in the door as a crackling like lightning slammed his eardrums.

Mission accomplished.

The secretary kept her fingers over her ears, her face screwed up in pain. Marcus felt something tickle his mind.

A warning. He ignored the now wide-eyed, terrified secretary and headed for the door. When he opened it, he thought he heard another sound, and he strained to listen.

The phone on the secretary's desk rang and she picked it up. Her terrified, shaky voice yelled into the phone, "Hyatt is here and he's done something! I don't know. A bomb or—what? What? Oh my God. Oh my God."

Her voice trailed off to a whisper as she dropped the phone.

"What is it?" he asked, aware his voice held menace.

With a stricken expression, her hands trembling, she warbled her answer. "Someone is shooting downstairs."

A flash-fire thought tore into his mind and gut. He knew only one thing.

Retrieve the Glock stashed in the bottom drawer of his desk and get to Tara.

* * * * *

Tara's heart pounded against her chest and her rapid breathing sent black spots across her vision. She sucked in deep breaths. She'd never fainted in her life, and she wouldn't start now.

Drake had come for her. Horror swept through her in an uncontrollable wave. Had he killed anyone? *Please, no.* If anyone died because Drake had come for her, she could never forgive herself.

The gunfire had ceased after those initial two bursts, and they sounded far enough away that he couldn't be right on top of her position.

Marcus. To have him with her now. She'd always felt so safe with him near.

No. No, that would mean Marcus would be dead. Drake wouldn't hesitate to kill Marcus. Nausea rose up in her throat, and she took two more deep breaths. She grabbed the phone on the wall and punched a line to the outside. Nothing. Static. She glared at the phone. Another try and she finally reached 9-1-1. She reported the situation with shaky breaths. When the woman on the other end asked her stay on the line, she realized she couldn't. The sound of gunfire came closer. Intuition told her that staying in the room might be fatal.

"He's probably looking for me. I have to get out of the building or hide so no one else is hurt."

She hung up before the 9-1-1 operator could protest. She had to get out of there.

The stairwell.

She couldn't stop on any floor. If she did, Drake could take out more people on the way.

But she'd be leaving Marcus here.

She took a trembling breath. If anyone could keep clear of Drake's wrath, Marcus could.

She opened the door cautiously and realized she hadn't heard gunfire or screams again in a minute or two. At least he wasn't firing continuously.

She removed her shoes and left them in the lounge. She peeked in both directions but saw no one. Nothing.

She eased into the hallway and ran as fast as slippery floor and hose would allow.

She reached the stairwell, when she heard Drake's insane bellow. "Tara!"

Chills of terror propelled her onward. She had to keep going. Straight down, through the parking garage and then escape.

Hurry. Hurry. Hurry. She slammed through the door and down the steps.

She'd gone down two flights before she heard Drake's cry. "Tara! Come to me!"

His shout served to quicken her feet. Drake's pursuit echoed down to her as he followed. She reached the last flight and hope.

She burst through the doorway leading into the parking garage. She didn't look back, her heart pounding in her ears. She spotted the empty guard shack and ran toward it. Her feet protested the treatment, but screaming fear pressed her forward.

She heard the burst of another gun, this one not automatic, and kept running.

Agony spread through her lower right leg, then right shoulder. Her leg buckled as she cried out. She crumpled and fell facedown.

As heat seared Tara's leg and shoulder, she gasped for breath. This was it. He'd found her and now she'd die. One soul-breaking thought slipped through her mind as she fought the pain. She hadn't told Marcus she loved him.

Why hadn't she told him? Mental anguish split her apart worse than bullet wounds. Tears of fury and pain threatened, but she fought them. She turned and sat up even as her wounds screamed and throbbed. Better to face the devil than be shot in the back.

Dizziness made her tremble. Nausea washed through her stomach. Thinking beyond the pain took effort.

A lone dark figure strode toward her, the gait unmistakable. If she ran, he might shoot again. She glanced at the wound on her leg. A horizontal gash across her right calf dripped blood. She couldn't see the shoulder wound, but felt warm blood ooze over her shirt. Through the fog in her head, she remembered the silk scarf around her neck. She stripped it off and tied it around her leg.

Drake took his time, and as he came closer, she sucked in breaths to slow down her heart and regulate the relentless throbbing.

His eyes held total lack of concern, the automatic weapon slung over his left shoulder. He stuffed another smaller gun back into a hip holster. He smiled and squatted down in front of her. Her vision fuzzed around the edges.

"Tara, Tara," he *tsked* and shook his head. "I'm sorry. You gave me no choice."

Her tongue felt like thick waded cotton as she tried to speak. "Who—how many people did you hurt?"

He winked. "Don't worry about that now. Do you know what's going to happen in the next few minutes?"

Fear tightened her throat and choked her voice. "No."

"Get up." His voice curled around her, soft and smooth.

She gritted her teeth as she worked her way to her knees. She used her left leg to push off the ground and rose up. She swayed and would have fallen, but he grabbed her left arm. Pain shot through her leg. Nausea threatened to make her throw up.

A serene smile crossed his face. "See, I knew you could do it."

He marched her across the parking garage. Each step sent renewed agony jolting her body.

"Where are we going?" she asked.

"'Bring the man or woman who has done this wicked deed to the gate of the town to be stoned to death.'"

"What are you talking about?" She heard the trepidation in her own voice.

"'Show none of them mercy, neither spare them or shield them; you are to put them to death, your own hand being the first raised against them, and then all the people are to follow.'"

Insane. He's gone insane.

They'd almost reached the stairs when the pain made her cry out. She fell and he let her drop on her butt.

"You shouldn't have given me an ultimatum." One of Drake's brows quirked. He crouched down beside her.

"What do you want from me?" she asked, voice quivering.

"You."

Suffering seized her in a long wave. Amazing how two gunshot wounds could make her whole body ache. She moaned.

"Hurts, doesn't it? Now you know what it's like to be in battle."

Battle? He'd never been in battle.

"If you...if you want me to come back to you, I need medical help. I don't know how much blood I'm losing."

His once-over held no desire, only contempt. "Looks like enough to cause you some problems."

He stood, then reached down and lifted her in his arms with ease. Her psyche rebelled against his embrace. "Where are you taking me?"

"You'll see." He strode toward the elevator.

Struggle. Do something.

Instead, she cleared her mind as best she could and tried to send Marcus a message.

Marcus. Can you hear me? Please help me. He's taking me to a room near the elevator on the first level of the parking garage.

First level parking garage.

First level parking garage.

She kept the litany, her eyes closed. Instinct told her to play the weakling. If he thought she'd passed out, he might wait to kill her.

She let her head flop onto his shoulder.

"Hey, you okay?"

She didn't answer, and weakness made it easy to fake unconsciousness.

"Tara. Damn it."

He sounded worried, and that surprised her. She didn't think he possessed an ounce of humanity in his pinkie finger.

"Come on. Wake up." He shook her a little, and as pain rippled and arched, she couldn't help but moan. Still, she kept her eyes closed and hoped Marcus received her message.

* * * * *

Marcus found chaos when he reached word processing. As he'd run down the stairs, he'd was swept up in the massive exodus as people scampered down the stairwells evacuating the building.

He heard wild stories all the way to word processing.

Terrorists.

He didn't bother to correct anyone. Whatever or whoever had infiltrated the building didn't matter. Finding Tara and keeping her safe dominated his thoughts.

That and not getting killed.

"It's him!" One of the women word processing cowered and screamed as Marcus edged into the area and made sure the gunman wasn't there.

"No! It's Marcus," Cecelia said, her eyes wide with shock.

He looked around, knowing he must look wild-eyed. "Where's Tara?"

People had already started to help each other. Two people suffered serious leg wounds, but Drake hadn't killed anyone on this floor so far as Marcus could tell. He didn't know about other floors. Marcus went right to his desk drawer and removed his weapon. He loaded it and started down the cubicles.

"Holy shit!" A man not originally from word processing said. Fear sketched the man's face. "He has a gun, too."

Several women stepped back, clearly terrified.

Marcus kept walking. "Don't be afraid of me. I'm an agent for the government."

"That creep wanted Tara," one lady said. "He was asking where she was, too."

Marcus thought his heart might stop on the spot.

Drake.

Through every assignment he'd experienced with the SIA, he'd never felt anxiety eating him alive from the inside out. He allowed determination to override fear for Tara.

"Which way did the bastard go?" Marcus asked.

Someone called out, "He went down the hall toward the employee lounge."

Cecelia appeared at his shoulder. She grasped his forearm, and he tensed. Tears filled the woman's eyes as she trotted to keep up with his long stride. "Please help Tara."

He continued without saying a word, unable to feel sympathy for Cecelia when Tara's life hung in the balance.

First-floor parking garage.

Tara's weak voice, filled with pain, echoed in his mind. Rage threatened. The bastard hurt her.

I need you, Marcus.

Exhilarated that he knew where to find her, he quickened his pace to a run.

Tara, you stay alive, you hear me? Do whatever he wants. Tara? Tara?

No answer.

Chapter Twenty

ဢ

"We're here." Drake's voice rumbled above Tara's head as he set her down on a hard surface. "Alone."

Hot brands across her leg and shoulder brought her back to full awareness. Her eyes opened. She blinked as her senses tried to come online. She'd never fainted in her life, and she took in a heavy breath, struggling to regain strength. She couldn't wimp out now.

Tara's heart humped a sluggish beat in her chest, her world rotating in a slow spin. He'd propped her against a hard wall. She looked around and spied concrete walls that narrowed down to a long passageway. An electrical-type box stood near to them. Where were they? Two naked light bulbs hung from the roughly twelve-foot ceiling, harsh light hurting her eyes. Maybe this was a maintenance corridor. Did he plan on taking them down this way? How did he know where it led?

"Where are we?" she asked.

"Somewhere to hole up for a few minutes."

"Where does this hallway go?"

"Shut up." He said it with cool confidence and the harsh parent-to-child tone he'd used on her so many times before.

Anger roared up inside her. "I'm not the same woman you knew, Drake. I don't take orders."

"The hell you say?" He laughed. "You'll fuckin' take mine now."

She opened her mouth to protest, and he cracked her across the face with his open palm. Her cry of surprise and pain echoed down the walkway.

Just like old times. Frustration and fury gnawed at her insides. Playing subservient to this creep grated on every nerve she possessed. Her skin stung like hell, and her jaw ached.

A cockeyed grin covered his mouth. For a moment, he seemed the Drake she'd known so many years ago. The man she'd thought he was when she first knew him.

His boyish grin faded, but the stone-cold killer didn't return. "I'm sorry."

She swallowed, and her throat hurt. She could humor him longer and forget the ache that never ended, and the knowledge she could die. She knew Marcus must be looking for her, and that gave her some hope.

"Sorry for what, Drake?"

"Sorry I shot at you. I mean…" His gaze darted away. "I want you with me. If you bleed to death, you'll be…"

When he didn't finish, she said, "I'll be what?"

He stood and started to walk down the hall, then back again, an animal in a long cage, pacing out his minutes.

"I'll be what, Drake?" she asked again.

He continued walking, his footsteps firm and certain. "If you die, you'll be with the Lord, our God."

She nodded. "Is that where you want me to be?"

Back and forth, back and forth he paced. "I want you with me."

She shuddered as sickness eased into her bones. "Then why did you shoot me?"

"Because I was angry."

"Are you angry now?"

"No."

"Then…if you want me to stay with you, I need to stop the bleeding. My shoulder's on fire and my leg is—"

"No!"

His harsh growl made her jump. *Pacify him. Don't escalate the situation.* "All right. What do we do now?"

He stopped halfway down the cold, lonely hallway. "We wait for your lover to come."

"What lover?"

"That long-haired shithead."

"He's only my friend."

"Bullshit."

She cringed inwardly, fighting for anything to say to calm his wrath. "Why do you want to hurt Marcus?"

"That's his name? Should be fuckin' obvious why I want to hurt him. He's a pussy. And you and I are meant to be together forever. You broke those vows."

"I didn't break them. You beat me and the cops arrested you. They put you in prison for almost killing me. We're divorced."

She held her breath and waited for his reaction.

"Tara, you know that's not true. If you'd been a dutiful wife and followed God's law, none of this would have happened." His eyes glittered as he returned to her, then crouched down to peer into her face. "You really worry me. It hurts me when you make dumb-ass accusations. Hell, my own sister wouldn't even defend you. She knew you were wrong."

As weakness threatened to close her eyes, she struggled to stay conscious. "All right. Whatever you say."

She would fight, to keep alive for Marcus and for what she wanted to do with her life. She needed more than what she'd had so far, and if she made it out of this alive, she'd make those changes permanently.

A slight tap on the door made her jump. Drake started, too, and swung toward the door with his automatic weapon.

"Drake!" Marcus' solid, deep voice rang out. "It's Marcus Hyatt."

Tara's heart sang with a terrible mingling of sheer joy and wrenching anxiety. She almost opened her mouth to speak, then saw Drake tense.

"Hyatt! Ain't this a treat?" Drake laughed his voice heavy with contempt.

"Let me speak to Tara."

"Uh, I don't think so. She's out of it right now."

There was a long pause before Marcus replied. "Is she all right?"

Drake kept his back turned to her, so she couldn't see his expression. "No, she's not. But she understands now that she belongs to me. She's staying with me." He turned toward her. He held up his weapon and pointed it right at her. "If anyone tries to get in here and take you away from me, they die, then you die. I'll kill myself after." He sniffed. "Hate to say it, but it's the ol', 'if I can't have you, no one will'."

He turned back around and stared at the door.

Renewed trepidation quickened her breathing. Pain knifed her shoulder, and she yelped. Drake glared at her.

"Drake, I need to see Tara." Marcus' voice came on strong.

"You're kidding, right? You don't think I'm opening this door, do you? You'll have to come in and get me."

"There's no one else out here but me. You've got an automatic weapon. I'm no threat to you." Marcus' voice rang out. "Drake, you know that a SWAT team has this place surrounded. You know they'll think of a way to infiltrate this building and come down on you hard. I'll make you a deal."

"No deals."

"Don't refuse until you've heard the deal."

"You're more than a long-haired pussy, I'll bet. You got a military background, Hyatt?"

Tara wondered how Drake knew, but it seemed many men in the military could sniff out each other like bloodhounds.

"I was in the Marines," Marcus said.

Drake snorted. "Fuckin' pansies."

Marcus kept silent for several moments, then his voice came again. "What it is you want?"

"My wife to come back to me. You aren't taking her away, so you can fuckin' forget it."

"I understand. How do you think you're getting out of here with SWAT surrounding the building?"

Drake didn't answer. He glanced back at her.

"How *are* we getting out of here?" she asked.

Drake sneered, then turned back to the door. "I've got a proposal for you, Hyatt."

"Yeah?"

"We fight to the death. Best man wins the woman. What do you say?"

"You're on. No weapons."

Tara's heart slammed in her chest. *No, Marcus. Don't.* She sent the message out to him, shrieking it in her mind.

"No weapons," Drake said. "I'm going to open the door and come out. You make any false moves, and I'll shoot her. You understand?"

Tara trembled with gut-wrenching worry. Marcus and Drake fighting? She had no doubt Marcus could win, but what if Drake hurt him? Shivers danced over her skin as a hard knot welled in her throat.

"Drake, don't," she said in a last-ditch effort.

A confident glint entered his gaze. "I'll kick his ass."

Drake adjusted his weapon and held it at the ready. "I'm comin' out!"

Drake opened the door. As he looked around the edge and then stepped out, she eased her body off the floor. Her body hurt like a mother. Sweat beaded her forehead. She took several deep breaths, searching for control. She could run off down the hallway, run as fast as she could, but she didn't know if the left turn she saw at the finish was the end of the hallway.

She took two stumbling steps toward the door, savage pain raking her leg. She collapsed to her knees and crawled. Every movement jarred her leg and shoulder, but she didn't care. When she peeked around the door, she saw Marcus had placed his weapon on the floor near a wall. Tara noted Drake's weapon balanced against another wall. The men stared at each other like two boxers ready, several feet between them.

Despite Drake's muscular body and the anger dripping off him in waves, Marcus looked like an avenging angel. His gaze flicked to her, and then whipped back to Drake. He stood with feet braced apart, arms akimbo, leashed power ready to explode. Testosterone filled the air, livid male energy on the edge.

"Here's the wager," Marcus said. "The man who wins takes Tara."

Drake shook his head and put his hands on his hips. "You're crazy. I'll kill you."

"Maybe. Maybe not."

Scared out of her mind for Marcus, she sank down by the door and watched.

Marcus was willing to die for her.

The impact of that reality hit her in the gut and sucked away the rest of her air. She trembled uncontrollably, aware that even if she took off running now, she'd never make it to safety.

"Come on, pussy. Let's do it." Drake launched forward at a run.

Marcus sprang into action, and met him in the middle. He feinted to the side and clothes-lined Drake. Drake landed hard on his back with a grunt, coughing as he clutched at his throat. Marcus didn't attack, and she watched in fascination as he circled Drake like a panther teasing his kill.

With a roar, Drake sprang up and jumped on Marcus. Marcus staggered under Drake's weight, but moved with a blur that sent Drake crashing to the floor. Both men were quick, but

Marcus defined incredible grace and strength. Tara's breath staggered in her lungs, and she held back a cough. She felt weak, so tired, but she stayed riveted on the struggle. Drake tried another move. Marcus landed a rib-cracking punch. Drake's moan of pain echoed in the parking garage. A growl built in Drake's throat as he dived for Marcus' legs. Marcus went down in a heap with Drake on top of him.

Tara reached out in panic. "Marcus!"

Drake and Marcus rolled, grappling, their punches and jabs brutal. Marcus finally jumped to his feet, and when Drake came up to challenge, Marcus landed another punch to Drake's face. She heard a sickening crack. Drake flew backwards, sprawling on his back with legs and arms out spread-eagle.

Marcus, breathing hard and with blood on his face, walked toward Drake and knelt down. He checked the pulse in the other man's neck. He turned toward Tara at the same time he reached into his pants pocket for a device that looked like a cell phone.

His hair tossed around his shoulders and blood over his right eye dripped down onto his cheek. His shirt stained with blood, one knee on his pants ripped.

He held the cell phone up to his ear and spoke into it rapidly as he walked toward her. "This is SIA operative badge number 8888. The hostage situation is resolved." He asked for paramedics.

Shaky with relief, and hanging on with her last reserves, she watched him walk toward her. Stark concern laced his features. She struggled to her feet before he reached her. His arms went out and around her as her legs started to buckle. He held her tight.

"Tara," he said, his voice ragged as he buried his face in her hair. "Oh God. I was so damned scared for you."

Hearing the raw emotion in his voice set her off. She couldn't stand it any longer, and the dam burst. She choked on sudden tears, her entire body shuddering with pain and release from fear.

"Shhh, easy sweetheart. Easy. I've got you. He's never going to hurt you again." He crooned to her, his deep voice tender and reassuring.

"Drake. What if he—?"

"He's not going anywhere. He's dead." He cupped her face. "Where are you hit?"

"Leg and shoulder."

"Oh Christ." He eased her down to sit on the floor. "Here, let me see. Good job on binding your leg."

"I think it's just a graze, but it hurts like hell." Her voice quavered. "My shoulder is worse."

"Damn, I'll bet it does hurt." Anxiety lined his features as she looked at her shoulder. He tore her shirt. "Looks like he nicked you, but it's a deep wound. The bullet didn't penetrate."

A wave of dizziness flowed over her, and she put one hand to her head. "I'm not feeling…"

Her eyelids flickered and she tilted to one side as consciousness ebbed away.

Marcus' frightened voice edged through the encroaching darkness. "Tara, damn it, stay with me." His arms embraced her, his hand cupping her face. "Open your eyes. Tara, you're scaring the shit out of me. Don't do this. I need you with me. I need you."

She managed a tiny smile of pure happiness before the shadows won.

Epilogue

⁊⊙

Tara stepped out of her car and watched purple rain clouds gather above the sharp peaks around her. A storm approached as wind rustled the huge pine trees circling the beautiful cabin hideaway in front of her. She drank in a deep breath of bracing, rain-scented mountain air. She stretched and winced as her still healing wounds reminded her about events little over a week ago. Events where she'd found and lost love in one heartbeat. Tears prickled at the back of her eyes, but she inhaled another long breath and refused to buckle to self-pity.

She opened the trunk and pulled out a small roller-type suitcase. She grimaced under the weight.

Mom, Dad and her sister had about had a card-carrying fit when she'd told them from her hospital bed they didn't need to come out to Colorado, and that after a couple of days in the hospital she had some serious sick time scheduled in Bettina's summer cabin.

Thank goodness for Bettina. She'd been a lifeline during the last week when things could have crumbled under brittle emotions. The doctor said she should stay home and rest for two weeks, but home sounded boring. Lonely. Too lonely. No, coming up here would clear her mind and repair her body.

She rolled the suitcase along behind her as she walked. She marched toward the door and once inside the cabin, put her suitcase in the standing position and closed the door. Bettina's summer cabin went beyond rustic into pure luxury. It wasn't large, but the cabin featured two bedrooms, two bathrooms, a beautiful kitchen, dining area, and living area with fireplace. Here she wouldn't worry about phones or the television. She'd brought her cell phone for emergencies, but planned to keep it off most of the time. On the agenda for two weeks? Sleep, reading and trying to forget about Marcus.

Forget about Marcus? Right. Like that's going to happen anytime soon.

She grabbed her suitcase and rolled it into the bedroom and started to unpack. Unbidden memories filled her thoughts. When she'd woken up in the hospital a few hours after Drake's attack, she found Bettina by her side. Bettina explained that Marcus had been there, watching over her for hours, until he received an urgent call. He'd dashed away after making Bettina promise to watch out for Tara. The next day came with no sign of Marcus, and then that evening, he called her. She remembered his words with a bittersweet pang and the joy that had filled her for one moment.

"Tara, I'm so glad you're all right. Do you feel much better?"

"Yes. I was...I was hoping you'd be here."

"Yeah. I know. Tara, I'm not even in Colorado."

Disappointment had speared through her like a new, fresh wound. "What?"

"My boss...my real boss, sent me to Florida in connection with Jason Forte's case. It turns out he used to work at a company down here before he came up there. Two women turned up dead, just like Sugar. He disappeared before anyone could make the connection between him and the women."

"He was a serial killer?"

"Yeah. Of a sorts. He's not your ordinary serial killer."

"How is that?"

"It's a long story. And Bettina isn't exactly an ordinary supervisor. She's very special."

She'd rubbed her aching temple. "Bettina said something about the Shadow Realm and she'd explain it to me someday. That she's not from this dimension." She laughed, but there wasn't really any humor in it. "If I didn't love her to pieces for being so supportive and kind, I'd think she'd completely lost her mind."

"She's going to work for the SIA now because of her special talents."

"Bettina didn't explain much about it. She said the SIA is a special branch of the government."

"That's right."

"Is it like the CIA?"

"Not exactly."

"You'd tell me but then you'd have to kill me," she said dryly.

"No. Look, we need more time to talk. I'm so damned sorry I'm not right there—"

"Don't worry about it. You had to go." She'd gripped the phone receiver tighter as disappointment and irritation overtook her. "I'm pretty confused right now about what's happened. I don't think we should see each other for a while, okay? Give me time to process everything."

"What? Please, listen—"

"All this time I thought you were my friend and then we got involved, and I find out you're undercover for some secret squirrel organization. For all I know, the Marcus I thought I knew doesn't exist."

"Tara, wait—"

She'd replaced the receiver gently.

As she opened her suitcase and stood there in the bedroom, she wondered why it felt as lonely here as it had back in her apartment in the city. She sank down onto the king-size bed and covered her eyes. Her heart ached so deep, she didn't think she'd recover.

But nothing wounded her more than that last conversation, where she hadn't given him the benefit of the doubt and had acted so immature. She'd wanted him with her now, kissing her, telling her what he truly felt for her. Her head ached thinking about how stupid she'd been. She could have called and apologized, but taking this vacation to sort out her true feelings may give her time to understand what motivated her to push Marcus away.

She lay back and fell asleep, exhaustion and encroaching tears wearing her down.

A knock on the front door startled her out of sleep sometime later, and she jackknifed into sitting position. Her shoulder ached, and she gasped. Her heart pounded, adrenaline streaking through her. Old fear arose like an avenging eagle, talons sharp and unremorseful.

"Tara?" Marcus' voice rang out. He knocked on the door again. "Tara, are you all right in there?"

Joy and apprehension tangled inside her. She'd better answer him or he'd probably find a way in with some secret squirrel device or break down the door.

"Just a minute," she said loudly.

She hurried to the living area and opened the door. In the afternoon sun, his dark hair lay about his shoulders, gleaming and healthy, his ocean eyes soul-deep with worry. Gone were the glasses and the attempt to look like a nerd. He looked delicious enough to eat with a green T-shirt pulling across his broad shoulders, curving to his biceps and stomach. He wore new jeans and hiking boots.

She'd never seen a man sexier or with a deeper glower on his face. "I was about to bust down the door."

A smile escaped her before she could stop it. "I was asleep. I didn't hear you." She let him in, butterflies in her stomach swooping and diving. "What brings you here?"

He stepped inside, the frown growing stronger. "You have to ask?" He came into her personal space, invading her with his nearness, and his purely masculine heat. She knew he'd give his life for hers, and yet right now he looked dangerous and angry. "You're up here alone?"

"Of course. Bettina thought it would be a great place for me to recover."

He surveyed the vaulted ceiling and the furnishings. "It's nice. But it's too damn isolated."

She shrugged. "What's the problem with that? Drake's dead. I don't need a bodyguard anymore."

"You were just shot. I don't think you should be up here alone."

She planted her hands on her hips and dared to stare into his eyes. "I didn't invite you to baby-sit me, and I don't need help. I'm fine. The wounds weren't as bad as we thought."

Muscles in his jaw tightened and released. He swallowed hard. "You lost a lot of blood. When we were in that parking garage and you passed out like that, I was... I thought..."

He didn't finish the sentence, his gaze haunted.

He walked toward her until barely a foot separated them. His nearness wreaked havoc with her ability to stay cool and unaffected. "Tara, you hung up on me the other day and didn't let me finish what I had to say. I'm going to finish saying it here. Now."

She sighed. "I thought you were a word processing clerk like me, and now I know you're some sort of secret agent for a mysterious government agency I've never heard of. Bettina said you were sent in to investigate Jason Forte, and I still can't believe what she told me about Jason."

"It's all true. I did lie by omission, but I was undercover."

She nodded. "I could have gotten past that. But when I woke up in the hospital you weren't there, and then you didn't show up later."

He reached up and cupped her face with one hand. His thumb caressed her gently. The warmth of it captured her breath and held it prisoner.

"I know," he said. "I was in Florida then. I wanted to be with you."

He gave her cheek one last tender stroke, then dropped his hand back to his side.

She asked him if he wanted something to drink, and he declined. They settled on the couch. He sat close and put his arm on the back of the couch. She could feel his exciting heat, and as her stomach fluttered, she wondered if she could ever forget the wonderful feeling of being near him. "There's something new you don't know. Drake's sister heard about what happened to her brother and she contacted Douglas Financial Services. She got in touch with Bettina that way."

"Kendra." A slow burn started in her gut. "How is she?"

"I think she'll be fine now that she's away from her twisted family. She went to a women's shelter, and she's getting help."

"Good. That's great." A pause came between them before Tara spoke again. "Bettina said she had something else to tell me about herself, but then she never got around to explaining how she got out of that room after you used the...the..."

"Particle weapon."

"Right. The particle weapon to eliminate Jason."

"This might come as a shock, but Bettina isn't exactly from around here."

"You're not going to tell me she's an alien or something? Not that other dimension story she told me?"

He grinned. "No, she's not an alien in the conventional UFO sense. When I set off that particle device, she literally disappeared before she could get caught in it. She really is from another dimension. Jason was a doppelganger and used mind control. She was sent from the other dimension to hunt for him. She's been trying to think of a way to control him, without much success. She's not going back to the other dimension now that she's bagged Jason."

"But you bagged him."

"I'm giving her credit for him." He shrugged. "She's staying. She said she likes it better than where she's originally from."

"And you didn't realize she was from the other dimension?"

"Not until she disappeared. Then I knew something weird was going on. By the way, she's really two hundred and fifty years old."

"That's incredible." She couldn't wrap her mind around it, but Bettina's presence here, in this dimension and time, would always be a gift to Tara.

They went silent, and Tara wondered how she could ever absorb all the bizarre things she'd learned about her coworkers in the last few days.

Raindrops started to drum on the roof. Marcus' eyes continued to look a bit sad. "I don't know how I can ever make it up to you for leaving you defenseless. When I realized Drake had you, I thought I was going to choke to death on my fear. I told you I'd protect you. I failed. I can't forgive myself for that."

The ache in her heart this time came from one source. She knew she couldn't let him suffer like this. "It wasn't your fault. You saved my life."

Tears welled up and threatened. God, she'd give anything to stop being so weepy, but seeing him torn up like this wore a hole straight through to her heart.

"My job with the SIA can be dangerous sometimes and take me away long hours, or even weeks or months. A woman has never wanted to put up with that. But there is something I want you to know because it's the truth." Rich and husky, his voice vibrated with raw power and heartfelt emotion. Tenderness filled his eyes. He took her hand in his. "No matter what you do or where you go, if you need me, I'll always find you, I'll always be there. You only have to call me."

Tears came, whether she wanted them or not. She shifted away and stood. She limped a slight distance away. When she looked at him, no words would come. Her throat tightened.

His gaze went intense and filled with wanting. He stood and walked toward her until he could slip his arms very gently around her waist. She knew he was concerned about her shoulder wound, and his touch was so tender. As his chest pressed against her, and his hips nestled into hers, she felt the power of his arousal. His cock swelled against her belly, and she inhaled sharply at the passion of her desire. She wanted to strip him, kiss him, make him forget the bad dreams they'd experienced. Maybe, here in this cabin far away from everyone, they could have a new beginning.

"Say something," he asked hoarsely.

Happiness swirled inside her like a beautiful, multicolored dream. She never wanted to wake up. "You're wrong, you know."

Uncertainty and vulnerability grew in his eyes. "I'm crazy for you and it's driving me nuts because if you can't love me—"

"Shhh." She put her finger over his mouth, then spread her fingers over his hard pecs, relishing the sensation of muscles flexing under her touch. "I'm so sorry I made things difficult for you. When I was in the hospital too much had happened, and I was missing you so much when you were gone."

His eyes filled with heat and ardor. "Yeah? You really missed me?"

She palmed his face and savored the prickle of his five o'clock shadow over her sensitive skin. "Really. I'm sorry I hung up on you while I was in the hospital. It was stupid. After what we'd been through, I should have listened to you."

He kissed her nose and gave her a heartbreaking smile so handsome, her toes almost curled. "Apology accepted."

His gaze heated, and she recognized that feral, hungry look. He slipped his hand into the hair at the back of her neck and kissed her. Her mouth opened to his insistent touch, his tongue dipping in and out and caressing her with intense sexual rhythm.

When he drew back, she was panting.

He groaned and drew her closer, burying his face in her hair. "Oh shit, honey. I love you so damned much." He nuzzled her ear, whispering in a hot, drugging voice that set her on fire. "I want to watch you come while I'm deep inside you. I want to love you until you can't think of anything or anyone but me for the next sixty to seventy years."

As he peppered kisses along her face, she quivered. Fine tremors of ecstasy filled her lower belly and set her on fire. "I think it's already too late."

He drew back slightly and frowned. "What?"

She reached up and pulled his head down for another drugging, sensual kiss. When she let him up for air, she said, "It's too late. I already can't stop thinking about you. I think I've been in love with you for weeks and didn't know it."

He grinned. "Hell, I like the sound of that. We'll make this work, Tara. I'll do everything in my power to make it work between us. I'll do anything."

Tara couldn't remember the last time she'd been this happy and this certain about anything in her life.

"Come here, then," she whispered against his mouth. "Let's get started on that sixty or seventy years right now."

The End

About the Author

అం

Suspenseful, erotic, edgy, thrilling, romantic, adventurous. All these words describe Denise A. Agnew's award-winning novels. Romantic Times Book Review Magazine called her romantic suspense novels "top-notch" and her erotic romance PRIMORDIAL received a TOP PICK from Romantic Times Book Review Magazine. Denise's record proves that with paranormal, time travel, romantic comedy, contemporary, historical, erotic romance, and romantic suspense novels under her belt, she enjoys writing about a diverse range of subjects. The fact she has lived in Colorado, Hawaii, and the United Kingdom has given her a lifetime of ideas. Her experiences with archaeology have crept into her work, as well as numerous travels through England, Ireland, Scotland, and Wales. Denise lives in Arizona with her real life hero, her husband. Visit Denise's website at www.deniseagnew.com

Denise welcomes comments from readers. You can find her website and email address on her author bio page at www.ellorascave.com.

Why an electronic book?

We live in the Information Age — an exciting time in the history of human civilization, in which technology rules supreme and continues to progress in leaps and bounds every minute of every day. For a multitude of reasons, more and more avid literary fans are opting to purchase e-books instead of paper books. The question from those not yet initiated into the world of electronic reading is simply: *Why?*

1. *Price.* An electronic title at Ellora's Cave Publishing and Cerridwen Press runs anywhere from 40% to 75% less than the cover price of the exact same title in paperback format. Why? Basic mathematics and cost. It is less expensive to publish an e-book (no paper and printing, no warehousing and shipping) than it is to publish a paperback, so the savings are passed along to the consumer.

2. *Space.* Running out of room in your house for your books? That is one worry you will never have with electronic books. For a low one-time cost, you can purchase a handheld device specifically designed for e-reading. Many e-readers have large, convenient screens for viewing. Better yet, hundreds of titles can be stored within your new library — on a single microchip. There are a variety of e-readers from different manufacturers. You can also read e-books on your PC or laptop computer. (Please note that Ellora's

Cave does not endorse any specific brands. You can check our websites at www.ellorascave.com or www.cerridwenpress.com for information we make available to new consumers.)

3. *Mobility.* Because your new e-library consists of only a microchip within a small, easily transportable e-reader, your entire cache of books can be taken with you wherever you go.

4. *Personal Viewing Preferences.* Are the words you are currently reading too small? Too large? Too… ANNOYING? Paperback books cannot be modified according to personal preferences, but e-books can.

5. *Instant Gratification.* Is it the middle of the night and all the bookstores near you are closed? Are you tired of waiting days, sometimes weeks, for bookstores to ship the novels you bought? Ellora's Cave Publishing sells instantaneous downloads twenty-four hours a day, seven days a week, every day of the year. Our webstore is never closed. Our e-book delivery system is 100% automated, meaning your order is filled as soon as you pay for it.

Those are a few of the top reasons why electronic books are replacing paperbacks for many avid readers.

As always, Ellora's Cave and Cerridwen Press welcome your questions and comments. We invite you to email us at Comments@ellorascave.com or write to us directly at Ellora's Cave Publishing Inc., 1056 Home Avenue, Akron, OH 44310-3502.

THE
✶ ELLORA'S CAVE ✶
LIBRARY

Stay up to date with Ellora's Cave Titles in
Print with our Quarterly Catalog.

TO RECIEVE A CATALOG,
SEND AN EMAIL WITH YOUR NAME
AND MAILING ADDRESS TO:

CATALOG@ELLORASCAVE.COM

OR SEND A LETTER OR POSTCARD
WITH YOUR MAILING ADDRESS TO:

CATALOG REQUEST
c/o ELLORA'S CAVE PUBLISHING, INC.
1056 HOME AVENUE
AKRON, OHIO 44310-3502

erridwen, the Celtic Goddess of wisdom, was the muse who brought inspiration to storytellers and those in the creative arts. Cerridwen Press encompasses the best and most innovative stories in all genres of today's fiction. Visit our site and discover the newest titles by talented authors who still get inspired - much like the ancient storytellers did, once upon a time.

Cerridwen Press

www.cerridwenpress.com